"So what do I owe you for the rescue, my lord?" she asked, wriggling into a more upright position, her knees pulled tightly toward her chest.

"You can't even approach what you owe me, Julia."

"Very well, then. I'll simply say thank you and leave it at that."

Leave it at that? Indeed, he supposed he should. But he wouldn't.

"Not on your life," he said and was foolish enough to touch her.

He stroked her shoulder where the skin was exposed. A bolt of unexpected lightning coursed through his veins and his fingers flexed. She was warm, soft. Somehow he hadn't expected that. It seemed after becoming Mrs. Fitzgelder she should have turned as cold and serpentlike as her damned husband. But she hadn't. Her skin was as perfect as he remembered it.

His hand ached for more of her, so he slid his fingers down to hook the blanket. Slowly, he dragged it lower until it hung off her shoulder, and she had to clutch it against herself to remain covered. She glared at him, her dangerous eyes tempting and warning at the same time. He'd be an absolute fool to continue.

Then again, he'd always been her fool, hadn't he? He'd believed her lies; he'd fallen for her deception. He'd promised to make her his wife, for God's sake. And even after three years, the woman still occupied his mind and tortured his dreams.

PRAISE FOR
Mistress by Mistake

"Sparkling with superbly crafted characters, humor, and deliciously sexy romance, Heino's debut . . . is splendidly entertaining."

—*Booklist*

Berkley Sensation Titles by Susan Gee Heino

Damsel in Disguise

SUSAN GEE HEINO

BERKLEY SENSATION, NEW YORK

THE BERKLEY PUBLISHING GROUP
Published by the Penguin Group
Penguin Group (USA) Inc.
375 Hudson Street, New York, New York 10014, USA
Penguin Group (Canada), 90 Eglinton Avenue East, Suite 700, Toronto, Ontario M4P 2Y3, Canada
(a division of Pearson Penguin Canada Inc.)
Penguin Books Ltd., 80 Strand, London WC2R 0RL, England
Penguin Group Ireland, 25 St. Stephen's Green, Dublin 2, Ireland (a division of Penguin Books Ltd.)
Penguin Group (Australia), 250 Camberwell Road, Camberwell, Victoria 3124, Australia
(a division of Pearson Australia Group Pty. Ltd.)
Penguin Books India Pvt. Ltd., 11 Community Centre, Panchsheel Park, New Delhi—110 017, India
Penguin Group (NZ), 67 Apollo Drive, Rosedale, North Shore 0632, New Zealand
(a division of Pearson New Zealand Ltd.)
Penguin Books (South Africa) (Pty.) Ltd., 24 Sturdee Avenue, Rosebank, Johannesburg 2196,
South Africa

Penguin Books Ltd., Registered Offices: 80 Strand, London WC2R 0RL, England

DAMSEL IN DISGUISE

A Berkley Sensation Book / published by arrangement with the author

PRINTING HISTORY
Berkley Sensation mass-market edition / August 2010

Cover art by Jim Griffin.
Cover design by George Long.
Cover hand lettering by Ron Zinn.

For information, address: The Berkley Publishing Group,
a division of Penguin Group (USA) Inc.,
375 Hudson Street, New York, New York 10014.

ISBN: 978-0-425-23598-0

BERKLEY® SENSATION
Berkley Sensation Books are published by The Berkley Publishing Group,
a division of Penguin Group (USA) Inc.,
375 Hudson Street, New York, New York 10014.
BERKLEY® SENSATION and the "B" design are trademarks of Penguin Group (USA) Inc.

PRINTED IN THE UNITED STATES OF AMERICA

10 9 8 7 6 5 4 3 2 1

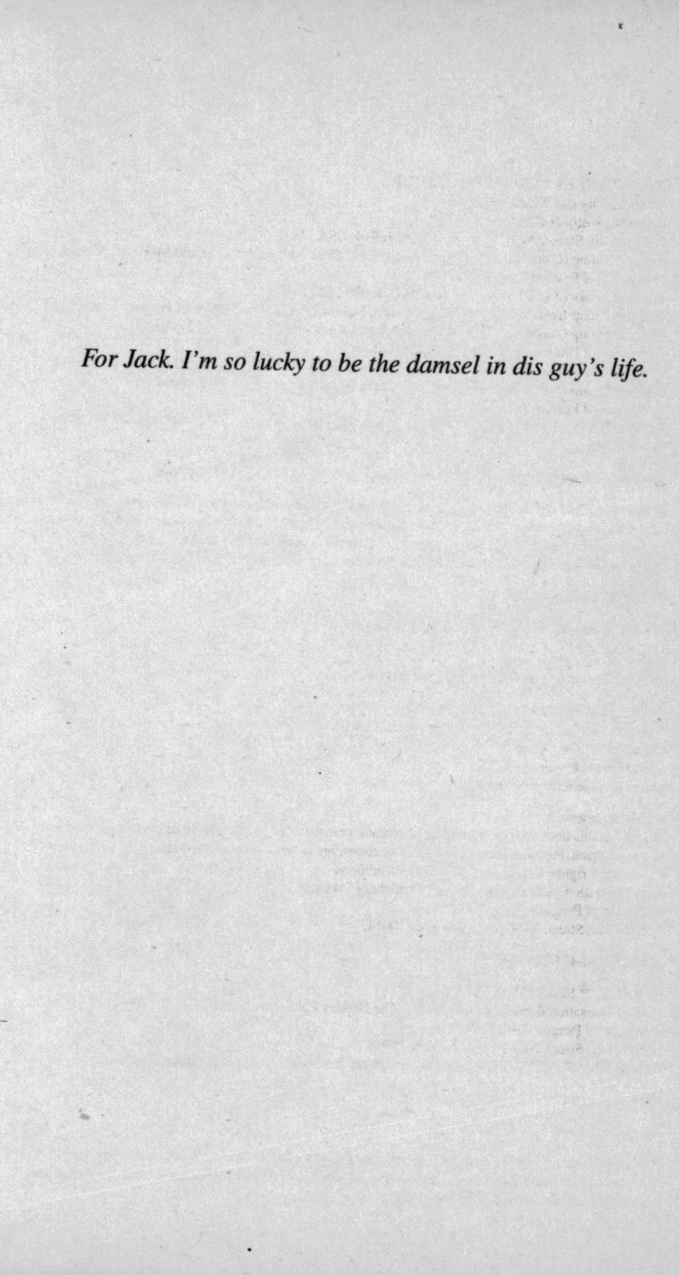

For Jack. I'm so lucky to be the damsel in dis guy's life.

Chapter One

WARWICKSHIRE, ENGLAND,
15 JUNE 1816

Julia St. Clement had never tried to eat soup through a mustache before. It was dashed difficult, she found. No wonder the awful embellishment had gone out of favor with modern men. Three days now she'd hidden behind the blasted thing, and already she felt weak and malnourished from struggling to strain any decent sustenance through it. Why ever had she let Papa talk her into this dreadful disguise?

Because she'd had no other choice—that was why. Papa had whacked off her long dark hair, fashioned a sorry little mustache from a lock of it, and threw a pack of clothing at her.

"Change quickly, *ma chérie*!" he'd ordered. "Fitzgelder will know my face, but he's not seen you before. With this, he'll never suspect who you are."

And it was true. The man they both feared—for good reason—had been completely deceived. He'd not caught a glimpse of Papa, and Julia had faced Fitzgelder alone. She was properly introduced as Mr. Alexander Clemmons, and the foul little man had no reason to guess his new friend was as much a sham as the shabby facial hair. Papa had escaped. This bloody mustache, it seemed, had saved his life.

And now, God willing, it would save a few others'. Hopefully, Julia's would be one of them. Provided, of course, she didn't succumb to starvation first.

"You've got soup on your whiskers," her pretend wife, Sophie, announced with a girlish giggle.

"Of course I do," Julia grumbled. "I've got soup on my chin, soup in my cravat, soup everywhere but in my mouth. Blast this disgusting mustache!"

"But you look quite dashing, you know," Sophie said as she daintily spooned plenty of soup safely into her own mouth. "Really, it's a pity mustaches aren't more the style."

"I feel wretched, and I look worse," Julia assured her. "It's a monstrous thing, and Papa will never hear the end of it when we finally meet up with him again."

"*If* we meet up with him," Sophie corrected, her sweet voice quavering. "The coachman has been so slow, miss. What if Mr. Fitzgelder catches us?"

"He won't. Surely that locket you stole from him isn't so important he'd come chasing us all the way out here."

"I didn't steal it!" the girl insisted for at least the dozenth time. "When he attacked me, it must have torn off in the struggle and fallen into my apron."

"Little that will matter to him, will it? But I doubt he'll be looking for you, Sophie. That locket is the least of Fitzgelder's worries just now. He's got bigger things on his mind, I'm afraid."

"Such as killing your friend, you mean."

Julia shushed her. They were sitting off alone in the crowded common room of the posting house, but still it couldn't hurt to be cautious. There was no telling who might be listening in. Fitzgelder had men out and about, and they could be anywhere right now. The room was quite full of strangers, not all of them respectable-looking.

"Anthony won't be killed if I can help it," Julia muttered under her breath.

Sophie gave a dreamy sigh. "He must be very special to you."

Lord, she'd quickly disabuse the girl of that deranged notion. "The man is a selfish lout who doesn't have an honest breath in his body," she announced. "He very nearly deserves to be murdered."

Sophie wasn't swayed. "Then why have we spent the last three days traveling all the way out here to warn him?"

"I said *nearly*," Julia had to admit. "No one deserves what Fitzgelder has planned for him; murdered on the highway by cutthroats and left there to rot."

Sophie shuddered, momentarily forgetting her soup. "Are you sure we shouldn't just find the local magistrate and tell him? I'm not too keen on all this cutthroat business."

"I told you to wait back in London, didn't I?"

Now the girl was offended. "What? And leave you to come out here alone? I couldn't do that, Miss Clement! You saved my life."

"Well, I certainly didn't save you from Fitzgelder just so his hired thugs could do you in on the road," Julia said and stared longingly at the two shriveled potatoes in her bowl. "It's getting dark. I think we should let the mail coach go on without us and spend the night here."

"Here? But surely we're getting close to—what's that place where your gentleman friend is staying?"

"Hartwood; it's likely some musty old estate. The lord of the manor had Rastmoor stand up at his wedding, and no doubt they're all still reveling. Since we've not yet passed through Warwick, and as difficult as the roads have been, it's bound to be another full day's travel for us."

Sophie sighed. "Well, I suppose we ought to stay here, then. I just hope, for the sake of that selfish lout you want to rescue, we get there in time."

"So do I, Sophie," Julia agreed, making another brave go at the soup. "So do I."

Almost as irritating as this blasted mustache was the worry that Fitzgelder's men had already reached the destination and accomplished their goal. True, she and Anthony, Viscount Rastmoor, had not parted on the best of terms, but she'd give anything right now to see that he was alive and well. If he could just walk through that door safe and sound, she'd . . . well, she'd be very relieved.

Then she'd knock him on his arse and ask what in the hell he'd been thinking three years ago when he'd wagered—and lost—her at the gaming table. Good God, as if she was chattel he could own and barter at will! Well, he'd owned her, all right—owned her heart and soul—right up until that night when Fitzgelder marched up to Papa, waving Anthony's vowels and claiming that *he* was her fiancé now. As if such a thing could be legally binding.

But it was the fact that Anthony had done such a thing, even as an angry jest, that had broken Julia's heart. She knew what it meant. Anthony had found out the truth about her identity and wanted no part of such a wife. He'd cast her off like the rubbish he believed her to be and Julia had never seen him again.

Indeed, Anthony Rastmoor simply had to remain alive. If Fitzgelder's men got to him first, how would Julia ever get her revenge?

"IT'S BROKEN," ANTHONY, LORD RASTMOOR, SAID AS he inspected the underside of their carriage.

"Damn," his companion, the Earl of Lindley, fumed. "I just bought this phaeton three weeks ago. Quite a piece, don't you think?"

"I think you got taken." Rastmoor dusted the dirt off his hands and trousers. "Most of the higher-quality conveyances have axles that actually attach to the wheels."

"It certainly was doing that when I bought the blasted thing," Lindley said, fairly diving onto his hands and knees to crawl under the carriage. "Are you saying there's been shoddy workmanship here?"

Rastmoor was perfectly content to let his elegant friend get muddy. It was, after all, Lindley's carriage. He should have been the one down there investigating in the first place, although what Lindley would have investigated, Rastmoor couldn't say. The stylish earl likely wouldn't have known the difference between a broken axle and a hay rake. Still, Rastmoor was happy enough not to be the only one with dirt on his knees.

Lindley swore, and Rastmoor had to chuckle. While most

men might let out a string of colorful words over the condition of the axle, Lindley was more likely upset over what he'd just done to his clothes. He probably wouldn't even notice it was some very shoddy workmanship, indeed, that put them in this predicament.

In fact, it hardly looked like workmanship at all. No, if Rastmoor didn't know better, he might even wonder if the damage to Lindley's carriage was intentional. But that was ridiculous. Who would tamper with Lindley's carriage? Unless, of course . . .

But that was ridiculous, too. Surely dear cousin Fitzgelder would not stoop to something like this, would he? No, this had to be merely an accident.

Damn, but it was rather coincidental, wasn't it? Mother sent a message warning he'd best get himself to London for some unnamed trouble Fitzgelder was stirring up, and now something so unusual as this threatened to delay him. Could it be mere coincidence? He wanted to believe so, but somehow he just couldn't.

What was Fitzgelder about, this time? The terms of Grandfather's will had been well settled these two years. Surely his cousin couldn't think to dredge all that up again, could he? Then again, Rastmoor had learned the hard way not to put anything past Cedrick Fitzgelder.

The horses fidgeted nervously, so Rastmoor went to calm them.

"What rotten luck," Lindley said finally, uttering a few more oaths and crawling out from under his carriage. "I don't suppose you have a spare axle or whatever you said that was?"

"No, I don't," Rastmoor said. "But if you have some straps or the like, we might be able to bind the thing well enough to get it back to that posting house we just passed. We won't be riding, though."

Lindley bit his lip and glanced around at the dusky trees lining the road on either side of them. "That's slow going, isn't it?"

"I suppose, but with that axle broken, we're done for the night, I'm afraid."

"Yes, it appears that way, but I'm not sure my horses are up for pulling dead weight. Even if we bind it, that axle won't turn very well, will it?"

So Lindley did have some basic understanding of the mechanics of the thing. Well, he couldn't very well blame the man for not wanting to overtax his cattle. The only thing finer than Lindley's wardrobe was his stables, and these two goers were as good as they got. It would be a shame for such proud horseflesh to be dragging a lame carriage all the way to that posting house.

"All right, help me loose them, then. We'll walk the horses and send someone back to get your precious phaeton."

Lindley agreed, then noticed his muddied condition. "Bother. My valet will have my hide over these trousers."

Oh, not the valet again. Rastmoor rolled his eyes. "I don't see how you abide the man. From what you say, he sounds like a ruddy tyrant."

Lindley smiled. "That he is, but I assure you I'd never make it without him. Which reminds me."

He left Rastmoor with the horses and went around to the back of the carriage. He dug through a box stowed there.

"Ahem, but we unharness the horses up at this end," Rastmoor called.

"Yes, but the weapons are back here."

"Weapons?"

"Here, take this," Lindley called out, tossing Rastmoor a lethal little pistol.

"What's this?" Rastmoor asked.

"It's a pistol," Lindley informed him.

"I know it's a pistol. What in God's name is it for?"

"For shooting anyone who might come out of those trees after us." Lindley glanced at said trees and shuddered. "You never know what sort of persons are about these days, and it's very nearly dark out."

"Good grief. Is it loaded?"

"Of course. What bloody use would it be empty?"

Rastmoor shook his head, but he accepted the pistol and slipped it into his pocket. He was a bit taken aback when Lindley casually tucked his own pistol into the front of his trousers. This image of the always elegant Lindley with a pistol wedged at his waist was more than a bit humorous.

"What is it?" Lindley asked.

"Aren't you worried that will ruin the lines of your tailoring?" Rastmoor asked, not bothering to hide his smirk. "Whatever will your valet think?"

"Should a highwayman leap out after us, I would prefer to have my weapon where I can get at it," Lindley said, stepping up to help with the horses. "A few wrinkles can always be ironed out. Blood, my valet tells me, is a bit more dicey."

"I'm sure it is," Rastmoor had to agree.

No highwaymen did leap out, though, and they pushed and pulled until the phaeton was safely out of the roadway. Leading Lindley's fine horses, the men headed off to the posting house. The evening was dreary and still, yet not nearly so dreary as the day two months ago when Rastmoor had traveled this same road.

He'd been traveling with his friend Dashford, on the way to what was supposed to have been a quiet house party. Some house party, though. There were floods and fiancées and fiascos until the bloody thing ended with Dashford's wedding. Rastmoor still wasn't sure how he felt about that.

The whole concept of matrimony hadn't exactly worked out very well for him and, to be honest, he was still not convinced any man ought to put much stock in the institution. From what Rastmoor had seen so far, women were an untrustworthy lot. He hoped Dash wouldn't have to learn that the hard way.

Rastmoor sighed as they plodded along. Damn, but with Dashford trussed up and married now, Rastmoor would likely have to settle for Lindley's persnickety company more often. Oh well. For a game here or there at the club or a visit to the races, no one could fault Lindley's sportsmanship or his overall entertainment value. But if Rastmoor had to have one more discussion about where to find the best gloves or which bloody knot would look best in his cravat . . . Honestly, what could Dashford have been thinking to go and get leg shackled?

"You know what I'm thinking?" Lindley said after they'd walked in silence quite a while, the horses plodding nervously along behind them.

He hated to imagine. "No. What?"

"There'll likely be women at this posting house."

"Probably so."

"That suits me just fine. With luck, there'll be a couple for both of us. Which do you prefer, the blonds or the brunettes?"

"The ones who do their job and disappear before daylight."

"I reckon that'll be all of them," Lindley declared with a hopeful laugh. "I think I'd favor a blond tonight. Unless of course there's only one available, and blond is your preference, then naturally I would—"

"No, thank you. Have any woman you want. I think I'll just sleep tonight."

"What? But you've been stuck up there at Hartwood for nearly two months, and I saw the sort of guests they had—not exactly fresh and accommodating, as they say. Surely now that you're getting out and about again, you'd want to prime the old pump handle, if you know what I mean."

"I know what you mean, damn it," Rastmoor grumbled. "But I'm not interested, all right? Good luck to you and your pump handle, but I'd rather sleep. Alone."

Lindley frowned as if that was a foreign concept. "Alone? But you're not ill, are you?"

"No. I'm fine."

"You don't sound fine. You sound—blue deviled. My God, but you can't possibly still be pining after that girl? That little French actress of yours—St. Clem, or something, wasn't it?"

"St. Clement," Rastmoor corrected before he caught himself. The last thing in the world he wanted was to discuss Julia right now. "And I'm not pining. I'm just not interested in some dirty whore at a posting house, all right?"

Lindley gave a slow whistle. "You *are* still pining! Dash it all, Rastmoor, that was years ago. And didn't she end up marrying your cousin or something?"

"Yes."

By God, what would it take to not have this conversation? Was he going to have to use that pistol on Lindley?

"That's right, and then she died in childbed, didn't she?" Lindley went on.

Rastmoor gritted his teeth. "That's what I heard."

Oh, he'd heard the story, all right. Then he'd gone and gotten roaring drunk. Dashford's father had taken ill and died some short time thereafter, and the two of them were roaring drunk together. Things hadn't gone so well for them after that, as he recalled.

Eventually, Dashford pulled himself together, and Rastmoor had simply learned to pretend. He supposed, in a way, it had been easier for Dash. He'd been mourning a devoted father, a man who left behind fond memories and warm emotions. Rastmoor, however, had been grieving something altogether different.

When Julia St. Clement died, all she left behind were bitter wounds and heartbreak. It was hard enough knowing she'd left him for another man, but with time he might have recovered. It cut deeper than that, though. Julia left him a scar that would never go away. The whore may have died in Fitzgelder's bed, but the child she'd taken to the grave with her had been Rastmoor's. She'd carried *his* child and still left him for another, passing the child off as Fitzgelder's.

How did a man ever recover from that?

"I CAN'T WAIT TO SEE THIS LORD RASTMOOR'S FACE when he meets you again," Sophie was saying as they finished their supper.

Julia cringed. "Hopefully that will never happen. With luck, we'll find he's safely at Lord Dashford's home, and I can simply send a warning message. He'll find out what Fitzgelder is about, and you and I can be off to meet Papa."

"You don't want to see him again?"

"Heavens no!"

"We've come all this way, and you're not even going to see the man?"

"Exactly."

Sophie was downcast. "That's so sad. I was hoping the two of you might . . ."

"Sorry, Sophie. That only happens in novels."

It was a shame to disappoint the poor girl, but better she get such foolishness out of her mind now before she started expecting grand romance for her own life. Indeed, women like them should harbor no such hopes—Julia had learned that the hard way. Perhaps the truth would come easier for Sophie.

"We'll be done with this before you know it," Julia went on, hoping her light tone and warm smile would both encourage and distract her young friend. "Then we'll find Papa, and you'll become a part of our troupe. You're quite a hand at sewing, but perhaps we can coax you into acting, as well."

"Acting? Oh, I'm sure I could never be so very good at that. All those lines I'd have to memorize!"

"You've been playacting the part of a blushing bride for three days now, and so far, the audience seems quite enthralled," Julia said, sweeping her arm wide to indicate the patrons of the posting house, a few of whom had traveled this last leg of the journey on the mail coach with them.

Sophie looked around the dim room and frowned. "I believe our audience would be no less enthralled were I simply a chicken tucked under your arm. They've hardly taken note of us at all."

"There, you see? You've played your part to perfection. Who's to say you might not make a memorable Juliet or Ophelia or—"

"Lord Lindley!" Sophie said suddenly.

"Lord Lindley? I don't believe we have any scripts with Lor—"

And then Julia glanced up to realize what Sophie meant. The doorway was filled with the elegant form of a man they had briefly met in London just as they were making their hasty escape. Lord Lindley—a good friend and confidante of the evil Fitzgelder.

Sophie's eyes were huge and terrified, and Julia wanted to slide under the table. Good heavens, if Lindley recognized them, he'd notify Fitzgelder of their whereabouts! They had to hide, to get out of here this very instant.

But there was nowhere they could go, nowhere in the room to hide. They were trapped. Julia's pulse pounded, and she struggled to think up some scheme to protect them. What could she do? Where could they . . . ?

Suddenly all coherent thought ceased.

A familiar broad-shouldered form appeared behind Lindley. Julia's lungs contracted, the air squeezed out of them in a whimper. Around her, the world disappeared, and she was aware of only one thing: Anthony Rastmoor was still alive.

Thank God she wasn't too late! Fitzgelder's men hadn't succeeded in their plan. Anthony still lived and breathed and wore that smile of half amusement, half boredom she'd come to know so well three years ago. Three long, painful years ago.

He was alive, and he was beautiful. And he was cold. When his gaze fell on her, she recoiled, both inwardly and out. The chill that emanated in his hazel eyes was as unfamiliar as the image that had been greeting her in the mirror since she and Sophie had taken up this masquerade. Indeed, the Anthony Rastmoor who followed Lindley into the poorly lit common room was a man much changed from the man who had taken Julia's virtue—as well as her heart.

His gaze didn't last long on her, though. Quickly it moved on, as if she were of little importance to anyone. This surprised her more than even the fact that she was seeing him again. How could she be struggling for air, feeling as if the universe itself would collapse around her, and yet his gaze simply swept over her as if she'd been nothing more than furniture? It was unthinkably hurtful.

Then his gaze did linger, but not on her. She had to physically turn her head to see what he was seeing. The air swept back into her lungs and burned like fire.

He was gazing at Sophie.

Her brain began functioning again. Mostly her thoughts were torn, though. Should she gouge out the man's eyes or grab up a dull knife and castrate him here? God, but how he was staring at Sophie! The nerve of him!

Funny, Julia had never contemplated how fetching the girl must appear to those of the male persuasion. Yes, Sophie was pretty, she supposed. Gentlemen would notice that, of course. But, by God, what was that charming expression forming on Sophie's fresh, youthful face? Why, the little tart was actually smiling at Anthony Rastmoor!

Julia's stomach roiled, and she put an involuntary hand up to her mouth. Damn, but there was soup in the mustache there. She hated the itchy thing all the more. Of course Anthony would not look at her in the same way he was ogling Sophie—soup-stained gentlemen were hardly his type. Gullible little misses like Sophie were. Just as Julia had been, once.

"Why, Mr. and Mrs. Clemmons," Lindley said, noticing them and coming their way.

Julia had given the false name at the spur of the moment as they were leaving London. It had seemed convenient to use as they'd traveled, and now she was glad they had. No one would think it amiss to see the quiet Clemmons couple being greeted by an old acquaintance here, and no awkward explanations would have to be given at mistaken names.

Anthony, too, would likely not recognize the name.

Or maybe it didn't really matter. He'd likely forgotten her altogether, judging by the way his attention was now given entirely to her companion. Indeed, why should he so much as spare a second glance to Julia's severe haircut and soupy mustache, while Sophie was sitting there in front of him, all blond and dreamy and feminine? Damn his eyes.

"How odd to run into you here," Lord Lindley said when he reached their table. "I had no idea you were traveling this way, else I would have invited you to share my carriage."

He, too, had his eye on Sophie. What pigs these men were. Didn't they realize Sophie was supposed to be a married woman? How dare they stare like this! If it kept on, Julia feared she'd end up having to call at least one of them out or risk exposing herself as a fraud. What husband could sit calmly while virtual strangers drooled over his wife? Shame on them. How on earth had Julia ever thought Anthony Rastmoor to be a decent, worthwhile human being?

"We had a rather sudden change of plan," Sophie was saying. "Didn't we, Mr. Clemmons?"

Julia cleared her throat. "Er, yes. We came this way rather spur of the moment." She worked at keeping her voice low and hoped Anthony might not recognize it.

She needn't have worried. His focus was all on Sophie, to the point the poor girl must have noticed and was finally starting to appear uncomfortable.

"Forgive me," Lindley said, at least trying to tear his eyes from Sophie and act respectably. "Everyone has not been introduced. Lord Rastmoor, this is Mr. Alexander Clemmons and his lovely wife, Mrs. Sophie Clemmons. We met a few days ago in London."

Rastmoor made a polite bow and allowed Julia a quick nod before turning his attention back to Sophie. It had been highly unnecessary for Lindley to recall Sophie's first name, but obviously he had. Sophie was looking decidedly anxious now. The girl might be too pretty for her own good, but at least she appeared to have some sense. She knew enough not to trust the flattery of blackguards.

"How do you do," Julia said, not pausing long enough for Rastmoor to speak before directing her next question to Lindley. "Will you gentlemen be staying for the night here?"

Lindley sent a quick look toward his partner, and Rastmoor gave the reply. His voice sliced Julia to the heart. Odd that a voice could have so much power.

"We're undecided as yet, Mr. Clemmons. Will you be staying?"

Julia fixed her eyes firmly on her soup bowl. *Mr. Clemmons*. He still hadn't recognized her. Lord, but that, too, hurt far more than it should have.

"We haven't entirely decided that, my lord," Julia replied. It was true. If she found the men would be here, she'd simply leave a note of warning for Rastmoor with the innkeeper then get herself and Sophie back on the road and far away from the lusty lords.

But Sophie had her own ideas. She smiled brightly for the men. "The roads have been so very difficult, though. I do truly dread getting back in that coach to be jostled along to the next posting house. Perhaps if Mr. Clemmons knew some of his gentlemen friends were to be staying here tonight, I could stand a better chance of convincing him."

Julia gaped at her friend. What was she doing? Now that Lindley was here, they needed to leave, not settle in for the night! He was the one who could unmask them! Maybe Sophie didn't have so much sense, after all.

Lord Lindley gave a rumbling chuckle and turned his gaze onto Julia. "Shame on you, Mr. Clemmons, forcing your young bride to travel under these conditions."

His attention was short-lived. He returned his focus—and a disgustingly warm smile—back on Sophie. "Rest assured, Mrs. Clemmons, if it will gain you a few hours' respite from the torment of travel, Rastmoor and I will do our best to persuade your husband to obtain a room for the night. In fact"—here Lindley smiled at Rastmoor, who gave a slight nod—"I'll go see to making arrangements with the proprietor. Don't worry, Clemmons, tonight will be at my expense."

Lindley made a showy bow then went off in the direction the innkeeper had last been seen. Blast, what had Sophie done? It was true the small purse Julia had on her at the time of their departure was growing a bit thin right now, but certainly she couldn't allow Lindley to assume their expenses. Even more certainly, she couldn't spend the night under the same roof as Anthony Rastmoor! What if the man tried to engage her in conversation? How long could she expect her disguise to hold out if Rastmoor ever did decide to take his eyes off Sophie long enough to question Mr. Clemmons's bizarre mustache and feminine voice?

But so far Rastmoor hadn't reached that point. He was still staring at Sophie and smiling in delight as he called out to Lindley, "See about getting us a private dining room, as well. I'm sure the Clemmonses will wish to join us in a quiet supper."

Oh, Lord. What next?

Lindley nodded and disappeared into a back hallway where the innkeeper had last been seen to go. Julia glanced nervously at Sophie. The girl just batted her wide blue eyes and shrugged. Well, Julia would just have to find a way to get them out of this.

"There's no need for a private room, sir," she protested. "Mrs. Clemmons and I have just finished our meal, as you can see, and now we'd like—"

"Oh, but dearest," Sophie interrupted, innocent and darling. "Surely that little bowl of soup was barely enough for a strapping man such as yourself. Why not join your friend Rastmoor over a hearty meal?"

Ah, so *that* was Sophie's angle. The chit was meddling. Julia would put a quick end to that. And just what on earth did the little hussy mean by calling Julia "strapping"?

"I assure you, my precious, that soup was quite adequate for my frame," Julia said. "We have no need to remain here any longer. I simply need to give a note to our innkeeper, if you recall." Now she gave Sophie a glare that should have wiped the pink smile from her rosebud lips. It didn't.

"What's our hurry, dear? Surely you can think of *something* interesting to discuss with these fine gentlemen," Sophie suggested.

"No, actually, I'm sure I can't," Julia assured her.

"Fear not, Clemmons," Rastmoor said, leaning casually against a nearby table and leering down at Sophie. "I'm sure we'll find plenty to occupy our time. In fact, a private room will be just what we need. There is a particular matter I'm certain you'll be most eager to discuss."

Now, that erased the pink smile. Sophie slid a nervous glance at Julia. What was Rastmoor hinting at with that glinting eye and ominous tone? Had he found them out? Preventing any hasty escape Julia may have contrived, Lindley returned with the proprietor.

"Yer in luck," the innkeeper said with an eager grin. "I got a nice room just waiting for ye, and my wife'll bring a good, healthy stew."

Julia tried to demur, but Lindley gracefully swooped in to loop Sophie's hand through his arm and assist her up from her chair. When Julia glanced over at Rastmoor, she found him, at last, looking her way.

"Come, Clemmons," he said. "I doubt you'll want to miss this."

Indeed, from the way he spoke, she was fairly certain she *did* want to miss it, whatever *it* was. She was fairly certain, too, he was not about to let her. Helpless, she followed Anthony Rastmoor through the big, safe common area into a private dining room off the dark corner under the stairs.

Chapter Two

Rastmoor was even more uncomfortable in the small room Lindley had obtained than he had been in the common. This Clemmons fellow was one odd duck. He fidgeted incessantly, and his doelike eyes seemed to stare everywhere but at Rastmoor. Sophie perched at the edge of her chair with hands wringing in her lap like a scolded child. Every now and then she'd catch her husband's eye, and she'd shrink a little more. It was more than enough to convince Rastmoor things were not quite as they should be with this couple.

Not that he'd expected any different. He knew who this Sophie Clemmons was. Just days ago he'd promised his friend Dashford he'd find her. He hadn't been exactly relishing the task, either, especially since he and Dash both knew the likelihood of his efforts producing nothing more than bad news. From what Dashford and his new wife, Evaline, had said, their cousin Sophie Darshaw had fallen in with a dangerous crowd and was likely long lost.

But then Lindley showed up at Dashford's wedding and mentioned he'd run across a girl of that very name and description in London. Seeing her before them now, Rastmoor had no doubt this Sophie and Dashford's Sophie were one and the same. The resemblance between the new Lady Dashford and her long-lost cousin was uncanny; Rastmoor had been quite stunned by it when he first laid eyes on Sophie. The women could have easily passed for close sisters. But finding her here, less than one day's drive from Dashford himself, was an unbelievable coincidence. In fact, Rastmoor didn't believe it was coincidental at all.

He presumed it must be Clemmons's doing, and Rastmoor had a fair idea of why. Clemmons must know all about Sophie's connection to Dashford. He'd no doubt whisked her away from her dismal life in London with the hopes of profiting. It could safely be assumed Dashford and his lady would pay handsomely to secure Sophie's welfare, not to mention to keep their relationship to her a secret.

Clemmons was, no doubt, taking Sophie to Hartwood with nothing short of extortion on his mind. Whether Sophie was a part of this scheme or not Rastmoor was still uncertain. Evaline claimed her cousin was merely an unfortunate victim of circumstance, but Rastmoor's understanding of women left him wary.

Either way, though, Rastmoor willingly put the heaviest portion of guilt on Clemmons. In fact, he could barely stomach looking at the man with his shifty eyes under those impossibly long lashes. He wore a dreadful mustache, too, which did not speak well at all. His mannerisms were so effete even the greatest dandy would find them disturbing. And the warning glances he kept sending to Sophie spoke volumes. Whether it had been her idea or not, clearly she was in on the scheme and harbored a guilty conscience.

"So, Clemmons, what brings you out here to Warwickshire?" Lindley asked as they all sat down together and waited for the innkeeper's wife to bring the promised stew.

Clemmons hesitated before answering. "Nothing, really, sir. We're simply passing through."

"Oh? You're not on your way to pay a call on Mrs. Clemmons's family?" Rastmoor asked.

Clemmons actually wrinkled his brow, but Sophie caught

Rastmoor's attention with a quick little gasp. *A gasp?* So the girl hadn't expected anyone to know about that. Well, she'd find Rastmoor knew a great deal.

"I wasn't aware Mrs. Clemmons had family in Warwickshire," Mr. Clemmons said quickly.

Sophie dropped her gaze to her lap. "I don't. My grandmother used to live not a great distance from here, but she passed away. I've no more family anywhere."

"Your grandmother?" Mr. Clemmons said with oddly believable compassion. "I'm sorry. I didn't realize that."

"It's all right," Sophie replied sweetly. "You couldn't have known."

Blast it, but the couple were passable liars. Yet why should that be surprising? Lindley told them Clemmons was an actor; indeed, the man must have taught the trade to his little wife. Well, it was time to call them on their charade.

Rastmoor cleared his throat before he continued. "And just where have you been living, Mrs. Clemmons, in the years since your grandmother passed away?"

Sophie had the good grace to look confused. Likely she was trying to determine in her mind how much Rastmoor might know about her background before she fabricated an answer. Mr. Clemmons appeared even more unnerved. The poor little man seemed desperate to think up something, but his creativity was apparently dried up. Silly man, clearly he was out of his depth in this. Well, Rastmoor would be only too happy to help them both on the point of discussing Sophie's past.

He couldn't help but smile when he asked casually, "Were you at Madame Eudora's brothel for the entire past four years, or did you find work elsewhere, too?"

Sophie's mouth pursed into an astonished little button, while Mr. Clemmons's jaw fell slack. Rastmoor could almost have believed the man knew nothing of Sophie's past, except for the fact he could hardly imagine where else a scheming and effeminate man like this might obtain a wife but at a brothel.

"A *brothel?*" Clemmons sputtered.

Sophie jumped to her feet and started backing away, accidentally trapping herself in a corner. The fear on her face was clearly more than good acting this time.

"That's none of your business!" she sputtered. "I'm not there anymore, and I won't go with you . . . either of you!"

Now Mr. Clemmons leapt to his feet in a rage, turning on them. "Leave her alone!" he demanded in a high, girlish voice. "Hasn't she been through enough with the likes of you? Take your filthy minds and your petty accusations out of here this instant!"

Rastmoor had never seen a hysterical man before, but he was fairly certain he was looking at one now. If Clemmons had not been so delicate and so—well—pretty, he supposed the man could have been almost fearsome. As it was, though, the man's passion was convincing. He did not appreciate such talk about his wife.

Rastmoor made the mistake of taking a step toward him. "All I'm saying is—"

He didn't get to finish all he was saying. Clemmons lunged and swung at him, catching him off guard and forcing him backward, into Lindley. Both gentlemen toppled over, leaving Clemmons free to rush into the corner for his still whimpering wife.

"Come, Sophie," Clemmons said gruffly, leading her out of the corner and around their table. "The mail coach is still in the yard. Let's get out of here."

Lindley was helping Rastmoor to his feet. "Damn it, Rastmoor—"

For half a heartbeat Rastmoor had a chance to wonder why on earth Lindley would be cursing him when it was, after all, Clemmons's fault they were sprawled on the floor, but his thoughts were interrupted. Glass shattered, and a loud concussion ripped through the room. The chair between Rastmoor and Lindley splintered violently as a bullet came through the broken window and lodged there, narrowly missing both men. Sophie and Clemmons screamed. They sounded remarkably alike.

"Get down!" Lindley yelled.

Rastmoor dropped to the floor, Mr. and Mrs. Clemmons

tumbling down near him. Lindley shoved the table over on its side to provide some measure of protection should more bullets come hailing through the only window in the small room. They did not, and Rastmoor called over to Clemmons.

"Are you hurt?"

"Are you?" Clemmons asked in return.

His huge, feminine eyes flashed with concern, and for a moment Rastmoor was caught in them. What sort of God put eyes like that in a man's face? He could make no sense of it. Quickly, though, Clemmons turned away. He gave his full attention to his wife, making sure Sophie had not been harmed.

Rastmoor looked at Lindley. "What the hell was that?"

But Lindley was already scrambling to his feet. "I don't know. I'll go check the front; you go out the back."

"Very well," Rastmoor agreed, since he really didn't know what else to do in this sort of situation. He gave Clemmons another glance. "Stay here, and stay down."

Mr. Clemmons didn't seem particularly happy with those instructions, but Rastmoor didn't bother to stick around to hear his complaints. Crouching, he followed Lindley out of the room and into the hall. The innkeeper ran smack into them and demanded to know what they'd been doing in his best room.

Lindley ignored the man and simply headed for the front door that would lead him out into the yard. Rastmoor muttered a warning that the man had better get out of sight somewhere and pushed past him to head for the back. He doubted the innkeeper—or any other innocent bystander—was really in danger. Rastmoor hadn't seen the shooter, but he had an idea who the fool had been aiming at: *him*.

JULIA WATCHED THE MEN RUSH OUT OF THE ROOM. Tables and chairs were overturned, shattered glass lay about the floor, and Sophie was starting to tremble. Heavens, what on earth had happened?

It must have been Fitzgelder! No, not Fitzgelder, but one of his hirelings. Fitzgelder was too cowardly to do the dirty work himself. But somehow his men had found Rastmoor and very nearly succeeded in their goal. Just how did they find him?

Lindley, it had to be. Once he met up with Rastmoor at that wedding, he must have gotten word to Fitzgelder's men. He pretended to be Rastmoor's friend all the while he'd been leading him into a trap. And heavens, he'd just taken Rastmoor outside! Lindley had said he was going one way and told Rastmoor to go the other—to his doom, probably.

Oh, but this was dreadful. While she cowered here under a table, Anthony was being murdered behind the posting house! No, she couldn't let that happen.

"Wait here," she called to Sophie as she clambered to her feet.

Sophie protested, of course, but Julia paid no mind. Thankfully, climbing in and out from under furniture was much easier in trousers than in her usual gowns, so she was on her feet and running into the hallway long before Sophie had time to collect her voice. Julia simply had to get to Anthony in time and warn him, to tell him that Lindley was in league with Fitzgelder.

She burst through the back door just in time to realize this was a very bad idea. Whoever was waiting there to kill Anthony would no doubt be just as glad to kill her right along with him. She paused on the back stoop and scanned the area around the posting house. The sun was getting low, and the trees cast long shadows over everything. Anthony was nowhere in sight. Everything was still. Too still.

Suddenly someone burst from the shrubbery beside her and pulled her to the ground, dragging her into the dim, musky seclusion of the overgrown foliage. Her face was pressed into the dirt. The whole thing happened so fast, she couldn't even struggle. All she could think was how positively annoying this helplessness was. Anthony needed her somewhere!

But then he spoke in her ear. "Keep quiet, Clemmons."

Thank heavens, he was all right. He was grinding her into the ground, pressing his knee into her back, but at least he was all right. So far.

"It's Lindley," she tried to say, though with all the dirt in her mouth she wasn't sure it came out entirely intelligible.

"Shut up," he hissed. "And pay attention. I don't believe for one second you and your little missus are just passing through here for the joy of it. I know who she is, Clemmons. Now, I'm going to give you one chance to tell me why you've come out here and how you're involved in what just happened. I'd better like what I hear. Start talking."

But heavens, what could she tell him? He seemed to know more about Sophie than she did. A brothel? Poor Sophie! But did Rastmoor really believe Sophie's unfortunate past had anything to do with the attempt just made on his life? She struggled to make sense of it all.

"It's Fitzgelder," she said. Her voice was weak with Rastmoor's weight cutting off her air supply. "He's hired men to find you and kill you!"

"Oh? I take it you're in league with him?"

She could barely draw enough breath to reply. "No! It's Lindley. Lindley's in it."

"What?" His knee let up just a bit.

"It's true. I heard Fitzgelder planning it. Lindley was there."

There was silence. She could hear voices calling out from the front of the inn, but Rastmoor didn't seem to care. "What were you doing with Fitzgelder?"

"My troupe was putting on a private performance in his house. I, er, happened to accidentally overhear him talking with some men. We barely got away."

"You're sure Lindley was in on it?"

"He was there while Fitzgelder was plotting your murder, for pity's sake. He didn't speak up to protest on your behalf, either."

Rastmoor moved himself off of her, and she drew in a deep breath. Indeed, she'd forgotten how heavy the man was, tall and solid as he was. Her cheeks went warm at the memory, and she was glad for the shadows and the prickly shelter of the shrub. She pushed herself up to sitting, keeping her face averted. Rastmoor stayed near.

"So what do you want from me?" he asked.

"I want you not to get murdered."

"A most noble cause. Now tell me what you really want. Money? An appointment for your troupe? To blackmail your way into Sophie's family?"

"She says she doesn't have any family."

"We all know that's a lie. I swear, Clemmons, I won't let you—"

But he stopped short. The voices were clearly coming around to the back of the building. He gave her a warning look then started to get up as if he'd leave the shrub. Julia grabbed his sleeve.

"No! It's Lindley!" she said.

He shot his hand out to cover her mouth. He smelled like midnight and leather. He was warm, and his skin was rough. She battled back the memory of how his hands felt on other parts of her body, as well.

"Keep quiet," he said, and she recognized the threat in his voice. Rastmoor rose and pushed his way out of the shrub.

"Did you find anyone?" he called as Lindley's footsteps approached.

"No, but a couple of the grooms saw someone on horseback riding away just after they heard the gunfire."

"No one they recognized, I suppose?" Rastmoor asked.

One of the grooms—she supposed, since it wasn't a familiar voice—answered. "Sorry, milord. I didn't get a good enough look. And anyway, lots of folk were here just then, drinking and such. They mostly all took off when they heard the shooting. The gent I saw might have just been one of those. You might do better to ask them still inside what they saw."

"Yes, we might," Rastmoor said.

Lindley thanked the groom for his trouble, and Julia heard one set of footsteps heading off. Her heart sped. Rastmoor and Lindley were alone out there. What could she do if Lindley pulled out a weapon?

"You don't by any chance know who was supposed to get shot tonight, do you?" Rastmoor asked.

"To tell the truth, no," Lindley said.

Julia cursed him under her breath.

Lindley went on. "But I do know it's not safe around here for you, Rastmoor. Fitzgelder's been stirring up trouble again."

"I know. I'm on my way back to London now to deal with it."

"Might be better to wait, all things considered," Lindley cautioned.

"*All things*? And what would those things be?"

"I don't know, but he's got something on his mind. Look, you shouldn't stay here tonight; it's too dangerous. Why not head back out to Dashford's and take our long-lost Sophie with you."

"And you?" Rastmoor asked.

"I'll head after that man the groom saw."

"He said he wasn't sure that was our shooter."

"Who else would it be? You just get yourself to Dashford's."

"And take Mr. and Mrs. Clemmons with me."

"Right," Lindley said then laughed. "If there's any chance of losing the mister along the way, that's what I'd propose."

Julia cursed him again. *Well!* This Lindley fellow was as unpleasant as they came. He might cut a fine figure, but that was plainly as far as his value went. She supposed the only reason he didn't just garrote Anthony where he stood was a fear of smudging his shirtsleeves.

But Rastmoor seemed oblivious to the danger or the difficulty he might have "losing the mister along the way."

"Fine," he said. "That's what I'll do."

Julia wondered if she ought to curse him as well. Then again, she'd done plenty of that these past three years.

"Good," Lindley agreed. "You go collect the Clemmonses, and I'll see if I can get a fast horse."

"You'll go off on your own, Lindley? Isn't it a bit dangerous?"

"Don't worry. I can handle it."

The cocky assurance in the man's voice was more than enough to convict him, as far as Julia was concerned. She'd seen the man, and he gave no appearance of one familiar with rough-and-tumble. Clearly he must know he was in no danger, chasing off alone on horseback in the dark after a would-be assassin. Likely this Dashford fellow where Lindley was so keen on sending them was in on it, as well, and would finish the botched task when Rastmoor arrived. Obviously, Anthony Rastmoor could stand to make some better friends.

Lindley's heavy footsteps crunched rapidly off toward the stables, and Julia wondered what would happen next. Surely Rastmoor wasn't fool enough to follow Lindley's instructions, was he?

"Clemmons," Rastmoor called. "Get out here."

She couldn't come up with any reason to argue, so she staggered out from behind the shrubs. A wayward branch nearly ripped off her mustache, but she managed to get it to stick back in place. Bother, but she must look an absolute sight.

"I take it you heard that?" Rastmoor asked as she emerged, dusting herself off as best she could.

"I did. The man cannot be trusted."

"He wasn't exactly threatening me."

Dear heavens! Was it possible the mutton-headed dullard was still choosing to trust Lindley? Unbelievable.

"I'm telling you, he's in on it!" she said. "He was helping Fitzgelder plan your murder!"

Rastmoor just gave her a cold glare. "I don't believe you."

"So, what are you going to do? Drag Sophie and me off to this Dashford person, where Lindley probably has a trap set for you?"

"Nothing's going to happen to you or your wife," Rastmoor said.

"Really? His lordship seemed to suggest otherwise. Lose me along the way, will you?"

"He was funning."

"I didn't find it humorous. Nor would Sophie."

"Look, it's not my first choice, but Lindley was right. We do need to get Mrs. Clemmons safely to Dashford's home. And you, too, I suppose."

"We'll do nothing of the sort. My wife and I have nothing

to do with this Dashford, and it's likely just a ruse to get you killed."

"Nothing to do with Dashford? Do you think I'm a fool? I told you I already know all about Sophie Darshaw and where she comes from."

"Then you know more than I, sir," Julia said, hoping the little bit of truth she dared share with him would be enough to convince him. "As far I was aware, Sophie worked as a housemaid in Fitzgelder's home, and the man used her abominably. She left with me as a means of escape."

"You know nothing about her connection to Lord Dashford?"

"*Lord* Dashford? I swear, if Sophie wished to claim any connection to one of your ruddy lords, don't you think she would have done so? Maybe he kept her before Fitzgelder; I don't know, and I don't care. But if Sophie doesn't wish to associate with the man, then who are you to drag her back there?"

"He wasn't her protector, damn it," Rastmoor growled. "He's her cousin. So is his new wife. Lady Dashford has been looking everywhere for the girl, and she practically begged me to lend a hand in the search. They want to help the chit, not abuse her some more."

Julia studied him. Could this be true? Sophie had a family? Good, decent family who cared about her? It was hard to believe. Since Lindley was keen on reuniting Sophie with her family—and getting Rastmoor there as well—Julia figured she likely shouldn't believe it. Or trust anyone.

"We'll ask Sophie if she knows about this," Julia declared, careful not to let Rastmoor meet her eyes. "If she says this cousin is someone she can trust, then perhaps we'll go there. But if your Dashford is friends with Lindley . . ."

"I'd trust my life to Randolf Dashford," Rastmoor announced.

"You might be doing just that," Julia cautioned, falling in step behind Rastmoor as he strode up to the back door.

Chapter Three

The innkeeper was swearing under his breath as he swept up the broken glass. Rastmoor glanced around the room where he'd been nearly killed just minutes ago, but it was clear that no further clues could be gained. Not that he needed them. He knew Fitzgelder was behind this.

There were a couple things he didn't know, however. One was whether Clemmons could be trusted about Lindley's involvement. The other was a bit more immediate.

Where the hell was Sophie?

"She was right here just a minute ago!" Clemmons announced, pushing Rastmoor aside and hurriedly examining the room.

"Weren't nobody in here just a minute ago when I came in with my broom," the innkeeper said. "Damn mess you people made in here, though."

"We didn't make the mess," Rastmoor grumbled. "We got bloody shot at here in your fine establishment. Now where is Mrs. Clemmons?"

"Pretty little thing with the yellow hair?" the man asked, scratching his greasy head. "Don't know. Guess I figured she went off with you."

Rastmoor could feel the tension rising in Mr. Clemmons. Indeed, he had a bad feeling about this. The posting house wasn't that big. They'd just come through the common room, and Sophie wasn't there. She hadn't been with Lindley, either. If she wasn't there and she wasn't here, where in God's name was she?

And just why the hell did the scrawny fool Clemmons leave his wife alone when someone was going around shooting at people?

Unless maybe that was part of the plan. Damn it, maybe that shooting incident didn't have anything to do with Fitzgelder's attempt at revenge. Maybe it was simply a distraction—directed by none other than Clemmons himself.

"You left her alone in here, Clemmons? With a gunman running loose?"

Clemmons was all twitchy and uptight. His gaze darted around the room, out into the hall, through the broken window, anywhere but at Rastmoor. He had guilt written all over him.

"Where's Sophie, Clemmons?" Rastmoor asked.

"I don't know!" the man exclaimed.

Finally he looked up at Rastmoor and, by God, those almost looked like tears in his sensitive eyes. Hell, he sure could play a part. Rastmoor wasn't buying, though. It was too convenient. Clemmons showed up to warn Rastmoor that Fitzgelder was after him, just as Sophie mysteriously disappeared? What a perfect way to set up a kidnapping—a fake kidnapping for the purpose of extorting money from Dashford.

Rastmoor eyed the young man. Damn, those eyes were disturbing. What did they make Rastmoor think of? Hell, he hadn't seen eyes like that since . . . he couldn't place it. Clemmons looked away.

"She might have gone to use the necessary," the innkeeper suggested.

While her husband was off doing battle with a would-be murderer? Not likely, Rastmoor decided. And surely if this really were a well-orchestrated ruse and the girl had gone off to hide, she would know that might be the first place searchers would check. Then again, he couldn't very well discount anything just yet.

"All right," he said. "We'll look around."

That took all of about five minutes. Sophie was not on the premises. Clemmons was making a valiant show of being distraught, however.

"She's just not here! Someone must have taken her!" he spouted, pacing.

It was too much. They were in the yard where the mail coach had just left—after Rastmoor had made a thorough check for the missing girl. She wasn't in the coach; she wasn't in the necessary; she wasn't in the stable; she wasn't in any of the upstairs rooms; she wasn't in the kitchen or the pantry or the cupboard with the lard. She just plain wasn't anywhere.

"What are we going to do? We've got to find her!" Clemmons ranted.

Rastmoor took him by the shoulders and gave a good shake. Damn it, they didn't have time for theatrics.

"What did you do with your wife, you shifty-eyed weasel?"

But still Clemmons didn't look at him. The man was touched in the head, or something, the way he simply refused to look in one direction long enough to make eye contact. Rastmoor grabbed his face and pulled it up so Clemmons had no choice but to meet his eyes. And he did.

God, there it was again. The minute Rastmoor's gaze caught on those warm brown eyes, something kicked him in the gut. Disturbing, most disturbing. What the hell was it Clemmons reminded him of? Someone he'd known, perhaps? Someone like . . .

Shit, he almost said her name. *Julia*. Damn it, but Clemmons's eyes were just the same mellow shade of nut brown, just the same shape. Staring up at him the way she did that last time they'd . . .

Hell, that was three years ago. And Julia was dead now.

Clemmons broke from his hold. "Don't touch me! Don't ever touch me again, Rastmoor."

Rastmoor was brought to reality. There were red marks on the man's smooth face where Rastmoor's fingers had been. He hadn't meant to grab on to him quite so firmly. Lord, but the man was soft. How old was this Mr. Clemmons, anyway? Rastmoor was only too glad to accommodate his "no-touching" rule.

He wasn't, however, ready to give up the Sophie issue.

"Is this your doing, Clemmons?" Rastmoor demanded. "You think Dashford will pay handsomely to get his cousin back from some hired kidnapper?"

"No!" Clemmons insisted. "You're wasting time. Someone took her—your friend Lindley, I'll wager."

"Lindley's got better things to do than dabble at kidnapping. Your little wife may be an attractive tart, but I assure you she's safe from Lindley."

Clemmons slapped him. *Slapped him?* Indeed, the man could use a lesson or two in more manly arts.

"Don't talk about her that way," Clemmons ordered. "Anything she may have done in the past is hardly your concern. She's not a tart."

"You going to call me out, Clemmons, or are you going to tell me where your wife is?"

"I don't know where she is, and we're certainly not going to find her standing around here. If you think your Dashford would care so much about her, then maybe you ought to quit accusing me of things and start helping me find her."

With that, the man turned on his heel and started off toward the stable. Rastmoor shook his head and followed. But following was uncomfortable. The man walked like a girl. If Sophie Darshaw had married Clemmons to escape the unwanted attentions of men, she'd likely been quite pleased in her decision. There was nothing manly about Alexander Clemmons. In fact, the man's coloring, shape, and bearing reminded him of . . .

Rastmoor shuddered. God, but he must be getting desperate.

Chapter Four

Julia did her very best to ignore Rastmoor. It wasn't easy. She'd been burning from his touch since the minute he'd laid his hands on her. Heavens, how could he still have this hold over her?

He couldn't. She simply wouldn't let him. Right now the only thing that mattered was finding Sophie. Whether Rastmoor liked it or not, he was going to have to help her find the girl.

She'd just have to be extra careful to keep up her guard around him.

"I need a conveyance," Julia said to the first stable hand she could find.

The man just looked at her, so she repeated herself.

"A carriage, or something! Hurry! My, er, wife has been abducted."

Rastmoor came up behind her, and the stable hand looked at him as if for confirmation. Blast it, apparently just posing as a man wasn't enough. She should have made sure her costume identified her as a man of means and importance.

"You heard the man," Rastmoor said.

She was inclined to be grateful for his support. Not too grateful, though. The stony set to his jaw said he didn't trust her as far as he could throw her.

"Sorry, sirs," the stable hand said with a shrug. "There's nothing to be had. Half our hands have been sent up the road to bring in a gig with a broken axle."

"Damn," Rastmoor said. "Horses then. Surely you have a few of those for hire?"

"I can scrounge something up for you there, sir. They won't be winning no derby, you understand."

"Fine. Just saddle us the best you've got, and we'll take those."

Julia swallowed hard. They were to be riding? It would be interesting to see how that worked out. She'd never been astride, and she absolutely could not think up any reasonable excuse for Mr. Clemmons to request a sidesaddle.

Rastmoor handed the man some coins, and suddenly he became almost enthusiastic about finding them decent mounts. Two grooms rushed about readying two horses, and before long Rastmoor swung himself up into the saddle of a large bay. Julia was presented an enormous chestnut gelding that she would have sworn was a close relative of the elephants she'd once seen depicted in a book. The thought of hopping all the way up there under her own power was quite daunting.

"Don't take all night about it, Clemmons," Rastmoor said. "Unless perhaps you already know Sophie faces no real danger?"

Oh, the man and his ugly suspicions were damnable. She placed her foot up in the stirrup like she'd seen her father do hundreds of times and pulled herself up into the saddle. By God, it was almost graceful. She glared at Rastmoor.

"Shall we, then?"

"Which way?" he asked.

She frowned. *Which way?* How was she supposed to know that?

"Which way did your friend Lindley go?" she asked.

"South, I believe," he said.

"Then we should go south."

He didn't bother to discuss it but simply spurred his horse into motion. Lovely, they were to do this at a fast clip, it appeared. Julia clung on as best she could and kicked her mount into the same quick pace Rastmoor had set.

He didn't bother to look back and make sure she was following, but she was glad for that. This gave her time to accustom herself to this unusual riding posture. She was glad to find, in fact, it was not nearly so impossible as she'd imagined. True, she didn't have the benefit of the usual leg prop, but she was pleasantly surprised to find much more control seated this way. Indeed, before long she felt confident to urge her horse a bit faster. She was beside Rastmoor in no time.

"Are you certain this is the way Lindley came?" she asked, happy to show off her new talent. Not that Rastmoor seemed to notice anything unusual about a man sitting atop a horse. Still, she was quite proud of herself.

"The groom said he saw someone go this way, and it was Lindley's intent to follow. I didn't actually see him, but I'm going to assume the man did as he said."

"So, for all we know, we could be going in exactly the wrong direction."

"Are we?"

Julia fumed. "Look, I did not have anything to do with this! I don't know who took Sophie, but Lindley would appear to be our best suspect. Who else knows about her connection to this Dashford person?"

"You tell me."

"I did tell you! I didn't know about this—I don't think Sophie did, either. Certainly, she never made any mention of it to me."

Rastmoor eyed her. She ripped her gaze from him and tried to tip her face into shadows. It wasn't clear how much longer this disguise might last under his scrutiny.

"How well do you know your young wife?" Rastmoor asked.

"Well enough," she said quickly.

He simply laughed at her. "Oh, I truly doubt that. Tell me,

did you take her from that brothel out of the goodness of your heart, or has she promised to make it worth your while?"

"I didn't take her from a brothel," Julia snapped. "I don't know why you insist on talking about her that way."

"Because it's the truth. The girl's nothing more than a cheap whore, and you know it."

"No! She was working as a respectable maid in Fitzgelder's house when I met her. He blackened her eye one day because she was nothing like the cheap whore you keep calling her."

"And so you married her?"

"She needed to get away from there."

"I'm sure she did. But just exactly what were you doing there? Your obvious intimacy with the likes of Fitzgelder doesn't do much to make me trust you."

"Believe me, there was no intimacy there," Julia assured him. "I told you; I was there professionally. Our troupe had been hired to perform at a private party. I met Sophie that evening, and I could see the difficult position she was in. I asked my father to give her employment with our troupe."

"How very noble. So she's an actress as well."

"No, a seamstress, and very good at it."

"I'm sure she's been a real asset. How lucky for your father you found her and . . ."

His voice faded, and Julia knew he was looking at her again. She could almost feel the tension in the air rising up around them. Evening was gone and darkness was settling in, but she knew he could still see her. Had he at last figured it out?

"Your father is the leader of your troupe?" he asked after a moment.

"Yes." She held her breath, waiting for the storm.

It arrived slowly, with Rastmoor letting out a long, slow growl.

"My God. Your name's not really Clemmons, is it?"

Her legs began to tremble, and she tried desperately to pretend she hadn't heard him. He pulled his horse up and grabbed the bridle on hers, bringing them both to a stop in the middle of the moonlit road.

"Is it?" he demanded again.

"No," she admitted in an embarrassingly tiny voice.

"It's St. Clement," he finished for her.

She nodded.

"Albert St. Clement is your father," he went on, and she nodded again.

He was quiet, and she concentrated on staying in the saddle. She counted the heartbeats—eleven. Why didn't he say something? He could yell or curse at her or call her all manner of foul names. Anything would be better than sitting here in silence, afraid to look at him but wondering what on earth was going through his mind.

Finally he spoke. "Julia was your sister?"

What was that? *Her sister?* Good heavens, could it really be he still didn't know? It was a miracle! Her chest heaved as she was finally able to draw a deep breath.

"Yes, that's right."

"I should have guessed. You favor her."

"Thank you."

"It's not a compliment. She was a whore, too."

Well, that was painful. She deserved it though, she supposed. She hadn't been exactly truthful three years ago. It was only natural he might not have a very high opinion of her, considering all that had transpired.

Rastmoor urged his horse forward again. Julia followed quietly.

"You're not going to defend her?" he asked after several moments.

"I'm sure she had her reasons for doing what she did," she said.

"I know she did," he replied. "That's what made her a whore. But I suppose it pains you to hear me speak ill of the dead."

"Yes. It does."

"Then I won't. She gave enough offense while she lived; no sense in allowing her any more now."

All was silent save the hoof steps again. Julia risked sliding a quick glance over at Rastmoor and found his face hard, cold, and unreadable. A shiver of concern ran down her back. He was a different man than the one she had known. This Anthony Rastmoor could be capable of just about anything. What would he do if he ever found out the truth?

She didn't want to know.

A loud crack rang out through the still night, and Julia practically jumped out of the saddle. Her horse shied and danced sideways. Rastmoor was struggling to keep his from bolting at the unexpected sound.

"What was that?" she asked.

"Gunfire."

Cold dread filled the pit of her stomach. "Sophie!"

She couldn't move. Part of her wanted to prod the horse forward, to rush ahead around the next bend to see what had happened. The other part of her—the sensible part—warred to turn tail and run.

"Come on," he was saying, grabbing her horse's head again and pulling them off the side of the road.

It made sense—whatever was ahead held danger. They had to hide. She followed Rastmoor's lead and hurried her horse off the road, into the thick forest that lined it. Rastmoor slipped out of his saddle and motioned for her to do the same. She did. Her desperate descent was not nearly so graceful as her careful ascent.

They moved farther into the safety of the woods, pulling the unwilling beasts along with them. It was noisy, and Julia hoped that whoever might come along would not hear them. She needn't have worried. When the gunfire was repeated it was much closer, but it was also accompanied by the noise of a thundering carriage and several shouts.

Their horses snorted in nervousness when Rastmoor finally stopped. He fixed the reins to a tree, and Julia followed suit. Hopefully they would be safe here, off the road and out of sight. But what of Sophie? What were the chances this gunfire had nothing to do with all that happened at the inn tonight?

Holding his fingers to his lips and motioning for her to follow, Rastmoor began moving slowly back toward the road. Drat. He was intending to go out there, wasn't he? Julia's breath caught in her throat. She wasn't too keen on being shot at, but of course if Sophie was in trouble, they had to go and help. She had no choice but to follow Rastmoor toward the danger.

They made their way quietly. Soon the sounds and voices were directly in front of them, no longer moving along down the road. The noisy carriage had stopped rumbling, and Julia could make out men's voices. They didn't sound too happy, either.

"Damn it, wrong carriage!" one of them called out.

Another man swore loudly, and there was the sound of a scuffle. The carriage horses stamped and whinnied. Then Julia heard a baby cry. A baby?

A woman's voice called out, "Don't touch my baby!"

The baby's crying turned more to whimpers. Julia could scarcely believe her ears. She pushed up into the thick undergrowth, desperate to see what was happening. Rastmoor was beside her and motioned for her to keep silent.

"What the hell are we going to do with this?" one of the men said.

Julia could barely make him out. He wore a dark coat and a mask over his face. Highwaymen! Two of them, it appeared. They had stopped the carriage and apparently killed—no, injured—the driver. He lay slumped on the ground, groaning.

One highwayman held the lead horse, his gun trained on the driver while the other man grasped a young woman by the hair, poking his pistol at the crying bundle she clutched desperately. Julia clenched her fist. What monsters, to threaten an innocent babe like that! By God, if Rastmoor didn't do something pretty soon, she would.

"This was supposed to be 'is lordship's carriage," the man at the horses said.

"Well, it ain't," the other replied. "We must have missed him. Damn. The boss ain't goin' to like that."

"What are we going to do?" the first man asked. Even from this distance, Julia could see his gun hand shaking.

"What do you think we're going to do? His nibs likely don't want no witnesses."

The woman with the baby made a frightened little squeak, and now another woman appeared in the window of the carriage. She let fly a string of words Julia had never heard come from a woman—she was quite impressed by it, really—until the man simply reached through the window and smashed his fist into the woman's face. The tirade stopped immediately, though the baby's mother made more squeaking sounds. Her child began crying again.

"He's going to kill them!" Julia hissed to Rastmoor, glad for the baby's distracting cries.

"No. Here's what we'll do," Rastmoor said, leaning in very close so that his voice was hardly a whisper. "I'll take the man at the horses. You step out and aim this at the other man."

From somewhere he pulled out a gun. It looked huge and heavy and frightening. He handed it to Julia. She shook her head violently.

"No, it's too dangerous!" she protested.

"You'd rather stand back and watch innocent people die?"

"No."

"Good. Can you handle a pistol?"

"No!"

"Of course not. All right, I'll set it to ready for you. Now, damn it, be careful where you aim, then pull the trigger."

"All right," she said, but it sounded more like she was being strangled than preparing to boldly overpower the enemy.

He growled out a sigh. "Miss Darshaw certainly got a bargain with you, didn't she, St. Clement?"

"You have no idea," she replied, but wasn't sure he heard.

Rastmoor was already moving away, pushing slowly and silently through the bushes. Julia didn't want to, but she followed. The minute he stepped out into the open, he'd have two guns aimed at him, and as far as she could tell, he'd just handed her his only weapon. If she didn't get herself out there and convince those bloodthirsty highwaymen she knew what she was about, Rastmoor would soon be shot full of holes.

Likely they'd all end up that way.

Rastmoor made his move. Julia had no idea a highborn gentleman could move so fast or so silently. Almost before she knew what was happening, he leapt out of their cover and dove at the first highwayman. They tumbled to the ground. Julia was vaguely conscious of the encouraging fact that there was no immediate responding gunshot, but she couldn't get too hopeful. There was still another man with an evil-looking pistol nearby, and she'd better do something to subdue him.

"What the hell?" the man near the carriage yelled as Rastmoor grappled with his friend.

Julia watched as he leveled that evil pistol in Rastmoor's direction, and she tried to replicate his quick and stealthy movement. Crouching to make herself less visible—not to mention a smaller target—she scurried out of the brush.

And managed to trip over her own ungainly boots.

With an unmanly cry, she crumpled to the ground. Drat, she was mucking this up already! Rastmoor would likely curse her up one side and down the other. If he lived long enough to curse anyone, that was.

Her clumsy actions had one unaccounted benefit. Both highwaymen were immediately distracted. This gave Rastmoor the opportunity to gain the advantage and take possession of his opponent's gun. In an instant he was on his feet, the weapon aimed squarely at his foe.

The downside of this was that now Julia found herself thrashing in the dirt, her pistol uselessly flung somewhere several feet ahead of her in the overgrown weeds. The man nearest her grinned. She could see his yellowed teeth in the moonlight. Very unsavory. His eyes fell on her just long enough to realize she was no threat. Mostly his attention was on Rastmoor.

With practiced skill he raised his gun. Julia could already imagine it firing, the bullet lodging somewhere in Rastmoor's body and sending him to the ground. It was all too obvious what would happen after that.

Unless, of course, she did what she was supposed to have done right from the start. Her fingers dug and clawed at the earth, and somehow she managed to get her feet under her. She hurled herself forward, arms swinging wide, and somehow her hand contacted the cold metal of her pistol.

She grabbed it up. Their assailant was ignoring her, still

training his weapon on Rastmoor when she felt the powerful recoil. She had fired.

It hit the man dead in the chest, up high toward the throat. The hideous scarlet stain was instantaneous and heavy. He staggered back, his pistol dropping into the roadway and an odd, gagging gurgle sounding in his throat. It was the most wretched sound Julia had ever heard.

Good God, what had she done? The man stared at her wild-eyed, his arms flailing to his wound and his legs buckling beneath him. He collapsed, but not quickly. The whole dreadful scene was playing out slowly, etching itself in her mind. Those damn yellow teeth were becoming red with blood, and he glared at her as if that in itself could avenge his injury. Perhaps it could. She felt a churning in her gut and the taste of bile.

The woman with the baby shrieked at some point and pulled herself away from the man, covering her child. There was blood on the woman's clothing, but Julia was fairly certain it was not hers. Or the babe's. It spattered off the man as he gurgled there, sinking pitifully into the ground. His lungs were full, and bloodied air was escaping through his chest. Lord, it was positively hideous what she had done to another human being!

She put one hand over her mouth and crawled backward, wishing she could get far, far away from this place but unable to take her eyes from the man. He was completely prone now, twitching and still gurgling, but the sounds were getting weaker. The woman in the carriage had reappeared, and she had blood on her face, too. The mother and child rushed to her and they whispered and cried and consoled one another. The baby had been frightened into silence by the sudden gunfire, but now he was howling for all he was worth. Julia took that to be a good sign, all things considered.

The driver of the carriage was moving, groaning, and awkwardly trying to get to his feet. Rastmoor had his quarry firmly under control. Good, because Julia was completely useless now. Dropping the spent pistol back into the weeds, she climbed to her feet and turned her back on the group. The bile finally got the best of her, and she cast up tonight's dinner.

Heavens, it certainly hadn't felt as if she'd gotten that much soup inside her, but here it was now to prove she had.

The heaves kept coming long after the soup was gone. She dug a handkerchief out of her coat pocket and tried in vain to tidy herself, succeeding only in displacing her mustache. It was no use salvaging it. Between creeping through the forest and now this, the fragile bits of hair Papa had fashioned into this theatrical disguise were ruined.

She fumbled with it but soon realized Rastmoor had come up beside her. All she could do was crumple the wilted thing in her handkerchief and hope she could keep her face averted. Between the loss of mustache and the tears he would obviously see streaming down her cheeks, only a fool could still believe her to be a man.

And Rastmoor was no fool.

"You did what you had to do," he said from behind.

"I know."

"Your aim was excellent. He didn't suffer long, if that makes a difference."

"It doesn't."

"You saved several lives tonight."

"He only had one gun," she pointed out. "I saved *one* life tonight."

"Well, if you hadn't, most likely you would be the one lying in the dirt right now."

His tone was so oddly gentle, so compassionate, it made her forget her guard. She glanced up at him. Too late she realized he hadn't yet noticed the absent mustache. He did now, however. She saw the moment it registered. His eyes grew wide, then narrowed.

She gathered her courage and returned his stare. "He was aiming at you when I fired, Anthony."

His voice came out brittle. "And yet you did fire. I wonder why?"

For just a moment he remained there, his eyes locked on to hers. But then he broke away, turning to the others and calling to make sure they were all right.

The carriage driver, though favoring one arm and limping

slightly, had a pistol in his good hand now and was keeping it on the one living highwayman. That fellow sat in the dirt, staring at his departed companion and shuddering every now and then. The ladies were recovering and now began to express concern over Julia.

"Is your friend there all right?" the older one asked.

"He'll be fine," Rastmoor remarked without interest. "He likes to make as if he's a sensitive sort, but I daresay it'll take more than murder to really affect him."

Julia ground her teeth. He hated her. Indeed, it had been evident in his eyes, and she could hear it in his voice. He hated her, and no doubt this was far from over.

But at least he was going to let her keep up this charade while in public. She had no doubt it was, of course, purely for his own benefit. What plausible excuse could he have to explain his romp in the forest at night with a woman in men's clothing? To save face in front of these others, he'd let her remain Alexander Clemmons.

And it was just as well. She was in no great hurry to face a furious Lord Rastmoor as herself, that was definite. She hadn't done it three years ago, and she certainly didn't wish to do it now.

RASTMOOR SWORE UNDER HIS BREATH AND STALKED back over to the remaining highwayman. He had to question the man, find out who he was working for and who he'd been hired to target. He doubted he'd like any of the answers he got.

Damn it, though, he couldn't think straight.

She was alive! God, it was too fantastic to believe. Julia was *alive*. How could this be? She'd died in Fitzgelder's bed three years ago. He'd seen the announcement in the paper, heard family members discuss it in hushed tones. Lady Fitzgelder had died and was buried, her newborn child with her in the ground. *His* child.

But she wasn't! She was here, standing just yards away, pale and shaking and still retching from the trauma of just having watched a man die at her hand. Apparently this was a new experience for her. Perhaps she'd always managed to disappear before having to face the consequences of her heartless actions—just as she had three years ago when she tore his heart out and tromped on it in her haste to become Fitzgelder's wife.

Damn it, Julia was alive! He'd been grieving her all this time, and she'd never even been dead. If he hated her before, he hated her more now. What game was this? What sport could she possibly find in tormenting him this way?

Or perhaps it was more than sport. Perhaps she was here at Fitzgelder's command, a part of his plan to remove the cousin who held all the title and fortune a bastard like him could only dream of inheriting. Indeed, that actually made sense.

It was far more likely he had Julia to blame for all this than that he should suspect Lindley. God, but she would have to pay for this. For all of it. Not now, though. First he needed to figure out what other dangers might still be lurking, and he doubted Julia would be eager to inform him.

Rastmoor stalked to the one remaining highwayman and loomed over him. The man was young and scared for his life. Unlike Julia, cooperation would come easily here.

The carriage driver had found some rope and begun binding the criminal. The poor driver had been hurt in the earlier struggle, and he was only too grateful to let Rastmoor relieve him of this duty. The driver leaned with a heavy sigh on the carriage, still keeping his pistol at the ready should anyone need an assist. Rastmoor bent to further restrain the nervous highwayman.

"Over here," he said, grabbing the man and strategically moving him to sit where he'd have an unobstructed view of his friend's tortured body lying in the bloodied dirt. This turned out to be a wonderful motivator for the young man.

"We wasn't supposed to be killing no women and children," he said quickly, his eyes begging Rastmoor to believe him. "I swear, that wasn't what I signed on for. Just a simple robbery of some London gent, that's what I was told."

"Just a simple robbery, was it?" Rastmoor asked, yanking the ropes unnecessarily tight.

"Ouch! Yes, a robbery," the man said and gave another

yelp. "Well, all right. It was supposed to look like a robbery, but Hank said the boss really wanted this man done away with. But I swear I didn't know about that until we got out here. I don't go for that none, killing and all, so Hank said he would do the deed."

"Yet you were content to share the purse, no doubt."

"A man's got to make a livin', don't he?"

"And murder makes a hefty living, I'm sure. But tell me, who is this boss you were working for?"

The man shrugged. "Don't know, and that's the honest truth. Hank did the meeting with him, and it don't look like he's talking much more tonight, does it?"

"No, it doesn't," Rastmoor had to agree. "So I guess you'll have to do his share. Where did he meet this boss?"

"I don't know! I swear it, sir, I don't. Warwick most likely, but to tell the truth, I don't know. Hank just comes back from meeting him and he says we've got to get this carriage tonight, on this road at this time. So we do, only it turns out to be the wrong carriage."

"Obviously. So tell me, which London gent were you expecting to find here?"

"Don't know, sir. All Hank says is we've got to come up and down this road looking for a bloke with a broken axle; that would be our man. But we got confused. We found this here carriage sittin' still and thought it must be the one. It wasn't. I guess they was just taking a rest, or something. Soon as we come up on them, off they go. Hank says we'd better follow, so we did, and now here we are."

Well, that was information enough to confirm his suspicions. That axle had been broken intentionally, and *he* had been the intended target of this ambush. Damn, but it had to be Fitzgelder's doing. He must have found someone to sabotage the carriage axle. But how? Rastmoor and Lindley had left Dashford's just this morning. Could Fitzgelder have gotten to one of Dashford's servants and persuaded him to do this? It seemed impossible; Dash's men fairly worshipped him, and Mother's letter clearly placed Fitzgelder in London. How else could he explain this, though?

Well, he and Lindley had stopped for a quick luncheon break in Warwick, hadn't they? That must have been where it happened. Yes, that made perfect sense. Their carriage had been left in the care of strangers for half an hour at least. Anyone could have tampered with it, damaging the axle to weaken it. These outlying roads were heavily rutted and rough. Anyone would have known the axle had no chance of lasting through their journey; they'd be left as easy prey for these thugs. By God, it was purely luck they hadn't met up as intended.

Unless, of course, it had not been purely luck. Lindley certainly had been in a hurry to get them off the road, hadn't he? Rastmoor would have been just as happy to work at attempting to bind the axle and see if they couldn't get the horses to drag the carriage along with them to the posting house. It had been Lindley's idea to abandon it. He'd been the one to insist on carrying weapons, too, hadn't he? Perhaps that was all just coincidence—Lindley didn't really strike him as the adventurous sort, after all—or perhaps there was more to it.

A ridiculous notion, though. Why on earth would Lindley have done anything to jeopardize his own safety? If he truly was in league with Fitzgelder, as Clemmons—er, Julia—suggested, he could have done much more to see to it that Rastmoor had been exactly where they wanted him.

Then again, perhaps he had. That bullet in the posting house had not been merely imaginary. Lindley had suggested that private room, too. Damn, Rastmoor hated to suspect his friend, but things were just not adding up. Exactly what was Fitzgelder up to, and who did he have helping him? Julia *and* Lindley? Then how did Sophie figure in?

Lord, it was enough to give a man a headache.

"Are you all right, sir?" one of the women said, coming up to him.

He'd been rubbing his forehead, but now wiped all trace of his emotions from his face. These women had been through enough tonight. There was no sense in causing them greater worry or concern.

"I'm fine," he said. "How about you?"

The woman's face was still swollen where the highwayman had struck her. She held a cloth to her lip to stop the blood, but it appeared she would recover well enough. Her eyes were worn, though.

"We're fine," she said. "Thank you so much. I can't even imagine what would have happened if you and your friend hadn't come along when you did. However did you happen to be out here?"

"We were coming up the road and heard the commotion," he explained. "Our horses are tied in the woods."

She seemed surprised by this. "Really? And did you see . . . er, are you certain there is no one else around?"

"I'm sure any others that may have been working with these two are long gone, ma'am. I believe you and your companion are safe."

This appeared to give her relief, and she sighed. "Thank you. Poor Mrs. Ashton is quite overcome, fearing for her child, and all."

"I can certainly understand. You both have had quite a difficult evening," he said. "Where are you bound? Perhaps my friend and I might accompany you."

"Oh, but surely you don't feel that's entirely necessary, do you? I couldn't bear to put you out of your way. You were headed south, no doubt, and we are on our way north."

"It's really no trouble for . . . er, how did you know we were headed south?"

His question seemed to confuse her. "I didn't, I suppose," she said with a frown then a wince at her swollen face. "I suppose since you had time to hide your horses I assumed you must have been coming ahead of us."

"I think perhaps we've all traveled enough for this day," he said, deciding his brain could stand a rest if he was now starting to question the answers and motives of these innocent and abused women. "There is a posting house nearby. Would you care for an escort there?"

"That would be lovely, sir," she said with the best smile her battered face could muster.

"I'll go speak with your driver," Rastmoor said. "We can

take our uninvited guest there and inform the local magistrate what has occurred."

The woman's face clouded. "Oh, yes, I suppose we will have to do that, won't we?"

I'm sure it will all be over soon," Rastmoor assured her. "The situation is clear. The law will have no difficulty determining the charges."

Indeed, the local magistrate would likely thank them for ridding the world of one unsavory highwayman. The ladies would soon be back on their journey and Julia would probably not even need to reveal her true name. Rastmoor glanced over at her, still carrying herself in that dreadful impersonation of a man as she made small talk with Mrs. Ashton and pretended to be busy inspecting the horses. It was laughable, really. How had he for one minute thought her to be male? She moved with that supple grace she'd always had, a feminine, feline quality that seduced him right from the start.

He'd not be seduced now, however. He knew her for what she was. His heart was safe from her this time. He suspected, though, that was because he no longer had a heart.

Chapter Five

They accompanied the ladies back to the posting house. Julia wasn't entirely sure it was wise to return, but most likely their assailant from earlier had gone. If anyone had seen them leave, they certainly would not have expected them to return. She supposed they'd be as safe here as anywhere else, considering she had no idea who was after them.

But what of Sophie? How safe was she? The longer they waited, the farther out of their reach Lindley could carry her. She hoped once Rastmoor had their prisoner turned over to the magistrate and the ladies settled in for the night, they could be off again, unpleasant as it seemed to go riding off into the darkness. Unfortunately, that was not to be the plan.

It was well after eight o'clock now, fully night. The magistrate was not able to attend them yet. They'd been asked to spend the night and meet with him in the morning. Julia had nothing to do but pen up her impatience and be glad for the fact that she and Rastmoor were sitting in a crowded common room. At least here he had little opportunity to confront her about, well, everything.

He would, no doubt, have questions. And they would not

be pleasant, she could be sure. Though, she couldn't blame him for hating her, not really. Heaven knew she'd hated herself plenty over these last years. She'd been foolish and irresponsible, and it cost a man his good name. Moreover, it had cost a good friend her life.

Julia sipped at her warm ale, staring aimlessly at the floor. Rastmoor sat nearby, but neither of them cared to talk. Other patrons in the room laughed and enjoyed themselves around them. Their merriment sounded foreign to Julia's ears. Then again, she doubted any of these others had just killed a man. Or seen the cold reality of hatred on a lover's face.

No, she wasn't much up for conversation.

Their prisoner was being kept safely in the stable, and the two ladies they had rescued were settled upstairs in their room. They were a Mrs. Smith and her young friend, Mrs. Ashton with baby Sam. Julia forgot where they said they were traveling, and really, it didn't matter much. She and Rastmoor would see the magistrate and then she'd be gone in search of Sophie long before the ladies were up and about tomorrow. Fortunately, though, they *would* be up and about come tomorrow morning, rather than the alternative that damned highwayman had planned for them.

Julia supposed she looked as morose and depressed as she felt, so naturally she was surprised when a jovial older man came into the room and moved to sit at the table near her. His ruddy face seemed to indicate he'd not necessarily waited until arriving here to refresh himself with spirits of some sort.

"Sorry lot we've got in here this evening, isn't it?" he said.

Julia realized he was speaking to her, so she nodded in polite agreement. He seemed to take that as encouragement for small talk. Indeed, his breath proved her earlier speculation had been accurate.

"I 'spose you're traveling somewhere?" he asked.

Julia nodded again, wondering why of all the others in the room this man had descended upon her. Probably because everyone else was already engaged in conversation or flirting with the four or five women who appeared to be here for no other reason than to provide friendly conversation—and perhaps a little bit more.

"Coming from something or going to it?" the man asked.

"Pardon me?" she responded.

"Traveling to," Rastmoor said from his position two chairs away.

"Ah, traveling together?" the man asked.

"Yes," Rastmoor said before Julia could answer.

Well, that was a bit presumptuous. So far she got the idea Rastmoor was as eager to be rid of her tomorrow as she was of him. Now he was declaring them travel companions? Well, she'd see about that.

"My companion and I are traveling together on business," she said, making it very plain this was not a pleasure trip. "Are you also traveling?"

The man appeared genuinely glad for someone to talk to, and he launched happily into a recounting of his days on the road. They'd been remarkably uneventful, yet somehow he found much to say about them. Julia was keeping herself awake by drawing on her acting skills and feigning interest, but she did have to admit at least it was better to be bored to death by the man's repetitive rambling than to be sitting here just a few feet from Rastmoor and not have a clue what was going on in his head. Right now it was easy to see what he was thinking, though. He was bored to death, just as she was.

Good. Served him right.

"I say, you've got deuced long eyelashes for a bloke," the man said, abruptly breaking off his discourse and staring at Julia.

"I, er, it runs in the family, sir," she said, and wished—oddly enough—she had that blasted mustache back to hide behind. The man was studying her so carefully she wondered if he wasn't beginning to figure her out.

"Had a dog once with deuced long eyelashes," the man said.

Rastmoor laughed. Julia glared at him. At least she knew what was running through his mind now. He was enjoying the thought of comparing her to a dog. Well, she could name off half a dozen unsavory beasts she might choose to compare him to, as well.

"She was a fine little bitch," the man went on, a sweet, nostalgic smile coming over his puffy lips. "I loved that pretty little bitch."

"I find it's often the pretty little bitches who tend to get rather nippy," Rastmoor said with a benign smile. "They take up with other masters now and again, too."

"You know, it's getting late," Julia said. She'd had just about enough for one night. It was bad enough she was forced to hold off her search for Sophie until morning, but putting up with his insults was too much. "I think I'll retire."

"Not just yet, my dear Mr. Clemmons," Rastmoor said. "Sit. Stay."

"I think not," she replied to his impertinent little commands.

"I was thinking, once things quieted down in here, you and I could have a nice long chat," Rastmoor said. "I'm sure you would hate to miss out on that."

She most definitely would *love* to miss out on that.

"You two are not sharing a room here tonight?" their gentleman friend asked.

"No, it appears this establishment has quite enough rooms for us to each have our own," Julia said. That was the one thing that worked out well for them tonight. "And I'm afraid I must go up to mine now. You'll recall, sir," she said with a pointed look at Rastmoor, "your room is at the end of the hall on the right. I'll be in the room on the left."

There, that should let the blackguard know how she felt about his little chat or anything else he might have planned for tonight. With what she assumed was a manly swagger and a final, friendly smile at their wordy companion, she left the common room. If Rastmoor wanted a chat, it was going to have to be with someone other than her tonight. Or ever, if she could help it.

THE AIR IN HER ROOM WAS COOL, BUT THERE WAS AN extra blanket, and Julia decided she'd likely be warm enough in the night. Fresh water had been an oddity, apparently, at the last two inns where she and Sophie had stayed, so she'd decided to take advantage of the luxury here and wash her underthings.

They were hung about the room to dry, and Julia, dressed in nothing more than what God had given her on the day of her birth, slid under the covers. The innkeeper had promised they'd been washed recently. She could only hope that meant sometime this month. Still, it would be worth it in the morning to slip into clean clothes. Their flight from London had been so sudden there'd not been time to pack any bags or grab extra clothing.

Oh, but how on earth was she going to sleep? She'd found Anthony again. Bother, but she'd have to stop thinking of him that way. He was no longer her Anthony. He was a cold, unfeeling nobleman who had used her for his own purposes. He'd always been that; she'd just never realized it until that night Fitzgelder came to speak with Papa.

She'd been hesitant to believe it even then. Surely Anthony would not have done that horrible thing, wagered her over a silly game of cards. Surely he'd show up to set things straight. Surely he wouldn't be angry at her forever for misleading him as she had about her true identity.

Of course she'd been hesitant to admit the truth—she was a mere actress, for heaven's sake. She'd only hoped by the time he found out he might come to love her enough to see beyond what society would say. Well, she'd clearly been wrong.

Still, he wasn't all bad. He'd been quite amazing tonight, as a matter of fact. Without thought for his own safety, he'd tried to find that first shooter, then gone with her after Sophie. When they came upon those women in trouble, he hadn't hesitated to get involved. She had, but Anthony hadn't.

No, he wasn't Anthony. She must think of him as Rastmoor now. She needed to separate the present from the past. What had gone on between them three years ago was over and done. He was Lord Rastmoor, and she needed to remember he would always be that to her and nothing more.

Still, she knew she wasn't going to get any sleep for all the wishing.

There was a soft knock at her door. She'd locked it up tight, though she'd never actually expected Rastmoor to pay any heed to it. She figured he'd likely end his night with one of the women patrolling the common room downstairs. That would be his way, to take what was easiest and get what he could from it. Yet who else would be knocking on her door at this late hour?

Only one way to find out. "Who is it?" she called softly.

No one answered, and she had just about decided she must have imagined that knock when she heard it again. Well, perhaps whoever it was couldn't hear her. Or perhaps it was Anthony—Rastmoor—and he was choosing not to draw attention to himself by answering her. Indeed, if he felt there were danger of some sort, he would wish to keep as quiet as possible.

She yanked the blanket off the bed and wrapped it around herself. What danger could it be? Heavens, was someone trying to kill him again? She hurried to the door and fumbled at the lock. Her nerves didn't help things, but at last she got it open.

It wasn't Rastmoor. It was the older man from the common room. His face glowed redder than ever, and he smiled.

"Good evening, sir," he said cordially. "Mind if I step in for a moment?"

Julia hugged the blanket tightly against herself. Heavens, this was certainly not what she'd expected! Apparently the man still believed her disguise, although how he could possibly now with her standing huddled under a blanket, she couldn't fathom. Certainly she had no intention of inviting him in.

But apparently he had no intention of waiting for an invitation. Without so much as a by-your-leave, he pushed past her and tottered into her room. She was too dumbfounded to protest. As a gentleman, of course, she could hardly get all missish over this. As a woman, though, she could hardly let him stay. She struggled to find a manly pose under her blanket and tried to be subtle.

"I'm surprised, sir. It's rather late, and I thought you'd likely be in your own room by now."

He didn't get it. "Ah, sorry about that, lad. I just didn't want to be too obvious about things with your friend downstairs. He seemed particularly interested in making sure I didn't follow you up here. Are you certain things are simply professional between the two of you?"

"What? Er, yes, of course."

"Well, that's a relief. He's not the sort of man I'd like to go up against, if you know what I mean. But if the wind ain't blowing that direction, then I've got nothing to fear, right?"

She really wasn't sure what he was talking about and didn't know if she wanted to. Something about the whiskey-fueled gleam in his eye and the smile on his face as he scanned her blanket bothered her. Why was he here? Had he figured out her ruse? She was not at all comfortable right now.

"Sir, I must tell you my friend is hoping to get an early start on our journey tomorrow, so . . ."

"Shush, don't worry, my boy. I'll leave you long before your traveling partner rouses himself for the day. He's snug in his room by now, and he'll likely sleep late tomorrow, guessing by how much he tossed back tonight. So smile, my fine young colt, we have the whole night ahead of us."

"The whole night for . . . ?" Oh God, she thought she began to understand. "Sir, I'm afraid you might be mistaken."

He grinned and came toward her, shutting the door behind him. "No mistake, lad. I may not be in my prime, but I assure you I don't exaggerate when I say 'the whole night.' Indeed, I'm a bit above average in that area, if I do say so myself."

She staggered back, tripping on a corner of the blanket. Drat but now she tumbled back onto the bed. Lord, this was not the position she needed to be in just now!

"There's a good lad, getting right down to business," the man said, still advancing on her.

She tried to roll out of his way, but he was remarkably quick for a large drunk person. Her escape was further hindered by the blasted blanket. She'd been clinging to it like a lifeline, but now it only served to bind her and keep her from getting away.

The man seemed to mistake her squirming for enthusiasm,

and he began reciting all the marvelous things he would do to her tonight. Dear saints above, but she did not want to hear it, let alone experience any of it! Why, oh why, had she been nice to the man in the first place?

"So very clever of you to let me know which room was yours, dear boy," he said, looming near. "I wasn't sure until then that you would welcome me. But come now; let's see what we've got under this silly blanket."

"Not what you're expecting, I'm afraid," Julia mumbled, groping to retain her blanket.

"My, what a feisty little fellow you are! I like that."

"Stop it! You misunderstood, sir!"

Bother, in her nervous thrashing she'd only become more tangled. The man was removing his coat now, humming to himself! Oh, but this was dreadful. How could he not recognize she wasn't an eager participant in this marvelous plan of his? It must be the drink. Heavens, but he was advancing on her! What would he do when he finally got the blanket off and realized his mistake? It would be just her luck the man played on both sides of the fence.

He sat beside her, his thighs spilling onto her blanket and pinning her securely. Dear heavens, she was trapped face-down. Her breasts were smashed into the sparse mattress, and the only parts of her she could move were her feet and her head. She felt him shift as he reached for the blanket, slowly uncovering her legs.

"I say, you are a young thing then, aren't you? Pink and smooth like a little girl. How enticing."

She supposed he'd meant that as flattery, but it merely served to make her want to retch again. She forced herself to be calm and draw in as much breath as she could in this stifling position.

"Sir, you've got to stop. I insist that you stop!"

"Ah, affecting you so much already, is it? Affecting me, too, laddie boy."

"No, it's—no!" she cried as his hand slid up her leg, approaching her buttocks.

"Ah, yes, yes!"

Bother, this man was hopelessly obtuse. Somehow she had to make him stop. She gathered her strength and was just about to call out at the top of her lungs when suddenly the man jolted.

"What the hell—" he exclaimed.

No, wait. That hadn't been his voice. It was another voice, a voice she recognized. Oh, thank God. She was saved. Rastmoor was here!

She could just barely twist her head enough to see him standing there, his sturdy and glorious form dominating the room. She was so happy she could have danced, except of course that she was still wrapped in a blanket and pinned facedown to her bed by a mountain of rutting pervert.

"I say, you could have knocked first, my good fellow," the man said.

"When I heard the commotion, I thought it unnecessary," Rastmoor replied, dryly. "What the devil is going on here?"

"Anthony, he's—" she began, but the man propped his elbow on her while he struggled to climb off the bed, and all the air left her lungs.

"What does it look like, man?" the mountain said. "We're two grown men engaging in love play, and I'll thank you to wait your turn, if you don't mind."

To her amazement, Rastmoor simply shrugged. "Fine with me, although I think there's something you ought to know."

Rastmoor marched himself to the side of the bed and pushed the man aside. Julia was ready to fling herself into his arms, but he simply took her by the shoulder and rolled her over. Before she could struggle up into a less vulnerable position, Rastmoor grasped the top edge of the blanket and yanked it down. Good God, but now her breasts were exposed!

"Anthony!" she cried, pulling the blanket back up and clutching it around her. Damn him! How dare he humiliate her this way!

"By God, he's a female!" the man stammered, hopping up from the bed as if she'd been a scorpion. His gaze shifted from her to Rastmoor then back again. "What sort of game is this, madam? If I'd have wanted a ruddy woman, I'd have bought one downstairs!"

With a great huff he readjusted his clothing and stomped to the door. "At least I found out the truth before I did something regrettable! Honestly, parading yourself around like a man when all this time you were . . . I declare, you people are just not natural."

At that, he flung the door open and left. It slammed loudly behind him. Julia was too stunned by all of this to have anything coherent to say. She blinked at the door, then slowly shifted her gaze up to Rastmoor and blinked at him. True, he'd just saved her from the most wretched thing imaginable, but somehow gratitude wasn't exactly what she felt right now. Blinding rage, perhaps, but not so much gratitude.

"So, Julia," he said, and his voice was far too light and casual, given the situation, "I see you've not changed a bit since last we saw one another. Still convincing gentlemen you're something you're not."

"And you're just the same, too," she replied, matching his tone. "As eager to get me naked as ever."

He stared at her, his eyes shifting their gaze from her face down to the blanket and her abysmally suggestive pose, tangled there in the bed with her shoulders and legs all exposed.

"Yes," he said calmly, bringing his eyes back up to meet hers. "I suppose I am."

BY GOD, SHE WAS RIGHT. HE *DID* WANT TO RIP THAT damn blanket off her and take up where their overheated friend had left off.

He wouldn't, of course. That would be the height of stupidity. But, damn, even with her luxurious chestnut hair cropped and gone and that shabby blanket wrapped around her, Julia was a stunning woman. Her nut brown eyes were large and round, with just the hint of an exotic angle at the corners. Her original expression of terror was now being replaced by a defiant calmness.

She clearly recognized the desire he still felt, and she knew she held control. As it had always been between them. Damn and damn again. When would he ever be free from her?

"So what do I owe you for the rescue, my lord?" she asked, wriggling into a more upright position, her knees pulled tightly toward her chest.

"You can't even approach what you owe me, Julia."

"Very well, then. I'll simply say thank you and leave it at that."

Leave it at that? Indeed, he supposed he should. But he wouldn't.

"Not on your life," he said and was foolish enough to touch her.

He stroked her shoulder where the skin was exposed. A bolt of unexpected lightning coursed through his veins and his fingers flexed. She was warm, soft. Somehow he hadn't expected that. It seemed after becoming Mrs. Fitzgelder she should have turned as cold and serpentlike as her damned husband. But she hadn't. Her skin was as perfect as he remembered it.

His hand ached for more of her, so he slid his fingers down to hook the blanket. Slowly, he dragged it lower until it hung off her shoulder, and she had to clutch it against herself to remain covered. She glared at him, her dangerous eyes tempting and warning at the same time. He'd be an absolute fool to continue.

Then again, he'd always been her fool, hadn't he? He'd believed her lies; he'd fallen for her deception. He'd promised to make her his wife, for God's sake. And even after three years, the woman still occupied his mind and tortured his dreams.

He'd bedded every whore he could afford, and yet none of them had been able to drive her away or soothe the burning he felt inside. By God, Julia was alive, and he'd just spared her a most unpleasant night. She owed him, just as he'd said. Damn it, he'd make her pay, too.

He jerked the blanket out of her fingers. She gasped. He did, too. Age and experience had only added to her appeal—her skin, her form, her every feminine curve was more tempting than ever. Apparently life with Fitzgelder agreed with her.

Damn the man to hellfire.

"Anthony, no . . ." she whimpered.

She lowered her eyes. He did, too, and gazed in awe at her perfect breasts, rising and falling with each nervous breath. Beautiful. How Fitzgelder must have enjoyed her over the years. The thought nearly made him sick.

"No?" he asked her. "Don't tell me you wish to remain faithful to my cousin."

"No, it's not that, it's . . ."

"I didn't think so. Faithfulness isn't your strong suit, is it?"

"Give me my blanket." She shot her eyes back up to glare hatefully at him. He was still too busy staring at the creamy mounds heaving before his eyes to care.

"I'm cold," she informed him needlessly.

He smiled. "Yes, I can see that. Perhaps you'd like me to warm you, then?"

"I'd like you to give me my blanket and leave."

"But why, my dear? Are you afraid a night with me will ruin you for the likes of your husband?"

"He's not my husband!" she said in defiance.

Now he was finally able to look away from her chest and meet her glare. "Oh?"

"It's a long story. Now, give me my blanket and go away."

"I want to hear the long story, Julia."

"No. Go away."

"Why? Are you running out of lies already? What a shame."

She lunged for the blanket. He dropped to sit on the bed and caught her, holding her shoulders so she was forced to meet him eye to eye. His eyes would have rather focused elsewhere, however. God, he had to get control of himself. What was it about her that could still do this to him?

Damn, but he wished he could be clearheaded about this. The only thing he felt clear about right now was that his body didn't really care if she'd lied to him and left him for Fitzgelder. She was here with him now, and that seemed just fine.

It *was* just fine. His hand followed his eyes, tracing a tentative line from her shoulder to her breast. She drew in a sharp breath, and he felt the energy surge through her and rush into his own being. His thumb made a slow circle around her delicate nipple.

"No more lies, Julia," he said. "I know about the child."

"The child?" She shuddered under his touch.

"My cousin told me. He took great pleasure in it, as a matter of fact."

God, his tongue splintered on the words, but he needed to speak them. She had to know he'd always been aware of the full measure of her treachery. The gentle movement of his hand on her breast kept her a captive audience.

"He came to me and gloated," he went on. "Fitzgelder thought it was some sort of grand triumph when he lured you away from me. When he found you were carrying a child, well, that just added to his sick pleasure. He bragged how easily you'd gone to him, how happy you'd been to trade in my proposal for his. The bastard was actually looking forward to raising my child as his own."

"*Your* child?"

She shrank back from him. Cold air filled the space between them, and he felt his head clearing. By God, what was he doing? This was insanity; he didn't dare extract his due from this woman. Nothing he could do to her tonight would make up for these past three years. He really was a fool, wasn't he? He had to get control of himself. For two minutes he'd say what needed to be said tonight then be gone, leaving Julia St. Clement behind him forever.

"I know all about it, Julia," he said. "That was *my* child. You may have chosen not to inform me of your condition, but Fitzgelder was glad to divulge it. You knew you carried my child when you abandoned me for him."

Obviously she couldn't deny his accusations. Her eyes were round with surprise, but she didn't utter a sound. So, she'd thought he hadn't known. Well, he had.

"Where is that child, Julia?" he asked. "I heard it died. But since I also heard you died, forgive me if I'm a bit skeptical."

"It's true. That child is dead."

"Yet here you are, no worse for the experience, apparently."

He'd meant his remark to cut her. It did, to judge from her expression. Her lips thinned as she struggled to keep from lashing out. A dark part of him enjoyed seeing her discomfort.

"What are you trying not to say, Julia?" he asked, glad to see he was rubbing salt in a tender wound. "That you never wanted my child? That you were glad when it was gone? Well, I suppose in a way I am, too. The poor thing is better off dead than being raised as Fitzgelder's offspring . . . with you for a mother."

Her color was gone, and her voice was hoarse. "You have no idea what would have been best," she said. "Fitzgelder would have given the child a name and a home, at least."

"And made it a monster. No, Julia. It's better this way. Better for my child, better for you. You have no ties to me, just as you wanted it. I suppose we should both be quite content with how life has gone."

He stood and moved toward the door. The blanket was still balled up in his grasp, so he threw it at her. She bundled it against herself. He turned away from the pitiful image.

"Where are you going?" she asked behind him.

"Back to London. My mother tells me Fitzgelder is causing some trouble for her there."

"What sort of trouble?"

He didn't dare risk looking back at her. "I would have expected you to know, since he *is* your husband."

"He's not! He's nothing to me."

Now he couldn't help but turn and glare. "Oh, don't give me that. You claim to know all about how he's been plotting to kill me. You obviously still have some association with him, despite the fact you're traipsing around in trousers now."

"I told you, I overheard his plot by accident."

"Give it up, Julia, and go back to Fitzgelder. You truly are his type."

He tried to leave again, but she stopped him. Damn, why couldn't he just keep going? But she called to him, and he was helpless.

"Wait! You can't be leaving tonight, can you? After someone tried to kill you? Twice?"

"That's all the more reason I'd better get back to London and look in on my mother."

"What sort of trouble is your cousin causing for her?"

"I don't know. Good-bye, Julia."

Finally, his hand was on the door latch. She was behind him and would soon be out of his life forever. By God, perhaps this brief reunion was just what he needed—he could finally see her for what she truly was. Perhaps he could, at last, wipe her from his soul and start over.

"I know what he's planning," she said softly.

His hand stayed.

"I mean, beyond just his simple plans to kill you," she went on.

Hell and damnation, but he turned to face her again. She was huddled there, wrapped in that foul blanket with her knees drawn up to her chest. She looked terrified. Every ounce of his being wanted to go to her and hold her, promise her all would be well. By God, if he didn't walk out that door this instant, he'd be lost forever.

"It, er, involves your family."

His hand dropped to his side.

"He said he'd kill me if I ever told you about it," she went on, her lip trembling.

She cowered into the blanket as he stalked back over to her. He knew the minute her dewy, dark eyes met his, he was doomed. Damn it, he did still have a heart, after all.

Chapter Six

Julia was shaking. True, she had her blanket back now, but it didn't seem to help. Lord, what had she done? She didn't know anything about plans Fitzgelder might have for Rastmoor's family. This was insane, making up more lies like this!

But she couldn't very well let him leave right now, could she? He'd go out into that dark night and get himself killed! And what of poor Sophie? How was Julia going to find the girl on her own? Like it or not, she simply had to keep Rastmoor around tonight. Oh, this was an awful muddle.

Then again, maybe not. She was amazed to watch as Rastmoor's face lost some of its fury. He was regarding her with a cautious curiosity, and he certainly wasn't walking out that door. Clearly he was intrigued by her words. It would seem her outrageous fabrication hit on something

"What are his plans, Julia?" he asked slowly.

Now, that was an excellent question; if only she had an excellent answer. Well, Papa had trained her to improvise. This seemed like a good time to make use of that skill.

"Fitzgelder, well . . . he knows something," she said cautiously.

She watched as one eyebrow arched. Apparently she'd guessed right; Fitzgelder *did* know something. She didn't, of course, so this was going to be tricky.

"Those secret papers. Mother was right to be concerned, wasn't she?" Rastmoor finished for her.

Secret papers? His mother? What on earth could Fitzgelder have over Rastmoor's mother? Well, that was interesting. Judging by the look on Rastmoor's face, it just might be something important. Likely it was damaging, too. Was there indeed some dark family secret hovering over the Rastmoor name? What on earth could it be?

Something shocking and sordid, she supposed. It was always that way with the upper crust, wasn't it? Well, unfortunate as this was for Lady Rastmoor, it certainly gave Julia a leg up. She'd make sure Rastmoor didn't leave this inn without her tonight.

"Yes, Anthony," she said, modulating her voice to a dusky and insinuating whisper. "He found out about those secret papers."

This was the right thing to say. Rastmoor's eyes grew dark.

"Damn it. He admitted as much three years ago, but I didn't want to believe him."

Rastmoor ran his hand through his hair and glanced around the room. She could feel the tension in his body; it was seeping into her own tired muscles. The urge to reach out and comfort him was no improvisation—it was real. She tamped it down.

"What does he want?" he asked finally, his eyes returning to rest on hers.

"Er, what does he always want?"

Rastmoor snorted. "Money, of course. The bastard is a veritable bottomless pit. I daresay he expected marrying you would solve his financial issues, the fool. He didn't exactly get what he thought he was getting, did he?"

"No," she said and decided to leave it at that. Better to change the subject. "He still hates you for inheriting, you know." This much of the story she *did* know.

"Let him hate me," Rastmoor growled. "The law is the law.

If his father had been man enough to marry his mother instead of merely bringing another bastard into this world, then Grandfather's title would have gone to him. I can't help that his father was a bounder and mine was not."

Everyone knew this aspect of the feud between Rastmoor and his cousin. Fitzgelder had always begrudged Rastmoor's birth. Rastmoor said Fitzgelder often ranted that *his* father had been the elder, so *he* should have inherited, not Rastmoor. Julia heard he even went so far as to falsify church records to make it appear that his parents had indeed been married. It didn't work. Thwarted, he turned to propagating rumors about Rastmoor's own legitimacy. He found no success, though. Rastmoor inherited the title and all that went with it, while Fitzgelder could do nothing but grind his teeth and look for opportunities to make his cousin's life miserable. Apparently he'd become quite adept at it.

"But what about you, Julia?" Rastmoor asked suddenly. "Where do you fit into this? Obviously my cousin's blackmail will benefit you as well."

"Benefit me?"

"You're his wife, after all. Is that why you agreed to help him like this?"

"Help him? I'm not helping him!"

"Don't think me a fool. It's obvious what he's done. He sent you out to find me, didn't he?"

"Of course not. I told you; I overheard his plan by accident."

"Forgive me if I find your word a little hard to take. If you merely sought to warn me, why the disguise? Why the deception? No, this is Fitzgelder's style. He likely thought dressing you in men's clothing could get you close to me; then, once it was too late, I'd fall prey to your charms." Here he paused and let his gaze roam over her again. "I daresay he knows better than any how irresistible you can be."

He hadn't meant that as a compliment, but still her cheeks flushed.

"He doesn't know I'm here," she assured him. "He thinks I'm dead."

Rastmoor cocked one eyebrow. "Does he?"

She nodded. "He has no idea I'm here."

He leaned closer. She clutched the blanket tighter.

"He didn't send you out to lure me into his trap, Julia?"

She shook her head. "I came out to *warn* you about his trap."

"And your ever-so-fetching disguise?"

"To avoid him."

He touched her again. He slid one long finger across her jaw and down the sensitive slope of her neck. She flinched, pained at how easily her body became his.

"So, he's not sitting over his cups somewhere tonight, wondering if I've bedded you yet?"

She shook her head again.

"He's not laughing at how easily I might be swayed by your soft skin or by the way your breath catches in your throat when I touch you just so?"

She tried to speak but couldn't; her breath caught in her throat when his burning touch traced the shape of her breast through the rough blanket.

"And he's not cursing himself for letting you out of his sight when there's a chance I might take you places tonight he's never been man enough to find?"

"No, Anthony, he's not."

His eyes were filled with burning ice when they met hers. "Then he's a bastard *and* a fool."

She wasn't sure who moved first, but in a heartbeat she was clinging tightly to Rastmoor's shoulders as his lips crushed hers with a three-year-old vengeance. She gave in willingly, and the blanket slid down between them. Warmth from Rastmoor's body spread into hers, his thin shirt all that separated skin from skin.

Heat raged to life inside her, and bringing Rastmoor closer, feeling him with her again after all this time, became the only thought in her mind. Whatever else happened tonight, she needed to hold him to her until the aching need could finally be sated. For so long she'd been numb; this brief taste of Rastmoor now was intoxicating.

He didn't bother with the niceties of conversation. With animal passion he once again pulled the blanket from her, letting his hands roam freely across her skin. She moaned when he pressed her back down into the mattress. He was kissing her, touching her, groping her as if his need was as great as hers. His legs parted her thighs, and he paused just long enough to fumble at his trousers. She gathered her wits and reached between them to assist.

He shoved her hand away. Clearly he did not need assistance; he made it very obvious when he thrust himself inside her a moment later he had things well in control. She bit back a surprised gasp. After wanting him so desperately as she had for these past years, how could she not be ready for him tonight? He'd caught her off guard. She hadn't been ready.

He didn't let that stop him, though. He hardly seemed to notice her sudden discomfort. She clenched her eyes and tried to block all thoughts and simply relax in the wonder of being with this man again. Yet she could not. She understood what he was doing.

Rastmoor was not making love to her; he was taking revenge on Fitzgelder. The passion he poured into her was not affection or even blind lust—it was bitter disgust. As his body heaved and thrust over her, his horrible cousin was occupying his thoughts. She was, basically, incidental.

"What's the matter, Julia?" he asked with a hard edge to his voice. "Am I not so much to your liking anymore?"

"Does it matter?" she replied.

He paused just long enough to shrug. "No, I suppose not."

And clearly it didn't. His enthusiasm for these primitive actions didn't seem diminished by her obvious uninvolvement. He kept right at it until she felt him find his release. He was careful to withdraw and spill his seed against her belly; just one more reminder his heart had been far from this. Fortunately, the whole event had not taken long. She wasn't sure how much of this cold, impersonal coupling she could have endured. Angry tears formed, but she fought them back.

Rastmoor slid off her and collapsed on the bed. She kept still, tugging as much of the blanket out from under him as she could. He tugged it right back.

"No. I prefer you naked."

"It's cold in here," she declared. He held the blanket firm.

"It's warm enough."

"That's because you've still got all your clothes on." *Beast.*

"Get some sleep. You'll probably want an early start if you're going after your friend Sophie."

"And where will you be?"

"I'm leaving tonight. For London."

He didn't move. She didn't either. He was beside her, but they were not touching. At any moment she expected him to do up his trousers and go, but as the moments ticked by, she wondered if perhaps he hadn't fallen asleep instead.

The inn was quiet. She could hear an occasional snore from one of the nearby rooms, and through the window a night bird called. Something clattered in the stable just beyond the yard—a restless horse, most likely. All human movement had ceased for the night, it appeared.

Rastmoor's breathing was slow and regular. The chill of the damp June air began to settle in her. Cautiously, she reached to tug at the blanket again.

"I said, I prefer you naked," he announced, his unexpected voice causing her to jump.

"I thought you were sleeping."

"I'm not."

"Apparently."

All was silent once more. When he spoke again, her body jolted violently. For heaven's sake, would this man make up his mind? Was he leaving, was he sleeping, or were they having a conversation? All his conflicting actions tonight wreaked havoc on her system.

"Just what does my cousin think you can convince me to do for him?"

"What? I told you, Fitzgelder believes I died. I'm not in league with him. Now, may I please have some blanket?"

"No. How did you happen to 'accidentally' overhear his plan, then?"

"It's a long story."

"It's a long night."

"I thought you were leaving for London?"

"I can wait until after you've explained."

She sighed in frustration. Well, perhaps if she gave him a few of the details, it might be enough to keep him from heading out to his death. The longer he remained here, infuriating as he was, the longer he might remain alive.

"Fine. I was at his home with my father's troupe. We were hired to put on a performance for a private party."

She could hear the disbelief in Rastmoor's voice. "Oh? That's odd. Last I heard, my cousin promised to murder your father if he ever saw him again. Apparently Fitzgelder was a bit miffed that the man helped mislead him regarding the true value of your dowry."

"Yes, which is very likely why he went to great trouble to keep his identity hidden from us. It was his steward who actually hired us. Papa had no idea whose home we were going to until we were there and it was too late. We were lucky to escape. If not for my disguise, I doubt I'd be here now."

"Ah, so that's where the mustache came from."

"Yes. Can I please have the blanket now?"

"No," he said, but he rolled onto his side and draped his arm around her.

By God, she wanted to hate him, but his touch was gentle and warm. He pulled her closer to his chest, and she snuggled there despite herself. What an idiot she was!

"Is this better?" he asked.

"No," she replied, but it was.

"So you were at this clandestine performance when you overheard Fitzgelder's plan to kill me? He was just chatting about it in front of all his friends?"

"Of course not. I was trying to help Sophie escape, and we were hiding in a hallway."

"And just what was Sophie escaping from?"

His posture was possessive, and his thumb brushed rhythmically over her breast. The nipple grew taut, and her body reminded her that the aching need was anything but sated. She drew a deep breath and tried to ignore him and his warmth and the feel of his hands on her skin. It took every ounce of her acting skills to keep still and not arch against him, begging for more.

"She needed to escape your ruddy cousin," she managed to say. "Sophie was a maid in his household, and he treated her shabbily—a behavior that must run in your family, as a matter of fact."

"I don't think you're the one to be giving lectures on proper behavior, my naked little player. Why don't you tell me the truth?"

"I am telling you the truth," she began, but her breath was caught again when his hand slid from her breast down to the hot valley between her thighs.

"You heard Fitzgelder say he would kill me, so you brought Sophie along to save me, is that right?"

"Yes, yes, that's right."

Heavens, was it ever right! He may have neglected her pleasure a few minutes ago, but he was tending to it now. Lord, if he kept this up, he'd have her admitting to the whole truth of the last three years.

"But just what made you so sure he would really do what he said?"

"He . . . he sounded quite determined."

"And what else is he determined to do? What will he do about Mother?"

"I don't know." She was fairly gasping for air by now. Oh, if only this interrogation could go on forever! "I suppose he's prepared to share what he knows about your mother with the public."

"But what good will that do if I'm dead? It's not as if he could ever stand to inherit. No, Julia, there's something you're not telling me."

Likely because there were many things she did not know. Why couldn't he quit demanding answers and just let her concentrate on what he was doing? His hands were so warm, his touch was so gentle, she could almost believe this time he cared.

But the ecstasy was over too soon. His caresses ceased,

and he turned her to face him. She kept her eyes on his shirt, although even that was painful for her, because she could recall all too vividly the perfectly formed muscular chest that lay beneath it.

"Why should Fitzgelder need me out of the way if he still intends to use his information against my mother? He would gain nothing—the fact of his illegitimacy would still be there."

"Perhaps that isn't his motivation this time."

"Well, what else is there? If I were dead, Julia, the only ones who could possibly be hurt by Fitzgelder's revelations would be my mother and my sister."

Indeed, she vaguely recalled Rastmoor had a younger sister. He'd spoken of her with brotherly affection a time or two. She couldn't imagine how the sister might fit into all this, but the sudden change in Rastmoor's expression and the ripple of tension that surged through his body said he was beginning to form an idea.

"You are sincere when you say Fitzgelder believes you dead?" he asked.

"Yes, but how does that . . . ?"

His smoldering eyes lit with a dark fire. "So he would be free to marry again."

"Yes, of course, but who on earth would ever . . ."

She paused. Indeed, Fitzgelder wanted revenge. Plus, he needed funds. How better to kill two birds with one stone than to marry judiciously—some vulnerable female who might fulfill both roles. Julia began to think she understood some of the concern washing over Rastmoor's face.

"Someone who was forced into it would marry him," he said.

My, but this really did sound like a devious plot, after all. If Fitzgelder truly did hold some damaging information over Rastmoor's family, surely a loving daughter—a very wealthy, loving daughter whose inheritance would go up exponentially were her only sibling to suddenly be found dead—might do anything she could to prevent a scandal or further injury to her mother. She might even stoop to marry the most despicable man on the planet.

"Your sister has a healthy dowry?"

"By God, she's swimming in it," Rastmoor said.

"And if you were out of the way . . ."

"Fitzgelder would be free to drag out all our secrets, ruining my mother and destroying Penelope's hopes for a decent future. Penny might think she'd have no choice but to give in to any demands he might have."

"But could he really destroy them? Is the information so very damning?"

"You don't think it's damning enough?"

She forced herself to meet his gaze. "I, er, I never actually heard what it was."

Now he actually smiled, and she thought maybe, just maybe, she detected some warmth to it. "No? By God, Julia, you are a damned good actress. Yes, the information is damning, provided, of course, he really does have it."

"Have what?"

"The proof."

"There's proof?"

"Damn it, Julia. Just how much of this did you make up?"

"I told you I wasn't privy to the details. What proof does he have?"

"I don't know. If he's got it, why hasn't he used it already? I didn't even know the item existed until I found it amongst my father's things after his death. How could Fitzgelder suddenly get hold of it now?"

"What is it?"

He laughed again. "You really don't know anything, do you?"

"I know Fitzgelder wants you dead, and now I think we know why. So what on earth does he have that's worth killing you for?"

"A locket," he replied after a slight pause.

He didn't have to repeat it. Fitzgelder's devastating proof was a *locket*? *The* locket? By God, it couldn't be this simple, could it?

"Did you say a locket?"

"Small, heart-shaped—yes, a simple little locket. But I'm not convinced Fitzgelder actually has it."

"No," she replied and watched his face. "He doesn't. But he did."

"What?"

"I've seen it—it must be the same one."

"You've seen it? Damn it, Julia! You know what's inside?"

"No, I didn't see inside it. But I saw it."

"Where is it, then?"

"Someone took it from him."

He frowned. "You?"

"No, someone else."

"For God's sake then, who took the locket?"

"Sophie."

HE HELD HER THERE, HER FACE CUPPED IN HIS HAND so she had no choice but to look at him. She was telling the truth, wasn't she? About three years too late, but finally Julia was telling the truth about something. Fitzgelder truly had found the locket, and Julia had seen it. Now, for some reason, it had run off with Sophie.

"We've got to find her," he said.

Julia smiled at him. "That's what I've been saying all along."

He let himself stare at her just a few moments longer. God, he still wanted her. Even after forcing himself on her and caring nothing for whether she wanted it or not, he was as hot as he had been. He wanted her, and he wanted to hear her panting and calling his name the way she used to. He wanted to drive her insane with pleasure, to know that for a short while, at least, Fitzgelder was far from her thoughts, and she belonged only to *him*.

He wrapped her in his arms and kissed her flushed lips. He convinced himself it was honest passion she felt as her body arched into his. He ran his hand back down to that place that was keeping her so distracted a minute ago. She reacted positively to that, too.

It couldn't be mere theatrics, could it? She wanted him; he was positive she did. He may have taken her too quickly earlier, but now he would take his time. Somehow, between now and when the sun rose, he'd find a way to curb this irresistible hunger for Julia. He'd have his fill of her if it took all night.

And by God, it just might. Loving Julia was every bit as easy as it used to be. Her body seemed to mold itself to his. He watched her in awe as the passion played itself out on her face. She was tranquil; she was thrilling; she was like no one he'd ever found before.

Carefully maintaining control, he teased her with his touch. It was as if his fingertips remembered every gentle curve, every graceful part that was Julia St. Clement. Perhaps they did. Lord knew she'd been etched forever in his brain.

He bent low to kiss the slope between her breasts. She sucked in a breath and released it, sounding very much like a contented kitten. He kissed her again just to hear the sound. She didn't disappoint.

She'd always been this way for him, responsive and oh, so engaging, yet without that jaded quality he'd found time and again in women of much casual experience. Oh, he didn't doubt there'd been many others besides himself with Julia, but somehow she always made him feel like the only one. Tonight, though, he'd put all that from his mind and just enjoy the fantasy.

And what a fantasy she was; her golden skin glowed radiant in the moonlight through the window, her short dark hair spilled around her like a chestnut halo. Long, lush lashes brushed those porcelain cheeks as her eyes shut tight. Passion had taken over, and her body rocked against his hands as they smoothed the taut flesh over her belly and thighs. She would come easily for him.

He didn't rush her, though, much as he might want to. She was obvious in her reactions, so he was able to judge the best ways to prolong her ecstasy. His touch brought her right to the edge of the mountain, then he let her settle back down again. His kisses fanned the inferno to raging again, only to back off just in time. She was left writhing and panting beneath him, her fingers clawing at his back in hopes of bringing him into her and finally quenching the flames. God, she made it hard to wait.

He was determined to draw this game out, though. He'd take great pride in having the upper hand as long as he possibly could. He was the one in control, not Julia.

Until she ripped his trousers down and sank her fingernails into his buttocks.

"If you don't get on with this, I'll murder you right now," she said.

Well, those weren't exactly the words of passion he'd expect at a moment like this, but he couldn't deny the effect they had on him. The desperation in her voice nearly undid him, and before he could stop to think, his animal urges took over. He plunged himself into her.

She cried out and he made rather a growling sort of sound. Together they grasped and clawed and wrapped themselves around each other. He was quite sure it had never been like this between them, never so wild and so carnal—but now was certainly not the time to reminisce. Now was the time to grind himself into her until the rest of the planet faded away into nonexistence.

And it did. His senses were full of nothing but Julia: her scent, her feel, the heat from her surrounding him—devouring him—and the sound of her ragged breaths. *"Anthony."* He heard his name in those ragged breaths, and it undid him.

The climax crashed over, washing away any coherent thoughts and reducing him to a plundering barbarian. But Julia was right there with him, which made it just that much more impossible to regain his control. She was gasping and moaning and calling out his name. *Again.* God, if he died right now it would be enough.

But he didn't die. He rode their passion until the wave finally passed. Slowly his world stopped spinning, and he could shove himself off of her, where he collapsed in a panting heap. So much for his earlier precaution. He'd poured himself into her with full abandon this time.

He watched her next to him. Her arms were limp at her sides, and her chest rose and fell in great heaving movements. Her eyes were still pinched shut, but her face showed plainly the glow of the passion he'd dragged out of her. She was sated and content. And beautiful. He stroked her cheek.

Her eyelids slid open, and she met him with a sparkle. "Do you suppose anyone heard that?"

He had to laugh. Indeed, the posting house was full tonight, and the walls were thin. How could anyone not have heard that? No doubt they'd get some rather curious stares at breakfast. Unless, of course, he left before breakfast as he planned. He really ought to leave, he knew. If Sophie truly did have the locket, then every minute he spent not hunting for her was a minute Fitzgelder had over them.

Julia must have read his thoughts. "If you think you're leaving now, I'm going with you."

"No, you should rest," he said and reached to pull the blanket up over her.

He'd stay until she was sleeping, then he'd drag himself away. Damn, but it was going to be difficult to leave her.

"I'm not letting you go without me."

So, she knew what he was about. He wasn't surprised.

"Go to sleep, Julia."

She reached for him and slid her hand under his shirt, stroking him in the sensitive spot she'd long ago discovered just below his rib cage. "Stay tonight, Anthony. It's too dangerous right now, and you need your rest, too."

A sensible man would ignore her. He hadn't been sensible for years. Hell, he'd been fooling himself to think he could walk away from her tonight. He was exhausted, and his resistance was shot.

"Very well. We'll leave in a few hours. We'll both get some rest."

No sense trying to deny how she'd affected him. Any idiot could see he was weak as a baby after their lovemaking. Julia had drained him in every sense of the word, but he wasn't complaining. Maybe, finally, he'd had enough of her.

She hugged the blanket to her and snuggled closer to him. "Good," she said through a yawn.

No, he decided, not good. This was bad. Even after taking her twice in rapid succession, he could feel the response deep down in his core as her skin contacted his. He hadn't had enough. He would never have enough.

Damn, this was not good at all.

He shoved the blanket aside and dragged himself out of her bed. "I'd better go back to my room. I'll call you in a few hours, and we can leave around dawn."

"Don't you dare! I'll not be left behind while you go off on your own to get yourself killed."

She moved as if she would follow him, and he had no doubt she would.

"I'm not leaving. I'm just going to my room. It appears neither of us will get any rest if I stay here."

She didn't seem entirely convinced. "You won't leave?"

"No. I'll stay until morning. Early morning."

Was she satisfied with his response, or was she just too tired to argue? He couldn't tell. Either way, she dropped back onto the bed and let her eyelids fall closed.

"All right then," she said without emotion. "I suppose I'll just have to trust you."

He had to laugh at that, too. "I'll call for you in the morning. Just remember, as far as anyone knows, you're still Alexander Clemmons."

"It's not as if I have a Mary, Queen of Scots, costume lying about. Of course I'll have to present myself as Clemmons again."

God, but even dead tired and poorly used, she was wonderful. He'd best put more than a simple wall between them tonight. He did up his trousers and moved toward the door.

"Get some sleep, Julia."

She nodded, sinking deeper into her pillow. "And don't you dare try to sneak away, Anthony Rastmoor."

No, he wouldn't. He couldn't. He was too tired, and they'd likely have a long day ahead of them. And if he didn't stop imagining just how much he'd rather stay in Julia's bed right now, he was going to have a long night ahead of him, too.

Chapter Seven

Sunrise was delayed by dismal gray clouds. They matched Julia's mood perfectly. Rastmoor had come pounding on her door first thing and ordered her to hurry so they could get on the road. As surprised as she had to admit she was to find him still here, she was even more surprised to see he appeared to have rested well enough.

She hadn't, though. She'd struggled as he left her last night to hide the hurt and the hollowness inside. It was a useless effort, though, she suspected. He wouldn't have noticed if she'd burst into childlike blubbering. He'd gotten what he wanted, then gone back to his own bed for a peaceful sleep.

She'd wept and blown her nose for the next two hours. How could she have been so stupid? How could she have let him take advantage of her like that? She knew what he was doing, that he'd simply been using her body for his own gratification. At first she'd even tried to convince herself she was doing the same thing, that being with Rastmoor again was nothing more than scratching an itch. It wasn't, of course.

Drat and botheration, it was far, far more that that. What on earth was wrong with her? How could she possibly still harbor any of those silly, stupid emotions she used to feel for him? By God, if it wasn't for poor Sophie out there kidnapped and needing rescue, she'd walk out of this inn and never so much as let herself think of Anthony Rastmoor again.

Of course that was a lie. She'd follow him wherever he went, if he asked her, or spend the rest of her life pining for him if he didn't. Blast, but she was hopeless.

She ought to put her mind to more important things, like Sophie, for example. The poor girl was out there somewhere, probably being manhandled by Lindley and being dragged back to London. Fitzgelder would get the locket, and then who knew what might happen to Sophie? Oh, but how could Julia have let herself get so distracted?

She tossed cold water on her face and did her best to look manly. No good. After last night, her skin had taken on a healthy glow, and there was a decidedly feminine gleam in her eye. Dash that man! He knew she wouldn't have been able to resist him. She never had been. She'd have to be on her guard every moment from here on out. Rastmoor might choose to make further advances, but Julia would be strong.

She'd keep her mind on Sophie, that's what she'd do. The only thing that mattered right now was finding her. They'd get her safely away from Lindley and see that Fitzgelder never got his hands on that locket. Then things would be over. Rastmoor could go his way, and Julia could take Sophie and go meet Papa. Life would fall back into place.

At least, as much into place as it ever had been since the universe crashed around her three years ago. But she would not allow herself to think about that. She'd become adept at pushing such thoughts from her mind—Rastmoor's betrayal, Fitzgelder's threats, and a good friend's sacrifice. By God, she'd made herself an expert at forgetting. Surely she'd find a way to do it again.

But she wouldn't forget Sophie. There was enough guilt to last her a lifetime; she would not add to it by letting another person suffer due to her reckless passions. She'd go meet Rastmoor, but it would only be to head out after Sophie.

She grabbed up her coat, pulled on her heavy boots, and

clomped over the floorboards out the door. Rastmoor would be waiting downstairs. No more dawdling. The quicker they could get on the road, the quicker this whole nightmare would be over.

Downstairs, the posting house was just humming into action for the day. Rastmoor didn't bother to look up at her when she approached him. He was seated at a long table, scrawling something that looked like a map on a scrap of paper.

"I may have word on Sophie," he said abruptly.

She dropped down onto the bench next to him. "Oh? Good word?"

"I believe so. The early mail just came through, and the coachman saw someone of her description in Warwick last night. He says a couple came to the inn there—a man and a young woman very much like Sophie—and some disturbance erupted."

"What sort of disturbance?"

"He wasn't sure."

"Well, what did the man look like?"

"He wasn't sure."

"Were they planning to stay in Warwick?"

"He had no idea."

"So how on earth can you believe this might be Sophie?"

"It's the best we've got to go on."

Finally he glanced at her, but his eyes held no sign of emotion. She should not have expected any, of course. She knew last night meant nothing to him, and certainly he had no particular concern for Sophie. All he cared about was getting that damn locket.

"Well, then," she said, pretending to yawn so he didn't hear how her voice splintered. "I take it we are off to Warwick, then?"

"Yes," he replied, casually going back to his scribbling. "Get yourself some breakfast, and we'll be on our way."

And that was that. Clearly he had nothing more to say to her. She left him there and went to find the innkeeper. Warwick wasn't far, but she'd best get something to eat before they set out. Rastmoor was not likely to entertain any complaints of discomfort or starvation along the way.

At least she didn't have the ruddy mustache to struggle with anymore. Whatever she got onto her spoon she'd be able to get into her mouth. Small comfort, though. Any appetite she'd had for food was long gone. It was replaced by a deep, yearning hunger for something else—something she didn't dare sample again.

WARWICK WAS A BUSY, BUSTLING TOWN. IT ALSO, INconveniently, had two prominent inns. Julia sat quietly as Rastmoor cursed himself for not getting adequate details from the mail coach back at their posting house in Geydon this morning.

"We'll just have to ask at both of them," she said.

"Obviously," he replied. "But let's not draw unnecessary attention to ourselves, shall we?"

"Then perhaps we ought to split up. You talk to someone at that establishment," she began, pointing to the building on the left. "And I'll talk to someone over there."

"No."

"I am capable of asking a few questions, you know."

"I don't care. We go together."

"I thought you didn't want to draw attention."

"We go together. Come, let's start over here."

There was little else she could do but sigh and let him yank the reins from her hands and direct her horse toward the inn on the right. He'd been surly all morning, and she knew it would be pointless to argue. If he thought she was so very incompetent, fine. Let him do all the work. Let him think her completely useless today.

He hadn't thought her useless last night, had he? The bounder.

She tethered her own horse and hurried to keep pace with him as he strode under a large swinging sign. The Guilded Barrow. It looked respectable enough.

It didn't take long for Rastmoor to learn nothing. The place was nearly deserted, and the proprietor claimed to have no recollection of any patrons arriving late last night or causing any sort of turmoil. This was not *that* sort of establishment, he claimed. Perhaps they should go across the way and introduce themselves to the proprietor of the Steward's Brake.

They did, walking their horses and finding the innkeeper. This gentleman was no more forthcoming than the first, until Rastmoor produced half a crown. Indeed, that brought a marked change in the man's memory. Ah, but of course he recalled just such an incident. At first, Julia was disinclined to believe him, but then he offered a convincing description of Sophie.

So the girl *had* been here. Thank heavens! And she'd been quite well, it seemed.

"Ay, the gentleman with her booked a good room for them," the innkeeper said. "He talked right nice to the girl; she seemed well happy enough to be with him, she did."

That was a good sign, Julia decided. She knew Sophie's feelings about Fitzgelder. If she had any notion the man with her was in league with her former employer, she would likely not have appeared "well happy," that was for certain. So who on earth was she with?

The man's description of Sophie's companion was a bit more vague. Apparently Sophie had left a much more memorable impression on the proprietor than her male counterpart had. Not surprising. Julia had seen firsthand the way men looked at Sophie; the way their eyes followed her as she moved, focusing with approval on her trim young frame and perky smile. Indeed, Sophie would have been far more interesting to this innkeeper than another of his kind.

"You say the man was slight of build?" Rastmoor asked after listening carefully to what little description the man could produce. "Was he near my height?"

"Oh, no sir," the man insisted. "The fellow was much smaller and wiry, not nearly yer size. And somewhat unkempt, if I do say."

Well, that clearly left Lindley out. Julia had only seen the man twice in her life, but no way could she imagine Lord Lindley ever appearing unkempt. Nor did she believe anyone could mistake him for "slight." Indeed, Lindley and Rastmoor were both quite tall. Rastmoor was broader and more athletic, of course, and his appearance was never so fussy as Lindley's, but comparison between the two would have been easy. The innkeeper's description left no room for doubt—Sophie had not been with Lindley.

So who the devil had the girl gone off with?

"And I think he was a few years older, too," the man went on.

Rastmoor had a few more questions, but they really learned little more than they already knew. Sometime in the night, a carriage had arrived, bearing Sophie and this mystery gentleman. Sophie followed him in of her own free will, and the man procured a room. Just one room. Julia couldn't help but be troubled at that notion, but if Sophie was not opposed to such an arrangement . . . well, perhaps things were not as dire as they'd feared.

However, the proprietor's story continued. Shortly after Sophie and her companion arrived, another man had shown up. He confronted the slight man, and the two skirmished. The smaller man was injured, and Sophie disappeared while the proprietor and his wife were tending to their injured patron. They assumed Sophie had gone away with the second man, but no one happened to notice which direction.

"Was there anything distinctive about this second man?" Rastmoor asked.

The innkeeper shrugged. "He was tall, like yourself."

"Oh?"

"Well-dressed, too. If it wasn't for all the scuffle, I'd have thought he was a right proper gentleman. A real somebody, you know?"

"Yes, I believe I do."

A heavy coach clattered into the yard outside, and the proprietor's attention was distracted. He claimed to have no further information and excused himself. Servants appeared, scurrying about in preparation for passengers in need of refreshment. Obviously there was nothing more to be learned here.

Rastmoor grumbled through clenched teeth. "It appears Lindley does have her now, after all."

Julia had come to exactly the same conclusion. "I told you he was in on this. He's probably dragging her back to Fitzgelder right now."

Rastmoor mumbled something more and turned away. He left the large common room where they'd been and headed back out into the yard. Julia trotted along behind him, skirting around the bustling servants and horses being changed out on the dusty coach. Rastmoor simply expected people to move out of his way as he strode along, deep in thought. Bother, why did the man have to walk so blooming fast? She must look ridiculous, scampering along after him this way. Not manly at all.

He rounded the building and headed to the stable tucked in the back. At first Julia wondered if she ought to remind him they'd left their mounts tied out front but very soon realized he was not here to reclaim their horses. Despite what they'd already discovered from their chat with the proprietor, Rastmoor was not finished asking questions around here. He headed for a pair of ostlers, busily rubbing down a stocky bay mare. They appeared eager enough to cease their labor in favor of the conversation—and coin—he offered.

"A scuffle last night?" one of the men said after Rastmoor recounted the story. "Ay, I heard about that, but I wasn't here for it."

"No, me neither," his coworker said. "Jeb was, though. He maybe would know what direction your folks run off in."

"Oh?" Rastmoor asked. "Where might I find Jeb?"

"Ain't here now. He's sent down to Geydon for to fetch something. Ought to be back for supper, though. You planning to be here then?"

"No, we're not."

The ostler shrugged his sloping shoulders. "Too bad. Jeb's the one that told us all about the excitement. He says he watched it real good, got to see everything. That first man was injured, he said. Bleeding in the leg."

His friend nodded. "Might have been shot, I suppose, though Jeb didn't mention it."

"Injured? Are you sure about that?" Rastmoor asked.

"Yes, sir," the first man replied. "Jeb was real sure of that. Hey, if you're looking for that man, you might think of looking in at the surgeon. Maybe the fellow found his way there."

"Yes, that's an excellent idea," Rastmoor agreed. "I think we'll do just that."

Julia was, once again, left to trot along behind Rastmoor like an obedient whelp. They got the surgeon's direction and left their horses in care of the helpful ostlers. The busy, narrow streets were crowded, and Rastmoor declared two men on foot would blend in and move more quickly than two on horseback. Well, at least Rastmoor was able to move quickly. His long strides carried him over ruts and mud holes with ease. Julia was not quite so fortunate.

"Slow down," she complained.

"I thought you were eager to find your friend."

"I am, but I'd prefer to do it without a broken ankle."

"Just watch where you're stepping, is all."

"That would be easier to do if we weren't sprinting. Can't you hold up just a bit?"

He not only held up; he stopped. She ran into the back of him. Slowly he turned to face her with a mocking grin. "What, are you having trouble keeping up with me? Poor Julia. Perhaps you should get more sleep at night."

She glared back. "I assure you, sir, it is my policy from now on."

His left eyebrow shifted slightly, but other than that, he gave no reaction. "Good. It's nice to know we are in agreement."

"For once."

Now the brow shifted again, but this time his lip twisted at one corner, too. "No, my dear, we've been in agreement many times, as I recall."

"Well, not anymore. Are we off to the surgeon or not?"

"We're definitely off," he replied and turned on his heel to resume his rapid pace.

She was left to amble along behind. Drat this man! He was infuriating. He was insulting. He was insufferable! And he was damn fine in those tight trousers, his long, muscular legs striding evenly, two steps ahead of her. Bother. If she didn't keep herself less distracted, she truly would trip and break an ankle.

Or worse, she'd succumb to him again and break something much dearer.

THE SURGEON—A ROUND-FACED MR. WARREN—WAS no help. He'd heard nothing of a late-night injury and had seen no one or no thing of interest this morning. Rastmoor was forced to admit they'd come up empty. He cursed under his breath all the way back to the Steward's Brake. Hell, they'd wasted nearly an hour here in Warwick and had absolutely nothing to show for it. And now it appeared Julia had given up on making any effort whatsoever to keep pace with him.

She dragged along as if her feet were made of lead. Twice he caught her hiding a yawn. Honestly, she looked exhausted, and he figured he ought to take some of the blame for that. He ought to be ashamed of himself, he supposed, but he wouldn't be. It was nothing short of ridiculous to trouble over a woman like Julia St. Clement. Late nights and lack of sleep were things she surely knew well.

He made a pretense of checking traffic on the street to give a worried glance over his shoulder at her. Her eyes were sunken, and her cheeks were pale. Blast. Very well, he'd make sure she got a break when they reached the inn. He'd order up a luncheon for them and insist she take a rest before they climbed back onto their mounts and continued after Lindley.

Or whomever they were after. Hell, he still wasn't ready to believe it. Lindley, in league with Fitzgelder? It made no sense. But the innkeeper's description of the man who arrived to cause such a disturbance in the middle of the night certainly sounded like Lindley. Damn. Just one more person Rastmoor had been wrong about.

"Come along," he said, opening the door for Julia when they finally made it back to the Steward's Brake. He pointedly ignored the hateful glance she sent up at him. "Have a seat, and we'll get some food."

She didn't protest. The proprietor was glad to see them back and ushered them into a private room, promising to bring only his best meal. It arrived quickly and, Rastmoor was pleased to discover, smelled almost enticing. He was happy to forgo conversation and focus on food.

"We should leave soon," Julia said, surprising him after the lengthy silence.

His mouth was full when he answered. "And where, exactly, should we go?"

"South," she said. "Of course Lindley's taking the locket back to Fitzgelder. Sophie, too, if she's still alive."

"Of course she's alive," he said, though of course he couldn't swear it was true.

"I hope so," Julia said and poked listlessly at her food.

Blast it, now she was ruining his appetite. So far, he hadn't really given much thought to Sophie's plight, but he supposed Julia was right. There was no reason for them to believe whoever abducted Sophie would feel the need to keep her alive once the locket was retrieved. Indeed, they'd seen more than enough violence these past few hours to assure them Sophie was, most likely, in very real peril. Damn. He'd been truly enjoying his stew.

"I suppose your disgusting friend Lindley might prefer to keep Sophie alive for a while yet," Julia said, startling him again. "Don't think I didn't notice how he was staring at her last night—how you were both staring at her last night."

"Of course we were staring at her. We were on our way to London to look for her."

"How lucky for Lindley you found her so easily," she grumbled and shoved her plate away. "I don't even want to think about what could be happening to her. We should go after them. Now."

"What, now? You haven't even touched your food."

"How can you think about food right now? Don't you care at all that your friend Lindley might have already killed a woman?"

"Lindley's no murderer."

"What about that fight here last night?"

"Fighting is not the same as murdering. Besides, we don't know for certain that second man who arrived was Lindley."

"You don't believe it was?"

Damn it, he couldn't lie to her. "Yes, I believe it was. Too many coincidences for it not to be Lindley."

"And I know for a fact he's in league with Fitzgelder, who plans to kill you and anyone else who doesn't strike his fancy, apparently. Any man who keeps friends like Fitzgelder would hardly have qualms about doing all manner of evil things to poor Sophie."

Rastmoor could well imagine what some of those evil things might be. "Perhaps he'd prefer her alive, then."

"That's not entirely comforting."

"We'll find her."

"Not sitting here, we won't."

"Eat your stew, Julia," he instructed. "You need your strength. If Lindley's goal was simply to kill her, he could have done that and been on his way. Instead, everything would indicate he's taken her with him—alive. We have no reason to believe he won't keep her that way."

"Do you truly believe that?"

"I do." Oddly enough, he sounded as if he meant it.

She was quiet. He watched her eyes as she pondered this. She seemed to take hope from his words, and he prayed to God they would turn out to be the truth. Lindley, despite his elegant appearance and dispassionate attitude, was a capable man. If he had any malicious intent where this Sophie was concerned, she'd be unlikely to put up any effective resistance. If Lindley wanted to murder an unimportant little tart to steal back the locket for Fitzgelder, he'd find a way to do it, and it wouldn't be right here where there were witnesses.

The fact that the innkeeper at the Steward's Brake believed Sophie was alive and well when she left in the night really meant nothing to them. Lindley could easily have taken care of an unwanted companion anywhere else. There were a hundred places in and around Warwick where a sturdy gentleman could hide a body in the middle of the night. Free from the hassle of a struggling victim, Lindley would already be well on his way back to London, and Fitzgelder would soon be holding the trump card. That would be bad for everyone.

Except that Rastmoor and Julia had not passed Lindley on the London road. True, there were other roads, but this would have been the fastest and most direct. Somehow Lindley's detour seemed significant and ought to be investigated.

He wasn't prepared to discuss this with Julia just now, though. She'd find this yet one more reason to worry and one more reason to tear off willy-nilly, despite her own exhaustion. On that count he was determined to give his guilty conscience some relief.

"We'll take a room here," he announced.

Her eyes darkened, and she pinned him with a defiant glare. Good thing he hadn't intended to make full use of that room. Any attempt to repeat last night's exercises would likely result in Rastmoor's body ending up dumped in a deserted place.

"A room for you to rest and refresh yourself. Alone," he clarified. "Sleep, Julia. I'll do some more asking around. If Lindley is on his way back to London already, he's taking a roundabout way. I'll try to discover it. Surely someone in this ruddy town saw something of them last night."

Of course she was hesitant to trust him, but he could tell she was rather enticed by the idea of refreshing herself. Good. She needed it, and he didn't appreciate being reminded of his beastly weakness every time he glanced at her. He'd had no right to force himself on her last night. By God, it would not happen again.

"I promise to find out all I can about Sophie and return to tell you the moment I have anything solid," he assured her when it was obvious her doubt might prevent her from agreeing to his proposal.

"Very well," she said at last. "I could do with a little rest. As long as I can trust you."

"You can trust me," he said.

She didn't look him in the eye. Instead, she merely nodded then stood. The proprietor had been hovering at the doorway and now rushed in to them. Rastmoor tossed him some coins and made the arrangements for the room. Julia didn't complain.

The proprietor left to prepare the room, and Julia seemed

eager to get up to it. She would have followed the man out if Rastmoor's hand on her elbow hadn't stopped her.

"I'll return in a couple hours," he said quietly. "Be prepared to leave if I've learned anything."

"Of course," she replied, then raised her eyes to meet his. "Just one thing, though."

"What is it?"

"Don't touch me."

She jerked her arm from his and left the small dining room. He let her go.

Chapter Eight

The sun was just an orange ball resting atop the trees on the horizon. Rastmoor had found no trace of Sophie—living or dead. He supposed that was good, but it didn't do much for telling him what to do next.

He knew what he wanted to do, but that had nothing to do with rescuing Sophie or getting that damned locket back before Fitzgelder got his grimy hands on it. He wanted to go curl up in bed with Julia.

He'd checked on her twice this afternoon, just to reassure himself she was still there. He'd been half afraid she'd disappear or that Fitzgelder might find her. Or that maybe he'd just imagined the last twenty-four hours, and she'd never been there to begin with. But she was.

Each time he'd checked, she was sleeping soundly, tucked neatly into the bed he'd procured for her. To judge, the woman was dead to the world. It must have been a long while since she allowed herself to rest. He found himself ridiculously glad to have been able to afford her this luxury. He was a fool.

He still loved her, didn't he? God, he'd never admit that to anyone, most especially not to himself. Best to spend his time thinking about that locket.

He spent the afternoon hunting around the alleys and side streets near the Steward's Brake, alternating between searching for Sophie's cold, mutilated body and checking on Julia's warm, inviting one. He spent a fair amount of time remembering last night, too, but that was another thing he preferred not to admit to himself. The hours ticked by, and he let Julia sleep. Thankfully, he did not find Sophie's body. It seemed Lindley had other plans for the girl than a quick demise.

So just what was Rastmoor going to tell Dashford? He'd promised his friend he'd find the girl, but he never dreamed it would entail all of this. And what if he failed? How could he explain this to his friend? Well, perhaps Dashford wouldn't be overly shocked. They all knew Sophie had not led a charmed life. Perhaps she did not truly want the rescue Lady Dashford so firmly believed she needed.

It would be a great disappointment to them though. Even despite the fact that Sophie had spent the last several years in a brothel, Dashford and his new bride were more than eager to locate their cousin and welcome her into their embrace. Ridiculous, of course, to think such a person could ever be accepted into society, but Rastmoor supposed he understood. He hadn't exactly been thinking of society's intolerance when he himself had become engaged to an actress, had he? Of course, he hadn't known right away the full truth of who—and what—Julia was, but in the long run, it hadn't mattered to him. He'd been only too happy to plan a future with her, right up until she ran off with Fitzgelder.

Damn, but he was a fool to let his mind wander over such things. Finding that locket was all that should matter to him right now, and so far, he still had no idea where it was. It seemed Lindley could have taken any number of roads out of town, and Rastmoor was without a clue.

More frustrated than ever, he turned his horse over to the ostler and headed back into the inn. There was still no sign of the return of this Jeb fellow who supposedly might have additional pieces of information, though the stable hands assured him the man was expected anytime. Basically, the entire day had been wasted.

Weary, he made his way up to Julia's room. He'd simply check on her again then leave her be. There was no sense waking her when he had no information to share. He supposed when she did wake, they might as well simply head to London and hope to meet up with Lindley there. It would surely be too late to prevent Fitzgelder from getting the locket, but perhaps Lindley could at least give them news regarding Sophie.

The door latch shifted easily, and he stepped quietly into the room. It was dim, the worn curtains blocking most of the last golden rays of sun. Julia still slept peacefully, curled like a kitten in the center of the large bed. He'd made sure the proprietor gave her the best room he had.

She was every bit as beautiful now as she'd been that first time he'd ever laid eyes on her. He should have known when their eyes locked in that crowded ballroom that no one who appeared that beautiful, that perfect, could possibly be all she seemed. But he was completely taken in, believing every lie she told him about a privileged life and a fabricated pedigree. He'd been a complete dupe for her.

By the time he learned the truth, he had already published the announcement of their betrothal. He felt a bit foolish that she hadn't confided in him, but he thought he could understand. He was heir to a title; surely she'd been ashamed to admit she was nothing more than an actress. He quietly forgave her and ignored anyone who tried to reason with him. Julia St. Clement would be his wife, actress or not.

And then she'd met Fitzgelder. Even as she planned her wedding to Rastmoor, she conducted a clandestine affair with his devious cousin. She must have assumed Rastmoor would never marry her once he found out. Foolish woman. Rastmoor had been such a sap, it probably would have been worth her while to at least beg him for forgiveness. Easily he would have given it.

Damn, but he'd been her fool right from the start. Even now, years and lies later, he was captured by her soft features. Where were the harsh lines of guilt or the haggard marks of shame? She was still as fresh and peaceful as a child. He studied her as she slumbered, seeing again the glowing woman he'd danced with those long years ago.

They'd met in London, at a ball. Ridiculous that he allowed himself to still remember it so well, but he did. She'd worn a silk gown in pale, silvery blue. It made the chestnut warmth of her hair stand out in the crowd, and her enormous dark eyes drew his attention. The graceful and ample curves of her tempting body would not let him ignore her, but she was so enthralled by the opulent luxury around her, she hardly seemed aware of her own loveliness.

He quickly mistook her for one of the giddy debutantes that swarmed the room, but still he was not deterred from making her acquaintance. No one he knew was able to provide an introduction, so he simply waited until he saw her wander off alone. He cornered her in a hallway.

But their meeting had been all innocence. In fact, she made him feel perfectly at ease, and he'd been happy to simply discuss with her the row of portraits that lined the hall. He'd never in his life found portraiture or hallways so damned absorbing. When she declared it was time to go and that her father would be looking for her, he fairly begged her to meet him the next day. She agreed.

From then on, he'd been lost.

Even when he'd learned about her background, found out she'd merely been posing as a gentlewoman and had not even been invited to that blasted ball, he was determined to marry her. He didn't tell her he'd learned the truth. So what if she was, in fact, an actress? He didn't care. She was his, and that was all that mattered.

He leaned over her and touched her hair. She still felt like his.

She stirred in her sleep, and his heart felt like lead. She'd been his, she'd carried his child, and she'd gone off to marry Fitzgelder instead. What a stupid bastard he'd been. Any man who could still love something like that deserved what he got for it.

He left the room. She'd made it clear he wasn't welcome

there, and he ought to thank her for that. He had better things to do with his evening. He had to figure out which direction Lindley must have gone. He had to contemplate ways to circumvent Fitzgelder's schemes. He had to worry how this all affected his mother and sister. He had to think of places he had not yet searched for Sophie's body.

Mostly, though, he thought he'd just rather get thoroughly drunk.

JULIA WOKE WITH A START. WHAT TIME WAS IT? SHE had no way of knowing. Her room was dark. It took several moments before she even remembered where her room was.

Of course, she was at the Steward's Brake. But where was Rastmoor? She was alone. How long had she slept? Good heavens, it must have been all day!

She'd slept in her clothes and now scrambled to her feet and tucked her shirt hurriedly. Drat that man, he promised he'd come and tell her when he found something! Had he found something? Surely that Jeb fellow from the stables had returned. Had Rastmoor gotten information from him?

What if he had? Blast him, what if he learned where Lindley had taken Sophie, and he'd left her here to go off after them? By God, she never should have let herself fall so soundly asleep. But it had been so long since she and Sophie left London, barely ahead of Fitzgelder's men, and she'd not dared let herself fully relax until now.

She yanked on her boots, horrible things. They were heavy and noisy and uncomfortable. No wonder men were so often in foul moods. They wore such dashed unpleasant clothing. She ran to the rusted mirror in the corner to do what she could with her hair. Hopeless, she decided, even for a man. No wonder Rastmoor had left her alone all afternoon.

But what if he hadn't come to tell her what he'd learned because he hadn't been able to? What if while she'd been sleeping, Fitzgelder had caught up with him? Good heavens, what if he'd been hurt—or worse! She gave up on her appearance and threw her coat over her shoulders. Lord, she'd never forgive herself if she'd slept through Rastmoor's murder.

She had to find him. She tore the door open and charged into the hall. Something blocked the threshold, though, and she tumbled down on top of it. It was hard, and lumpy, and it groaned. By God, it was Rastmoor!

"What the devil . . ." he started.

"Anthony!" she exclaimed, clambering off of him and studying him over for injuries. "Are you all right? Have you been hurt?"

He pushed himself up into a seated position, and his eyes narrowed at her. The light was burning at the top of the stairs nearby, and though he looked a bit shaggy, the man was happily whole.

"Julia?" he asked. "What in God's name are you doing out here in the hall?"

His words were slurred. He smelled like whiskey. Indeed, she'd been around enough actors in her life to recognize the symptoms. Rastmoor was staggering drunk.

She smacked his chest and pushed away from him. "Here I am thinking you've been murdered by Fitzgelder, and really you've just fallen down drunk in the hallway."

His brows furrowed. "I have not fallen down. I sat down here for the express purpose of avoiding falling down."

She sat back on her heels. "So this is what you've been doing all day? You've been sitting around drinking while Lindley does who knows what to poor Sophie?"

"Face it, m'dear, anything Lindley has been going to do to poor Sophie he's done it already. For my part, I'll wager he's shagged her good but left her none the worse."

She smacked him again. Harder. "Don't talk that way!"

He had the gall to laugh at her; then he was fool enough to think she'd actually allow him to help her up once he got himself into a standing position. True, he looked fairly sturdy there, but she had no use for him. She managed to stand just fine on her own. She wasn't the one who'd been swigging back whiskey all day.

"I take it you had a good nap?" he asked.

"Yes, but I was expecting you to come tell me when you'd found Sophie."

"I didn't find her, which you should be glad of, since I did everything but drag the river. I'm fairly convinced she's still alive."

"And being shagged by Lindley," she said, making sure her smirk was obvious.

The floor in this inn was remarkably dusty. Julia's trousers were a sight, and she stooped to pat as much of the dust off them as she could. Rastmoor tried to help, but she slapped his hands away.

"Just making myself useful," he said, matching her smirk.

"You'd do better to make yourself sober."

He shook his head. "No, then I'd realize how damned uncomfortable it is sleeping out here against your door."

"Well, don't think I'm going to invite you in," she assured him.

"I wasn't trying to get in. I was trying to keep anyone else out. I doubt you'd like a repeat of your visitor from last night."

Last night? Heavens no, she didn't want anything that happened last night to be repeated, that was certain. So is this why she found him out here, slumped on the dusty floor? He thought he was protecting her? That was actually very sweet. At least, it would be sweet if she could believe it.

She didn't. More probably the man was simply on his way to rouse her for another tumble when the whiskey got the better of him, and he passed out. Given how things stood between them, the idea that Rastmoor would sacrifice his comfort for her personal safety was more than a bit unlikely.

"I don't need you watching over me," she declared. "You ought to be this concerned about Sophie."

"I was never engaged to be married to Sophie. Besides, all Fitzgelder really wants from her is that locket. Lindley could have had that off her in five minutes, yet we had a report he'd been seen with her all the way up here in Warwick, didn't we?"

She decided to ignore that first comment. He was drunk. Nothing he might say could hold any meaning for her—even if it did make her catch her breath for one split second and wonder if there was perhaps the slightest chance he didn't entirely hate her.

"He must be taking her to Fitzgelder to find out what else she knows," she suggested.

"So why didn't we pass them along the way? Who was Sophie with that she ended up here before Lindley found her?"

"I don't know. How should I know? *You* were the one out gathering information all day. Why don't *you* know anything? Oh, I should have never let you talk me into coming up here to rest."

"You needed it. Didn't you and Sophie stop anywhere after you left London?"

"Of course we did. I just . . . I thought it would be safer if one of us kept a watch on things at night."

"So you didn't bother sleeping. How noble of you. Now why don't you head on back to your bed and finish out the night? It's got to be after one o'clock. We'll see what we can find when the sun comes up."

"And what about you?"

"I'll be right here." He leaned against the door frame and pointed to his spot of floor.

"Don't be silly. No one's going to bother me. Go to your own room, for heaven's sake."

"Can't. I gave it up."

"What? Really, I'm flattered, but . . ."

"Don't be. I didn't give it up for you; I gave it up for those two women we met during that unfortunate altercation on the road last night."

This caught her off guard. "What? The women with the baby?"

"The same ones. They arrived a few hours ago, and mine was the only room that didn't already have people sleeping in it. So there they are, and here I am."

"So you really weren't out here to protect me from marauders in the night."

"There is that added benefit, and you said yourself you find it flattering."

"You're an ass."

"You mean drunken ass."

"I mean every kind of ass. Did you even attempt to find out any more about where we might possibly find Sophie?"

He nodded. It came off somewhat sideways. "I did. But that Jeb fellow hasn't showed up yet so I've got nothing more to add to our collective pile of information. There's nothing more to do until morning."

Julia rolled her eyes. "It's hopeless. We may never find her now."

"Go back to bed, Julia. It's late."

So that was all there was to it? This was as much as he could do for Sophie, even with his own family secrets at stake? He truly was a drunken ass.

"I will. I'm going back to bed, and I don't care where you sleep."

She marched past him and back into her room, but he made no attempt to follow. Funny, she expected that he would. Now, damn her female weakness, she was disappointed he hadn't.

"Good night, Julia," he said, sober as a schoolmaster.

"You're really going to sleep on the floor?"

He gave her that smile, and she wanted to kick herself for melting under it. "I'll be right out here if you need me," he said.

She took two more steps into her room, and he started to pull the door shut. She stopped him. Even an ass shouldn't be left to sleep in the hallway, she supposed.

"Wait. It's a big bed, and you're drunk. No reason we can't both get a decent night's sleep."

He eyed her first, then the bed. His gaze slid back to her. "The bed's not *that* big, and I assure you I'm not *that* drunk."

A thrill ran up her spine. "You're going to wake everyone in the building if you insist on continuing this conversation in the hallway. Now get in here."

He strode into the room. That excitement coursing through her spine fanned out to include every inch of her. He was here, and there were still several hours of dark, seductive nighttime ahead of them. She closed the door, blocking out the thin light from the hall. They were alone and Rastmoor was nothing more than a shadow now, a huge, perfect shadow with an aura of moonlight silhouetting him against the faded window drapes. She moved toward him.

"I suppose you can take the right side of the bed, and I'll take the left . . ."

"No," he interrupted. "I don't play that game."

And once again he was surrounding her, taking her into his arms and pulling her close. She gave up her lips to his crushing, heated kiss. Longing overwhelmed her, and she tried desperately to draw his very being into her soul.

He pulled her shirt over her head and struggled at the fabric she'd used to bind herself. He swore when he could not remove it, then resorted to ripping the thread and literally tearing it off of her. Thank heavens. She needed to feel his hands on her skin.

She also needed to get rid of his clothing this time. Unfortunately, he was a bit too tall for her to drag his shirt up over his head, but she could certainly reach his trousers. So she did, having become an expert at undoing the blasted things over the past few days.

With one half of the front flap unbuttoned, they fell low, bunching around his muscular thighs. His smile glowed in the moonlight.

"I take it you'd like me to remove them?"

"Yes, please."

"Well, fair's fair, my dear," he said, going to unfasten her own trousers.

They did not bunch at her thighs. Most of her padding seemed to be in the rear area. She probably looked ridiculous, but Rastmoor didn't seem to care. He was studying her pale body in the faint light with an obvious appreciation.

He was studying it up close, in fact, and his hands slid down the full length of her as he knelt down to finish removing the trousers. She was standing over him; the perfect position for removing that shirt once and for all. She gathered it and tugged it up and over. He shrugged his arms through.

"Does it bother you that we're removing exactly the same

articles of clothing from each other?" she asked, hoping he didn't make a habit of that sort of thing.

"Not in the least, so long as this is what I know I'll find underneath," he said.

With that, he reached around to grasp her buttocks and pulled her toward him. By heavens, the man buried his face in her most intimate area! She was about to push him back, when the sensation of it all distracted her. Overpowered her, in fact.

He was kissing her there. How odd . . . how wonderful! A mite too wonderful, in fact. It was making her legs go weak. She had to grab his shoulders for support.

"To your liking?" he said, tipping his face to look at her.

She nodded. Really that was all she could do. Her voice was lost somewhere.

"Come here," he said, rising to stand before her.

She couldn't help but notice he was standing all over, too. Last night had been too quick and too furious. This time she could get a full view of him. At least, as full a view as the partially hidden moonlight would allow.

"Just a moment," she said and turned away from him to move to the window.

She pushed the draperies aside and let the bright moon filter in. Ah, that was much better. Now she could get her full view.

A sound from the yard below the window caught her attention, and she ducked back. So there were still servants at work down near the stable? Well, it would simply not do to let herself be seen this way.

She moved closer to Rastmoor. Let the world go on around them. She had all she needed right now. There'd be plenty of time tomorrow to think about servants and Sophie and strange goings-on at night.

Rastmoor smiled. It appeared she was not the only one who appreciated the stronger lighting. His gaze roved over her, and she reveled in his approval. He might be an ass, and he might think awful things of her, but by God, the man wanted her as much as she wanted him.

He took her hand and pulled her to the bed. She went willingly, of course. She'd always gone willingly. Right from the start, she'd not been able to maintain discipline around Rastmoor. Heavens, she'd only known him three days when she first let him have his way with her. In a carriage, of all places. She supposed she should have been terrified, as cautious as she'd always been about such things, but she wasn't. They were in love, and that first time with Rastmoor had been wonderful.

Even now, the love might be gone, but the wonder was not. Her senses sparked at his touch, and her intimate places burned when he pressed her down into the mattress, covering her body with his and ravaging her mouth with more fiery kisses. Thankfully, her physical being had completely taken over any rational thought. She could enjoy the moment without a single thought to how miserable she'd be when this was all over and Rastmoor was gone from her bed—and her life—again.

Well, she tried not to think about that, anyway.

His constant attention to her most sensitive areas was most helpful in distracting her. She did her best to be just as distracting in return. It appeared she was successful. Rastmoor's kisses trailed hot over her body, leaving her panting and moaning for more of him. He didn't seem to be in any hurry, though.

He stretched his long, solid body along beside hers. Slowly and methodically he explored her arms, her shoulders, her thighs, her back. She conducted her own excursions into the wonders of his perfectly sculpted chest and the manly parts yet farther south. He sucked a deep breath through clenched teeth when she fisted one hand firmly around him.

He was kissing her lips again then. For minutes or hours or days they remained like that, intertwined, breathing the same air and possessing each other's body. She felt him grow harder still in her hand, and she rocked against him. When their release finally came tonight, it would be untamable.

Then Rastmoor shifted. He held her hips in his strong hands and practically hoisted her off the bed and up onto him. For a moment she paused there, unsure what to do. But then it became clear.

Always in the past their coupling had been hurried, secretive, and usually fully clothed in whatever space they could risk being found in. This was something completely new. She gazed down at him and stroked his powerful form. Then she raised herself slightly to find just the right position.

And lowered back down onto him, bringing his manhood into her body and shuddering at the sensations that flooded her throughout.

Indeed, they'd certainly never done this before, with Julia leading the way. Fortunately, again, the animal instincts took over, and she did not have to contemplate the deeper meanings and implications of her actions. She let passion guide her and went to grating her body against his and memorizing each powerful angle of his frame with her hands.

Pleasure became the ocean around her, rolling her on waves of feeling so intense in their beauty that each time the sensation increased, she could barely survive it. She wasn't sure she had survived it. When the climax hit her, she called out, rocking against him to the point of exhaustion and struggling to breathe.

Rastmoor was throbbing inside her, roiling beneath her, crushing her against him as the waves of release ripped groans from the depths of his being. That only served to heighten the sensation for Julia, feeling his climax while experiencing her own. Her muscles gripped him, and the cool night air around them was charged with the fury of their passion.

At last she was fully spent and crumpled against him. His arms encircled her, heavy and damp. She would have gladly stayed this way forever.

But she couldn't. Eventually Rastmoor put her off of him. She hated even an inch of air between them, but suddenly air was all she felt between them. He did not reach for her or hold her close as she might have expected. It really was over already.

"By God, you've learned a bit over the years, haven't you, my dear?" he said at last.

It stung. There was no emotion in his words, only the same satisfied tone he might have used after winning a friendly game of cards. Had she really been fool enough to expect more than that from him?

"I think we should get some sleep," she said before she had to answer, before the pain could show in her voice.

"Yes, we should. Thank you."

With that, he simply pulled up the covers and turned to face the opposite wall. Just like that, she was forgotten and discarded. An ache burrowed deep into her soul. It wasn't likely to go away any time soon, either.

And, damn him, she couldn't even be certain he had thanked her for a most enjoyable tussle, or simply for suggesting they leave off such foolishness and get some rest. Either way, she could never, never allow herself to give in to this man again.

Pray God he never asked.

WELL, HE'D DONE IT AGAIN. HE'D LET HIMSELF BE Julia's bed toy once more. She'd turned those deep, dewy eyes on him, and he'd crumbled. Now all he wanted was to lie here, holding her against him forever.

He wouldn't, of course. Forever for them ended three years ago.

That left nothing for him to do but lie there, staring into the darkness and fighting every instinct. Nothing could erase the past, and nothing could bring back what he'd lost. He'd lost Julia long ago. More accurately, the Julia he'd given his stupid young heart to had never even existed. He'd do well to remember that.

Any enjoyment he got from joining his body with this woman was purely biological. She was an actress, after all, skilled in using her body to deceive. She'd simply picked up a few new skills in the time since he'd last known her.

Likely she'd picked them up from Fitzgelder, damn his bastard soul. Rastmoor struggled to keep his breathing even. He was never going to let Julia know she did this to him, that such hate surged through him at the thought of another man touching her. He'd rather die than let her know she still owned him.

He'd have to be on his guard. No more whiskey, and no more losing control with Julia. He'd find his bloody cousin and get that locket back—and give the man his wife while he was at it.

She'd made her choice. Now, damn it, she needed to live with it. So what if she hated Fitzgelder, or if he was cruel toward her? Nothing that bastard did to Julia could ever be half so painful as what he himself would be living through every day of his life.

This night was just one more reminder of what he would never have. Julia was fortunate she had never loved him. Love was torture. Lucky girl to have been born with no heart.

Chapter Nine

Julia wished she *had* died in Fitzgelder's bed three years ago. It would have prevented her from ever ending up in Rastmoor's again.

Oh, but this was terrible. The heartache was as painful as ever. What on earth had she been thinking, inviting him in like this and daring to hope he might somehow still care? He'd stopped caring for her years ago. If he ever had cared for her and not simply for her lies.

She listened to him breathing beside her, separated by infinite space. He was sleeping; had been for hours, it seemed. He'd turned away from her when their lovemaking was done and simply fallen asleep. She'd been the one to lie here and regret.

Her own heartbeat pounded in the darkness. Wait, that was not her heart. Someone was walking along the corridor outside their room. Odd, the house had been silent for hours. It couldn't possibly be nearing dawn already, could it? No, the moonlight was still strong through the window.

Julia felt her ears perk. Somewhere a door creaked, and there was the lightest padding on the floorboards in the hallway. A second set of footsteps? Smaller, lighter. A woman's footsteps, and they followed the first set down the corridor and down the stairs.

Servants, most likely. Or perhaps it was some patrons at the inn who decided to leave without paying their bill. Surely that happened from time to time. Well, it was not up to Julia to find them out.

The footsteps faded into the night, but soon another sound caught her attention. Voices, just outside the window. A man's and a woman's, from what she could tell of them. So the footsteps had indeed gone outside. Whoever they belonged to were leaving.

No, they were arguing. The voices were speaking in hushed, angry tones. And one of them was familiar.

Sophie? Good heavens, could it really be?

Julia slid out of bed and moved silently to the window. The curtains were still parted, and she peered out, hoping the moonlight would be enough to illuminate the speakers below. It would have been, she supposed, except that the voices were coming from the shadows right up against the building. From her angle, Julia could not see them.

Her window was partially open, so she could hear them, though. The words came out as jumbled hissing sounds. Both parties, apparently, were struggling to keep their voices low while obviously quite at odds with one another. By God, it certainly sounded like Sophie.

Who could she be with, though? And for heaven's sake, why was she whispering so? Why didn't she just cry out for help? Obviously, though she was not at all pleased with her companion, she was not in need of rescue from him, either. What could it mean?

Julia could call down to them, of course, but if they were already going to such troubles to keep their argument secret, she doubted they'd stand there and shout back their explanation. Perhaps Sophie did indeed need rescue, and notifying the argumentative gentleman that they were being watched would only give him notice to abscond with the girl again. That would not be good.

Best to keep quiet and find out how things stood.

She glanced at Rastmoor. Damn him for sleeping so peacefully! Well, she didn't need him. She'd find Sophie on her own then perhaps the two of them could put these useless men behind them. They'd leave the locket here for Rastmoor and be gone. He could sleep all he wanted, and Sophie's friend could find someone else to argue with. She grabbed up her clothing and dressed as quickly and as quietly as she could. Rastmoor didn't stir.

She tiptoed out of the room and went down the stairs. The house was still slumbering around her, and at each little creak of the floor, she wondered that no one noticed. They didn't, however. She made it out the door unseen and crept around the building to find the place the voices had been coming from.

They were gone now. Drat. Where could they be? It had not taken her long to reach this spot, but somehow they had vanished. Julia ducked into the shadows and glanced up to make sure she was below the correct window. It appeared she was. So where did the arguing couple go?

A clattering sound near the stables caught her ear. They must be preparing to leave! She stayed in the shelter of shadows and moved quickly in that direction. A hedge at the corner of the stables sheltered her while she tried to locate the source of the sound. No light spilled out from the doorway, and she was hesitant to dash in blindly.

Had it really been Sophie she'd heard? Cowering in the darkness, her trousers fastened crooked, her shirt hanging loose, and her memory fading, she was not entirely sure it had been. Also, she was not entirely sure it had been such a good idea to rush out here in the first place. Perhaps she'd been a bit rash, in fact. At the very least, it might have been sensible to rouse Rastmoor.

But now there was a light. Indeed, the flickering glow of a candle or even a torch, perhaps, lit the area at the far end of the stable. It got brighter. Julia wasn't sure if this made her more at ease or more nervous. What was Sophie up to out here?

Then a figure appeared, silhouetted in the flickering glow. Indeed, it was a torch. The figure carried it and moved swiftly.

Right behind him came another figure who also carried a torch. Both persons were male; at least they were dressed that way from what Julia could tell. Had Sophie taken to wearing a disguise? No, neither of these men were Sophie. And they didn't appear to be arguing, either. They were in perfect accord as they matched steps and moved from the corner of the stable toward the main building.

Julia barely had time to wonder where they were going with such bright torches when the first man paused, then tossed his flame high into the air. It crashed against a window, scattering glass and sparks out into the night. The second torch was tossed in precisely the same window. Immediately the room inside became lit with a bright glow. By God, the curtains were aflame, and the room was on fire!

Worse, it was the room where Rastmoor slept like a log.

The figures who'd thrown the fire darted away, but Julia didn't care. She was already screeching at the top of her lungs and racing back toward the inn. She had to get him out of there before he burned to death. Heavens, there was no doubt the fire had been intentional and that Rastmoor had been the target. Please God, let her get to him in time.

The yelling or the crashing or the roaring flames had managed to rouse some of the building's occupants. As Julia pounded through the door, she ran smack into the proprietor, staggering, bleary-eyed and confused. She pointed toward the back stairs and shouted that there was a fire. His eyes unbleared immediately, and he began barking orders to no one in particular.

Servants appeared, and doors banged open at the top of the stairs. A woman screamed, and running feet clattered from everywhere. Julia couldn't make her way up the stairs for the crowd of nightshirted patrons who were making their way down it. She scanned their frightened faces; none of them was Rastmoor.

She could smell the smoke now. Surprisingly, though, the air was still quite clear. This could only mean Rastmoor's door was still shut tight. He was locked in there, still tucked in bed asleep and soon to be that way forever. If the flames didn't get him first, the heat and the smoke would. They'd creep into his lungs, burning him and causing untold damage. She simply had to get to him!

Julia plowed her way through the crowd only to be knocked back by the first servant to rush by carrying a bucket of water. Two more followed. She found herself in step behind them.

At the top of the stairs, smoke began to billow. The door must have been opened. She couldn't even see her way to Rastmoor's room, but the sound of shouts and coughs gave her direction. She felt along the wall until she found it. A servant stomped her toe as he practically fell out of the room, still clutching his now-empty bucket. He clambered down the stairs, hopefully to return right away with more water.

The fire seemed to have taken hold rapidly. The faded, dusty draperies at the window must have provided ample fodder for those fiery torches. Had the bedclothes caught just as easily? Was Rastmoor still alive? She couldn't see through the smoke.

But then she could hear. He was calling her name! Through the smoke and the shouting and the melee all around them, she could hear him calling her name.

"Julia!"

She pulled her shirt to cover her nose and mouth then moved toward the sound.

More servants pushed past, bringing water. At last Julia could make out forms and bodies in the smoky room. The cool night air outside seemed to be drawing the fire to it, and as more buckets of water were doused over the flames, the room cleared just enough so that she could see him plainly.

He was naked. Two men held his arms, pulling him back from the bed, which was on fire. Rastmoor struggled against them, not trying to escape the room, but glaring with a fury at the burning bed. He caught one of his would-be rescuers with a hard right swing and broke free, diving into the bed.

Her lungs burned, but Julia took a deep breath and ran to him.

"Anthony!"

He hardly seemed to notice when she dug her fingernails into his shoulder and tried to pull him away from the flames.

"He's looking for some woman, someone named Julia!" one of the men near her yelled above the noise, taking Rastmoor's other shoulder.

Together they dragged him from the dangerous bed, but he pulled the blankets with him. Julia had to dodge embers that coursed through the air around her. She grabbed Rastmoor's chin to yank his face toward hers.

"Anthony!" she shouted. "Look at me, Anthony."

It took nearly a full second before he seemed to recognize her. The wild gleam in his eye faded into recognition, and he dropped the burning bedding. His arms swung around her, and he held her to him in an inescapable embrace. Whatever air she'd had left in her lungs was crushed out. But she would never complain.

The concern for a missing woman had spread to others around them, however. Servants hurried to douse the bed, searching the linens for this mysterious Julia he'd been shouting after. The smoky air became heavy with added moisture.

Someone found Rastmoor's trousers and tossed them to him. Julia pried herself away and tried to look manly and concerned instead of terrified and weepy, as she felt. Rastmoor glared through the haze as he pulled his trousers on. She choked for trying to breathe.

The danger was past. The smoldering bedclothes and window drapes were tossed out through the broken window. Servants in the yard below stomped out the remaining flames. Servants above poured their final buckets over the darkened woodwork and furnishings. The terrible glow of flames was at last replaced by smoky darkness and stinging air.

The inn's structure had been spared, as had all the guests. Heavy soot coated everything from Julia's hair to the walls around her, but thankfully all of it would be fine after a thorough cleaning. Rastmoor was alive and well. Thank God.

Julia was not likely to forget the scene any time soon, though. What would have happened had she not been awake and had not thought she'd heard Sophie? She shuddered to think of it. Indeed, the outcome could have been very different. Their would-be murderers might have succeeded.

Damn that Fitzgelder! She had no doubt this was his doing, but who else was involved? Sophie? Had that truly been her voice outside? Julia didn't know what to believe. Things were jumbled inside her head, and nothing made sense right now. She needed some fresh air.

"Come on," Rastmoor was saying, tugging at her elbow.

She followed him out, past the servants who hurried by. He led her down the stairs and out into the cool, damp night. Her lungs ached, and she coughed in great gulps of the heavenly air.

But he didn't let her revel in it for long.

"Where in God's name were you?" he demanded. His own voice was hoarse and gravelly.

"There was someone talking . . . in the hallway. Then they came out here, so I followed them."

"You came outside in the middle of the night because you heard someone *talking*?"

"It was Sophie! She was arguing with a man."

"Sophie? Does she still have the locket?"

He was already looking around, scanning the sooty faces cluttering the yard. She hated to disappoint him. True, she might have saved his life tonight, but she had the distinct impression he'd much rather have had her save that locket.

"Sorry, I can't be sure it was even truly her. It sounded like her voice, but when I came outside, they were gone."

"They? Who was she arguing with?"

"A gentleman—I don't know. I couldn't hear what they said."

"And the fire?"

"That I did see. Two men. They threw something burning up into the window. They were trying to kill you!"

He glanced up. From where they stood, the blackened window frame was easily visible. There were three other windows on this side of the building, but only one showed signs of fire. Clearly it was no accident those torches had landed in his room.

Now his gaze returned to her. She felt oddly self-conscious. What was he thinking? He stared at her intently, yet his face showed no emotion.

"Too bad you didn't find our missing Sophie, Julia," he began. "But how fortunate you were out here safe and sound when someone was trying to burn me to death—in your bed."

Now his expression made her take a step backward. She had a sinking feeling she knew what was running through his head. Oddly enough, she really couldn't blame him. He believed her capable of terrible things; why should murder not be one of them?

"Lucky they knew exactly which bed I'd be in, Julia," he went on. "Considering I gave up my room after everyone else had gone to sleep. Unless perhaps you'd like to convince me those flames were meant for you."

She stared back at him and forced herself to blink back tears. By God, she would not cry for him, no matter what he accused her of. And certainly she'd never propose that she had been the arson's target tonight. She knew as well as he that very few people on the planet cared whether she lived or died.

RASTMOOR HAD TO WALK AWAY FROM HER. HE'D BLAtantly accused her of wanting him dead, and she'd said nothing. She'd batted her eyes at him and stood there, cold as stone—beautiful under the shapeless men's clothing and the layers of soot—but heartless and dispassionate as marble.

Damn. She'd enslaved him again, hadn't she? She'd wrapped herself around his soul, and there was nothing he could do about it except lash out with harsh words then turn his back on her and hope to forget her for a moment or two. God, all he really wanted was to hold her against his chest and feel her heart beating.

He'd been nearly insane when he'd awakened in that smoky, smothering room. In his sleep-befuddled state, he simply could not comprehend that she was not with him, that she was not somehow trapped there, tangled in the fiery bedding, suffering and dying. He'd made a complete fool of himself, hadn't he?

He always did when Julia was involved.

"Sir!" A dirty little scullery maid came scurrying up to him. "They say you was looking for a woman?"

Blast. Now even the kitchen help labeled him desperate. "No, thank you."

The girl dropped her hoarse voice low. "'Cause if you was looking for a woman—for a particular woman—I might know something about her."

"What?"

She leaned closer, and her words came out in a whisper. "A certain woman might have just left here a little bit ago."

"Left here?"

He quickly glanced over to where he'd left Julia. She looked every bit a ragged hand at this point and was busy helping tend to some of the mild injuries several servants had suffered in the battle. She was paying no mind to Rastmoor, and it irked him, despite the fact that he shouldn't have cared.

But the maid before him was happy to continue her story. She nodded up at him, her eyes bright with conspiracy. "She left in a carriage, sir."

"A carriage?" Well, that would be an odd thing at this hour. He certainly hadn't noticed any carriage waiting in the yard, although he had to admit he'd been rather preoccupied surviving a fire and holding himself back from throttling Julia for endangering herself. Whatever could the little wench be talking about?

"What woman? Which way did she go?"

The girl shook her head, and the dingy cap she wore wobbled atop sooty hair. "I don't know, sir. I didn't see her myself; I just heard about it."

"From whom?"

The girl pursed her lips and took a step back. "Oh, don't make me tell you, sir. I don't want him getting in trouble. He's a good boy, sir, and he never meant to be helping no criminals!"

"Blast it, what criminals? Tell me what you know. Who set this fire?"

The girl's eyes were wide, and she nearly shook the cap right off her head. "Oh, sir, I don't know anything about that; I swear! My Jeb was just doing what he was told, he was—"

"Jeb? The one who's been gone all flipping day on some errand or other?"

"Yes, sir. He just got back a little while ago. Brought up that pretty carriage he'd been sent after down in Geydon."

"He went to Geydon to bring back a carriage?"

She nodded and grinned as if her beau had done something truly remarkable. "Yes, sir! He brought back the finest carriage you can imagine. A phaeton, and he drove it himself!"

By God, it couldn't be, could it? This Jeb had been sent to bring Lindley's carriage up here? That could only mean Lindley was around, and was expecting to be here at some point tonight or tomorrow to retrieve the thing! Hellfire, had Rastmoor been scouring the whole bloody countryside while Lindley was hiding Sophie someplace right here under his nose?

Could Julia have been right about hearing their voices?

"If those people who left in that phaeton had anything to do with this fire, sir, you can be sure my Jeb didn't know anything about it. He was too busy getting things ready for the gentleman and his woman. Honest, it never crossed his mind the pair of them might be up to no good."

"Who are they?"

"By faith, I don't know, sir."

"Well, what did they look like, for God's sake?"

"I didn't see them, sir," the girl replied quickly, and her lip was trembling now so he could barely understand her words. "I only heard them, sir. The gentleman comes in to call for his carriage, and he tells my Jeb he needs it right away. Then he goes out to the yard, and we hear him arguing with this woman."

"What woman?"

"I don't know, sir. Likely the one what left in the carriage."

"Did they leave before the fire started?"

"No, sir. It was after; I'm sure of it."

"So you believe they started it?"

"They must have, sir. Wasn't nobody else around. We

thought they left, though, 'cause it got really quiet out here, until there was yelling about a fire, and all."

"So you didn't actually see them start the fire."

"No, sir! Else we would have called the mistress and master straightaway!"

"But you did hear a man and a woman arguing in the yard."

"Yes, sir, that was for certain."

Well, that seemed to match up with Julia's story, didn't it? Of course, that could mean nothing. Julia herself could have been arguing with someone and simply told the story of hearing it to provide a nice tidy alibi for herself. Or perhaps she simply paid this hapless wench to corroborate her version of things. Just because he was an idiot and wanted desperately to believe that Julia was an innocent bystander in all this didn't mean he was about to take a stranger's word. He'd done that before, and look where it got him.

"What were they arguing about?" he asked the girl.

"I don't know, sir. They was trying to be hush about it, I think. But I could tell from the tone they wasn't getting along well."

"And you didn't bother to come out and see what was going on? Are women accosted here so often you tend to ignore it?"

The girl actually looked indignant. "Oh, no sir, it wasn't any sort of argument like that. No, that woman wasn't arguing 'cause she was in trouble or nothing. She just didn't like something the gentleman said, I figure. That's how it sounded to me, sir."

"But you didn't at least look out here just to be sure?"

"My Jeb and me, we know enough to keep our noses out of affairs of the quality, we do. And anyone could know from the way that gentleman used his words, he was quality. If he and his woman want to stand out in the yard and have a spat, my Jeb and I won't tell them they can't."

"Very noble—and convenient. So you didn't actually see this argumentative woman?"

"No, sir."

"Nor him, the gentleman of quality?"

"No, sir."

"Yet you heard his voice clearly enough to form an opinion of his heritage?"

"I did, sir. I was . . . well, I was in the stable there, and I heard him talking to my Jeb when he came in to call for the carriage."

"But you didn't get a look at him?"

She twisted her sooty apron in her hands. "See, sir, the master's kind of funny about us kitchen girls coming out here to the stable. But my Jeb and me, well, we didn't figure it would be so very bad if I come out here to visit him every once in a while. Just once in a while, mind you, and we never let it interfere with our duties, I promise!"

"Oh, I'm sure of it. But naturally when that gentleman came in, you figured it might be best if he didn't catch you."

Her cheeks flushed deeply under the ash and grime. "I wasn't exactly in a right state to be greeting the patrons, sir, if you understand."

"Yes, I grasp the situation. Tell me, though, how much time passed between when you heard the arguing and when the alarm was raised for the fire?"

More blushes. The girl couldn't quite give him a definite answer. Apparently she and her darling Jeb had been otherwise engaged during that time. Hellfire, it was a wonder the couple bothered to surface at all despite the raging inferno in their employer's establishment. The girl's story gave him none of the answers he needed right now.

"And what of the woman?" he forged on. Unlikely he'd get any solid information at this point, but he might as well ask. "You said she left. What do you mean?"

She brightened. "Oh! She left. In the carriage, sir."

"So you've said."

"With the gentleman. My Jeb got it all ready for him right quick, just like he said. He's an honest man, sir, and if he'd have known he was getting it ready for some scapegrace fire starters . . . well, he wouldn't have done it. But they must have come in and took the carriage while we was all out fighting the fire."

"Then you saw them leave?"

"My Jeb did, sir. He noticed them just as they turned the corner out of the lane. He said it looked as if they was in a hurry—the woman's yellow hair was hanging out from under her shawl and the man was driving the horses for all they was worth."

At last, something solid. "She was blond?"

"It's what my Jeb says, sir. Do you think that might be the self-same woman you was looking for?"

"I believe it was," he replied, surprised by his own truthfulness. Sophie was blond. Perhaps Julia had been right; perhaps the girl had been arguing with a man in the yard just before that damned fire.

God, he hoped so. He'd really much rather have been nearly assassinated by Sophie and Fitzgelder's flunky than by the woman he loved.

Used to love, he corrected.

He fumbled in a pocket for some coin to reward the girl.

She shuffled nervously but accepted the offering. "I suppose you'll have me tell the master now, wouldn't you, sir?"

"Tell him?"

"How I come by knowing who might have set this fire. Then the magistrate can be called and someone sent out to find your lady friend and that gentleman. They wasn't just trying to warm up your sleeping room, after all."

"No, they weren't. I'm sure your master would very much like to get his hands on them for all this damage."

He wouldn't mind getting them to answer a few questions for him, either. But what would that accomplish? If this really was Sophie, and her companion really was Lindley or even if the instigator was one of Fitzgelder's minions, they could simply deny their involvement. Surely Fitzgelder had enough money or friends in low places that could easily protect him from conviction. Any accusations Rastmoor might make—unfounded since he himself had seen no trace of anything that might formally tie his cousin into this—would only serve to drive Fitzgelder to more drastic measures. And that could mean more than just Rastmoor's life was in danger.

No, at this point he'd prefer to keep the magistrate out of it. This was between him and Fitzgelder. No one would gain anything by dragging family skeletons out into daylight. He'd deal with things his own way.

"No, I don't think your master needs to know," he told the girl with a forced lightness. "The damage inflicted here was aimed at me, so I'll be responsible for the repairs. That should ease your master's worries. I see no need to burden him with tales of kitchen maids and stable boys in the night."

Her eyes lit, and she smiled. She was almost pretty. "Oh, thank you, sir! Thank you and bless you!"

"But tell me," he asked. "Which direction did your Jeb see them go?"

"That way, sir," she replied, pointing to the south.

London, of course. Damn. Fitzgelder would get that locket and have the proof he needed to set his schemes in motion. Things would not go well for Rastmoor's mother and sister. For their sake, he had to get that locket back before it reached its destination. Which meant, of course, he'd be heading south, right into the lion's jaws.

He'd have to hurry, though, if he hoped to overtake them before Fitzgelder could get his filthy hands on the locket. And there was something more, too. Something far more dangerous would be traveling with them to Fitzgelder. Sophie carried the truth of Julia's identity!

God, that meant Fitzgelder would know, too. If any part of Julia's story was true, and she really was on the run from Fitzgelder, she could be in even graver danger than Rastmoor. He simply stood to be murdered by his cousin; there was no telling what fate the hateful man might have planned for a wayward wife.

Rastmoor glanced over to where Julia carefully poured cold water on the arm of a slightly singed servant. She must be forgetting she was playing a part just now; her actions were gentle and feminine, not those of the man whose clothing she wore. Perhaps she was not such a fine actress, after all. Perhaps she really was just a woman who'd been another victim of the bastard, Cedrick Fitzgelder.

But those were dangerous thoughts. He'd best not let himself ponder along those lines. People got hurt when they gave Julia credit for having a heart.

"If I may say, sir, you'd be wise to let her go," the scullery maid was saying.

He couldn't quite pull his attention back to her. "What?"

"Your lady friend, who just ran off on you," she said. "It was awful what she did to you."

"Yes, it was."

"But you should let her go. I daresay it could be dangerous for you if you don't."

The wench had no idea how right she was. "Indeed, it would be."

"A broken heart will heal, sir."

Now he finally took his eyes from Julia and turned them on the girl. She was entirely too young to have any idea what she was talking about, but he appreciated her concern. He wished he could take the advice she offered, but he knew he wouldn't.

"Here," he said as he managed to dig out a few more coins. "Keep track of these. You and that Jeb fellow might find a good use for them someday."

She curtsied and thanked him repeatedly so that he was enormously uncomfortable. He finally found some excuse to get away from her and wound his way through a gauntlet of well-meaning patrons who milled about the yard and asked after his welfare. Each one thanked God for his safety and expressed their astonishment that such a thing could happen in a respectable place.

No one seemed to have seen anything to indicate what might have caused the fire, and it appeared the general populace had not been enlightened to the fact that it was intentionally set. Well, he was in no hurry to inform them. The last thing he needed was public panic and local constabulary entanglements. He'd just quietly look into things.

The first thing he needed to do was verify the servant girl's tale. Had someone actually come to request Lindley's carriage in the middle of the night? Was it indeed gone now? That would be easy enough to determine.

He slipped into the carriage house. No carriage. He hadn't really expected to find it there, of course. The girl would have known he might look.

He snagged a passing hand and asked the boy what he knew of it.

"Aye, it's a mystery to me, sir," the young man said. "Jeb had to go all the way down to Geydon to get it. Waited there all day for them to fix it, too . . . An axle was broke, or something. He finally got it back here tonight and last I saw it sat right here in the carriage house. Real pretty and fixed it up right nice. Don't see many of those high-perch phaetons here, we don't. You might go ask Jeb what happened to it, though. He'd be the one what knows."

"Jeb, is it? I might just do that."

Indeed he *would* do that. A few questions ought to quickly absolve Lindley and his impeccable wardrobe, else they'd damn him for sure.

Rastmoor only had to question two more sooty servants before locating the infamous Jeb. He wasn't surprised to find the man strapping and well-featured, but he was disappointed in his understanding of gentlemen's attire.

"Well, how am I supposed to know who tailored his clothes?"

Rastmoor took a deep breath and wished to God for something to drink. "I don't give a blow who the bloody tailor was," he said with false calm. "All I asked was if the man appeared well-tailored or not."

"I don't know from tailors, sir," Jeb defended. "Truth of the matter is, I didn't happen to notice the man's clothes. If you ask me—and begging your pardon, sir—one quality gent's the same as another."

Quality. There was that word again. "So he was quality, was he?"

"With a gig like that? He's quality for sure."

"But how were you certain it was his carriage? Couldn't anyone have come in and ordered you to harness it up?"

Jeb straightened up his shoulders and set his jaw. "I don't give out a gentleman's carriage to just any bloke that comes along to ask for it, sir. He's the self-same man what told us to go fetch it from Geydon. By God, the self-same man and no one but him."

So, that was his proof. It had been Lindley, after all. His own friend was a part of the plot to kill him. Damn! And it sounded as if Sophie was with him, willingly. This meant that very soon Fitzgelder would know Julia was here. That is, if he didn't already know. At worst, Lindley and Sophie would reach London just after noon tomorrow, taking that locket and everything they knew straight into Fitzgelder's drawing room. Fitzgelder could have people after Julia within an hour of that.

A set of ill-fitting men's clothing would hardly protect her then.

He left Jeb to mutter about the oddness of the upper classes and meandered back to where a few servants and patrons still milled in the yard. For the most part, it appeared guests and servants alike were returning to normalcy. Rastmoor found Julia's gray form among the others and watched as she bade a polite good evening to the two ladies they had met on the previous night. Thankfully, they and the sleeping babe appeared unharmed by the recent events.

Of course, they would be. They had been safely across the hall, in the room Rastmoor should have had. Only Julia had known which room Rastmoor was truly occupying tonight. The thought gnawed at him.

Could he really credit her with plotting his demise? Every part of him revolted at the thought. He watched her gracious smiles and tender glances at the still-slumbering babe. Fool that he was, he simply couldn't imagine Julia capable of murder. He waited until she was alone then slid up beside her.

"Everyone survived?" he asked casually.

"A few minor burns and disturbance of the lung. Nothing serious. We'll all have sore throats for a day or two, I expect," she replied, clipping her words and keeping her eyes on anything but him. "Quite fortunate no one here knows you well. They were most eager to save your life."

"Yes, I'll have to thank them," he said, ignoring the slight.

"Did you have a nice conversation with the scullery maid?"

He did not ignore the pointed tone to her voice and hoped it was something akin to jealousy. "Yes, as a matter of fact, I did."

"Lovely. She seems quite your type."

"Quite yours, as well," he replied. "She corroborated your story to the letter. Oh yes, I heard all about the male and female voices arguing in the darkness. Pity this chit didn't manage to get a good look at them, either."

"Perhaps now you believe me?"

"I believe Lindley and Sophie are involved, and they drove off together while everyone else was fighting the ruddy blaze."

"What?"

"Says your kitchen wench . . . and her hot-tempered beau in the stables there."

"They saw them?"

"They did."

"I told you it was Lindley! I told you!"

"Yes, so you did. As I suggested, we might not be so quick to absolve Sophie from all wrongdoing."

"Insufferable man," she hissed. "Obviously she was arguing with Lindley because he is holding her against her will. Now he's taken her away again! We must find them. Which way did they go?"

He didn't answer immediately.

"Well? Which way? Surely you did think to ask, didn't you?"

He pulled his brows low. If he told her the truth, she'd no doubt head off on some foolhardy crusade to save her friend. If he told her nothing, she'd simply go find out from Jeb and his wench all on her own. If he lied and suggested they hurry off in the wrong direction, there might be a chance he could get her to safety.

And Fitzgelder would have the locket along with all the family secrets it contained. One thing he wouldn't have, however, was Julia. Rastmoor's gut tightened at that thought. He could still keep Julia from Fitzgelder, whether she wanted it or not.

She was glaring up at him, one skeptical eyebrow cocked at an angle and one smudged fist jabbed into her hip. Her cropped hair stuck out in odd places. Her clothes sagged. Her feet were bare but nearly as black as the earth. By God, he could have laughed at her if he hadn't wanted so fiercely to drag her back up to their burned-out room and get another fire going. Murder and scandal be damned.

"They went north," he lied calmly. "I'll see about hiring a conveyance."

Chapter Ten

He'd hired a dilapidated gig. It was all the ostlers could muster for them in the middle of the night, and Julia supposed she should be grateful. As much as she'd rather not be wedged here so tight against Rastmoor's warm, solid body like this, she knew she'd never have been able to stay atop a horse. Every muscle ached, her throat was raw, and her tired eyes simply would not keep open. Indeed, she was thankful for the secure seat beneath her bottom, uncomfortable though it might be.

They'd been driving for hours. The pink glow of dawn was just now beginning to erase the darkness of night, and the first songs of morning birds could be heard in the trees and hedgerows around them. The bony nag that plodded along before the gig tossed his shaggy mane, and the harness jingled. A mist clung low to the ground; its origin was the river that ran quietly along beside the narrow road.

"Are you sure they came this way?" Julia asked, more to keep herself awake than to actually get an answer.

Rastmoor shifted the reins in his hands. "I know Lindley. I know where he's going," he said.

That's what he'd said earlier, too, when they'd passed

through a sleeping Warwick without so much as pausing at the crossroads to wonder if Lindley had turned off. They'd passed one lonely farm cart along the way, and Julia urged Rastmoor to ask whether the driver had seen Lindley's fine carriage pass by, but he flatly refused. Stubborn prig.

They had been only a few miles past Warwick when Rastmoor turned onto another, smaller road. It twisted and wound along beside the Avon, and she asked about his decision but, as usual, he'd simply assured her he was convinced he knew Lindley's destination. Of course she'd reminded him the most logical thing for Lindley to do would have been to take Sophie—and the locket—directly back to London, but that only seemed to make him ill-tempered. He'd told her to keep quiet and use the remaining travel time for resting. As if she could.

Being jostled back and forth against him like this was not exactly conducive to resting. The small conveyance was clearly built for short daytime jaunts and wide-awake persons who were not the least bit attracted to one another and who didn't mind having to hold on to the seat for dear life. If she did happen to take his advice and allow herself to rest, she'd likely tumble right out of the gig to lie in a snoring heap on the side of the road. Rastmoor would likely leave her there, too.

Or worse, she might find herself snuggled up next to him mumbling in her sleep how much she'd missed him these past three years. By God, she was *not* about to let that happen.

"How can you be so sure you know where Lindley is headed?" she asked again. "You didn't exactly perceive early on that he was a part of your cousin's plot to murder you."

"Trust me. I know what I'm doing."

Well, certainly he knew what he was doing. She only wished he'd share it with *her*. Where were they going? What did he think they'd do when they got there? Did he really understand they were most likely heading straight into honest-to-goodness danger? Instead of being short with her, he ought to be spending their travel time planning and considering the situation. All this ridiculous brooding was quite irritating and certainly unproductive.

But she was too exhausted to persist in conversation. Besides, despite her worries for Sophie, it would honestly be a relief if they got wherever it was they were going only to find Rastmoor's assumptions were wrong. No doubt it made her a bad friend to poor Sophie, but a large part of Julia truly hoped they were heading quite the opposite direction from the people who wanted Rastmoor dead.

But poor Sophie. It was impossible to believe she would ever be a willing accomplice in what had occurred. Julia may not have known her long, but she simply couldn't imagine Sophie hurling torches up into Rastmoor's room. No matter what he might say about the girl's character, Julia knew Sophie's involvement with Lindley was not by choice. If Julia were a true friend, she'd have not settled for Rastmoor's brusque replies. She'd have pestered him to hurry the nag, beg information from locals, and overtake Lindley.

She hadn't, though. She simply let their little gig clatter slowly along, secretly hoping they were miles and miles from Lindley and poor Sophie and plots against Rastmoor. Oh, but she ought to be ashamed of herself. Once again she was willing to sacrifice a friend on account of Anthony Rastmoor.

The slow, rhythmic hoofbeats altered their tempo. Rastmoor tugged the reins, and Julia tried not to be aware of the taut muscles in his arm when she was forced to lean against him as the gig lurched. They were leaving the main road and turning onto another lane.

Julia frowned. Their gig felt especially shabby as they passed by an imposing stone gatehouse. No one appeared to stop them, and Rastmoor gave no indication of hesitating. For the first time since leaving that posting house in Geydon, he urged the horse to pick up the pace. Julia's chest tightened.

The lane was every bit as wide as the road they'd been traveling, yet obviously it was a private drive. This, no doubt, was the entrance to someone's grand estate. They'd apparently reached their destination.

"Where are we?" she asked.

"Hartwood," he replied.

"That tells me nothing," she grumbled. "What is Hartwood?"

"The home of a friend."

"Lindley?"

"No. I said a friend."

"A friend *like* Lindley?"

"No. A friend who doesn't generally try to murder people."

"Generally?"

"You'll be safe here."

She was momentarily distracted by the expanse of manicured lawn around her and the glory of dawn reflected off the still waters of a lake just to their right. Then his words sank in, and she turned to glare at him.

"I'll be *what*?"

"This belongs to my friend Dashford. You'll be safe here."

They rounded a stand of trees, and an enormous house appeared before her. No, it was more of a palace. Huge, rambling, well-tended, and luxurious; whoever this Dashford was, he certainly did well for himself. A person could get lost in a house this vast. Apparently that was exactly what Rastmoor had planned.

"You think you're going to leave me here, don't you?" she said, her voice remarkably controlled for the sudden rage that was welling up.

"I *am* leaving you here," he replied. "And you're going to be polite about it."

"I most certainly am not!"

"You are. Dashford and his new lady are friends of mine, and they'll keep you safe. I can't introduce you as Alexander Clemmons—they've heard that name and think you're Sophie's husband, for God's sake. So we'd best come up with another pseudonym. How about, oh, I think Percival Nancey should do nicely. You'll make a convincing Mr. Nancey, I should imagine."

"I will not! If you believe for one minute that I'll stay here while you go and get yourself killed, well, you . . ."

"You *will* stay here until I send word it's safe for you to leave. This is not a matter open to discussion, Julia. You are staying with Dashford, and under no circumstances will you reveal your true name or your gender to anyone. Is that clear?"

"Oh, it's clear enough," she said with clenched teeth.

By God, she could scarcely believe her ears. He was leaving her here? Expecting her to quietly agree to his preposterous commandments? He was a fool.

No, *she* was the fool. How on earth had she not seen this coming? Of course Rastmoor hadn't needed to hurry his nag or question passersby along the way. He'd known since the very start that Lindley did not come this way. By God, he'd been bringing her here to dump her off like yesterday's refuse all along! He knew Lindley had done the logical thing and taken Sophie south, down to London. All this way Rastmoor had simply been bringing Julia up here to abandon her, to get her out of his hair.

The opportunity to fume at him was lost as footmen darted out of the huge house to greet them. Rastmoor handed the horse over to them and let Julia clamber down from the gig under her own power. He gave her a dark look of warning then strode comfortably up the wide steps to the broad front door. More servants appeared and greeted him. It seemed Rastmoor was recognized and loved by everyone, although Julia felt more than a few curious stares directed her way as she trailed Rastmoor into the expansive foyer.

"How nice to see you again, my lord," the Dashford butler said, hurrying to welcome them.

"Thank you, Williams," Rastmoor replied, handing his sooty hat and gloves over to a curtsying maid. "Forgive our sudden invasion, but as you might assume, we've encountered some difficulties in our travel."

"Indeed?" Williams replied, valiantly ignoring their ragged condition. "I'm sure his lordship will be eager to know of your arrival."

"Yes, I'm sure he will. If you would be so kind as to let him know I've brought along my good friend, Mr. Percival Nancey."

Julia cringed. Damn him. The very least he could have done was let her choose her own alias—something a bit more, er, masculine. How was she to keep her gender a secret while prancing around with a name like Nancey?

The butler went off to inform his master of the arrivals, while Rastmoor and Julia were led by a Mrs. Kendall—the housekeeper, she assumed—into a cozy room to await their host. The house seemed to be bursting at the seams with curious servants, and in no time a tray of muffins and tea was brought in for them. Surrounded by such luxury and opulence, Julia felt supremely self-conscious.

Soot clung to her every inch, so she dared not sit on the furniture. Rastmoor, too, she noted, stood uncomfortably in the middle of the room. His face was lined, even more so thanks to the dirt and grime he'd not quite been able to wipe off. The man needed rest. She hoped his friend Dashford—if indeed the man was a true friend—would convince him to refresh himself before attempting the ride to London. If Rastmoor was to survive any further attempts Fitzgelder might have waiting for him along the way, he'd need to be wide-awake and in full control of all his faculties.

Besides, if Rastmoor could be prevailed upon to stall his departure, that might give Julia time to contrive a way to accompany him or at least to escape Dashford and follow at an undetected distance. But stay here with ruddy strangers? As Percival Nancey, no less? She thought not.

"You're awfully silent," Rastmoor said at length.

"I'm plotting," she admitted.

"Well, stop it. When I tell Dash he is to keep you here at all costs, I assure you he'll do just that."

"He might certainly try."

Rastmoor took an angry step toward her, and she had to force herself not to cringe. "Damn it, Julia, I'll not let you—"

But the door opened and interrupted whatever furious demands Rastmoor had been about to make. It was just as well—she'd not have paid heed to them, anyway, considering her attention was immediately drawn to the tall, disheveled man who entered.

He was dark, long-limbed, and striking. His hair was thoroughly tousled, and he carried his coat thrown over one arm.

His shirt, Julia noted, was only partially tucked into his trousers, while the shirt points hung limp at his neck with no cravat in sight. Clearly his lordship—she had no doubt this was Dashford himself—was only just roused from bed to greet them. She supposed she shouldn't be surprised. Even by country standards it was, after all, still very early in the morning.

The gentleman didn't seem to mind guests at such an hour, though. He appeared altogether cheerful and alert when he moved to clasp Rastmoor by the hand.

"Anthony! What the devil brings you back here so . . ." Then he paused, taking in Rastmoor's muddled condition. "Good God, man! You look like hell."

"Don't worry, we haven't mucked up the upholstery," Rastmoor said. "Sorry about dragging you from bed so early, though."

Dashford shrugged. "No trouble. I was awake. But tell me, what on earth happened to you?"

Julia reminded herself to play her part as Dashford's curious gaze scanned over her filthy attire. She held up her chin and tried to look manly. It wasn't easy. Compared to these two gentlemen, she must certainly look a poor example of masculinity if not a sham entirely.

"This is my friend, Nancey. Percival Nancey," Rastmoor announced.

Julia had the presence of mind to bend at the waist rather than curtsy, but Rastmoor continued before she had opportunity to greet their host.

"You'll have to forgive him; he doesn't speak. He can't."

What? Blast the man! Now he was taking away her ability to speak? Oh, she could simply choke him. Perhaps Dashford would leave them soon, and she might have opportunity to do just that.

Dashford, however, seemed perplexed by Rastmoor's words, so the ruddy liar continued. "There was a fire in the posting house. Nancey took in too much smoke, unfortunately. Likely it'll be days before he can find his voice again."

Curse him! Oh, she'd find her voice again soon, indeed. He could be sure of that.

"Dash it, I'm terribly sorry," Dashford said with conviction. "A fire, you say? Were there any other . . . Say, where the duce is Lindley?"

"Don't worry, he survived. The scoundrel is halfway to London by now, I suppose," Rastmoor said. "These last two days I've been traveling with Mr. Nancey."

Now Dashford frowned and gave her a suspicious look. At least, it felt to Julia like a suspicious look. She gave extra effort to a masculine pose. A quick glance at Rastmoor told her she was not succeeding. He rolled his eyes.

"Perhaps we might have the opportunity to refresh ourselves," Rastmoor said, drawing Dashford's attention again. "I'm sure Mr. Nancey could use some sleep, but if you're not too busy this morning, Dash, I'd appreciate a few minutes of your time."

Dashford nodded. "Of course. I'll call for someone to show you up to your rooms."

Well, at least she would have her own room in this expansive home. With luck it would be far, far removed from Rastmoor's. With a heavy lock.

Dashford moved to the bellpull, and Julia took advantage of his distance to scowl at Rastmoor. He smiled innocently. The snake.

She gritted her teeth and muttered so he alone could hear, "I'm not about to let you leave me here—mute of all things!"

"Hush, Mr. Nancey, don't strain your voice. Just think how that could ruin your opera career," Rastmoor said loudly.

Dashford frowned again, watching her. She feigned a sniffle and wiped her nose against her sleeve. There, was that manly enough? Apparently not. Rastmoor rolled his eyes again.

"That's rotten luck about your voice, Nancey," Dashford said after summoning his staff. "I'll call for the physician right away."

Oh, that was all they needed! Julia glared daggers at Rastmoor. Didn't the idiot realize his kindhearted friend would insist on medical care when he decided to make her a victim?

"No, really, there's no need," Rastmoor said quickly. "I assure you, Nancey was seen before we left Warwick. All he requires is a bed. For sleeping."

Julia glared harder, subtly pointing to her sooty, sagging clothes. Rastmoor got the hint.

"And if it wouldn't be too much trouble, I suppose we could both use another change of clothes. I'm afraid we've been rather separated from our bags."

"Of course," Dashford said politely.

The housekeeper arrived, and Dashford explained that the guests would need rooms for rest and refreshing, as well as fresh apparel. Julia tried not to blush as Mrs. Kendall surveyed her, obviously wondering where in the world to find men's clothing to fit such a peculiar body type. For Rastmoor it would be simple—he could likely wear some of Dashford's garments. For Julia, however, the staff would have to be more creative. Indeed, far more creative than they knew. She hoped she could keep it that way. At this point it would be far more troublesome to explain a change in gender than to simply keep up with the ruse they'd already started on.

Drat Rastmoor for his voiceless opera singer, though. If she thought for one minute she would be trapped here after he left, she'd be completely furious. As it was, she could do little but bide her time and choke back her anger. He'd get his tongue-lashing soon enough. And it would not be the pleasant kind, either.

Mrs. Kendall led them back through the grand entrance hall, and Dashford instructed Rastmoor to meet him in the office at his convenience. Julia hoped she was glowering enough that Rastmoor might get the idea he was not to leave this house without her. Stupidly, he seemed not to notice.

He did notice the figure floating down the stairs toward them, though. Julia glanced up and couldn't help but stare. For one minute she thought it was Sophie, but of course it was not. The hair was a somewhat darker shade of blond, and the eyes were very alike, but this person was a stranger. It must, of course, be the new Lady Dashford.

"Ah, here is my wife now," Dashford said, confirming Julia's expectation.

Lady Dashford met their group at the foot of the stairs and welcomed Rastmoor warmly. Too warmly. She threw her arms around him like some long-lost brother. He didn't protest, Julia was quick to notice.

Not that she cared, of course. Drat, she scolded herself for caring. It was none of her business whom Rastmoor let kiss his cheek or hang on his arm. But did Dashford not see the comfortable smiles the two shared?

Then the lady turned her smile onto her husband, and it was obvious that was where the real warmth existed. Julia was simply being a fool. Was she honestly jealous of Rastmoor? She must be soft in the head.

"What in heaven's name have you been up to, Anthony?" the lady asked, wrinkling her nose at Rastmoor's clothing. "My, but you smell like a chimney!"

Anthony? And just how long had this viscountess been on a first-name basis with her husband's good friend? Julia clenched her fists. Well, at least that would appear manly, should anyone notice. No one did. Lady Dashford easily monopolized their attention.

"I'm afraid we had a bit of difficulty on our journey," Rastmoor said. "Please excuse our appearance. There was a fire in the inn where we stayed last night."

Lady Dashford's bright eyes widened. "Heavens! Thankfully you survived it. Although, where is Lord Lindley?"

Rastmoor sent a quick glance at Julia, and she wondered exactly what he meant by it. Probably he was afraid she'd go and upset the lovely Lady Dashford by blurting out the traitorous truth about Lindley. Well, she was not so callous as all that. This lady was Sophie's cousin. Julia was not about to give her any more reason to fret than was necessary. Even if it was tempting to see that creamy complexion damaged by dark circles and worry lines.

"Lindley was not with us at the time," Rastmoor said. "He's taken another route to London."

"Another route?" Lady Dashford asked. "Has there been some news, then?"

Her husband interrupted. "Hold up, my dear. We should let

our guests have a moment's peace after their ordeal before we run them through an inquisition, don't you think?"

She looked embarrassed. "Oh, but of course. Forgive me!"

Now she turned to Julia and directed one of her generous smiles her way. "So you are a friend of Lord Rastmoor's?"

Again, Rastmoor jumped in before Julia might speak for herself. "This is Percival Nancey, a friend I met along the way. He's rather worse for the event, I'm sorry to say. Too much smoke from the fire has irritated his throat. The poor chap can't so much as utter a word."

"Oh, my!" the lady gasped. "How dreadful! Randolf, we must call for the physician right away."

"Already suggested and already rejected, my dear," her husband replied. "It seems our friend Rastmoor had the foresight to take care of simple details like that. All Mr. Nancey needs at this point is a fresh shirt and a place to lay his weary head."

Julia was left with nothing to do but nod dumbly. Lady Dashford quickly looped her arm in hers and began leading the way up the broad staircase. Their hostess seemed only too eager to lavish concern and compassion, and to be truthful, Julia was glad to accept it. She could certainly do with a little kindness right now. She wasn't planning to stay here long enough to get used to it, though.

"By all means, gentlemen. Mrs. Kendall will see to all your needs," the lady said as they ascended. "What a dreadful ordeal you must have had! I'm sure you will tell us all about it when you can, Anthony. And Mr. Nancey, feel free to rest here as long as needed. If there are any persons who should be notified of your situation, we'll be only too happy to post correspondences for you. Heavens, but your family must be quite worried. I'll send paper and ink up to your room so you may write. You may communicate in writing with the servants, as well. They will surely welcome the opportunity to assist you in any way possible. Gracious, but I can't imagine how frustrating it must be to lose one's voice so unexpectedly."

No, Julia was sure she couldn't. Lady Dashford seemed to rely heavily on the use of hers. Well, at least Julia would be afforded the privilege of consigning all her curses for Rastmoor to pen and paper. She might even find that more satisfying than a simple, verbal rant.

"I'm afraid Mr. Nancey's written English is not so good," Rastmoor said suddenly. "He is, rather, Italian."

Julia glared at him. *Italian?* Was he serious?

"In his homeland he is known as, er, Signor Nancini. He sings with the opera."

"Ah, Nancini the Italian opera sensation. Perhaps I've heard of you, sir?" Dashford said with just a touch of skepticism.

Was he mocking her? She couldn't be certain, and it was uncomfortable to study his unreadable expression. Instead, she occupied herself glaring daggers at Rastmoor. Damn the man twice for subjecting her to this!

But Lady Dashford didn't seem to notice the tension around her. "Opera!" she exclaimed. "How wonderful! But all the more reason we simply must call for the physician. Oh, it would be tragic if you could not get your voice back—especially as it is your livelihood."

"He'll be fine, just so long as he rests the throat," Rastmoor said with authority. "You will help us see that he is undisturbed and is not tempted to speak? At all?"

"Oh, but of course," Lady Dashford agreed quickly. "I'll inform the servants. Fear not, Mr. Nancini. I'll see to it no one bothers you or causes you to further damage your vocal abilities."

Well, so much for that. Rastmoor had seen to it she'd be left alone and ignored. Wonderful. Likely even the servants would avoid her, fearful of incurring their mistress's wrath should they provoke the great Signor Nancini into speech. Damn damn damn.

"I'm sure he's very thankful, my lady," Rastmoor said. "You can see how he'd love nothing better than to tell you himself just what your support of his prolonged silence means to him."

He was damn right she'd love nothing better than to tell them all a thing or two! But best to let Rastmoor think he'd won this time. Really, all he'd done was succeed in giving her ample time alone to plan the next course of action. Indeed, she'd use Rastmoor's own scheme against him. No way he was leaving this estate on his own. If Rastmoor was going off to face Fitzgelder's thugs on the road, Julia was bloody well going to be there.

Right now she wasn't entirely sure whose side she'd be on, either.

Lady Dashford consulted with the housekeeper, and they decided on two rooms for their guests. Unfortunately, Julia's room was right on the central hallway—no sneaking away in dark corridors—and entirely too close to Rastmoor's for comfort. They were right next door to one another. She'd been hoping for a separate wing.

Lord Dashford had initially appeared to be leaving them with the housekeeper, but when his wife had made her appearance, he continued up the stairs with them all. Now he was speaking low with Rastmoor, and Julia could not hear what was being said. Drat, she would need to know Rastmoor's plans if she was to know when he would be leaving here.

Well, perhaps having her room right next to his would be a good thing, after all. She would hear when he left to go downstairs. It would be the simplest thing just to follow. She'd merely have to make sure she washed and dressed quickly, that's all.

With one searing look at Rastmoor, Julia let the housekeeper usher her into her room. My, but it would be heavenly to scrape off the soot and slide into some clean clothes. Her hair could use a good washing, of course, but she could wait for that. The most important thing was to be ready to follow Rastmoor at a moment's notice.

She couldn't help hoping, though, that it would be a nice long moment. The room she was offered was fresh and tidy and full of a huge, soft bed that practically screamed out to her. Perhaps it would be safe just to rest on it for a moment while Mrs. Kendall collected some clothing. Just a few moments relaxing there would be like heaven.

It had been a long night, after all. A short rest would be good to clear her head. She nodded her thanks to the housekeeper and Lady Dashford, then sank down into blissful comfort as the door closed behind them. Yes, this truly was like heaven.

For half a minute she wondered if the bed in Rastmoor's room was just as comfortable, but then gave in to the overwhelming urge to close her eyes for just a moment. Or two.

RASTMOOR'S HAIR WAS STILL DAMP AS HE MADE HIS way into Dashford's office. His friend was seated there behind his enormous desk. He looked up and smiled.

"You still look like hell."

"I feel like hell," Rastmoor admitted. "What's it been since I left here, three days? It feels like three weeks—and I haven't slept much."

"Fitzgelder?"

"Yes, and Lindley's with him."

"What? I don't believe it."

"Believe it," Rastmoor assured him and sank into a nearby armchair. "Jul—er, Nancini saw them together in London and came to warn me. I didn't believe him, but then someone shot at me and tampered with the axle on Lindley's carriage and sent highwaymen out to waylay us and finally tried to burn me in my bed. Yes, I believe him now."

"Good God, what the devil is he up to? Murdering you won't gain him anything. Fitzgelder is a damn bastard, and everyone knows it—he can't inherit a penny he hasn't already gotten. Why would Lindley be helping him? The man's a bloody earl, for heaven's sake."

Rastmoor ran his hand through his hair and tugged at his too-tight cravat. "I know; it makes no sense. But Fitzgelder's got something, something damning against my family. Maybe he's got something on Lindley, too. Besides, we all know Lindley's sire played fast and loose with the family fortune."

Dashford frowned. "True. But what sort of thing could he have to drag a cove like Lindley into criminal activities?"

"Who knows? For me, it's information I found in my father's things. And a locket. Presumably, there's something inside, though he never mentioned it to me. I believe my mother knows what it is, but she won't say. Just that we've got to get it back before Fitzgelder can use it against us."

"That hardly seems worthy of murder. So you've got some scandal in your family history—who doesn't?"

"All I know is Mother's more than a little concerned. She really didn't even want me to stay here for the wedding; she said they needed me in London. That letter she sent here just before the parson arrived didn't say, but I wonder if what Fitzgelder has planned might involve Penelope."

"Your sister? She's hardly old enough to have any great scandal to hide. What could Fitzgelder possibly have to hold over her?"

"She's eighteen now, Dash, and Mother's been trotting her out to the marriage mart this season. She's furious I'm not there to do my duty as elder brother and all that rot, as a matter of fact. But it seems to me if Fitzgelder got me out of the way, then Penelope would be a very wealthy young woman without a sturdy protector. If he's got some terrible family secret tucked up in that locket, I daresay he might be able to convince Penelope to do pretty much whatever he wants under threat of exposure."

"And of course he'd want her to marry him and hand over the Rastmoor fortune."

"Of course he would, and if that secret is bad enough, she might think she had to."

"That's rather far-fetched, Anthony."

"Yes, to you and me, because we're rational people. But Fitzgelder? It might seem perfectly logical to him—he's more than eligible for Bedlam and has been for years, if you ask me. I'm not prepared to gamble my life—or my sister's—on Fitzgelder's capacity for rational thought."

"I see your point. But wasn't your mother able to give you any better notion of what this scandalous element is that Fitzgelder is dangling over her head?"

"She can't write that in a letter, and I haven't seen her. We didn't exactly get as far as London."

Dashford contemplated this, then nodded. "No, I suppose

you wouldn't have had time to get that far and come back. So where did you go?"

"South of Warwick. That's when things started going badly. We spent the night in Geydon then headed back to Warwick and spent the next night there."

"That's hardly a full day's ride. What held you in Warwick?"

"Sophie."

"Sophie? *My* Sophie? You actually found her?"

Here Rastmoor sighed. He wasn't about to confide in Dashford anything concerning Julia, but he needed to tell the man his fears where Sophie was involved.

"Yes, she was traveling this way."

"On her honeymoon?"

"No," Rastmoor confessed. "Sorry, Dash, but that Clemmons fellow isn't really her husband. They were just posing as husband and wife."

"That blighter! Well, I'll force him to do right by her. She's a Dashford by birth, and I'll see that he . . ."

"Wait. There's more to it. Sophie has the locket."

"What? *Your* locket? I thought Fitzgelder had it."

"Apparently he doesn't have it anymore. Somehow it came to be in Sophie's possession. I'm still unsure how that happened, by accident or by purpose, but now Lindley has abducted Sophie—unless she's gone with him willingly—and they're on their way to London to return the locket to Fitzgelder."

"Good God, do you know what you're saying?"

"That everyone I know is conspiring against me? Yes, that's pretty much what I'm saying, I suppose."

"Well, I'm not conspiring against you. Evaline and I had no idea Sophie was involved in anything like this—I still can't quite believe it."

"I'm not lying to you, Dash." *At least, not the parts about Sophie.*

"I never suggested you were. So what do we do? Why did you come *here*?"

"Nancini. He needed a safe place, so I brought him here."

"Yes, so you did. And just who the hell is this Signor Nancini, anyway?"

"Just someone I met once in London," he said, drifting into half-truths. "He risked his life to come tell me about Fitzgelder's plot, so I owe him, that's all. But he's got to stay here. I can't take him with me."

"No, that I can understand. But how do you know he's not actually working with Fitzgelder?"

"He warned me, didn't he?"

"Did he?"

"Look, I need you to promise he'll be safe here. I know you and Evaline would probably rather be alone here right now—hell, you probably only just got rid of your wedding guests and your mother—but there's nowhere else for him to go. Tell me he can stay here, and that you'll leave him alone. Let him rest and don't pester him with questions, all right?"

Now Dashford was staring at him intently. Perhaps he'd been a bit too forceful with his instructions. Perhaps he made it sound as if he cared a bit too much about the strange, female-shaped man. Blast, Dashford would wonder about all of it. He wasn't stupid; he'd know things were not all Rastmoor declared them to be.

Or maybe it was still too early in the morning for Dashford to be his usual perceptive self. With a heavy shrug, Dashford simply turned the conversation away from his mysterious houseguest. Apparently he decided a mute opera singer merited no further discussion, thankfully.

"All right, he's safe here. But what are you going to do?"

"I've got to head for London," Rastmoor answered.

"Not until you've gotten some sleep, my friend."

"They've already got a half day's head start over me."

Dashford didn't seem to care. "I can understand you want to end this, but going off half-cocked won't help anyone. Take some rest. I'll get necessities together for you; horses, a dozen or so sturdy footmen . . ."

"I don't need all that. I just need to know Nancini will be safe here."

Dashford chuckled. "Hell, that's the least of your worries.

Of course we'll keep the pup safe. How hard could that be? But who the hell's going to look after you?"

Rastmoor had to admit his friend had a point. Odd, he really wasn't worried about himself. It was these dashed women in his life—he needed to know they were protected. He needed to know his mother and sister would not suffer some horrible scandal, or that Fitzgelder would never again get his filthy hands on Julia. Damn, he wished he could confide the whole bloody story to Dashford. Dash would understand. No matter what happened to Rastmoor, Dash would look out for Julia if he was asked to.

But he couldn't very well ask him, of course. He still wasn't sure for himself how much Julia was involved. Saddling Dash with her for anything more than this very short-term situation could easily be putting him and his new bride in danger. Rastmoor would never do that to them. Someone on this blasted planet deserved to live out a happy ending, didn't they? It sure as hell wasn't going to be Rastmoor.

Chapter Eleven

Julia's arm had gone numb. It felt clumsy when she moved it; then she understood why. She'd fallen asleep literally where she'd tipped over from exhaustion onto this beautiful, comfortable bed. Her arm had been bent in an awkward position beneath her, and now it tingled and twinged as if coming back to life. She rubbed and worked it carefully. Drat, but she hadn't meant to doze off like that.

Judging from the sunlight streaming through the window, it was now much later in the day than when she'd been directed to this room. How long had she slept? Dear Lord, had she let Rastmoor make good on his plans to abandon her here?

She leapt to her feet, discovering that one leg was also sleeping. It crumpled beneath her, and she was forced to clutch the bedpost for support. This was awful! What if while she'd been blissfully slumbering away, Rastmoor had slipped into clean clothes and ridden off to his doom? She could have kicked herself—if she'd been able to control the useless muscles in her twitching leg that is.

It took several minutes of stomping around her room before her various limbs felt normal again. What an idiot she'd been to drop off that way! And still in her filthy clothes, to make matters worse. Now Lady Dashford's fresh counterpane smelled of smoke and two days' travel. Lovely.

At some point the servants had brought in fresh water and a change of clothes, so she quickly made use of them. It felt a bit odd, pulling on trousers that had come from God knew where, but miraculously they fit and gave every impression of being clean. She simply chose to concentrate on fretting over Rastmoor's possible departure rather than let her mind dwell on the past life of her new outfit. She did her best to look—and smell—presentable and even put an extra knot in her cravat.

She studied the effect in her reflection. Not bad, for a slightly rounded, smooth-faced, effeminate young man. Was the disguise enough to keep the household convinced? Oh well, this was the best she could do.

She yanked the door open and hurried out into the hallway. It wasn't until after the fact that she realized she'd half expected to find herself locked in—it would be so like Rastmoor to come up with an excuse for such a thing. The fact that he hadn't done so struck her as rather ominous. Perhaps he hadn't needed to secure her in her room. Perhaps he was already long gone. How many hours had she slept? He could be miles from here by now!

Not sure what to expect, she kept her footfalls as silent as possible when she made her way down the stairs. How on earth did gentlemen spend their lives clomping around in these heavy, noisy boots? When this was all over and done, she would never again begrudge any of her fussy female apparel.

There had not appeared to be any sign of Rastmoor upstairs, so she thought she'd best go down. Hadn't Dashford said something about Rastmoor meeting him in his office? Yes, but where on earth was his lordship's office? She had no idea how to find her way in this enormous house. Did she dare risk uncovering their lie and actually speak to someone to ask for directions? Before she could do that, she'd first have to find someone, wouldn't she? That, too, could be problematic.

Well, what could it hurt to do some of her own investigating? That blasted office had to be somewhere, didn't it? She made it to the bottom of the stairway and realized she had two options: one archway opened onto a wide corridor that led to the small drawing room they'd initially been ushered into, and one archway opened to a narrower corridor that snaked around toward the back of the house. Likely the office was along one of these.

She peered first around one archway then the other. Each corridor held several doors that likely opened into music rooms, libraries, retiring rooms, or whatever else one needed a room for in a giant house like this. Clearly Dashford had rooms to spare in this place. But which way would take her to the man's office?

Voices caught her attention. She peeped back around the first archway. The door to the one drawing room she had been in was only partially closed, and she could distinctly hear voices inside. Not Rastmoor's, though. These were female voices. Well, surely they'd know where to find Rastmoor, wouldn't they? She tugged her coat into place and headed for the doorway.

Then she remembered she couldn't speak. Rather, she wasn't *allowed* to speak. Lady Dashford would likely intend to enforce that, as concerned for her guest's well-being as she'd appeared to be. And, of course, Julia's written Italian was rather lacking. Indeed, it was nonexistent. Rastmoor would have known that, of course, drat his ruddy hide.

She paused outside the doorway, wondering what to do. Her silent pondering gave her accidental snatches of the conversation inside. Rastmoor's name came through particularly clearly, trilled on the tongue of some youngish female. More precisely, his *Christian* name was trilled on the tongue of some youngish female. And spoken with a fair measure of affection, as a matter of fact.

Julia leaned in toward the door to accidentally hear more.

"Yes, Anthony can be quite vexing at times," the female trilled on with a wistful sigh. "But I do love him, of course."

"Of course you do," what was likely Lady Dashford's voice replied. "He was merely surprised to have you arrive here, that's all."

"Well, he needn't have been so cross with me when we arrived!" Trilling Female Voice said, sounding far less affectionate and rather more petulant. "What did he expect, that I would stay back in London and wait? He was supposed to have come to us a month ago."

"It must be very frustrating for you," her calmer, less petulant hostess said. "But Dashford and I were so glad Anthony could be with us for the wedding."

"I was supposed to be planning my own wedding already, if Anthony had done as he should by me."

"Of course. And I'm sure Lord Rastmoor will see to making that happen just as soon as he can," Lady Dashford said.

Her voice continued, soothing the obvious irritation in the first lady. Julia could not tell if she was successful or not, but she did detect a rather distinctively unsoothed irritation in her own person. And she didn't like it.

So, Anthony was getting married, was he? She hadn't heard that. She shouldn't be surprised, of course. She'd always known he'd marry someday; it was inevitable. The man had his duty to think of. Indeed, there was a title and entailments and that ridiculous wealth that needed an heir. Of course Rastmoor would feel the need to marry, if not the urge. Then again, if the petulant triller behind the door was even halfway attractive—and Julia expected she was—Rastmoor likely felt the urge.

And this, of course, explained why Fitzgelder was suddenly so motivated to rid the world of Lord Rastmoor. If Rastmoor married, it would only be a matter of time before the world was riddled with more little Rastmoors, and each one of them would put Fitzgelder just one step farther away from getting his greedy hands on any more of the unequally distributed Rastmoor money. It made perfect sense. Rastmoor was to marry.

But what was his fiancée doing here? It didn't seem as if Rastmoor had expected her. The girl said he'd been cross. Well, Julia didn't wonder. He'd no doubt been more than a bit surprised—not to mention uncomfortable—to learn that his former and current fiancées were suddenly ensconced under the same roof with him. The whole thing could be really humorous, actually. If, of course, Julia didn't feel so utterly wretched clear down into her bones.

How could Anthony possibly be marrying that little twit? And did this mean he had run even more swiftly from this place, or did this new circumstance mean he was bound to extend his stay? Julia would not relish seeing him fawn over his dearest intended. No, at this point she rather hoped he had gone already. She'd be the one to follow him, not insipid trill girl.

First, however, she'd have to deal with the throat-clearing personage who just materialized behind her. Bother, she'd been caught eavesdropping, hadn't she? Slowly, she turned.

A stern-faced matron stood there, glaring expectantly.

"Are you looking for someone?" she asked.

Julia had no idea who this was, but the woman's regal bearing and feathered turban convinced her immediately she was not one to trifle with. Unfortunately, trifling was all Julia could do at the moment. Her throat was dry, and she made a rather odd sound when she tried to come up with some logical reply.

"Well?" the woman said, obviously taking pleasure in Julia's discomfort.

Julia's throat gurgles and the woman's impatient foot tapping must have been enough to alert the ladies behind the door that they had company. The door swung open to reveal Lady Dashford. She smiled at Julia and then at the turbaned mother superior.

"Ah, Mr. Nancey . . . or would you rather that we call you as they do in your homeland, Nancini? I trust you had a nice rest. Lady Rastmoor, this is our guest, Mr. Nancini. He's a friend of Lord Rastmoor's, from Italy."

"How nice." The lady pinned Julia with her stare. "And do you always make it a habit of listening at doorways, Mr. Nancini?"

Julia couldn't help but stare back. This was Rastmoor's mother? The poor man had his current fiancée, his former—and disturbingly recent—lover, and his *mother* all converge on him at once? Indeed, she was quite sure he must have gone at the earliest possible moment. And she really couldn't blame him, either.

"Poor Mr. Nancini cannot speak, my lady Rastmoor," Lady Dashford said kindly, opening the door and stepping aside to invite Julia in. "I'm afraid he was overcome by smoke in a fire recently and is under strict orders not to use his voice until his throat heals. You are a singer, are you not, Mr. Nancini?"

Julia nodded and bowed, trying to be as manfully gracious as possible in the hope that Lady Rastmoor would stop glaring at her. Good heavens, she'd sooner face six Fitzgelders than one Lady Rastmoor who might determine her true identity!

Then her eyes caught on the real terror in the room.

A young woman perched primly on a sunny settee near the window—she was nothing short of stunning. By God, this creature was the epitome of gentle breeding. She turned compassion-brimmed, doelike eyes in Julia's direction, and her expression held not only concern and purity, but there was depth and intelligence, as well. She was everything Julia had once aspired to be. No wonder she had failed miserably.

"Oh, how dreadful!" the young lady said with honest sweetness. "How distressing for you, Mr. Nancini. Surely the doctor has given every hope you'll soon regain your voice?"

Julia hated her. Never in a hundred years, not with all the theatrics in the world, could she herself have become the mixture of beauty and sincerity and innocence that was Rastmoor's future bride. Indeed, the man had done remarkably well for himself. She hated him, too.

And she hated this ruddy cravat. Standing here, surrounded by silk wall coverings, ornate furniture, and three cultured, noble-born ladies, Julia felt more out of place than she had ever been. She tugged at the cravat and wished to God she'd stayed up in her room. And to think, this was the world she would have entered to become Anthony's wife! What a fool she'd been.

"Rastmoor assures us he will heal," Lady Dashford said. "But only if we are careful to insist he not strain himself. No, you mustn't speak, Mr. Nancini. Perhaps you can use gestures if there is something you must tell us."

"Yes, please do!" the stunning one said brightly. "It will be most amusing. Almost like a game!"

Julia rejoiced to see the girl's halo tarnished by a smidgen of insipidness.

"If Mr. Nancini has something to say, can he not simply draft us a note?" Lady Rastmoor suggested.

"No, I'm afraid he only writes in Italian," Lady Dashford explained. "It is your native tongue, is it not, Mr. Nancini?"

Julia nodded, hopeful no one would test her in this. Italian was as native to her tongue as ancient Sanskrit.

"Pity," Lady Rastmoor said with a frown. "I'm afraid my Italian is incomplete. I should love to hear all about this dreadful fire my son claims was hardly more than a spark from the stove. Odd that a simple spark should cause you so much pain, isn't it, Mr. Nancini?"

Julia wasn't certain how to answer that. What did the lady suspect? Did she suspect Julia's ruse, or was she aware of Fitzgelder's scheme? Likely she had no idea her son's life was in danger. Should Julia give up this pretense and warn her? Would any of these fine people believe her? More likely they'd be appalled by her lies and throw her out on the street.

Curses on Rastmoor for putting her through this. He should never have brought her here. They should be on their way to London right now, rescuing Sophie and getting that dratted locket back.

"I think fires are perfectly terrifying," the young lady in the settee said with a sigh that hinted she could do with a bit more terror in her well-ordered life. "Now I wish I had learned Italian instead of all that useless French. Pity you don't write in French, Mr. Nancini."

Yes, pity she didn't. Except that she did. As a matter of fact, Julia's French was every bit as good as her English, spoken *or* written. Indeed, Rastmoor had said nothing about French, had he? Perhaps Mr. Nancini had just found his voice after all.

Julia nodded profusely for them. Her lips formed a rather exaggerated *Oui*.

* * *

"*WE*? WHAT DO YOU MEAN, *WE*?" RASTMOOR ASKED his friend, glaring across the mahogany desk in Dashford's private study.

"I mean *we* will leave for London in the morning," Dashford replied, studying the whiskey he'd just poured himself. "I discussed it with Evaline while you were catching up with your mother. She agrees that you need me more than she does right now."

"That's not exactly what one wants to hear from one's new bride, Dash," Rastmoor chided. "I can handle Fitzgelder on my own."

"Perhaps, but I'm going with you just the same."

"Likely you're simply looking for an excuse to leave this house full of women."

"I do seem to be outnumbered—my mother will be most disappointed she left when she did and missed all this excitement. Then again, there is Nancini to keep me company . . ."

"No! You assured me he'll be left alone. Dash, it's very important no one interferes with his rest."

"And no one will. By God, you're on edge. What aren't you telling me?"

"I just wasn't expecting my mother and Penelope to show up here, that's all."

"Yet here they are. That proves things are worse than we thought, which is why I'm not letting you go back to London alone."

"But . . ."

"The matter is settled," Dashford said with convincing determination. "I've already dispatched men. They'll see what they can find out about Lindley's involvement and then wait for us at my town house. You can gain nothing more by charging off before morning."

"Dash, I appreciate it, but this doesn't concern you."

"Of course it does. My unfortunate young cousin and my thick-headed friend are both involved, so I'm concerned. End of discussion. If you'd like to explain this Nancini person to me, however . . ."

Rastmoor was about to inform him there was nothing further to discuss about Nancini when they were interrupted by a knock at the door. A footman appeared.

"Excuse me," he said with a bow. "Lord Rastmoor asked to be informed if Mr. Nancini left his room."

Dashford sent Rastmoor a questioning look, but Rastmoor ignored him. He tried to remain calm as he questioned the footman. "Has he?"

"He's gone to the drawing room, sir, with the ladies. I was only just made aware of it, but Mrs. Kendall says he's been in there half an hour."

Hellfire. What was Julia up to? He did not need this right now.

"Thank you, Hal," Dashford said.

The footman excused himself with another bow and pulled the door closed behind him. Rastmoor gripped the arms of his chair and wished he hadn't already downed his whiskey. He needed a drink. Damn, but he'd like to get his hands on Julia right now and . . . No, it would not be helpful at all to think about what he'd like to do to Julia right now. Best to think about whiskey, instead. Just as soon as he figured out what to do about what must be happening in the drawing room.

"So, shall we adjourn there?" Dashford said after an uncomfortable pause.

Rastmoor nearly leapt from his seat. He really needed to work on being more subtle, but right this moment, all he cared about was getting to Julia and finding out what damage she'd done. If she'd given his mother and sister greater cause for worry, why he'd . . . he'd . . . well, it wouldn't involve anything that required him to lay hands on Julia's person. Somehow every punishment he dreamed up involving hands and physical contact ended with her in his bed wearing nothing but a satisfied smile.

He followed his friend out into the hall, through the grand entrance area, then under another archway into the hallway that led to the drawing room. Why in heaven's name couldn't the man walk faster? This damned enormous house made it impossible to get anywhere in a timely manner. There was no telling what Julia might be saying. Dash it all, if she gave his mother reason to suspect her true identity . . . well, he might be walking into a catfight, the likes of which the world had never seen.

The nearer they came to the drawing room, the more he was convinced this must be exactly what was occurring. Female screeches issued from the partially opened door. Dashford glanced at Rastmoor with a raised eyebrow, and Rastmoor pushed him out of the way. He bowled through the door prepared to dodge anything from flying bric-a-brac to fainting matrons.

He found neither, however. It was much worse.

Julia, he discovered, was cleaned, combed, trousered, and disguised in immaculate linen and a well-tailored waistcoat. She was behind the settee, fairly leering over a cow-eyed, giggling Penelope. The other two ladies cackled from their perches at either side of his sister, blinking with adoration at the dandified young man Julia appeared to be. Bits of scrawled handwritten paper were scattered about them and clutched in their hands. The women's mirthful rumpus silenced just long enough for them to glance up and take in Rastmoor's blustering presence. Then, with sidelong glances at Julia, their hilarity started all over again.

By God, were these women laughing at *him*?

"What the devil is all this?" Dashford asked.

"Hello, my dearest," Lady Dashford replied in her sweetest tone. "Mr. Nancini has been very kindly telling us how he and poor Rastmoor survived that terrible fire."

Somehow "poor" Rastmoor had a feeling Mr. Nancini must be embellishing the truth somewhat. From his recollection, there had been nothing funny about that damned fire. What the devil was Julia doing? She was supposed to be tucked safely away in her room. Mute.

He glared at her. "Mr. Nancini is not supposed to be speaking. He's supposed to be resting his voice. Upstairs. Alone."

"Don't be such a worrier," his mother said, waving away his concern with a flick of her fan. "Mr. Nancini has been very careful with his voice. He's written it all on paper."

He narrowed his eyes at Julia in case she hadn't yet noticed how angry he was. "Oh? But Mr. Nancini cannot write in English, if he might recall."

"English isn't the only language on earth, you know," Penelope announced. "Mr. Nancini has been writing in French. And very prettily, I declare. He's kept us well entertained this half an hour. Did you know he's a poet as well? He wrote me a sonnet! In French!"

"Oh, did he, now?" Rastmoor clenched his fists and stepped back to rest his weight on one leg. His jaw twinged where he ground his teeth to keep from saying just exactly what he thought of Mr. Nancini's decision to become French.

But his fury was apparently lost on these women. Penelope burst into more giggles, and she actually had the nerve to point one long finger at him.

"Look, Mr. Nancini," she cried. "He's doing it, just as you showed us! And there's that little tic in his jawline, just as it always is when he's very upset. My, but you have such a talent for pantomime."

Julia dared bow in appreciation of Penelope's praise. Rastmoor unclenched his jaw and straightened his stance. He did *not* assume this pose whenever he was upset, and he *never* had a tic, despite what all the ladies in this room seemed to think.

"Indeed," Lady Dashford said, equally smitten with Julia's apparent talent. "I had no idea a life in the opera could develop such observational skill. No wonder Lord Rastmoor has been so gracious to sponsor you in society and promise your introduction to the London stage."

Now Rastmoor's eyes widened in surprise. He had been doing *what*?

His mother smiled at him. "I'm proud of you, Anthony. You should have told me you'd become so interested in the arts."

"And that home for orphans!" Peneloped chimed. "How generous! Please say you'll take me there someday so I can bring gifts to the poor little children you support."

He wasn't sure he heard that right. "What?"

Dashford literally choked. "By God!"

"Oh, I know you're too modest to brag," his mother said,

beaming. "But Mr. Nancini told us all about it. How you've turned your back on the usual pursuits of privilege and earthly pleasure—it's quite commendable, Anthony. And now you've become a temperate! Indeed, a mother can be proud. I'll see to it all strong drink and temptation are removed from Rastmoor House the minute I go home."

"You certainly will not!" Rastmoor announced. "What the devil has Mr. Nancini been saying to you?"

"Not saying, dear, *writing*," his mother corrected. "But I understand you don't wish to discuss it. He explained how you've been simply trying to assuage the plaguing guilt over your treatment of a certain young lady some years ago, but we will say no more on *that* tender subject."

"He said *what*?!"

Julia just smiled demurely, while Dashford's laughter drowned out the oaths Rastmoor muttered under his breath. By God, he'd murder the devious, storytelling female! How was he ever going to live any of this down? Obviously, based on the adoring way his mother and sister were ogling him and the rugged back-patting he was getting from Dashford, he wasn't.

"I had no idea you were such a philanthropist," Dashford was saying and seemed to find the whole notion more than a bit amusing.

"I'm a bloody victim, that's what I am," Rastmoor muttered. He tried to pin Julia with another killing glare, but she had become too distracted with fluffing her cravat to notice.

"It's impressive, all these upstanding things you've been doing, Anthony," Penelope said with a hint of sisterly skepticism. "I can nearly understand why Mr. Nancini was willing to put aside all thought of his own safety and plunge into that fire to save you—even if you were completely ape drunk."

"I beg your pardon?" Rastmoor could hardly do more than gape at his sister. Never mind the fact that this was completely fabricated information, where in God's name did Penelope learn a phrase like that?

"Oh, he didn't mean to insult you," Penelope went on, blushing. "We had to beg him to tell us all about that dreadful fire."

"And now I wish we hadn't," his mother added. "It's just awful to think what might have happened if Mr. Nancini hadn't been there!"

"But he was," Penelope reminded her. "And now he's here. Our hero." She twisted in her seat to flutter her lashes up at Julia, and Julia did not have the good sense to appear in the least ashamed of her actions. Some hero.

Enough was enough.

"Indeed, I owe Mr. Nancini quite a debt," Rastmoor said, finally catching Julia's truthless eye. "And I'll start repaying him by reminding everyone he desperately requires rest and solitude."

He moved to Julia's side and dropped his hand down onto her shoulder. He felt her muscles tense, and she subtly cringed. Good. She ought to cringe.

"Come, Nancini," he said. "You must be completely fatigued."

Of course there was nothing she could say. She sure could glare, though, and she did. With a vengeance. He didn't care. Like it or not, he was in charge here, and for her own good Julia was going to do what he said. It would only put her in danger if anyone suspected her true identity. How did he know Dashford's servants wouldn't talk or carry the tale of a disguised woman into the nearest town? All it would take was a hint of that to get back to Fitzgelder or Lindley or any number of people who might have reason to hold a grudge.

He had too many other things to worry about to be distracted by that concern.

"Oh, but Mr. Nancini seems perfectly healthy to me," Penelope protested. "Except, of course, that he simply can't talk."

"Now, dear, if Anthony seems to think our new friend needs to rest, perhaps we ought to let him. I'm sure that was a harrowing experience for both of them last night."

"Of course it was," Lady Dashford said, rising to play the part of hostess. "Let me send for someone to attend you, Mr. Nancini."

"No need," Rastmoor assured her. "I'll escort Mr. Nancini up to his room and see he's tended to."

Julia's right eyebrow shot up into her forehead. Dashford seemed to find that amusing, too.

"I say, Rastmoor," he laughed. "Perhaps we ought to simply hire a nursemaid for poor Nancini. You seem to think the man can't be left alone."

"I absolutely think the man *should* be left alone," Rastmoor said. "Come, Nancini. You've written enough today. You're likely to get a cramp—with any luck."

Julia frowned at him but had the good sense to appear compliant. She gave a polite bow to the ladies and marched sedately out into the hallway. She was kind enough to wait until they were safely out of earshot of the others before she turned on him with a barely restrained hiss.

"And just what do you think you'll be tending to once you've dragged me off to my lonely cell, my lord?" she asked in a tone that left no room to question her thoughts on the subject.

He didn't answer. He didn't look at her, either. Just how exactly was he going to keep Julia safely in her room the rest of this evening and all through the long night ahead? Unless of course he intended to remain there with her, which he did not.

He made a particular point of reminding himself that he did not.

JULIA CHOSE NOT TO ARGUE AS RASTMOOR LED HER up to her chamber. She figured it was safer that way; clearly the man was furious with her. His ominous silence chilled her while his viselike grip never released from her shoulder as they left behind the relative safety of the Dashford drawing room and headed up the wide and deserted staircase toward the first floor. Even more unnerving, Rastmoor knew exactly which bedroom to direct her toward.

He followed her inside and shut the door behind them. Her heartbeat quickened, and she fought to forget the huge, well-stuffed bed looming just behind her. The huge, comfortable, well-stuffed bed. The huge, comfortable, *lonely*, well-stuffed bed. The huge, comfortable, well-stuffed bed that would be so very warm and inviting if Rastmoor would just . . .

Oh, bother it all! What was wrong with her that even after all his lies getting her here and his dreadfully rude manner toward her she could still think of such a thing? She was certain Rastmoor wasn't. No, clearly amorous thoughts were far from his mind.

He practically shoved her away from him and glared at her with fiery eyes. "Brava, Miss St. Clement," he said, crossing his arms over his chest. "Your impressive performance has won you some new admirers downstairs. Penelope, especially, seems absurdly infatuated."

"Obviously she has better taste than I was giving her credit for," Julia replied.

She took an involuntary step backward when he moved toward her. His arms cut through the air as he gestured in anger.

"Damn it, what did you think you were doing down there?" he stormed.

No, this was definitely not amorous behavior. Still, she held her ground. "I did not give away my identity or break your silly rule about speaking. I simply found a way around it."

"By God, this is not a game, Julia! What on earth were you doing, leading Penelope to fancy herself cow-eyed for some Italian prig who doesn't even exist?"

"What?!"

"Don't try to convince me you didn't see it. She was mooning over you."

Really? Well, that would serve the brute right if she had managed to catch the eye of his darling intended. Would serve him right indeed.

"She was mooning? I didn't notice."

"Like hell you didn't."

"What's the matter? Are you jealous?"

"No, by God, I'm bloody furious. What made you think to use my sister this way?"

Well now, that gave her pause. "Sister?"

His fists were clenched, and he was pacing with a vengeance. "Is that what you were doing? Taking out your anger at me by toying with her? An innocent, impressionable girl? That's reprehensible, Julia, even for you. Penelope's barely out of the schoolroom."

"Wait, I didn't . . . I mean . . . Your sister?"

"Of course she's my sister! Who in bloody Hades did you think she was?"

Well, she wasn't in bloody Hades about to answer *that*. Oh, but how could she have been so silly? She could see it now; she'd let the green-eyed monster get the best of her and spent a full half hour purposely making Penelope fall a little bit in love because of foolish jealousy. She simply couldn't bear the thought of the girl being any bit in love with Rastmoor. Good grief.

"You're overreacting," she said, hoping to end the discussion quickly. "I'm sure Penelope couldn't care less for Mr. Nancini."

"Penelope was worshipping Mr. Nancini!"

"You're exaggerating."

"Oh? I watched her bat her eyelashes at you, and I saw the way you fawned over her. You ingratiated yourself with my mother! You had to have known how that would appear to a starry-eyed eighteen-year-old girl."

"She seems a sensible sort. She would know it all meant nothing."

"You wrote her sonnets, Julia. In French!"

"Just one. And I fail to see what difference it makes which language I used."

"I told you to stay up here. Where it's safe."

"Safe? Safe from what, my lord? What horrors are stalking the halls of Lord Dashford's fine home?"

"You know very well what horrors I'm talking about," he said. "Unless, of course, you haven't been entirely honest with me about your own dealings with Fitzgelder. Perhaps the man really holds no threat for you. Is that it?"

"You don't believe that, else you'd have gone straight back to London and not bothered to bring me out here. You know I spoke the truth about my involvement with that man."

He scowled. "I'd like to believe you, Julia, but how can I, when you show such complete and utter disregard for caution? All we need is for one gossiping servant to head to the village, babbling about a mysterious woman in men's clothing hiding out at Hartwood. You've seen what Fitzgelder can do. If he indeed has as much against you as you claim, then why do you keep taking chances?"

She was taking chances, all right, just by meeting his eyes. Indeed, it was too easy to let his persistent talk of concern for her safety mislead her into believing he still cared. That smoldering heat behind his gaze could so easily be mistaken for concern—for tenderness, even. She turned away quickly and walked to the window.

"I'm sorry. I never meant to do anything to hurt your sister."

"So what do you propose we do about it?" he said, still doubtful. "Penelope is young and sheltered. This misplaced attachment could seriously damage her."

"Look, if there is any misplaced attachment, it will be easy enough to snuff," Julia assured him. "Just tell everyone I'm married. I have a wife back in Italy, and I'm devoted to her. Surely that will keep your sister from fancying any great affection, right?"

"You believe affections are so easily cast off?"

She'd had her back to Rastmoor but turned to face him now. He'd come up close behind her, closer than she'd expected. Oh, she hoped he might not see the hurt his words had caused her.

"No, I don't," she replied. "But circumstance cares little for affection, does it? Penelope might as well learn that sooner rather than later."

"Yes, I suppose that is one of life's harsh lessons she's bound to learn at some point," he agreed. "I just wonder why you felt the need to educate her yourself."

"I told you, it never crossed my mind that the girl might take a fancy to Mr. Nancini. I was simply enjoying their entertaining company after you so rudely trussed me up in here without so much as the ability to call for a fresh chamber pot!"

"And apparently I was the subject of your entertainment," he said.

As if he had any reason to be so offended. He was not the cross-gendered, wounded mute.

"And why not?" she snipped. "I thought it a topic that might amuse them."

"Oh?" he asked with a cocked brow. "Why should you have thought that? You just told me you had no idea who Penelope was. Why should a stranger be so amused by a discussion of my personal tics and endearing little quirks?"

"I don't recall anyone mentioning that they are endearing."

"Admit it. You did know Penelope was my sister."

"No, I did not. I thought . . ." She was fortunate to stop herself, but it was apparently too late. Rastmoor's interest was piqued. He reached to touch her cheek, brushing a stray hair back into its expected position.

"You thought what? Who did you think she was?"

Oh, bother. What was the way out of this? It would seem there was none.

"I thought she was your fiancée." There. She'd given him the answer he wanted. Perhaps he would not laugh too long at her.

He didn't quite laugh, in fact, but he did smile. Hugely. "My fiancée?"

"Introductions were a bit irregular, what with me being mute and Italian, and all."

Now he slid one hand around to the small of her back and tugged her gently toward him. For pity's sake, she couldn't seem to find the strength to resist. And how very tantalizing his breath was when he leaned in and breathed against her neck.

"And you were jealous, weren't you?"

"Don't be ridiculous," she said.

Her quavering voice negated her words, especially as she melted into him and tipped her head, allowing him to slowly unfasten her pitiful cravat. He dragged it from her, the fabric brushing against her and leaving her nerves tingling for attention. The cravat hit the floor, and Rastmoor pushed her ill-fitted coat from her shoulders. Unrestricted, her shirt fell open nearly to her navel.

"You thought to steal her from me, didn't you?"

His words were a low growl, and his lips teased their way along her collarbone.

"Er, you do recall I'm not really a man?"

"Yes, I do happen to recall that, as a matter of fact," he said, and the dusky warmth in his voice convinced her he was every bit as aware of their difference in gender as she was. She shuddered at the little tingles running up and down her spine.

"Admit it, Julia. You were jealous, weren't you?" he asked.

Of course, it wasn't really a question. His voice already held the triumph of knowing the answer full well. He knew she'd been jealous as hell. She thought Penelope was his fiancée, and she'd been determined to put herself between them out of sheer feminine envy. It really wasn't very nice of her, she did have to admit, and certainly not very smart. He was going to make her regret it now, in the most delightful ways possible.

"You know," he began after covering her with kisses, "it disturbs me how much I enjoy looking at you in these infernal men's clothes."

"Then why are you going to so much effort to get me out of them?"

He chuckled, ripping her shirt from where she tucked it so carefully into her breeches and pulling it swiftly up over her head. "Because I'm not at all disturbed to look at you naked."

With that, he grabbed the loose bit of the binding fabric she used to conceal her ample bosom. Clearly frustrated that it did not slide away so easily as the cravat, he gave a rough tug. As the fabric was wrapped twice around her body, this sent Julia spinning away from him. She couldn't help but laugh as she tumbled onto the bed. Likely he planned that, the devious letch.

Not that she was doing anything to slow his progress. Her trousers were unfastened half a second before his, and he was pinning her into the luxurious counterpane. She wrapped herself around him and gave up trying to pretend this wasn't exactly what she wanted.

His hands explored her, slipping inside her trousers to ignite the desire that seemed to perpetually smolder there. She happily returned the favor, although she had to admit his trousers were not nearly so accommodating as hers. Things were a bit more, er, crowded in his.

"Damn it, let's just dispense with the bloody things," he said, moving himself away from her long enough to see both sets of boots and unmentionables cast into a pile with the rest of their apparel.

Lord, now they were stark naked in the middle of the day! Julia was quite certain this had not occurred before. My, but how the daylight accentuated certain aspects of the man's personal, er, appendage. Not that things didn't appear remarkable enough by candlelight, but somehow the illicit nature of this mid-afternoon romp made everything just a bit more pronounced.

How wonderful.

She grabbed that delightful appendage and pulled it—and Rastmoor with it—closer to her. He did not seem to mind and obediently resumed his tactile exploration. She knotted her fingers into his hair and held him close, succumbing quickly to his deepening kiss.

She succumbed to everything rather quickly, as a matter of fact. Rastmoor overwhelmed her with the power of his passion, and before she knew it, she was panting, begging him to come into her and satisfy the yearning that two full nights of sharing his bed had not seemed to extinguish. He kindly obliged.

They lay there, tangled with each other and the tousled bedclothes. Julia basked in the warmth of his nearness and the glow of his loving. Sunshine beamed through the window, making Rastmoor's skin glitter with the tiny droplets of sweat his efforts had produced. It was beautiful—the whole world was beautiful.

At least it was until Rastmoor rolled over and spoke.

Chapter Twelve

"How often did you let Fitzgelder make love to you in the daytime?"

It was a horrible thing to bring up just now, but Rastmoor had to know. He was rapidly losing his very soul to this woman. Perhaps the vulgar reminder of her betrayal would help him keep his sanity.

No, clearly it would not. The pain was evident on Julia's face, and Rastmoor knew any man who would cause that in another human had already left his sanity behind. God, he wished he could take it back.

But he couldn't. He needed to hear the answer.

"I told you," she began, softly. "I never even met him."

It had to be a lie. How could this possibly be the truth? He'd seen the announcement in the paper; he'd heard Fitzgelder's own words. Why must she persist in this?

"It's rather impossible to be married to a man without ever meeting him, Julia."

"You don't know the whole story," she said. She turned her face away from him, but her limp body was still pressed against his.

"Don't I? What more is there? Julia St. Clement married Cedrick Fitzgelder almost three full years ago. Then she died. Yet, here you are alone, and you look damn lively to me. Why is that?"

It felt an eternity before she spoke again, and the words seemed to be dragged from someplace very deep inside her.

"Fitzgelder never married me," she began, slowly turning back to face him. "It was someone else."

"Oh?" Of course he was skeptical. Even a sane man would be, wouldn't he?

"It was my friend Kitty," she said slowly, trembling. "She went in my place."

His gut tightened. Her friend went in her place? Did she expect him to believe that? Ridiculous. He was not so easily duped. Even though he might want more than anything for this tale to be true, he was careful not to let any of his warring emotions be evident in his voice when he spoke.

"I'm surprised you didn't think to mention this before, Julia."

"Because I wish to God it had never happened."

"And why's that?"

"Because Fitzgelder murdered my friend, that's why."

Oh, so the story got even more sordid, did it? "Murdered?" he asked. "No one ever said Fitzgelder murdered his wife. She died in childbirth."

"That's what he'd have everyone think," she said, shaking her head and pushing herself away from him. The space between them was painful. "I never believed it. Kitty was fit as a horse—she came from a family with twelve healthy, sturdy children. She should have birthed her child well and easily."

Rastmoor reached for Julia, but she stayed out of reach. It was just as well. Touching her was dangerous. Still, her body was shaking furiously now. The least he could do was to drag some of the counterpane over her. She clutched it to her like a child and took a deep breath.

"She was an actress in my father's troupe. When her lover abandoned her in a delicate condition, she kept silent. I wish I'd known, but I didn't. Not until it was too late."

"Too late?"

"She was desperate. One day Fitzgelder sent a note backstage—to me. He wanted to meet, but I had no clue who he was and threw the note away. Kitty retrieved it. She went to Fitzgelder in my place and began an affair. He thought she was me! Kitty was so determined to have a name for her child that she convinced Fitzgelder to run away and marry her. She even stole some of my clothing and jewelry so he would continue to believe the deception.

"Once they were married, she must have realized what a monster he was. She warned me in a letter never to let him find me. I should have known she was in danger, but instead of finding her and helping her, I convinced Papa to stay in hiding. And then she died. I know it was at Fitzgelder's hand, likely because he learned she'd deceived him. And I allowed it."

Damn it all, but she played the part too well. She was more than believable; everything she said made sense. Was it possible this was real? That his cousin's claims were simply misinformation? His thoughts ran back through the years, no matter how hard he tried to stop them.

He'd been so convinced Julia was the one for him. Even when he learned the truth that she was nothing more than an actress, he still chose to believe her worthy of taking the Rastmoor name. His friends thought him daft, of course, but he would not listen to their warnings.

One night over cards, however, he was forced to listen. Fitzgelder had shown up, boasting that he'd been bedding Julia for weeks. Hell, he had one of her shawls—one that Rastmoor had purchased for her himself—to prove it. The shock of Fitzgelder's accusations wiped away any common sense—he'd believed the bastard's assertions without so much as confronting Julia, hadn't he?

He'd been humiliated. His friends said he was fortunate to learn the truth before he'd gotten shackled for life—she was nothing more than a greedy little bitch who'd played him for the fool. For the sheer fun of it he offered to let Fitzgelder deal a hand of cards—winner kept possession of the fair Julia St.

Clement. Rastmoor lost. He prayed to God she would find out one day how easily he'd wagered her away that night.

Was it possible all that had been a lie?

"How did Fitzgelder find out he'd been tricked? Did you tell him?" he asked.

"Certainly not! I may have been too cowardly to rescue Kitty when I had the chance, but I never did that. He must have figured it out on his own, pestering her as he did, night and day about that stupid locket."

"The locket?"

"Good heavens! Did he think I had your precious locket?"

"So you knew about the locket?"

"I only knew what Kitty wrote in her letters. I'd let myself forget all about it until now, actually. Apparently, right from the start Fitzgelder believed I had the locket."

"And you don't?"

"No! I told you, somehow Fitzgelder had it, and Sophie accidentally took it. I don't know how he got it."

"Why did he think you had it?"

Her slender shoulders shrugged under the covers. "I don't know. But Kitty knew how badly he wanted it, so she let him think if he married her she would get it for him. She was desperate. She was abandoned and knew she'd soon have a child to care for. I suppose she felt she had no choice but to play along with Fitzgelder."

"And so he married her. She must have been quite convincing, your little friend. Clearly, though, Fitzgelder knew the child wasn't his. Hell, he's the one who told me it was mine."

"He told you that?" She honestly seemed surprised. Then again, as she'd just reminded him, she was an actress, too.

"He did."

"And you believed it."

"I had good reason to believe it, didn't I? He seemed convincing enough."

He was propped on one elbow looming over her, but she didn't shy away. She did, however, pull the thin counterpane more tightly over her. He could see the outline of her breasts all too clearly. If she intended for this conversation to continue much longer, one of them was going to have to send for a bucket of cold water. How on earth could he possibly want her this badly again so soon?

"What have you done to make your cousin hate you so?" she asked.

"I was born, I suppose."

"Born legitimately, you mean."

"Yes. If his mother had been someone his father could have married, then he'd hold the title today."

"And what was so horribly wrong with his mother?"

Rastmoor was about to answer then had to laugh as he recognized the bitter irony of it.

"She was an actress," he finally replied.

Julia's voice was stone-cold. "No wonder you were so eager to be rid of me that you resorted to gambling."

He winced. "You found out about that?"

"Of course I did and, damn it, Rastmoor, all this time I'd hoped it wasn't true."

She shoved away from him and rolled out of bed. Oblivious to her nakedness and his obvious reaction to it, she marched across the room to collect her clothing. Watching her graceful form as she stalked about was absolutely painful for him, but he couldn't drag his eyes away. Never would any woman ever affect him the way Julia St. Clement did. Still.

"Well, I'm sorry. It is true."

"You found out I was a dirty little actress, so you got rid of me and thought to have a little entertainment in the process, did you?"

"No! I didn't care that you were an actress! Hell, I was such a fool back then, I'd have married a fishmonger."

"Well, thankfully Fitzgelder informed you of my profession before you did something so foolish as that."

She had her trousers pulled up and was tucking in her shirt. It was backward, but she didn't seem to notice. He left the bed and followed her around as she gathered the rest of her things.

"Damn it, Fitzgelder didn't have to tell me you were an actress, Julia. I knew about it the week after we met."

That gave her pause. She whirled on him and hesitated just a heartbeat as her eyes scanned his naked form. He supposed he should have been a bit more unnerved to know she must recognize how he felt about her—Lord knew it was obvious enough right now—but the fact that he detected the same sort of hunger in her own expression gave him a certain satisfaction. Not the type of satisfaction that he would have really appreciated just now, but some measure of contentment. As much as he wanted Julia, she wanted him, too. Again.

Surely they could build something on that, couldn't they?

"Then why did you gamble me away at the table that night and never so much as send a note of farewell?"

"Because he'd been shagging you the whole time I was!" he said bluntly. "At least, that's what he told me."

"And of course you believed him," she snapped and went back to concentrating on her costume. "You didn't even bother to find out if it was true."

"No. I was embarrassed and angry and drunk. He showed me the shawl I gave you, and I assumed that was proof enough, so I believed him."

He caught the hint of a smile cross her lips. "He had my shawl? I wondered where it went. It wasn't with your other gifts when I burned them. Well, I suppose Kitty borrowed it, and that's how he got it."

"You burned my gifts?"

"The ones I couldn't sell."

"Is that all you thought of them? Of what I thought we'd had between us?"

"Whatever we had between us got gambled away when you didn't care enough to trust me over your hateful cousin."

"But he had proof! And I already knew you'd lied to me about living in Mayfair."

"We were staying in Mayfair."

"You and your father were visiting the mistress he kept there! You led me to believe you were a gentlewoman, that you had decent connections and a proper station in life."

"No, you assumed all those things. I simply agreed with you."

"You acted a part to deceive me, Julia."

"That's what I do, Anthony," she replied. "I'm an actress."

Those, he realized, were the truest words she'd ever uttered. He made a lavish bow to her and smiled.

"I should have never endeavored to take you away from your true calling."

She threw his trousers into his face. "No, you shouldn't have. We lost everything when you caused Papa to give up his theatrical license."

"When I did what?"

"Put your clothes on, Rastmoor. You look like a randy racehorse."

"No. I need you to explain yourself. What do you mean, I caused your father to give up his theatrical license?"

"I suppose I can't blame you," she said, crawling halfway under the bed to retrieve a boot. This did nothing to reduce his so-called racehorse condition. "I lied. You were humiliated. I was merely a passing fancy to make your nights a little warmer, and I had the nerve to expect more. Of course you retaliated."

"You were a hell of a lot more to me than a passing fancy, Julia. It's true you ran away and married my damnable cousin, but I never . . ."

"*Kitty* ran away with your damnable cousin. *I* ran away with my father, since it was obvious you didn't care enough to give me the benefit of the doubt, and Fitzgelder seemed to want Papa dead."

"Fitzgelder wants a lot of people dead. You should have come to me with this, Julia."

"So you could have laughed to my face? No, Anthony. You don't believe me now; can you honestly think you would have believed me then?"

By God, yes, he would have believed her. It was all he could do right now not to grab her back into his arms and promise her the world. If he would have just let himself see her once more back then, he would have never let it end as it had. But he'd known that, and he'd been a coward.

He'd known that if he faced Julia again, he would have

forgiven her of anything. That was why he never sought her out, never attempted to steal her away from Fitzgelder. He'd wanted to, but he hadn't allowed himself. He stayed so drunk for two full weeks his valet had begun seeking other employ. He'd let Julia—or so he'd thought—go off with Fitzgelder, because he knew if he didn't, he'd spend the rest of his life trying to win her back. He'd be nothing more than her groveling slave until the day he died.

But damned if he was going to let that keep him from facing Julia today. Everything he thought he knew these past three years had changed. He no longer knew what was truth, but he was sure as hell going to find out. If there was the slightest chance Julia had honestly felt for him a portion of what he still felt for her, then he was most definitely going to find out if . . .

A quiet knock on the door stopped him from taking the two strides he would have needed to get her into his arms. She stared up at him, wide-eyed and terrified. Her slight little nod toward his still unclothed—and still prominent—self brought him quickly back to reality. The search for truth would get exceedingly more difficult if someone were to walk in here and find them together this way.

He dove for his clothes, scooping shirt, cravat, coat, and sundries into one wrinkled armload. Julia, still supposedly mute, of course, could hardly call out to the door and announce her status. She would have to open the door to gesture to the knocker. Bloody hell.

She shoved him toward the door, positioning him carefully off to the side where he would be completely hidden when it opened. Hopefully. If the person in the hall decided to make an uninvited entrance, it wouldn't do to have them find him here in his present condition.

JULIA DID WHAT SHE COULD TO TIDY HER APPEARANCE and opened the door. Rastmoor gave her one last, pitiful look that clearly begged her to be quick about this. He was rather cute, huddled there in the corner behind the door with his clothing, desperately trying to conceal what was really and truly far too huge to conceal. Quite flattering, actually, but certainly not something she envied having to explain to whomever was at the door.

As it turned out, their guest was none other than Lady Dashford.

"Oh, I'm sorry to disturb you, Mr. Nancini," she said politely, although her expression said she was more than a bit surprised to find her guest so disheveled.

Julia yawned, hoping she would get the idea he'd been doing nothing more sordid than taking a peaceful afternoon nap. Partially dressed. After having just woken from a nap barely one hour ago.

But if the viscountess noted anything amiss, she was too generous to point it out. "I just wanted to be sure you had everything you needed and to remind you that we keep country hours. Dinner will be early, if that isn't too much trouble for you."

Julia shrugged, shook her head, smiled, bowed, nodded, and did whatever else she could think that might assure her ladyship all was well. Lady Dashford's dewy green eyes swept the room and seemed content that all was as it should be. Julia yawned again.

"Very well," the lady said. "I see you have fresh linens. Shall I have the maid bring you water to wash as you dress for dinner?"

Julia nodded. Indeed, a bit of a wash was not at all a bad idea.

The hostess smiled warmly. "Fine. We'll see you at dinner."

Julia smiled her away and nearly heaved a sigh of relief when Lady Dashford turned to go. But suddenly she turned back to her.

"It will probably take the maid a full half hour to bring the water, Mr. Nancini. I'm quite sure the upstairs staff will be put to other tasks until that time, in fact. The hallway will likely be empty of everyone. I do hope that isn't, er, inconvenient for you?"

Julia shook her head. Why ever would Lady Dashford see

the need to discuss the actions of her upstairs staff, unless . . . And then she noticed the darting glance Lady Dashford gave to a spot on the floor just behind Julia. It was the spot, incidentally, where Rastmoor had left their boots.

Good heavens, there were two pairs of men's boots! And one pair was conspicuously larger than the other. Drat everything.

But the lady simply smiled and left. Did she know? Had she figured them out? Did she see through Julia's disguise? Or worse, did she *not* see through Julia's disguise? Oh, poor Rastmoor! How on earth was he going to explain this to his friend?

She shut the door and stood near it, listening for Lady Dashford's soft footfalls to fade away. Finally she glanced up at Rastmoor. Yes, without the door to block his view, his gaze had wandered over to the double pair of boots, too.

"Shit," he said with understated passion and dropped his pile of clothing.

Julia carefully held back the laughter. It probably wouldn't do to laugh at the man when he must realize what their hostess clearly suspected. If she told her husband, poor Rastmoor would be humiliated. Or worse. Then again, clearly he wasn't that upset. His cravat had not exactly reached the floor with the rest of the clothes. It had been, conveniently, caught. Waving like a white flag, it hung there, tantalizing her.

"You know," Julia said, catching her breath. "She did say no one would be around for at least half an hour."

RASTMOOR LET THE DOOR SHUT NOISELESSLY BEHIND him. He hoped their hostess had been correct, and no one was prowling the hallway. It could very well have been past that half hour she gave them, though. God, what Julia could do to a man!

He was glad dinner would be early. He needed sustenance.

"Patch things up, did you?"

The voice startled him, and Rastmoor was surprised to find Dashford waiting at the head of the staircase.

"Beg pardon?"

"Did you patch things up with Nancini there?" Dashford asked slowly. "When you brought him up here, you seemed a bit put out. Now I see you're smiling."

"Am I?" He quickly remedied that.

Good God, had Lady Dashford mentioned anything to her husband? Damn it, now how was he going to explain himself without giving Julia away? Indeed, Dashford could be trusted, but even the walls had ears, and as long as Fitzgelder might have honest reason to hate Julia, Rastmoor just couldn't take any chances.

"He's an odd pup, that Nancini," Dashford went on, blocking the stairs so Rastmoor was forced to stand in the hall and have a conversation. "Wherever did you dredge him up?"

"I told you, we met in London a while ago."

"Yes, you told me, but I thought I'd go ahead and ask again. Thought possibly I'd get a different answer."

"You won't."

"Fair enough." Dashford shrugged. "It just seems you might like to tell me who the pretty little bloke really is."

"The *bloke* is a bloody opera singer. If this isn't acceptable to you, then I suppose we can send for a carriage and be out of your hair before dinner."

"No need for that. Dash it all, Anthony, is it just this Fitzgelder thing that's got you so off balance, or is there something more? I'd like to think you consider me trustworthy if there's something more plaguing you."

"There's nothing plaguing me," Rastmoor said sharply. Even he thought it sounded decidedly plaguey. "I just didn't expect my mother and sister to turn up, all mixed into the situation."

"No, I would have expected Penelope to be enjoying her first season, not running away from it. They sent their regrets for the wedding, you know. How odd they'd show up three days after it."

"Yes, isn't it? The quicker we can get back to town to see what my ruddy cousin's up to, the better."

"But could it be possible that . . ."

Here Dashford paused. The butler stood at the bottom of the stairs and cleared his throat. Dashford glanced over his shoulder at the man.

"Yes, Williams?"

"Sir, there is a Mr. Thatcher here to see you," the butler announced.

Dashford frowned. "Thatcher? Do I know him?"

Rastmoor ran through his memory but couldn't think of any Thatcher that might have anything to do with his current troubles, so he decided this must be a legitimate matter for Dashford. Good. Last time the butler announced arrivals, it was Rastmoor's uninvited family.

"He comes from Findutton."

Yes, that was most certainly a business matter for Dashford. Findutton-on-Avon was a tiny village just upriver from Hartwood. Much of the property surrounding it was a part of the Dashford estate except, of course, for Loveland. That neglected heap was an old cottage, held dear by Lady Dashford because it once belonged to her grandmother. Oddly enough, though, that cottage was intended for cousin Sophie. Dashford and his wife were hoping to locate the girl and turn the title over to her.

Ironic, however, that Sophie was most likely going the opposite direction, on her way to London in the probable employ of Fitzgelder and that traitorous Lindley. Damn. Things were beginning to overlap. Perhaps Rastmoor ought to be concerned about this Thatcher fellow, after all.

Dashford, however, seemed to be waiting for more information. He simply stared down at his butler until the man finally gave further explanation.

"Mr. Thatcher was passing by the cottage, sir," Williams continued. "He says someone was there. He fears treasure hunters again, sir."

"But everyone knows there was no treasure," Dashford replied. "What makes Mr. Thatcher so suspicious he'd come all the way over here to warn me?"

Rastmoor had an odd, sinking sensation. Damn and damn again! Last time something was going on at that blasted cottage, he'd thought he'd lost his best friend. But all of Dashford's troubles were solved weeks ago. Who on earth could be pillaging Loveland this time? Unless, of course, it was someone in league with Fitzgelder; someone stalking him, waiting for the opportune moment to strike.

By God, couldn't they at least have chosen a new location this time?

"He says it looks like it might be a troupe of actors, sir," Williams went on.

Dashford seemed no less surprised than Rastmoor.

"Actors?" they said in unison.

"Yes, sir," the butler confirmed. "Perhaps if you would like to speak with the man yourself, he can give you details."

"Yes, all right," Dashford said. "Have him sent to my office."

That seemed a simple enough request, but the butler cleared his throat again.

"Yes, Williams?" Dashford asked.

"Thatcher is a farmer, sir."

"Is he?" Dashford asked, clearly wondering what that had to do with anything.

"Yes, sir," Williams confirmed. "Pigs, sir."

"Ah, well, my condolences for Mrs. Thatcher. Now please show the man in to my . . ."

The butler cleared his throat again. By Hades, was the man consumptive? Dashford really ought to look to better care of his servants' health.

"Yes, Williams?"

"He's coming from his yard, sir," Williams announced. "His pig yard, sir. The place where he keeps his pigs, sir. Several of them, by the smell of it."

Ah, now the butler's lung trouble made more sense.

"So you're saying Thatcher has brought bits of his labors with him, are you, Williams?" Dashford chuckled.

"Indeed, sir."

"So perhaps conferring with him out of doors might be the best course, eh, Williams?"

The butler gave a great sigh of relief. "Thank you, sir. If

you don't mind, sir. The staff would have a devil of a time removing that from your carpets, sir."

"Then by all means, for the sake of my carpets, let's go meet with Mr. Thatcher outside," Dashford said with a smiling glance at Rastmoor. "Care to join me? I can't imagine a troupe of vagrant actors would hold any interest for you, yet . . ."

"Yet then again, it might," Rastmoor finished for him.

Indeed, Dashford knew his past history with actors. Well, with one particular actress and her scheming father, to be more specific. Likely he, too, was wondering what this manifestation might have to do with whatever Fitzgelder had simmering.

Yes, Rastmoor would most certainly care to join him in the yard with the aromatic Mr. Thatcher. It would be interesting to see what they could find out about these mysterious actors who appeared out of the blue to take up residence in Sophie's former home. He was more than a little interested, also, to find out if perhaps Julia knew anything about it.

JULIA SLID THE DOOR SHUT AS THE TWO MEN DISAPpeared down the staircase at the end of the hallway. She'd poked her head out after Rastmoor left, curious as to where he would go. Of course she couldn't help but listen when Dashford practically announced his suspicions about her, and Rastmoor's gruff responses could have done nothing to ease Dashford's mind. The man was a horrible actor—out of the bedroom, anyway.

But what on earth was this? Someone had been speaking to them from the bottom of the stairs. The butler, she'd deduced, and it seemed he was talking about—had she heard it right?—a pig farmer. Well, that certainly was less than interesting.

But something else captured her attention. Actors. Both men had said "actors," and the way they said it convinced her there was some measure of importance. Someone was bringing word of actors.

Well, this could mean nothing, but then again, it could mean everything. Papa and his troupe should be safely in Gloucester, shouldn't they? Yet if Fitzgelder had found out about them, there was no telling what could be occurring. She simply had to find out what this was.

She quickly readjusted the binding that wrapped tightly around her chest, fussed with her clothes, and peeked out into the hallway again. Empty. Good.

It had sounded as if someone was here to speak to Dashford about these actors, and of course the likely place for that would be his office. Julia would sneak her way down there and, with luck, shamelessly eavesdrop outside the door. Hopefully this had nothing to do with her.

From the tension she'd heard in Rastmoor's voice when he agreed to accompany his friend to talk to whomever they were meeting, she didn't feel there was strong hope. Rastmoor appeared to believe this did have something to do with her. And the way her life had been going, it probably wasn't something good.

Chapter Thirteen

So, where the devil was that man's office? She'd hunted it earlier but found the drawing room, along with three chatty women. She'd rather avoid them just now, so she headed in the opposite direction this time. An elaborate archway beyond the grand staircase led her down a hallway she'd never been in. Well, there was no sign of Rastmoor or anyone, so she wandered.

This blasted house had rooms and doors and hallways at every turn, it seemed. How ever had Lady Dashford learned her way around? She'd seemed perfectly comfortable here, yet Rastmoor said the viscount and his lady had been wed just a few days. Then again, likely the new viscountess came from a house very much like this. These well-bred blue bloods arrived on the planet knowing about such things as gargantuan estate homes and flocks of servants. It would surely have taken Julia more than a few days to adjust to being lady over such opulence. Just as well, then, that she would never be faced with that particular hardship.

Thank Providence for small favors, she supposed.

She heard sounds from the room several steps ahead of

her but immediately knew it could not be Rastmoor. It was those women again. As much as she'd enjoyed their company, now was not the time. She needed to find Rastmoor and learn about this acting troupe. But the ladies' voices appeared to be heading for the hallway. Seeing her best hope of escape, Julia ducked into the nearest doorway, realizing at the last moment that she had no reason to believe this room was any less crowded than the hallway was about to be.

Nervous, she glanced around and found herself blissfully alone in the library. Books lined every wall and filled several low shelves placed here and there about the area. The room itself was oddly shaped, with alcoves and corners in unpredictable locations. Indeed, if one wanted to avoid detection, this would be the place. Could it be she'd actually gotten lucky? She tucked herself around the corner and held her breath as the women's voices got louder in the hallway outside.

"But what do you think of him?" Penelope was asking. "So beautiful and delicate, don't you think?"

"Yes, I suppose some would describe him as such," her mother replied.

"He's hardly the type my brother usually keeps as friends," Penelope went on.

Oh Lord, were they talking about her? Rather, about Mr. Nancini? Julia was not at all pleased to hear high praises from Penelope. Bother! She'd hate for Rastmoor to be proven right.

"Yes, he is at that," Lady Rastmoor said, agreeing with her daughter.

She did not sound particularly enthusiastic about it, though. What was that chilly edge to her voice? Perhaps she, like Rastmoor, had suspicions that Penelope might indeed be growing a bit too fond of this odd Mr. Nancini. Or worse, perhaps Lady Rastmoor was worried that it was her son who harbored a secret tenderness for the delicate gentleman. Well, on that point the lady could rest perfectly assured. At least, partially assured.

"I like him exceedingly," Penelope declared. "And I daresay he's quite a positive influence on my brother. I shall hope we see much more of him."

"He's an affable sort, indeed," Lady Dashford said with

hesitant agreement. "But we should remember that once he recovers from his vocal troubles, he must be back at his career. I'm sure we cannot depend on having him much underfoot, my dear."

The voices seemed to stop just outside the library door. Julia held her breath and crept farther away from the door, inching closely against the shelf-lined wall.

"Oh, but surely Anthony will take me to the opera to see him. Perhaps I might even visit him backstage!"

"Absolutely not," her mother announced. "I'll not have my daughter carousing with an opera singer!"

"It doesn't seem to bother you that your son is, though," Penelope pointed out.

"My son is a grown man. Whom he chooses for friends is his own business."

"Well, I'm an adult now, too," Penelope replied. Julia could practically hear her pouting. A silent tension filled the air, and Julia wondered if the mother and daughter were going to argue over her right there in the hallway.

But Lady Dashford was the perfect hostess and diffused the situation with a polite suggestion.

"Ladies, here's the library," she announced in an airy tone. "My husband keeps an excellent collection. Perhaps you'd like to select something to take up to your rooms as we dress for dinner?"

Oh, for heaven's sake! Julia scurried to hide behind a low bookshelf. She had to drop down and sit on the floor to be sure she was not visible behind it. It was a foolish attempt, though. All it would take was for the women to walk into the room and make one curious turn around the shelf to find her there in this unusual position. However would she explain herself then?

Once again she was in a most uncomfortable situation, and once again she had the viscount Rastmoor to thank for it. Well, she supposed if she were honest, not all of the positions the man had put her in had been uncomfortable—especially not that rather interesting one upstairs not so very long ago. But goodness, she'd best not dwell on that! She could feel her face flushing already. Indeed no—she needed to spend her mental energies on thinking up some logical excuse for what she might be doing here in case she was detected.

The ladies would surely think her a sight, crawling on the dusty floor as she was. She could only hope she'd chosen to conceal herself behind a bookshelf that saw very little use. *Oh please don't let the novels of gothic romance be shelved here! Surely that would be Penelope's first choice.* Julia quickly scanned the leather spines of the books beside her.

Thank the heavens. This corner appeared to shelve nothing more than abandoned miscellany. Why, on one shelf in particular a large medical treatise was upside down and haphazardly shoved between two volumes of poetry. In another place a thin and particularly well-worn book with no lettering on the spine was literally crammed between the shelf and the wall. Shame on Dashford for letting things go so out of order.

If she wasn't in mortal fear of discovery, she would have dug that little book out and found a proper shelf for it. Books were a luxury not all could afford; they deserved to be treated with better care. The footsteps at the doorway, however, reminded her to ignore her righteous indignation and stay still.

"I already have something to read, thank you," Penelope said pertly. "I saved all of Mr. Nancini's notes."

Lady Rastmoor grumbled something under her breath, and though Julia couldn't quite make it out, she had a fair notion of its meaning. Rastmoor had been correct after all—his sister was smitten. Dinner was shaping up to be regrettably awkward.

"Come along, then, Penelope," Lady Rastmoor demanded. "I suppose we should refresh ourselves."

The footsteps padded off, leaving Julia to breathe a sigh of relief as she heard the ladies' voices trail down the hallway and out toward the grand staircase. Thank heavens she'd been spared an awkward encounter. With Penelope safely upstairs, perhaps Julia could resume her search for the men.

First, however, she'd do the decent thing and right Dashford's bookshelf.

She had to work her fingers tightly into the space between the shelf and the wall before she could grip the worn volume tucked in there. Slowly, she worked it out. The words embossed on the binding were faded, so she casually flipped the cover open. There inside she read the book's rather intriguing title: *My Hours With the Fairer Sex: the informative notations of a Particular Gentleman.* For further clarification, it went on: *An Illustrated compilation of the memoirs of an English Gentleman. His most congenial relations carefully recorded and illuminated for instructive purposes.*

Congenial relations? Did that mean what she rather assumed it meant? Indeed, this gave her pause. Of course she should have been rushing off to find Rastmoor and learn more about those mysterious actors, but instead she cracked the book open to a page roughly in the middle. There, carefully engraved, was the detailed illustration of a certain unmentionable activity she and Rastmoor had engaged in not more than a half hour ago. Dear heavens!

She slammed the book shut and peeped up over the shelf to make sure no one had heard. No one was there, and no footsteps sounded in the hallway. Thank goodness.

She sank back down onto her knees and slowly opened the book again. It was purely to convince herself she could not have possibly seen what she thought she saw, of course. She couldn't, could she? What sort of book was this?

Indeed, it was *that* sort of book. And hers were not the first eager eyes to appreciate it, either. The pages were worn at the edges, and some careless scribbles appeared here and there at random places. Odd scribbles, she had to admit. They almost appeared to be intentional lettering, although certainly they were not from any language she had ever seen. Someone must have just been idly making marks as they pored over the contents.

And it was easy to see how the scribbler might have been too distracted to realize what he was scrawling. The book was fascinating! She read the title for chapter five, "in which a Gentleman comes upon the Key to rise beyond his peers."

Timidly, she turned pages to investigate just exactly how one could achieve such distinction.

Oh. By gracious! Each page gave detailed description—with the corresponding informative drawing—of certain things this Gentleman might do to ensure his, er, "Key" did indeed rise beyond his peers.

By Jove, this book was a primer! Sir Cocksure—if that indeed was the author's true name—had provided complete illustrations and descriptions of the most intimate things a gentleman might wish to know. Why, right here on page 75 was his suggestion regarding a narrow tube and some form of suction involving water pressure. Indeed, if the Gentleman had wished to "rise beyond his peers," this certainly seemed to do the trick quite admirably, although the more Julia studied the drawing, the less certain she was it could be considered entirely safe. She must remember to be thankful that Rastmoor did not employ such tactics. The man certainly had no need to endanger himself to, as it were, stand out among the crowd.

Then again, she really didn't have much of a crowd to compare him to, did she? She seemed to have rather been waiting for him all her life and then could not bring herself to consider anyone else once he was gone. It was actually quite unfair to assume all others were his inferior, wasn't it? Indeed. So, for the sake of fairness, she really ought to scan another page or two, oughtn't she?

Of course she should. Perhaps by comparison she might learn that Rastmoor was not nearly so special as she had always thought him. Perhaps he was really no better than average. That information would be good to know! It would certainly help to secure her resolve to push the man—and his damn "key"—out of her mind forever once this dreadful Fitzgelder business was over.

Two chapters and twenty pages later, Rastmoor still retained a high place of honor in Julia's memory. Heavens, how did she let herself get so distracted? Then again, how could she not? Sir Cocksure's book was certainly a page-turner. Illustration after enlightening illustration convinced her that the gentlemen depicted here in this book had absolutely nothing Rastmoor could be envious of. Fresh on her mind as he was, Julia could be quite certain her estimation of Rastmoor's abilities were not exaggerated.

Drat. Unless Sir Cocksure's primer was very incomplete,

Rastmoor was every bit as extraordinary as she'd always thought him. Plus, he seemed to have mastered every applicable page here. Julia's traitorous body, however, was only too eager to continue the man's education. Oh, but she should have shoved this book back on the shelf the moment she realized what it was!

The first page claimed it was "valuable to all Gentlemen who endeavor to gain some measure of a most useful carnal knowledge." Bother! All it seemed to have been useful for was to make her wish beyond all reason that she was *not* hiding in men's clothing and sneaking around in hopes of learning about actors who might in fact turn out to include her father, which would mean she must, with all haste, leave this place—and Rastmoor—to go off again into obscurity. And a cold bed.

Damn. She'd much rather locate Rastmoor and devote further mutual study to chapter six. She had the suspicion he would be inclined to agree. In fact, this titillating little primer might come in very handy, should she discover she needed something to distract Rastmoor if he decided it was time to abandon her here and take himself off to London.

Yes, this was just what she needed. Sir Cocksure was just small enough to fit nicely into her shirt—she could cart him back to her room and tuck the volume away for later. It was a lucky find indeed!

Of course, it had kept her from finding the men and learning what they'd been up to. She'd have to find a way to question Rastmoor later. For now, though, she'd best get herself ready to survive what was bound to be a most interesting dinner. Yes, she really ought to go freshen up for that. She'd certainly have to be in rare form. With Lady Dashford's obvious suspicions, Lady Rastmoor's motherly concern, and young Penelope's constant swooning, it was bound to be a taxing evening.

Pity Cocksure didn't have a primer for dealing with that sort of interaction.

RASTMOOR TRIED TO DROWN IT OUT BY CHEWING loudly, but his sister's endless prattle was not to be ignored.

It was nearly enough to ruin his appetite for the hearty spread Dashford's fine cook had prepared tonight.

". . . And if you had been there, I daresay you would have needed to call him out, the way Mr. Brumpton stared at my very best fichu all that night long," she boasted lightly. "Three times he begged me to dance, after I'd already stood up with him twice!"

"Am I to assume you make it a habit of dancing repeatedly with the same gentleman at any given ball?" Rastmoor asked, sliding his mother a none-too-subtle look of frustration.

"Don't glare at me," his mother snipped at him, cutting delicately into her trifle. "It's not as if I haven't told her what's appropriate and what isn't. Perhaps if you'd joined us in London this season as a responsible brother, your sister might not have attracted so much of the wrong sort of attention."

"And just what wrong sort of attention has Penelope been attracting, may I ask?"

As if he believed for one moment that Penelope had foolishly let herself fall into impropriety. He knew his sister better than that; she was too smart, too determined for that. The last thing she would allow was her brilliant season to be ruined by some hint of scandal. His mother was clearly trying to heap on guilt for the way he'd managed to avoid their little soirees and, no doubt, the marriage traps. Indeed, he had no delusions about the woman's ulterior motive for insisting his presence was necessary for Penelope's social success. She was planning to get both her offspring carted off to the parson this year.

Well, she'd just have to settle for one. Provided, that was, Rastmoor was able to settle this with Fitzgelder, and Penelope could safely go back to Town to finish out her season. Attracting the wrong sort of attention, indeed. No doubt she'd turn up her nose at any inappropriate suitor and settle for nothing less than a duke.

"She's been positively indiscriminate in her attentions toward admirers," his mother announced.

"Mamma, honestly!" Penelope said with a dramatic sigh. "I can't help it if gentlemen find me so irresistible."

Her mother simply sniffed in response. "Indeed? Well, you

at least should not find each and every one of *them* so very irresistible."

Rastmoor had made the mistake of stuffing a crust of bread into his mouth. He very nearly choked on it. By God, what had Penelope been up to?

"Well, how am I ever to select one of them for a husband if I can't so much as carry on a conversation?"

"If only conversation were all you carried on," their mother muttered under her breath.

At least, it's what Rastmoor thought she had said. Had she said it? He pinned his gaze on the innocent-looking Penelope. Had she been idiot enough to let some of those knock-minded pups in London lure her into disgrace? The last thing he needed right now was to learn that his sister had not been circumspect in her relationships.

No, that was not entirely correct. He glanced over to catch Penelope eyeing Julia with a coy smile. Holy hell. Now *that* was truly the very last thing he needed.

No, that was not entirely correct, either. Penelope's next words hinted at what was, indeed, the *very* last thing he needed right now.

"Well, how was I to know our cousin is an evil cretin who would never bother to marry me?"

Silverware clattered. Rastmoor's mother dropped her fork.

"This is not something we are discussing right now, Penelope," she declared.

Rastmoor found his voice to disagree quickly. "I'm sorry, but I'm afraid I'd rather like to discuss this right now, if you don't mind. Penelope, precisely which cousin did you have hopes of marrying?"

"Cedrick, of course," Penelope said with a mournful shrug of her shoulders. "But it turns out he's dreadful."

"By God, I'll say he's dreadful!" Rastmoor fumed, shooting a furious glare at his mother. "How in heaven's name did Fitzgelder come to be among my sister's pool of suitors?"

His mother merely gave a martyred shrug and had the nerve to reply, "I begged you to join us in London. There's no telling what a girl might encounter there in her debut."

"Well, she should certainly not have encountered someone like Fitzgelder. Good Lord, Mother, where were you when that snake was oiling his way up for an introduction?"

"I can't be everywhere at all times, Anthony," she snapped back. "And I highly suggest that if you have anything further to say on this subject, we wait until after dinner."

She was damn right to imagine he might have a few more choice things to say about this subject, but blurting them out here in front of Julia and the uncomfortable-looking Dashfords was probably not the best way to go about it. All right, he would wait until later when he and his family could meet alone. But, by God, he'd have plenty of words for them then!

The awkward meal continued in silence for several minutes. Servants bustled in and out with various courses, and they must have felt the tension in the room, too. None of them seemed the least bit interested in lingering. Rastmoor didn't blame them. What was the world coming to when his own sister might find herself romantically inclined toward the likes of Cedrick Fitzgelder?

He risked a quick glance at Julia. She was watching him. He supposed he could have expected a smirk, but instead he read concern on her sober face. Yes, that was to be expected. Julia might not care a fig for him beyond what he could do for her in the bedroom, but she wasn't entirely heartless. She wouldn't want an innocent like Penelope to be inflicted with the sort of misery Fitzgelder could provide. Dear God, if that story of her friend Kitty and her untimely demise was true, Rastmoor had best take this Fitzgelder threat a bit more seriously. It was no longer merely his own life that was in danger, so it would appear.

"So what's this my maid tells me of travelers camping at Loveland?" Lady Dashford asked, breaking the silence with a dramatic change of subject. "Are they gypsies, perhaps?"

Her husband shook his head. "Gypsies? No, they would appear to be actors, my dear. A farmer from outside Findutton came by earlier to inform me what he'd seen. It doesn't appear anything to worry about. I'll send someone out to roust them."

"Actors?" Penelope said, all brightness and curiosity despite the tension around her. "Do you suppose they're in the area to give performances?"

"I'm sure they're just passing through," Rastmoor grumbled in answer. "And I doubt any of them are your type."

She wrinkled her nose at him. "I only wondered if we could perhaps find a bit of entertainment, that's all."

"It would appear more entertainment is the last thing you need."

Dashford spoke before further sibling hostilities could erupt. "I can't imagine they'd be up to London standards, Miss Rastmoor," he said. "Given the fact that they must trespass to find lodging, I'd guess they're nothing more than a ragtag group of transients, sorry to say."

"How odd for actors not to approach us and offer their services in exchange for the lodging," Lady Dashford noted, her soft features pinched in contemplation. "Perhaps they simply don't know Loveland is attached to Hartwood. They might be a reputable troupe, after all, on their way to the theater at Stratford, perhaps."

Rastmoor saw no reason to think this at all. The news they'd gotten earlier from that man, Thatcher, gave no indication that the troupe was in any way known in these or other parts. Instead of outright saying so, though, Dashford had the good sense to treat his wife's suggestion with sensitivity. By Jove, the man had become a veritable mollycoddle when it came to that woman. Just one more reason Rastmoor needed to make sure his romps with Julia didn't become a habit.

"I suppose they could be on their way to Stratford, my dear," Dashford said. "But I doubt they are people we should wish to have into our home. Most likely a group of hacks, if you ask me. Certainly I've never heard of the Great Giuseppe and his Poor Players."

Julia choked on her wine. No one else seemed to notice, but Rastmoor had. She didn't look up from her plate, though, so he could not be quite certain if it was a simple matter of accident or if it was a reaction to Dashford's words.

"Is that what they call themselves?" Lady Dashford was asking her husband.

"Indeed, so says our farmer friend who informed me of them," Dashford replied with a chuckle. "I wonder just how prophetic that title is, though. The Great Giuseppe is auspicious enough, but His Poor Players leave one fearing they might be exactly that."

"But Giuseppe is Italian," Penelope announced. "How wonderful! Please, don't roust them without inviting them here to perform for us. Imagine—Mr. Nancini could have the pleasure of being with some of his own countrymen. Wouldn't that be delightful, Mr. Nancini?"

Rastmoor couldn't miss the worry in her eyes as Julia raised her head to meet the expectant gazes of the others. She seemed suddenly pale, too. Of course he couldn't blame her—one minute face-to-face with real Italians, and everyone present would know she was not one of them. He'd have to be very sure no invitation was extended to the group of actors camped at Loveland.

But suddenly Julia broke into a smile. She nodded most profusely for Penelope, holding her hands to her heart in some exaggerated expression of joy. By God, what was Julia up to? Surely she knew Dashford would never be so cruel as to deny Mr. Nancini something he believed he wanted. Julia was playing it too rich! Dashford would send for the actors immediately.

Unless, of course, that was what Julia wanted. Was it possible she knew this Giuseppe and his Poor Players? Bloody hell, that was clearly the case. She recognized the name when Dashford announced it. But just exactly what were the chances friends of hers might have shown up so near Hartwood completely by coincidence?

None, he'd wager.

"See? He'd love that very thing!" Penelope chirped. "Oh, please, my lord, do invite them to come perform for us. It would mean so much to poor Mr. Nancini."

"Penelope," their mother scolded. "Lord Dashford is certainly free to do as he sees fit with regards to these vagabonds.

I'm sure Mr. Nancini has no wish for unsavory strangers to be forced upon him just because they might possibly share a slight connection to the same geography."

But Julia was still making dramatic motions with her hands, wringing them, waving them, and holding them up to her face to display surprise and delight. It was disgusting. She certainly hadn't been that excited when she ran into *him* at that posting house two nights ago.

"Mr. Nancini, can it be you actually know this Giuseppe person?" Lady Dashford asked.

Julia nearly broke her neck nodding so profusely. Her eyes sparkled, too.

"How lovely!" Penelope said, giggling like a child. "Then we simply must call him to bring his troupe. Oh please, Lord Dashford, do let us invite them!"

Rastmoor caught Julia's eyes then simply rolled his.

"Very well, ladies," Dashford said, as spineless as jelly. "I'll send word to the troupe that we should like them to entertain us on the morrow. Shall I inform this Giuseppe that he can expect to find you here, Nancini?"

Rastmoor took at least a tiny morsel of pleasure from the quick hint of confused discomfort that swept over Julia's face, but then it was gone and replaced by a secretive smile. She shook her head and put one finger to her pursed lips. How any man could for one minute not realize those were the lips of a woman, Rastmoor had no clue. He did, however, have a clue why Julia wished Dashford to keep Nancini's presence a secret; whoever this Giuseppe was, he certainly had never heard of the newly invented Nancini.

Dashford simply shrugged. "All right, old boy, we'll keep that as a surprise. Are you content with this arrangement, my dear?"

His wife gave him one of her dazzling grins. "I can't wait. If this Giuseppe is a friend of Mr. Nancini, I'm sure we can trust him and his troupe to treat Loveland with care while they are lodging there. Indeed, it will be nice to have some drama around here, won't it?"

Personally, Rastmoor felt there'd been entirely too much

drama already. What the hell *had* Penelope been up to with Fitzgelder? And, by God, Rastmoor would see to it there was drama tomorrow if that Giuseppe person showed up and thought he could lay a finger on Julia. He'd heard about those damned randy Italians.

GIUSEPPE AND HIS POOR PLAYERS. IT WAS PAPA!

Julia could barely contain a giddy smile. The others at the table had gone back to making small talk, carefully avoiding any mention of Fitzgelder and just muddling through the meal until at last they could all excuse themselves. Rastmoor's expression was dark—obviously he was planning out what he'd have to say to his sister once they were alone.

Well, Julia couldn't let herself worry over their situation. She had her own to worry about. Papa was here, on this very estate! Oh, but this was wonderful.

A bit confusing, too. What was he doing here? And why on earth was he using that silly name, the same one he'd used several years ago when they were first hiding from Fitzgelder? It could only mean Papa and their troupe must be in some sort of danger.

But what sort of danger? Had Fitzgelder learned the truth? Had he discovered Papa in London? But she was sure he hadn't. Papa had disguised her and hurried away the minute they discovered the man was to be in their audience that night. The performance had gone on as planned; Fitzgelder enjoyed the entertainment and believed she was a young gentleman. It seemed he would have completely ignored her altogether if it hadn't been for that incident with Sophie.

The poor thing. Julia had noticed the maid's bruises as she bustled around before the performance, helping the actors to dress and organizing the few props they had brought into the home where they'd been hired to entertain. If only they'd known whose home it was! But somehow her disguise had gone undetected and they'd escaped. Thank heaven for that.

It had been close, though. At one point after they had overheard Fitzgelder's plan to murder his cousin on the road it seemed Lord Lindley might have discovered them. Fortunately, the man had not realized they'd overheard. He let them go without raising an alarm.

Likely he regretted his error later. It seemed Fitzgelder had not realized his precious locket was gone until she and Sophie were nearly gone. He'd raged about it but they made it out of the house and disappeared into the night without her identity ever being known. It had been nothing short of a miracle, actually.

The plan then was to go north to warn Rastmoor, then go to meet Papa at a friend's home in Gloucester. Then she would forget this had ever happened. Fitzgelder would never know how close he'd been to the family that made a fool of him three years ago. Very simple. Yet Papa was clearly not in Gloucester. What in heaven's name were Giuseppe and his Poor Players doing out here now?

Perhaps Papa found out Julia was in trouble. Yes, of course the other actors would have left after their performance and gone directly to warn Papa that Julia had very nearly been found out. When she ran away with Sophie heading toward Warwick, they must have realized something was wrong. They would have gotten word to Papa.

But of course that's what happened. Papa couldn't have been very far from London by that time; he must have gathered the troupe and set out to find her. Likely he'd been following her all along! Oh, dear, dear Papa. He must be worried sick.

Indeed, what if he discovered she was with Rastmoor again? Heavens, if he'd followed her here, he would most certainly know that. And he wouldn't likely care for it, either.

Well, she'd best see to it that Papa did not have reason to meet up with Rastmoor. For everyone's sake, that uncomfortable scene simply had to be avoided. She'd best find out where the troupe was staying and get herself there before Papa showed up here.

She'd have to leave in the night, obviously. Then they could disappear. She'd done what she'd set out to do—she'd warned

Rastmoor. Now it was up to him to save himself from whatever Fitzgelder had planned. He would be fine. Now that Papa was nearby, soon she would be fine, as well. Somehow.

All she had to do was choke down the last few bites of her dinner, then mime exhaustion and take herself up to bed. Would Rastmoor follow? No, of course not. He would be busy with his family tonight. This news about Penelope had clearly unhinged him. No doubt he would have much to discuss with his mother and younger sister. A merely convenient lover was probably the last thing on his mind right now, especially since she'd so graciously taken care of whatever basic needs the man might have had just a couple of hours ago. Twice, as a matter of fact.

So she'd have no distractions tonight—leaving would be the easiest thing in the world. She had no belongings to carry and no one she owed any explanations. Leaving was just a matter of walking out the door. Although, of course, she'd have to wait until the house was quiet and the servants were abed. Surely if anyone saw her attempting to leave, they'd alert Rastmoor.

That meant she'd have several long, empty hours to pass before she could escape. Pity she couldn't make the best of them. After all, once she was back with Papa, it was unlikely she'd ever speak with Rastmoor again. Or so much as look at him. Or do anything with him, for that matter.

And, by God, she did rather enjoy doing things with him.

She stabbed at the half-eaten fish on her plate. Good Lord, but what was she thinking? Papa was nearby, her own life and identity was right around the corner, and she would rather risk it all for another quick tumble with a man who despised her? Honestly.

She was a member of the gentler sex, wasn't she? Despite her circumstance, she'd been raised like a lady. She didn't need the constant pawing and groping of primitive urges. She'd do quite well on her own tonight—peacefully unmolested until such a time as she might slip away. Alone. The way she'd likely be for the rest of her life. Chaste and maidenly, as far as anyone else knew. Never to taste passion again. Ever.

So perhaps she'd best take advantage of things while she could, since it was going to have to last her a whole, loveless lifetime. Surely Rastmoor wouldn't need to spend the entire night lecturing his sister, would he? He had to go to bed sometime. And truly, if the man was worn out from exertion, he'd sleep much better and be less likely to hear her stealing away. Right?

Of course it was.

She carefully took up her spoon and just as carefully dropped it into Rastmoor's lap. It got his attention, of course. Even more so when she reached to retrieve it.

But before she could be sure whether or not he recognized the invitation, Dashford's stiff butler interrupted. Indeed, it seemed the butler was not the only thing in the room holding itself ramrod straight. However, he was the only one standing in the doorway clearing his throat as if he had something dreadfully important to say.

"You have a guest, my lord," the butler announced clearly.

"In the middle of supper? Who is it, Williams?" Dashford asked.

Julia sucked in her breath. Could it be Papa? Had he come already? She quickly withdrew her hand.

Would Papa cause a scene? Would he call Rastmoor out with dueling pistols as he'd threatened to do those three years ago? Oh, she hoped not! Were either man to be shot full of holes, that would certainly put a damper on any plans she had for a final night of unbridled passion. Oh, this was dreadful. If only it might turn out not to be Papa. Perhaps it was simply one of Dashford's tenants, or the local vicar, or . . .

"It is a Mr. Cedrick Fitzgelder, sir," the butler replied.

Oh hell. Now *that* put a damper on her night of passion.

The spoon slid off Rastmoor's lap. It clattered loudly onto the marble floor, but no one seemed to notice. Everyone was reacting in his own way to this unexpected news. Fitzgelder—the man who wanted to murder half of them and forcibly seduce the rest—was here!

Dashford glanced at his wife, and she shrugged. The dowager Lady Rastmoor glanced at her son, and he scowled. Julia happened to glance at Penelope. She smiled.

Really? Penelope *smiled*? Heavens! Perhaps once the murdering was done, Fitzgelder would encounter less resistance than expected in carrying out the rest of his plan. If only it had simply been her vengeance-seeking papa at the door.

Chapter Fourteen

Dashford had sent Fitzgelder on into his office. Rastmoor sent the sturdiest footman he could find to stand at the door and keep him in there. By God, he was not about to have that poxy bastard wandering his friend's home while Julia and Penelope were in it. What on earth did Fitzgelder think, showing up here like this?

And why didn't Dashford immediately offer the nearest shotgun to let Rastmoor deal with the vermin the way any reasonable man ought? Honestly, inviting the bastard in? Dashford was being too bloody polite—giving the ass a quiet place to sit, sharing a fresh decanter, treating him like he was actually welcome here. Useless. The minute Rastmoor knew all the women were safe in their rooms, he was going to see about undoing all Dashford's kindness and throw the bastard out.

But first he needed just a few quick answers from Penelope.

"So exactly how long have you let yourself be Fitzgelder's little plaything?"

His sister's eyes grew huge. At least she had the good taste to feign shock, although surely she expected this line of questioning when Rastmoor demanded she remain to speak with him while everyone else declared themselves well fed and scurried off to their various bedrooms. His mother had seemed reluctant to leave Penelope to face him alone, but eventually Rastmoor's stern looks won out. She'd retired with the rest of the group.

For her part, Julia had been only too eager to retire. Good. He hoped she was in no hurry to socialize with the man she claimed had married someone in her place. Just to be on the safe side, though, Rastmoor had another footman assigned to stand guard near her chamber with instructions not to let anyone in—or out.

All he had to do now was pry the truth out of his sister.

"Answer me, Penelope."

"I don't know what you expect me to say. Honestly, Anthony, I can't believe my own brother would think such things of me!"

She'd been too damn evasive for him to expect he'd like the truth when he finally heard it. By God, he was going to storm into Dashford's study and kill Fitzgelder with his bare hands in about five minutes.

"Just what am I to think, Penelope? You've been carousing with Fitzgelder, of all people."

"I most certainly do not *carouse*."

"Then how the hell did you end up on polite terms with the likes of Fitzgelder?"

She had the gall to roll her eyes. "He was presented to me at Mrs. Parkerstone's rout. Somehow the lady who gave the introduction must have had no knowledge of our connection. Well, I couldn't very well be rude, could I? He asked me to dance, and I felt there was nothing to do but accept."

"Oh, certainly. And if he had asked to take you off to a dark alley somewhere?"

"Of course I would have declined. It was quite raining and cold that evening—a walk through a dark alley would have destroyed the lovely new gown Mamma had made up for me, not to mention the adorable slippers to go with it."

The table rattled when he pounded it.

"By God, Penelope! What else went on? Did you meet him beyond that?"

"Yes, I met him. All right? He turned up everywhere we went. I know you've always hated the man, but he was nothing but charming toward me. All I did was respond with common friendliness in return."

"And just how much common friendliness did he get from you?"

She frowned at him. "You keep insinuating things. I don't care for it."

"And you keep avoiding things. Just how far did this relationship with Fitzgelder go?"

"I won't justify your accusations with an answer."

"Then I'm left to assume you have a great many things to answer for."

"Certainly nothing so sordid as the dozens of things *you* must have to answer for," she said, picking at a crumb on the table and coyly avoiding his eyes. "Perhaps we ought to compare stories, Brother dear? I would so love to hear the details of that little actress you were engaged to a couple years ago. Oh, that's right. She died, didn't she?"

Oh, but that was low. He took a long, careful breath before continuing. "We are not talking about me, Penelope. We're talking about you. What has passed between you and our cousin that convinced Mother to drag you away from the season and come rushing out here to find me?"

She sighed. "You're determined to think the worst of me, aren't you?"

"You're giving me little reason to think otherwise."

"You shouldn't need any reason to think otherwise! I thought you knew me, Anthony."

"Apparently not. But I do know Fitzgelder."

"Do you? I daresay there are some things you *don't* know about him."

For the first time she met his gaze. Why had he never realized she had the eyes of a grown woman? What on earth had he been doing lately while his innocent little sister was growing up? Perhaps Mother had been right. Perhaps he should have been with them in London.

"What don't I know about him, Penelope?" he asked slowly.

"You don't know that he claims to love me," she announced. "He says I have captured his heart."

"Bullshit. Fitzgelder has no heart."

"He says he wants to marry me, Anthony, but he knows you'll never consent. So he asked me to pledge in secret."

"By God, Penelope, you did no such thing!"

"He begged me not to mention it to you or to Mother."

"Of course he did! He has no idea of honoring that pledge beyond what benefits him. Besides, he knows I'll goddamn kill him."

"It might interest you to know he made a generous gesture of his love."

"Oh, Lord. Just how generous was his love, Penelope?"

"You have a disgusting mind, Anthony. It's nothing like that. He gave me a ring."

"A ring?"

"He told me it once belonged to our grandfather."

What? Fitzgelder had his grubby hands on some family heirloom, and he willingly parted with it? That hardly sounded believable. "Oh? And just what did he expect you to do in return?"

"See, there you go again, thinking poorly of me."

"I asked what he expects to get in return for his generous token!"

"All right. He expects me to ignore all other proposals until he has proven to you he's not the black sheep you apparently think him. That's not so terrible, is it?"

"That's all he asked for?"

"Well, that and the silly old locket."

"The locket? You mean, our father's old locket?"

"Yes, that's the one. He said it had been his father's before it was passed on to ours. He wanted it for sentimental reasons."

What? Penelope gave him the locket? The locket that was

the cause of all this current frustration and excitement? Damnation, so that's how the bastard got his hands on it. He knew what the thing contained, and he used Penelope to get it. Now he would use it against her—against all of them.

Dear Lord, did his little sister have any idea what that simple piece of jewelry contained? Obviously not. Mother must not have told her. He drew a deep breath, rubbed his aching temples, and wondered how his day could get any worse.

He shouldn't have wondered.

"I guess it was probably wrong for me to tell him where Mamma and I were headed, wasn't it?"

No, she couldn't possibly have just said that. Had she? She was the one who told Fitzgelder where to come find them all? Hellfire and damnation! Here he'd been wondering if Julia had done that, when the true culprit had been his own flesh and cotton-headed blood.

"Our mother took you away from London to keep you safe from that weasel, and you gave him permission to follow?"

Penelope just shrugged. "It only seemed right, seeing as how he is practically my fiancé."

"Like hell he is! I swear, Penelope, I never imagined you to be so want-witted. Good God, do you know what you've done?"

Now she actually smiled at him. "I believe I do, yes. Now, if you would just let me explain—"

"I don't want an explanation. I want you to assure me you've not gotten yourself into such a condition that I'll be obligated to force Fitzgelder into marrying you before I put a bullet through him."

There. He'd said it. He'd given voice to his worst fear, and now there was nothing but to anticipate her answer. She didn't keep him waiting long.

"Oh, honestly, Anthony," she replied with disdain. "Of course I haven't let *that* happen. Really now! As if I could ever be so stupid. A lady may flirt upon occasion, but she never gives up the merchandise without a bill of sale."

With a meaningful huff she crossed her long arms and pouted extravagantly. All Rastmoor could do was wonder where on earth a sheltered miss like Penelope had gotten such a colorful expression. Not that he was arguing with the results, actually, if it had helped keep her safely from ruination at the hands of Fitzgelder, but he'd see snowflakes in Hades before he let his sister go around speaking that way.

"That's hardly becoming of your station, Penelope," he reminded her.

"Oh? Well, perhaps if you hadn't always been so busy off chasing actresses and . . . and opera singers, you might have found a few spare moments to spend with us to help ensure I was provided with a proper understanding of what, exactly, is becoming of my station."

"Now don't try throwing this in my face, Penelope. You've been provided a most excellent education in all things maidenly and proper."

"Yes, and demmed boring it's been, too."

"Don't attempt to change the subject! We are discussing just what it is you and our bloody cousin have been getting up to together."

"And I told you. He wants to marry me, so I gave him Papa's old locket. Now, if you'd just let me explain . . ."

Dear God, they were going in circles here. It was making his head pound. He was just going to have to tell her, once again, that Fitzgelder was a bounder and a blackguard, and she was never to have anything to do with him again. His lecture, however, was interrupted before it began.

Dashford stepped into the dining room and cleared his throat. Hell, but if the man hadn't been born with the bluest of blood in his veins, he'd have made a fair butler.

"Our guest is getting a bit impatient, I'm afraid," he said, nodding his head back toward the direction of the study where Fitzgelder cooled his heels.

"Fine," Rastmoor said, rising to his feet. "I might as well go talk to him then, for all the straight answers I'm getting here."

"I'll go with you," Penelope offered, also rising to her feet.

"Like hell you will! No, you will go directly up to your bed."

She simply glared at him, apparently unconcerned with whatever impression Dashford must be gathering of her as he watched from the doorway. "I think I should be there when you speak with our cousin."

"And I think you should be safely locked away in a tower while I speak with our cousin. Go to bed, Penelope. I'll deal with Fitzgelder."

"That's what I'm afraid of," she grumbled.

But apparently she was not entirely lacking in gray matter. She glanced from Rastmoor to Dashford and clearly decided it was not worth the argument. With an overly dramatic sigh, she shrugged her shoulders and flounced toward the door.

"Very well, I'll retire," she said, although she sounded less than agreeable. "But I'll require an apology from you, Anthony, before I give any further explanation."

"Fine. Wonderful. When I'm in need of any further explanation, I'll sing or dance or whatever you require—should that day ever arrive. For now, just get up to your room and stay there."

She was not amused. Chin raised in an obnoxious show of defiance, she marched from the room. Rastmoor followed to make sure she found the stairs. She did, but then she dawdled around, taking forever to ascend. Dash the girl! He stormed up to grab her by the elbow and led her forcibly the rest of the way to her room.

"You're absolutely a tyrant," she declared when he flung her bedroom door open and waited for her to enter.

"If you would act like you had half a brain, I wouldn't have to be," he replied.

She merely sniffed disdainfully and sauntered past. Just before he could shut the door behind her, she whipped around and glared at him. "If you had any idea what you're dealing with, Anthony, you'd not be acting like this."

"Yes, yes; I'm dealing with true love, fate, destiny, the Montagues and Capulets and all that rot. Sorry, Penelope. I'm the very last person to give a fig for any of that, especially if it involves Fitzgelder. Now lock yourself in there and at least pretend to regret what you've done."

She huffed and slammed the door. Rastmoor slumped, staring at the polished oak and thinking how much pleasanter it appeared than his fuming sister. Dashford came up behind him, chuckling.

"It's so nice to see a family getting along." He smirked.

"She's going to be the death of me."

"She's young. Eventually she'll understand you've done her a favor by keeping that cockroach away."

"I hope so."

"She will. You'll manage things," Dashford said and seemed relatively certain of it.

Rastmoor wished he felt some of that assurance. He glanced across the hall toward the room that had been assigned to Julia. Her shock at the announcement of Fitzgelder's arrival had been honest—he could be sure of that now. It was Penelope who brought Fitzgelder here, not Julia. But could he take that to mean Julia had been honest about all the rest? She never really had betrayed him with Fitzgelder? All along Fitzgelder had been married to an imposter, while Julia and her father remained in hiding? It was so very far-fetched, although he had to admit the evidence seemed heavily in Julia's favor just now. He wished he could go to her now; find out if that look she was giving him at the dinner table really meant what he thought it did.

But he couldn't. He had to face Fitzgelder.

"I suppose our guest is eagerly awaiting me," Rastmoor grumbled.

"Getting more eager with every passing minute," Dashford agreed.

Well, nothing to do but go down there and see what the bastard wanted. He'd find out just exactly what Fitzgelder planned to do with that locket—rather, with what was contained in that locket—and ask him point-blank what he'd done to Penelope. Then, if Rastmoor hadn't already murdered him in a fit of rage, he'd throw the blackguard out into the street. It was only just now twilight. Perhaps Fitzgelder might find his way back to some local inn before cutthroats or wild animals waylaid him on the open road.

And Rastmoor could hardly take the blame for that, could he?

"You've not had any packs of feral dogs ripping into sheep or eating the occasional weary traveler about these parts, have you?" he asked his friend.

Dashford frowned. "No, not that I've heard of lately."

"Damn."

Dashford just shook his head. "Nor have we had any here inside my house. I say, Rastmoor, you've commandeered all my footmen."

Dashford gestured toward the two hearty-looking men Rastmoor had put on guard in the hallway here outside the women's chambers. Indeed, he'd set two more downstairs with Fitzgelder. Perhaps that was a bit overdone, but one could not be too careful where a snake like Fitzgelder was concerned.

"Might you spare one, at least?" Dashford asked. "I'd like to send a message out to those actors at Loveland before it gets too dark. Don't want to disappoint our ladies, you know."

"Yes, heaven forbid we don't provide them ample entertainment. Very well, I suppose you may take possession of your footmen. I'll go down and see to Fitzgelder myself. I doubt with two broken legs the man will be able to navigate his way up your grand staircase."

"There you go—that's the spirit, old man."

Dashford laughed. Interesting. Apparently he thought Rastmoor was joking. Well, they would see what sort of treatment Fitzgelder merited once Rastmoor dragged the truth out of him. He started down the staircase.

Dashford summoned his footmen to follow and began giving instructions on carrying a message to Loveland. Bother. It appeared those damn actors would be invited, and Rastmoor would have to endure watching Julia reunited with whomever the hell that Giuseppe person turned out to be. Rastmoor hoped he would not have to commit two murders in the space of a few short hours. Such a thing was bound to be hard on one's constitution.

They had barely made it to the ground floor when Fitzgelder appeared. It would seem he'd grown weary of cooling his heels in Dashford's study. What nerve, to come wandering about as if he were some invited guest!

"Ah, there you are, Cousin," he said when he spotted Rastmoor. He came toward them. Rastmoor held his ground, keeping his body firmly between Fitzgelder and the staircase.

"Have you finished his lordship's brandy already?" Rastmoor asked.

Fitzgelder gave a benign smile and seemed to completely miss the implied insult. "I was afraid you'd forgotten me."

"I've tried. It cannot be done."

Fitzgelder laughed as if that, too, had been meant in jest. "Indeed, I've missed you, Cousin. But come, spare me a few moments of your time. I'm sure you agree we have much to discuss."

Rastmoor wondered if the fury he felt toward this man radiated off him like smoke from smoldering rubbish. How could the bastard be so bold? What could he possibly hope to gain, arriving here like this? Any fool must realize civil discussion between them was hardly a possibility, given their history. And Fitzgelder was not a fool. He was a great many other things, but he was no fool.

Obviously he had reason to believe his goal—most likely that of attaching Penelope—was attainable. Rastmoor would have to find out why.

"Yes, I suppose we do," he agreed.

"Please, make use of my study," Dashford offered. "I'll join you there presently. First, I need to see about an errand that needs tending."

Rastmoor nodded, silently assuring his friend he would not need his assistance. Yet. It would be nice to have an extra pair of hands when it came time to drag the body out, but for right now, he was perfectly happy to keep his conversation with Fitzgelder a very private matter.

JULIA LISTENED AT HER DOOR. THE HALLWAY WAS quiet. Slowly and carefully, she cracked the door open just the tiniest bit. Yes, the footmen were gone. Vaguely she could hear the men's voices at the bottom of the staircase.

So, Dashford was going to send footmen to deliver a message to Papa? How wonderful! She crept into the hall so she could hear their voices more clearly.

Fitzgelder! She recognized his voice from that harrowing performance in London. So, he was still here. Somehow she expected Rastmoor to insist he be thrown out immediately. He hadn't, obviously. In fact, it sounded as though Rastmoor would actually be meeting with him to calmly discuss the situation with Penelope. Good Lord, what had the poor girl done?

Julia had heard the sharp voices in the hallway. It would seem Rastmoor was quite frustrated with his sister. Could that mean she'd fallen prey to Fitzgelder in the most horrible sense of the word? Perhaps Rastmoor would be forced to actually consider that marriage.

But didn't he realize the danger that would put him in? As Penelope's husband, Fitzgelder would be right in line to possess not only Penelope's dowry, but her share of inheritance should Rastmoor unexpectedly expire. That unthinkable event might not be exactly unexpected as far as Fitzgelder was concerned. Did Rastmoor still not believe her about his cousin's treachery? Even when he'd seen it firsthand?

She heard their distant footfalls as the men dispersed from the grand entry hall at the foot of the stairs. Rastmoor's steps appeared to go with Fitzgelder off in one direction, while Dashford took his footmen in another. Julia wondered what she should do. The footmen were likely to wait on Dashford while he wrote a note to be carried to Papa. Perhaps if she followed closely, she could make her way there, too. She could follow them right to Papa!

But was Rastmoor safe here, left alone with Fitzgelder? She hardly thought so. Perhaps she ought to find where he had gone.

Although, if Fitzgelder was about to complete his betrothal to Penelope, he would certainly have no reason to do away with Rastmoor. Not yet, anyway. If things were progressing in his favor, surely he'd choose to bide his time, wouldn't he? Of course he would. Fitzgelder was devious and supremely greedy. He'd play the game and make his schemes, up until he and Penelope were legally wed. Then he'd see about getting rid of his dear cousin turned brother-in-law.

That meant Rastmoor was safe for the time being. It also meant Fitzgelder might not be cast out of Hartwood as she'd expected. If the man was Penelope's new fiancé, Rastmoor might feel obligated to let Dashford invite him to stay. That would mean when Papa accepted Dashford's invitation and arrived here tomorrow, Fitzgelder was very likely to see him. If Fitzgelder saw Papa, Fitzgelder might recognize him, even if he arrived as Signor Giuseppe.

And that was bad. Very bad. The last thing poor Kitty ever did before her tragic end was to warn Julia. Fitzgelder had learned of the deception and was furious. Frighteningly so, from the tone of Kitty's letter. She begged Julia to never, never let Fitzgelder learn where she and Papa were hiding. Julia took her seriously enough to ensure that she and Papa were safe in a new town with assumed names, but by the time Julia got around to considering how she could help her friend, it was too late.

Would it be too late for Papa? No, not if she found a way to warn him. But how? She doubted she could very well convince Dashford's footmen to take her with them. Then again, she could probably send them with a note. Indeed, that should be easy enough. It was worth a try. She'd have to be quick, though, if she hoped to get it to them before they left. And she'd have to be careful if she didn't want Dashford or Rastmoor to find her out of her room, sneaking notes out with footmen.

Padding as softly as she could, she found writing paper and ink on a desk and dashed off a note for Papa. There was the worry that someone might intercept it and learn her true identity, so she was careful not to include her name. Papa would know her writing. To be extra careful, she wrote in French, hoping that any nosy footman or prying servant might not know that language. For an additional caution, she took pains to refer to Fitzgelder not by his name, but as "the troublesome gentleman from London." She instructed Papa to "meet his favorite young lady at the usual place."

There. Should the note somehow fall into the wrong hands, no one could link it to her or identify Papa by it. Hopefully, Papa would understand her meaning and leave for Gloucester at once. When she could finally get away from here, she would meet him there. With luck, by then this business of Fitzgelder and that locket might be sorted out. Sophie might turn up safe and sound, and Rastmoor would be saved. Penelope, too. No matter what the gullible girl may have already done with Fitzgelder, she certainly did not deserve a lifetime shackled to him.

Making certain the hallway was still empty, Julia tiptoed her way out and toward the servants' stairs. She didn't dare run the risk of bumping into Rastmoor or Fitzgelder down in the main part of the house. It would be better to stay hidden until she could find those footmen and present them with her note—addressed to Giuseppe, of course—without any disapproving audience.

She made her way down to the ground floor without running into anyone who might question her unorthodox presence and quietly wound her way toward where she thought she'd heard Dashford's voice disappear. She'd done well; just as she rounded a corner, she saw two footmen coming out of the room she recognized as the front drawing room. One of them carefully tucked a note into his livery and waited as Dashford's voice carried out of the room behind them. Julia ducked into a doorway to listen.

"Make sure they understand; two grooms carry that note. No one travels alone. And tell them to keep their eyes open."

"Yes, sir," the footmen replied.

"And then I need you back in here. I'll set a few others on watch outside, but as long as Mr. Fitzgelder is in this house, no one gets any rest, unfortunately."

His men didn't seem to complain. It appeared they would not be the ones carrying the letter, but they would take it to the stables and grooms would be dispatched. That was good. She was wondering how she was supposed to explain things to these footmen when they'd been told she was mute. The grooms out in the stables, however, would not likely have been given that information. If she made her way out there and gave her orders directly to the ones assigned to travel to Loveland, they would not be likely to think anything amiss. How convenient for her. All she needed to do was follow the footmen to find the way to the stables.

She tucked herself tightly up against the wall just inside the doorway where she'd taken refuge as she heard the footmen passing by. Dashford's footfalls went off the other way. She hoped he was going to check on Rastmoor. Julia did not much approve the idea of him meeting alone with the cousin who wanted to see him dead.

She would simply have to force herself to concentrate on the matter at hand. As soon as the corridor around her was silent again she went off after the footmen, the cryptic note for Papa clutched in her hand. She hoped he got it in time.

"I'VE ASKED HER TO MARRY ME," FITZGELDER WAS saying with an awkward grin that Rastmoor could only assume aimed to make the man appear besotted. Its actual result was to make the bastard look something more akin to demonic.

"And she has given me proof that she would love nothing better," the demon added.

"I know what she gave you, damn it," Rastmoor said, though the sound came out with rather a low hiss.

"Then you understand that things have progressed to the point where a marriage is necessary."

"Hell. I understand she gave you the locket. She's admitted to nothing else."

"Oh. Then I will forgo mentioning anything else."

You'd damn well better. "That locket was not hers to give. It is part of the estate. I'll take it back now, Fitzgelder, if you please."

"I'm terribly sorry, dear Cousin, but I'm afraid I cannot help you there. It seems I've managed to, er, misplace it."

"Well, that's rather careless of you, considering it was a love token from the woman you've planned to make your wife. One would think you'd keep better track of such things."

"Oh, I've been keeping track of it," Fitzgelder assured him. "I have a very good notion where I might find the thing, as a matter of fact."

"Do you now?"

"I would start by asking your friend Clemmons what he's done with his charming little wife."

Rastmoor felt his blood chill. Was Fitzgelder baiting him? Why mention Clemmons if he didn't know the truth behind Julia's false identity? The old suspicion raised its ugly head, but only for a moment. Julia was not in league with this man. His soul knew it indisputably. But if Fitzgelder was aware of Julia's presence here, she was in danger. He'd best play the game until he knew exactly how much Fitzgelder understood—and just what he planned to do about it.

"Who?"

"Come, come, Cousin. There's no need for silly playacting. I know you've been traveling with him. What's his game? Blackmail, perhaps?"

Blackmail? At that, Rastmoor couldn't help but laugh. Was it possible Fitzgelder really did not know who he'd been following? Could he possibly be in the dark about Julia's ruse? It was almost too good to believe.

His reaction must have shown on his face. Fortunately, Fitzgelder seemed to misinterpret that, too. Clearly Rastmoor had been giving the man's intellect entirely too much credit lately.

Fitzgelder's grin slipped into a menacing sneer. "Ah, it seems I've hit on something, haven't I? You're concerned about Clemmons. What's his hold on you, Cousin? Did he send his little wife off with the locket until you give him what he wants?"

Rastmoor wasn't sure how to answer that. A part of him wondered if he ought to just let Fitzgelder continue on with his confusion, but that could lead to the fool seeking out a confrontation with Julia. That might not go so well. If only he had Julia's talent for creative explanation! He needed a good one—fast—and was coming up blank.

"So that's why you're here," Fitzgelder said, apparently

coming up with his own creative explanation for things. "Clemmons wants the treasure."

"The *what*?"

"Oh, don't act stupid. I know all about the treasure. Your father and his bloody French allies hid it well, didn't they? I just can't figure how Clemmons plays into this. Does he hold part of the code, or something?"

"Code?"

"Damn it, Rastmoor! Don't treat me like I'm ignorant! I know all about the code. Your simpleminded sister should have been a little more cautious about handing me the code."

"The code was in the locket?" Rastmoor asked.

Funny, all along he'd thought the locket contained information of a more personal nature. After all, the papers he'd found tucked away with the locket had contained information about a certain payment that was being made every month to an anonymous account—and everything was written in French. At best, his father must have been supporting a French mistress. At worst, he was involved with the enemy during war times. This latter is what Fitzgelder had always implied. It didn't seem possible, but it would ruin his family should proof of such treason be produced.

But even after obtaining the locket, Fitzgelder had not produced that proof. A code, therefore, made perfect sense. If the locket merely contained damning evidence, why would Father have kept it lying around, leaving it for Mother when he died? No, if that were all it was, he would have destroyed it, and the thing would hold no value to Fitzgelder now. Indeed, Rastmoor should have realized there was more to it than they'd thought.

But if Fitzgelder already had the code, why was he still interested in the locket? What the hell sort of "treasure" had the man been talking about? It sounded just short of rubbish to him, yet Julia had been convinced Fitzgelder was willing to murder Sophie to get his hands on it again. Was he? Or was Sophie, in fact, a part of his scheme? Not likely, he supposed, if Fitzgelder still believed her married to a nonexistent man named Clemmons. Unless he was lying about that in an attempt to lure Rastmoor into supplying further details about the locket and its supposed code.

But Rastmoor had none. How did Fitzgelder come to know anything about this when Rastmoor had not? What made him so certain Penelope would be able to get it for him in the first place? Indeed, Rastmoor had a thousand questions, but they would have to wait. Right now, the only thing that mattered was making certain Julia and Penelope were safe from whatever treachery Fitzgelder might have planned.

"So, I take it since Penelope gave you the locket you've puzzled out the code already," he said. "You don't need Clemmons or his runaway wife."

"Unfortunately, the locket wasn't in my possession long enough for me to give it the attention it was due," Fitzgelder grumbled. "Clemmons's damn hussy took off with it. So, Cousin, it appears you and I have something in common."

"Oh, I very highly doubt that."

Fitzgelder sneered bigger. "How it must pain you to be reduced to an equal position with me. But truly, you and I are both at the mercy of this bastard Clemmons. So tell me, what are his demands?"

Botheration. This line of discourse could only draw Julia into a dangerous situation. "I'm afraid you've made some hasty conclusions. Clemmons and I are here together only by chance. He was seeking his wife, and I thought to help him. I'm afraid I don't fully understand what you say is his involvement with the locket Penelope offered to you."

Fitzgelder slammed his hand on the nearest table. The sputtering lamp standing on it rattled and shook precariously. "Like hell! Clemmons and his wife took the locket then headed out to meet you. Now here you are—together—just a stone's throw away from the treasure, and you claim it's coincidence? I'm not simpleton enough to buy that. What is Clemmons's business with you? Tell me!"

"The man's wife is gone. He's distraught. I took pity on the poor bastard, and there's nothing more to the story."

"I'll bet I could get something more out of Clemmons. Perhaps I should just go find the fellow and discuss this with him?"

"No! He doesn't know anything more than I've told you."

"You seem rather sure of that."

"I am sure of that. It's his wife. She's the one who wants the treasure. She was only using him to get it."

Fitzgelder seemed to pause long enough to consider this. "She doesn't seem the type. She's nothing but a dirty whore I pulled out of a brothel and let her work in my home because she amused me. She doesn't have the brains to comprehend what that locket is or just what it could mean for her."

"And Clemmons believed her a respectable servant. That just goes to show, no one can trust a pretty face. She duped you both."

"Let's go see this Clemmons and find out just who's the one who's been duped around here."

"I think we've done enough talking for one night, Fitzgelder. The locket is gone, and there is no treasure. I'm never giving my consent to your marriage to Penelope, and this is just a waste of our time here tonight. You should leave."

"Sending me away, are you? Shouldn't that be Dashford's prerogative?"

"I'm sure he'd approve. You were, after all, not exactly invited."

Fitzgelder was getting red in the face, and Rastmoor fully expected more table pounding. The knock at the study door interrupted them, however. The butler appeared.

"Beg pardon, sir," he began in his steady tone. "Your mother has asked me to bring you word. Something rather urgent, I believe."

He wasn't eager to receive urgent word from his mother right here in front of Fitzgelder, so he rose and went to meet the butler in the doorway. "What is it?" he asked quietly.

"There is a problem, sir."

Chapter Fifteen

The evening air was thick with moisture, and the heavy clouds blocked out what was left of the sunset. Julia had no trouble keeping herself concealed as she followed the footmen out into the yard where they made their way toward the stables. Dashford's luxurious estate had no shortage of hedges and garden foliage sending shadows every which way. Certainly all manner of secret undertakings could go on out here under cover of moonlight. She only hoped she would not lose the men as they carried out their master's orders.

Most likely they would simply deliver the note to a groom who would then carry it to Loveland. That would require time and effort to prepare a mount. Julia was counting on that in order for her own plan to work. She would wait until the footmen had gone back to their posts indoors and then stroll leisurely into the stables.

As she was convincingly dressed in trousers and a fine coat, the stable hands should have no trouble recognizing her as one of their master's houseguests. Hopefully, none of them had been informed of her status as a mute Italian. Why should they, after all? No one ever expected her to come out here.

She would simply present them with her letter for Papa and ask that it be delivered with the other. For good measure, she thought it best to announce that Dashford himself had authorized this addition. Who would question such a simple request? The grooms would happily oblige, and her letter of warning would be on its way to Papa in no time.

She waited quietly in the dark. The footmen delivered their message into the stable and, as expected, were soon heading back toward the house. Julia tucked herself behind a flowering shrub and waited. Thankfully, they didn't dawdle—she was alone again in mere minutes. She would be free to scuttle into the stable and speak to the grooms before anyone had left for Loveland.

Except that she wasn't alone. Someone was tugging on her coat.

Julia whirled around to find Penelope in the shadows behind her. Heavens, when did she get here? It was all Julia could do to stop herself from squeaking in feminine surprise. Penelope shivered in her light gown and smiled coyly up at her, one ivory hand still laid meaningfully on Julia's arm. Well, drat. This was a bother she certainly did not need just now.

"Were you looking for me, Mr. Nancini?" Penelope asked softly.

Julia shook her head. Vehemently.

"I was afraid you did not recognize the message behind my smile at dinner tonight," Penelope went on. "But I'm so glad you did."

Oh, but this was awkward! However was she to extricate herself from this without making an absolute cake of it?

"Come, come, Mr. Nancini. Surely this cannot be the first time you have met a young lady out in the garden in the night?"

Well, actually . . .

"They do have such lovely gardens here, don't they?" Penelope said as she slipped her arm into Julia's. "So very romantic. Are you quite fond of romantic gardens, Mr. Nancini?"

Julia was quite certain she would never be fond of gardens again. Oh, but whatever was she to do? She didn't dare give up her ruse, not with Fitzgelder so near, but she couldn't very well let Rastmoor's little sister seduce her out here, either. Heavens, but what a pickle.

She tried to gently pry Penelope's hand off her arm. It wouldn't budge. The girl might appear young and helpless, but Julia found quite an iron will behind that sweet expression. Wonderful. This was not going to make things any easier.

"My, Mr. Nancini, but you do have the softest hands," Penelope said then gave a wistful sigh.

Merciful heaven, she had to get out of this. What on earth had she done to cultivate this ill-placed infatuation? True, she'd been purposefully entertaining and perhaps a wee bit more charming than necessary, but did she deserve this? Penelope clung to her like a weedy vine, batting her eyes and smiling incessantly. Not good. This could only end badly for the poor girl, and Julia—though she would have never thought it possible—was beginning to feel like a cad.

Perhaps it was time for the truth. Yes, that was the only recourse. She would admit to her lies and hope Penelope might not run to Fitzgelder with the story. God, but this was a prickly patch she'd grown for herself.

"Mr. Nancini, you seem so tense," Penelope cooed. "Are you nervous here with me? Come, sit with me in this quiet corner where I might console you."

Console her? Good Lord, she was quite certain she needed none of that.

"No! No, I'm quite fine," Julia exclaimed. By God, just what sort of innocent and sheltered little sister did Rastmoor have?

And then she remembered that Mr. Nancini could not speak. Drat. She'd just cried out—in flawlessly executed English. What would Penelope make of that? Julia took a moment from prying those fingers off her arm to spare a quick glance at the girl. Indeed, she was perplexed by what she saw. Far from being shocked, Penelope's eyes showed she was laughingly amused. Really? Was the girl daft, or something?

She didn't get the opportunity to ask. Suddenly she was aware of human sounds nearby, and she looked over her shoulder just in time to find Rastmoor pushing his way through the foliage. He appeared to be wearing the shock on his face she'd expected to find on Penelope's. Oh, botheration.

"What the devil—" he began. "What are you doing out here?"

Julia wasn't quite certain if he'd posed the question for her or for Penelope, but she figured this was an excellent time to fall back into her role as a mute. Penelope, however, seemed to think this was an excellent time to provoke her brother.

"What does it look like we're doing?" she asked boldly.

Julia glared at her. Heavens, but the girl truly *was* daft. Didn't she understand what this would look like?

"Penelope! Who is this?"

Julia glanced over her shoulder again to find that Rastmoor was not alone. He was accompanied by—oh, Lord—Fitzgelder. Good grief. Things were not getting better.

"Why, Fitzy! I rather thought my brother would have turned you out to the elements by now," Penelope said.

Fitzgelder appeared to be having the same reaction to that ridiculous nickname as Julia was having to the way Penelope cuddled up against her. Rastmoor appeared unable to know exactly how he should be reacting to any of this. Julia tried to catch his eye and silently share some of the helplessness she felt just now, but he eluded her. Probably for the best, though. It certainly would not help matters if the others were to question why Lord Rastmoor and his male companion were making eyes at each other while the former's sister clung tenderly to the latter's arm.

"I was in the process of sending your dear 'Fitzy' on his way when I was informed you'd disappeared," Rastmoor told his sister. "What on earth is Mr. Nancini doing to you?"

What? He was accusing her of "doing" things to Penelope? Now he was daft, too. As if she was equipped to "do" anything to Penelope! Quite frankly, Julia was beginning to wonder if *anyone* was capable of "doing" anything to Penelope. It seemed to her Rastmoor's sister was the one most likely to be doing the "doing." And Julia, for one, would have very much liked her to stop.

It would seem Mr. Fitzgelder agreed. "Nancini? Hell, Rastmoor, so you would lie to your own sister? Poor, sweet Penelope. You've been deceived. Mr. Nancini is a sham!"

Julia's pulse pounded in her ears. Fitzgelder knew who she was! Somehow he knew, and he was furious. What would he do to her now that he'd finally found her? What would he do to Rastmoor or Penelope?

"He is?" Penelope said but didn't push herself away from Julia as one might have expected. Despite the implication of Fitzgelder's announcement, Penelope's voice remained sugary sweet. "Anthony, you've brought a stranger into our midst and lied about who he is? For shame!"

"This is pointless," Rastmoor said, finally trying to control the situation. It was a bit late by Julia's estimation, yet he continued valiantly. "Why don't we all go inside and forget about this?"

"*Forget* about it?" Penelope gasped at the mere mention of such a thing. "You expect me to simply forget what's passed between me and Mr. Nancini here tonight? Never! I could never."

Lord, but Julia was confused. Just what exactly *had* passed between her and the younger woman tonight?

"Damn it, his name is not Nancini!" Fitzgelder said. "He's lied to you, Penelope."

"I don't care," she declared. "Since the first moment our eyes met, I knew we shared a bond. Names mean nothing; underneath, I'm convinced we're two of a kind."

Well, Julia had to admit, Penelope did rather have a point there.

"He's a liar and a blackmailer," Fitzgelder announced.

"I don't believe you."

Now Rastmoor stepped in again. "Penelope, really. There are some things you don't quite understand."

"I understand more than you know," Penelope said, but her childlike pout and whining tone made it unconvincing. "However, I daresay if you hadn't interrupted us so rudely just now, I'd have understood a considerable bit more."

"Good Lord, Penelope!" Rastmoor said.

Julia was more than grateful they'd been interrupted when they were. There were some lessons she'd much rather not have a hand in teaching the eager Penelope.

"And how do you know what I do or do not understand?" the girl said, facing her brother. "You haven't been interested in anything—or anyone—since that, well, since that incident three years ago."

Here she sidled up to Julia again and slipped her hand through her elbow. "It's really quite tragic," she said softly for Julia's ears alone. "The poor sap's been nursing a broken heart all this time. I wonder if he's mentioned that to you?"

For the first time a shudder of understanding ran through Julia's spine. She briefly met Penelope's eyes and knew: Penelope was playing a game here. What it was, exactly, Julia could have no idea. But clearly Penelope was not as uninformed as they'd all assumed. Somehow she'd seen through Julia's disguise. She *knew* who she was.

Julia shot a glance toward Rastmoor. He still fumed at what he obviously assumed was his sister's headlong attempt at disgracing herself. Whatever Penelope was up to, she certainly hadn't informed her brother. Nor did Fitzgelder seem to have a clue. He glowered possessively.

"Don't listen to anything he tells you, Penelope," Fitzgelder warned. "You're too young and unsophisticated to recognize his lies."

Penelope frowned. "Really? I should think it would be easiest for those with a clear and honest conscience to recognize a lie when they hear one."

"Come, let's take this indoors. We don't—" Rastmoor began, only to be cut off.

"Oh, thank God, you found her!"

It was Lady Rastmoor rushing up beside her son. Penelope just smiled. She kept herself uncomfortably close to Julia, too, unfortunately. The lady took quick note of that.

"Hello, Mother," Penelope said sweetly. "Were you looking for me?"

"Yes, by God, we were. You were not in your room, and

with Fitzgelder prowling around . . . for heaven's sake, do stop hanging on Mr. Nancini like that. What on earth is going on out here?"

"I was just asking Anthony what he thought about me marrying Mr. Nancini," Penelope announced.

"You were not," Rastmoor said.

"I was about to!" Penelope shot back. "I think Mr. Nancini would make a wonderful spouse. He's so gentle and witty. And he has the softest hands!"

"Bloody hell," Rastmoor grumbled.

"But Penelope," Fitzgelder said, "you are going to be married to me!"

Lady Rastmoor sucked in a wheezing breath. "Gracious! Anthony, you most certainly did not agree to any such a thing, did you?"

"No, of course not, Mother. I—" Rastmoor said but was interrupted again.

This time it was Lord and Lady Dashford joining their little party. Julia thought to take advantage of everyone's distraction to try again to pry Penelope's fingers from her arm. It was useless. The girl had the grip of a falcon.

"Good," Lord Dashford said upon assessing the situation. "I see you've found the missing female."

"How silly that everyone thought I was missing!" Penelope giggled. "I've been here with Mr. Nancini all along. But I'm afraid Anthony thinks we must be married after this."

"I most certainly do not!" Rastmoor assured them all. Very likely he assured the entire county, the way his voice rose and echoed in the damp evening air.

Now Lady Dashford joined the other lady in gasping from shock. "Married?"

"You can't be married to him," Fitzgelder said firmly. "You're already engaged to be married to me!"

Penelope shrugged. "Oh, poor Fitzy. Our agreement was never official, of course. I said I might consider marrying you, but now that I've met Mr. Nancini, I'm afraid I've quite gone and changed my mind."

"But you can't," Fitzgelder said, seemingly stunned that his plan could possibly unravel this way. "He's . . . he's already married to someone else!"

Now Penelope finally dropped her hand from Julia's sleeve. "Already married?"

"Yes, I'm afraid so," Fitzgelder said, clearly relishing his role as bearer of truth. Poor man. Even when he tried to give accurate information it was, in fact, a lie. "I encountered him *and* his wife in London not three days ago."

Lady Rastmoor was struggling to make sense of this. "Mr. Nancini has a wife?"

Fitzgelder gleefully went on. "Oh, yes. But this man is not Nancini. His real name is Clemmons, and he's nothing more than an actor. His wife is a common harlot called Sophie."

Everyone seemed to be quietly taking this in. Lady Dashford, however, suddenly lunged at Julia and grasped her shoulders. "Dear heavens . . . you're *that* Mr. Clemmons? You're Sophie's husband?"

Julia nodded then shook her head. By God, she didn't know what to say.

"Where is she? Is she well?" Lady Dashford rattled on. "Is she coming to Hartwood with you? Oh, no . . . the fire! Was she hurt in that fire?"

The lady's questioning was quite enthusiastic. Julia looked up at Rastmoor for assistance. Fortunately, he nodded and took up the cause.

"Clearly an explanation is in order," he said, clearing his throat to commandeer their attention. "Perhaps *now* we should all return indoors to get things sorted out?"

Julia would have truly liked to see how he might propose to do such a thing. As far as she could see, any explanation at this point would serve merely to create further conflict, not sort things out. What were the chances she could steal a horse and find her way to that cottage where Papa was camped right now? None, she had to admit. Drat it all.

The group begrudgingly agreed to do as Rastmoor suggested and make their way back into the house. Lady Dashford, however, was impatient. She resumed her questioning right away, latching on to Julia with almost the same tenacity as Penelope.

"Is your wife truly Sophie Darshaw? The same one who, until recently, was, er, employed by a certain Madame Eudora of London?"

Julia glanced at Rastmoor. He shrugged. Oh, *marvelous*. The man had not a clue what they should do to get out of this.

Well, she supposed she had little choice but to give out as much truth as she dared. She nodded in reply to Lady Dashford's question. Indeed, Julia may have lost her Nancini identity, but surely she could cling to the story of her injury in the fire, couldn't she? No sense speaking and giving herself away as female until it was absolutely necessary. As long as Fitzgelder was still in the dark, at least her life wasn't in jeopardy. Provided Penelope didn't say anything to put it there.

Judging by the way the girl still smiled and clutched her arm, it seemed Julia may not have to fear in that area. Whatever game Penelope was playing, she seemed content to continue it. For now, at least.

But Julia had no opportunity to contemplate Penelope's motives. Their hostess was still barraging her with inquiries as to Sophie's well-being.

"Then where is Sophie?" the viscountess continued. "Why did she not accompany you? Is she well?"

Julia didn't even bother to look at Rastmoor this time. A fat lot of help he was proving to be.

"Yes, where is your young bride, Mr. Clemmons?" Fitzgelder asked, eavesdropping as Rastmoor ushered them all into the hall.

"You'll have to excuse him," Rastmoor said, finally—and thankfully—placing himself between Julia and Fitzgelder. "Mr. Clemmons has temporarily lost his voice. He was injured in a rather unfortunate fire at the inn where we stayed last evening. Perhaps you heard something of it?"

"No," Fitzgelder said. He was a good liar. "Nothing at all, though it sounds dreadful. I suppose it's fortunate you weren't killed."

"Yes, isn't it?"

The men glared at one another. Thankfully there were witnesses present, and Julia hoped that meant violence between the two might be avoided for a bit longer. She wouldn't have minded, however, if something had come up to take a bit of the attention away from her.

"Well, I for one would like to know why this Mr. Clemmons felt the need to deceive us," Lady Rastmoor said, giving severe looks to both her son and to Julia. "Italian opera singer indeed. Anthony, if this is just another of your larks, it has been in very poor taste. Think of what you've done to your dear sister!"

"Penelope is fine, Mother," Rastmoor said as the group found itself gathered in the grand entrance hall. "I've done nothing to her, and I can guarantee Mr. Clemmons hasn't, either."

His mother merely sniffed in disbelief. "I'm glad you can put so much faith in a man who uses false names and lies to young girls. I cannot."

Julia cringed inside. My, but wouldn't Lady Rastmoor be thrilled if she found out who Mr. Clemmons *really* was? What a dreadful encounter *that* would be. Julia vowed to make sure she was long gone when that revelation finally occurred.

"I understand, Mother," Rastmoor said. "And I assure you I will handle everything."

"Indeed you will," his mother responded. "You'll find out what Mr. Nan—er, Clemmons—has for intentions."

Julia didn't much care for the sound of that. Penelope simply giggled, although she stopped quickly when her mother shot a withering glare at them both.

"Come, Penelope. We shall retire," the older woman announced. "Forgive us, Lady Dashford. You've been kindness itself, yet my son has seen fit to populate your home with wretched intruders."

"Mother, really now," Rastmoor began. "This is not nearly so—"

His mother paid him no heed. "Come along, Penelope. This is no place for you."

Penelope pouted. "But I have the feeling things are only now going to become interesting, Mamma!"

"All the more reason we should be upstairs. Come. *Now*."

Even Julia recognized that was a tone one did not dispute. Penelope sighed her disapproval, but she dropped her hand from Julia and followed her mother toward the staircase. Lady Dashford seemed torn between following her guests to see to their comfort and remaining here, with her husband.

The latter won out. As Lady Rastmoor harrumphed her way upstairs with the quietly grumbling Penelope, Lady Dashford glared at Julia.

"But what of Sophie?" she asked with a barely controlled desperation. "Please, I must know if she is well. And, er, the baby."

Well, that certainly caught Julia off guard. "Baby?"

Rastmoor and Fitzgelder echoed her. Apparently they were just as surprised by this development as she was. True, she and Sophie had not enjoyed a particularly long acquaintance, but never had the girl mentioned a baby. Good heavens! There was a poor, innocent baby involved in all this?

THE LAST THING RASTMOOR WANTED WAS TO PROlong Julia's interaction with Fitzgelder. Unfortunately, he didn't see any way around it. Lady Dashford wanted answers and, quite frankly, she deserved them. Since he knew full well Julia didn't have any suitable answers to give, that left only Fitzgelder. Like it or not, Rastmoor would have to keep the man in their conversation.

At Dashford's suggestion, they all made themselves comfortable—at least, as comfortable as one could be when seated in close proximity to a viper like Fitzgelder—in the large drawing room just off the main entrance hall. Julia looked decidedly pale. As well she should. It had been beyond careless of her to speak. Fortunately, Rastmoor had covered it by reminding them all of the damage to her voice. With luck, anything recognizably feminine in her tone had been dismissed as part of her injury.

Still, he didn't much care for the way Fitzgelder was looking at her. Or Dashford either, for that matter.

"You can understand our concern for poor Sophie," Lady Dashford was saying. "I've been searching everywhere for her! Anthony was kind enough to agree to look for her when he got to London, but I'm afraid I didn't mention anything about the child to him."

"No, you didn't. Obviously Mr. Clemmons also knows nothing about it."

"Is this true?" Lady Dashford asked. "You did not know about the child?"

Julia shook her head. It was nothing if not believable, yet the Dashfords seemed unconvinced. Rastmoor really couldn't blame them. How on earth could a man not know his wife had a child . . . unless something tragic had happened.

"How long have you known Sophie, Mr. Clemmons?" Dashford asked.

Julia appeared at a loss. Rastmoor quickly answered for her.

"When I met Mr. Clemmons, he and Sophie had been married a matter of days."

Dashford glanced at him and slowly raised one eyebrow. "That doesn't really answer my question, does it?"

"The man can't speak," Rastmoor reminded him. "If you have any questions for him, I'll answer."

"You are intimately versed in Mr. Clemmons's private life, are you?" Dashford said, the implication obvious.

"I know enough to tell you he was never aware of any baby."

"So you are not the child's father?" Lady Dashford asked, turning huge, questioning eyes on Julia.

Julia shook her head.

"Then who is?" Dashford asked.

Julia slid her glance over to Fitzgelder. The others followed suit. For the first time it dawned on Rastmoor that this was the most likely explanation. No wonder Sophie was playing Fitzgelder's pawn in all this.

But Fitzgelder pushed himself back into his chair and fisted his hands. "Oh, no, don't think I'll be taking the blame for that one," he said. "The chit's only been in my house a matter of weeks, and I've gotten nothing but a swift kick to my articles out of her—the least damned agreeable slut I ever heard of. If she's got some brat tucked away somewhere, it sure as hell ain't one of mine."

Lady Dashford was somehow able to ignore Fitzgelder's vulgarity and simply went on, worried for her cousin. "But what might have happened? Sophie's last letter was posted in March, and she assured me the babe had arrived and all was well. She was leaving the, er, her previous employment and was going on to honest work for some gentleman. I suppose she could have meant you, Mr. Fitzgelder."

Fitzgelder shrugged. "That sounds right. But I never saw any baby. Madam Eudora didn't mention it, either."

"So, you are familiar with her former employer?" Lady Dashford asked carefully.

"I knew how the hussy earned her keep before she came to my service," Fitzgelder admitted. "Hell, a man's got to get references on his employees, doesn't he? Don't want someone who can't do the job that's expected, and all."

Rastmoor had a fair idea what had been expected of Sophie. Julia and Lady Dashford apparently did, too, from the dual glares sent in Fitzgelder's direction. Rastmoor wondered which lady was going to leap from her chair and pummel the man first. He'd rather enjoy watching that, as a matter of fact.

But of course there was no time for sport just now. They needed to satisfy Lady Dashford's concern for her missing cousin—and the little detail of that baby—and get Fitzgelder as far from Julia as possible. So far, the man was still in the dark, but Rastmoor knew better than to expect luck to hold out forever.

"I suppose she must have given the child over to someone's care," Lord Dashford suggested. "Surely that's done often enough. And we could hardly blame her for not mentioning it to her new husband, after all."

"Oh, but to feel she must leave her own child! Poor Sophie," Lady Dashford said, giving her attention back to Julia.

"Please, if you have any idea where we can find Sophie, you would tell, wouldn't you?"

"Of course he would," Rastmoor answered for her, although it was hardly necessary. Julia's dramatic head-nodding left no question as to her feeling on the matter. Indeed, now that a baby had entered the picture, Julia appeared all the more determined to absolve Sophie of any willful collusion with Fitzgelder and heap even further guilt on the man. Rastmoor was rather inclined to agree.

"So you're really going to fret over the likes of that gutter wench and her little bastard, are you?" Fitzgelder asked, watching Lady Dashford chew her lip.

"Of course I am," she shot back. "Sophie is my cousin!"

"And mine," Dashford added. "Any child of hers is a member of this family, and we'd appreciate whatever help you could give us in the matter of locating them both."

Fitzgelder wasn't too thick to miss the scent of reward in Dashford's statement. His hands unfisted, and he relaxed in his chair. "Well, now, my lord. Just how much do you imagine you'd appreciate my help in the matter?"

Lady Dashford nearly pounced on him. "You know where they are!"

"Don't trust him," Rastmoor cautioned, but it was a waste of breath.

Just one quick glance at the expression of desperate hope in Lady Dashford's face, and he knew beyond a doubt that Dashford would give Fitzgelder whatever the bastard asked for if there was even the slightest hope it would bring joy to his wife. And who could blame the man? Rastmoor knew he'd do exactly the same thing were this some beloved relative of Julia's lost in the world somewhere.

He looked over at her and found her eyes on him, full of nearly the same desperate hope he'd seen on Lady Dashford. But Julia never let her emotions be displayed for long. Quickly, she looked away, and her face became that passive mask she'd perfected so well. Still, for just a moment, Rastmoor had seen into her soul. She'd been watching him, trusting him.

He would not betray that trust. Not this time.

"No games, Fitzgelder," he warned. "If you know something, then tell us."

"Oh, I know quite a bit, Cousin," Fitzgelder said with a greasy smile, his voice sounding almost like a purr. "Are you so certain you'd like me to share it all?"

"The only thing I'm interested in is locating Mrs. Clemmons," Dashford said, thankfully shifting the topic back to his own concern. "And her child. Do you know where they are?"

"Possibly."

Rastmoor had a few choice words for his cousin, although for the sake of the ladies present, he skipped them in favor of further questioning. "I thought you said you didn't know anything about a child?"

"I don't. But if the chit did end up breeding, I have a fair notion where she'd tuck the brat."

"Tell them," Rastmoor ordered.

Fitzgelder frowned. "And how does this benefit me?"

"I might let you keep breathing," Rastmoor said.

"Not good enough," Fitzgelder said.

"What do you want, Fitzgelder?" Dashford asked. "I can assure you my wife and I will be very grateful should your information prove worthwhile."

Fitzgelder seemed to consider the offer. Rastmoor couldn't quite imagine what in hell the man thought he had to consider, but finally Fitzgelder spoke again.

"Tomorrow," he said.

"What?" Rastmoor asked.

"Tomorrow," Fitzgelder repeated. "I will have the information for you tomorrow. I'm waiting for word from someone; then I can tell you where they are."

"What the hell do you—" Dashford began, but his wife laid her hand against his arm and stopped him.

Rastmoor, however, had no doting wife to check his temper. "What the hell do you need to wait for?" he asked, rising and looming over his cousin. "Tell us where to find Sophie."

"No," Fitzgelder said simply. "I can't. The truth of it is, I won't know where the bloody little wench is until I hear from my man."

Now it made sense. "So you've got someone out hunting her even as we speak. To get that damned locket back, I presume."

"Hunting her? Oh, no, Cousin. It's much easier than that. I've managed to buy myself the one man she'll willingly follow to the ends of the earth—and it ain't you, is it, Clemmons?" Fitzgelder sneered at Julia.

"What the hell are you talking about?" Rastmoor asked.

"He's bringing her—and the locket—right where I want her. And when I get that damned locket, you can have your precious little whore," Fitzgelder said and actually had the nerve to laugh in Rastmoor's face. "Although what you'd do with her I can't imagine. Seems you're content enough with this half of the happy couple you've already got."

His condescending glance toward Julia was hardly necessary. Rastmoor knew what the man was implying, and it was not meant as a compliment. Still, he couldn't help but smile. The bloody bastard fool still thought Julia a man, did he? He obviously hadn't misinterpreted their relationship, but he thought Julia was a ruddy male. That was rich—Fitzgelder had been duped again. The woman deserved an award.

He'd see what he could do about showing his appreciation for her talents. Later.

"What sort of danger have you dragged Sophie into, Fitzgelder?" Dashford asked. "How much has she had to suffer just so you can reclaim this contemptible locket?"

"She'll be fine. Once I've got the locket, you just might be able to make it worth my while to tell you where she is," Fitzgelder said with a smug leer. "I don't care if she does have well-heeled connections or a limp-wristed little husband. That chit owes me."

"No, Cousin," Rastmoor said. "*I* owe you."

Chapter Sixteen

Julia could have done without the tension filling the air and constricting her chest. The longer she stayed here, suffering Fitzgelder's demeaning sneers and probing glances, the more inevitably she'd be found out. Fortunately, the Dashfords were far too distraught over their concerns for Sophie to give her a second thought, but how much longer could that continue? Her nerves were frayed, and it was just a matter of time before she'd forget the role she played and say something or do something to ruin it.

Fitzgelder's conceited posturing didn't help matters, either. If someone didn't shut him up soon, she'd be likely to slap him. Although, from Rastmoor's expression, it appeared he was only too eager to shut the man up—permanently—and Julia knew she really ought not condone that.

"So it would seem you won't have the satisfaction of tossing me out on my ear tonight, Cousin," Fitzgelder said, still smiling at Rastmoor. "I'm sure our gracious host would much rather offer me one of his luxurious beds than run the risk that I might not return with news of his dear Sasha."

"Sophie," several of them corrected together.

Fitzgelder shrugged and turned to Julia. His eyes narrowed. "Of course you are most eager to have the girl returned safely, Clemmons."

Julia nodded.

"Odd that she never mentioned anything about having a child, though," Fitzgelder went on. "Seems the sort of thing a husband ought to know, doesn't it? But then again"—here he turned to Rastmoor—"I suppose every couple has their little secrets. I know my wife—God rest her—certainly hid a few things from me. For a while."

It was something like pure hate that Julia saw in his eyes. Oh, but Fitzgelder must have raged when he realized Kitty had duped him, that they had *all* duped him. He'd made Kitty pay for it, too, just as he'd make Papa pay, if he ever found him. Lord, but Julia prayed she'd find a way to get her letter to him in time.

Fitzgelder turned his attention back to Julia. "Maybe you're not the sort to be bothered by such things, Clemmons, but most men don't enjoy being lied to by their wives. Then again, you don't appear to be like most men, do you? But I suppose my cousin, here, counts that a positive. Just exactly how have you been passing the time while your darling wife has been missing?"

The fool was purposely baiting them. Did he hope to push Julia into revealing herself? Or was he simply reveling in the thrill of humiliating Rastmoor in front of his friends? Likely that. She wouldn't entirely blame Rastmoor if he did defend himself by explaining things, though she truly hoped he wouldn't.

She doubted she'd be so well received by the lord and lady if they learned the truth. She was lucky they were tolerating her even now, after discovering her ruse as Nancini. What must they think of her, of her relationship with Rastmoor?

Surely they'd already had some unpleasant suspicions; now Fitzgelder's words were just fuel on the fire. Indeed, Rastmoor seemed fairly ready to murder the man. His jaw, however, was set, and Julia knew he forced himself to keep quiet. He would not expose their subterfuge, though he must be aching to do so. Did any part of that owe to his concern for her? She was probably a fool for wishing it. He had much at stake on his own; he didn't need to keep quiet simply to protect her.

Either way, though, she was glad he did.

"If there is nothing you can tell us about Sophie," Rastmoor said after drawing a long, calming breath, "then we have no reason to keep you from that borrowed luxurious bed you are so keen to employ."

Dashford took the hint and summoned his butler. "Indeed. I'm sure we are all ready to retire for the evening. I'll have someone take you to your room immediately, Mr. Fitzgelder. And don't worry that you might be disturbed during your rest. I'll see to it my best footmen are placed to keep watch over you. All night."

The butler appeared and was instructed to look after Mr. Fitzgelder. He seemed to quite understand that Dashford's instructions involved more than simply seeing to the man's comfort. Good. Julia would rest easier knowing someone was to guard his every movement. If she found herself able to rest at all.

Dashford also made certain his butler understood that word should be sent to him immediately if any messenger arrived for Fitzgelder. That was also a good thing. The two viscounts would learn anything about Sophie before Fitzgelder did. The unwilling prisoner, of course, grumbled over such treatment, but there was nothing he could do. He'd made it plain he was not interested in being civil, so why should the others waste any further time with him tonight? The footmen appeared, ready to escort him away.

"Your hospitality is too much, my lord," Fitzgelder drawled.

Dashford allowed him a gracious bow. "Oh, but it is the least I can do for such a guest as yourself, Mr. Fitzgelder. Let us hope it is enough."

"For your sake, Fitzgelder," Rastmoor added, "let's hope Mrs. Clemmons is being treated nicely—wherever she is."

Fitzgelder was able to smile at that. "Oh, don't worry on her account. I assure you she's been in very good hands. And so has that lovely little locket."

"That locket—and whatever is inside it—belongs to me," Rastmoor reminded him.

"You have no idea the value of that little bauble, do you?" Fitzgelder said. "None of you do, I'll wager. Ironic. All these years, it's been right under your nose . . . Well, after tomorrow, Rastmoor, if you ask me very nicely, perhaps I'll let you have the bloody thing back. I'll have no need for it."

Nothing more was said as Fitzgelder took his smug leave and let the footmen show him to his room. Julia thought the air in the room was suddenly a bit easier to breathe. Rastmoor, however, seemed little eased at his cousin's exit.

Just what did Fitzgelder mean by all that ramble about the locket's value sitting right under Rastmoor's nose? Nothing, quite likely. Words from Fitzgelder were nothing more than a waste of syllables. It was useless to give credit to anything coming from that man's mouth. She'd be better off to forget him and just be thankful Lord Dashford had such healthy—and menacing—servants.

Lady Dashford seemed to be of the same mind. She glared after Fitzgelder when he left, then turned back to her guests and sighed. She declared herself fatigued and suggested they all make an early evening. Julia could hardly blame her. The poor woman was wed only a matter of days, and yet she'd been invaded by this houseful of troubled strangers. It was a wonder she was putting up with any of them.

Rastmoor readily agreed with his hostess's sentiment and urged Dashford to see to his wife. Dashford, Julia noted, didn't need a second invitation. He bade a good night to Rastmoor and "Mr. Clemmons," tucked his wife's hand in his, and led her away. At the doorway she paused for one quick look back at Julia, and for a moment it seemed she would speak. She didn't, though, and with a silent nod, Lady Dashford followed her husband into the hall.

Julia was relieved. She knew she must be playing a very poor husband indeed to show so little concern for Sophie in the face of Fitzgelder's offensive tone, but she just didn't have it in her to put forth her best performance. She was tired, and the strain of it all was taking a toll.

The sounds of footsteps and human activity faded in the hallway. Once again, she and Rastmoor were alone. Oddly enough, the tension in the room only increased.

"I can't believe no one's separated him from his vitals," Rastmoor said through tightly clenched teeth. "Damn him for what he's done!"

"To your sister? Did he . . . did he hurt her?"

He shook his head. "She claims he's done nothing but court her, although I find that difficult to believe. She's not acting herself."

"Yes, when she found me in the garden she was acting a bit, er, strange."

"Oh? You did nothing to instigate that?"

"Certainly not!"

Rastmoor chuckled at her. "I know. Your tastes lie elsewhere, don't they?" he said, moving to wrap her into his arms.

She wanted to melt into his comforting warmth, but how could she? Fitzgelder was here. He was scheming, plotting, and at any moment he could realize who she was. He could find Papa. She pried herself away.

"I'm worried for what people will think of *your* tastes," she said, glancing around the room, letting her eyes linger on anything but him.

"There's nothing at all wrong with my tastes," he said, not letting her escape him so easily. "How about if we see how you taste tonight?"

He pulled her back into his arms and nuzzled her neck. She felt the warmth of his tongue tracing the edge of her earlobe. She shuddered and desperately tried to remember why she should not be doing this.

"But what if Dashford should find us this way?" she said in feeble argument.

"Dashford is escorting his wife to bed. I highly doubt we'll see either of them until morning."

Yes, he was probably right about that. But what of Papa? She still hadn't sent word to Papa that Fitzgelder was here and had men roaming about. Oh, but she couldn't let herself get so distracted she forgot about Papa, could she?

Then Rastmoor's hands were sliding her coat aside, slipping beneath it to skim the thin fabric of her shirt. His thumb brushed across her nipple, and she felt her body strain against the binding fabric she used to disguise herself. Oh, how she longed to be out of this disguise! But she couldn't . . . not now, not while Papa might be in danger.

"My, but how ancient some of the furnishings are in here," she said, desperate for a distraction that might keep her from being so distracted.

"And how soft the skin is here, just below your ear," Rastmoor was saying as he kissed that very spot.

Oh, bother. However could she think straight while he was doing this to her? She blinked furiously to keep her eyes from sinking shut. Fortunately, her gaze caught on something that did manage to keep her attention.

"Look, that appears to be an old map of the entire estate."

Rastmoor mumbled something but didn't bother to take himself away from the task that occupied him. At this present moment, it seemed he was working his way past her cravat. She swallowed, sighed, and forced her eyes to focus on the map.

"And is that Loveland?" she said, realizing that it, indeed, was.

Yes, the finely drawn map that Dashford had hanging beside his desk showed quite clearly the lay of Hartwood estate. The road to Loveland seemed quite prominent.

"I'll show you far better things than Loveland, my dear," Rastmoor said in a low, rumbling tone. She knew he could very well make good on his promise, too.

Her cravat was askew, and her shirt gaped open. Rastmoor pulled her tightly to him, then hoisted her up to seat her trousered bottom on Dashford's desk. He leaned forward to brush kisses on the heated skin of her chest. She drew a long breath and cursed the tight binding cloth.

"I'm surprised it is so close," she said, her words coming out slurred. "At dinner I assumed it was much farther."

He made no reply to this and seemed to be ignoring her completely. He'd managed to push the tight fabric aside, and at last his lips found the tip of her eager breast. She couldn't help but lean into him, arching her back to present an easier target.

She sighed and was easily lost in the sensation Rastmoor's touch always brought her. His hands moved over her body, and she allowed hers to do the same to him, tugging and untucking his shirt so she could contact his heated skin beneath. He nipped her lightly, and she moaned, gloriously mindless. She reached for his trousers.

He stopped her there, though.

"Careful, my dear. We should save some things for upstairs."

"Upstairs?" she asked.

"Of course. You don't think I mean to tumble you here on Dashford's desk and be done with it, do you?"

"You don't?"

He smiled and gave her a sweet, gentle kiss on her lips. "No. You deserve so much more than that, Julia. I'm going to take you to your bed and keep you there until they send someone to find us."

Oh, but his words reminded her what she ought to be focused on. She didn't want anyone to find them! And indeed, if she didn't do something, Papa would soon turn up here to be found by Fitzgelder. Drat, but she could not afford to spend her night wrapped up with Rastmoor in the soft, expansive bed upstairs. She had to save Papa.

And now that she'd found this map, she stood a chance of doing just that. It was far too late to hope to get her note carried there by Dashford's grooms, but she could find the way herself now. All it would cost her was this one last night with Rastmoor.

Oh, but she hated that. If only they could work around it . . .

"But how can you get into my room upstairs, Anthony?" she said, reaching to toy with the fastenings on his trousers again. "Dashford put guards to keep watch over Fitzgelder. Someone would surely see you."

"Let them. The truth will eventually come out, Julia."

That's what she was afraid of! "It doesn't have to come out, Anthony. No one need ever know about us. We can be discreet. In fact, I've got an idea you might like."

She slid from the desk and went down onto her knees. She'd seen this in that amazing little book she'd found in the library. Indeed, if Sir Cocksure could be believed, this was something highly favored by most gentlemen. She unfastened one side of his fly.

Again, he stopped her. "Good God, Julia!"

She stared up at him, confused by what she heard in his voice. Had she shocked him? Was he disgusted, even?

"Is this what you think I want? You servicing me like some paid-for whore?"

"Shh! Keep your voice low," she said. "You don't want this? But I thought most men—"

And now he was furious. He pulled her up to her feet and glared at her. "What do you know of most men?"

"Well, I, er . . ."

She didn't know what to say. Had she done something wrong? Apparently so. Her gaze flicked back to the map—a reminder of what she should have been doing instead of getting carried away.

Rastmoor was watching her. He growled and stepped away.

"You're right," he said. "We can't be found out. You'd better just get on up to your room. We've got a lot to sort out tomorrow. You need your sleep."

"But we could—"

"No, we can't. This was a bad idea, Julia. Go to your room."

She tried to think of something to say but couldn't. What did one say when something ended that never really existed at all?

"Good night, Anthony."

She gave the map one last look and left the dark, masculine study. Rastmoor said nothing more. She wondered if he realized he'd never see her again. She refused to let herself wonder if he'd care.

* * *

HE WATCHED HER GO. DAMN, BUT HE WANTED TO call her back so badly he physically hurt. And not just because what had started out as a passionate moment had ended. He ached because he knew deep down that what he wanted with Julia could never be. She was making love to him, but her mind was elsewhere. He hadn't known where until he saw that map.

It wasn't just a map of Dashford's estate, but it showed Loveland, as well. Those damn actors were there—that Giuseppe person who brought such a smile to her face. Was he Julia's current lover? No wonder she was so curious about Loveland. Her body might be here, but her heart was there.

She'd made a valiant attempt to cover it, but he'd seen through it. She'd been simply going through the motions with him, hesitant to commit to a night in his arms. Her hopes rested elsewhere, apparently.

Oh, he had no doubt she'd enjoyed their energetic trysts, but tonight's display had been proof that she thought of him as nothing more than just one man in a string of many. Sadly, he had no one to blame but himself. He could have married her three years ago and made sure she belonged to him alone. Now it was too late. Julia had moved on.

But she'd left something behind. Not just the heartbreak and painful memories, but a thin, folded paper. It lay before him on the floor, just where Julia had been. He bent to retrieve it.

God, he wished he hadn't. There, in Julia's own hand, was a note. Addressed to Giuseppe. The words were cryptic, but he could make out the meaning. Julia was warning her love—in French, no less—that she was here and that she was with the "troublesome gentleman from London." He supposed that must refer to him. Did she think by stating it that way her lover would not be jealous?

Well, this lover was very jealous. And troublesome, indeed. He decided to go right after Julia and spend the rest of the night wiping that damn Italian actor out of her mind. But he didn't. What would it gain him? He'd already been with Julia for three days, and still her eyes sparkled when Dashford announced Giuseppe was close by.

If he really did care about her at all, he'd let her sleep tonight. Alone.

"Giuseppe, you damn well better deserve her," he muttered as his eyes fell on the collection of decanters Dashford kept prominently on the table behind the desk.

Thank God for good, stiff libations.

IT WAS FAR TOO BRIGHT THIS MORNING. RASTMOOR'S head ached and his legs felt none too steady. Coming down here to the breakfast room had been a mistake. What on earth made him think food might help? His stomach turned at the mere sight of it there, laid out on the buffet table. No, miserable or not, he should have stayed in bed.

Or better yet, he should never have finished off that bottle of whiskey—all of it. But what else could he do to numb that gnawing agony inside him last night? It had been more than he could bear. He'd as much as declared himself to Julia, and she'd rejected him.

And the worst of it, he couldn't blame her. After the way he'd doubted her, left her, treated her badly, it was no wonder she found it impossible to care for him as she once had. Hell, despite the throbbing in his head and the squinting, blurred vision, he could see it all so clearly. She had loved him once, and he'd betrayed her—by listening to Fitzgelder, of all people! Damn. He deserved the way he felt this morning.

"Good heavens, Anthony," Penelope shouted, stomping into the breakfast room and pounding over to the window. "It's so dark in here! Heavens, I feel like a mole. Let's open these drapes, for goodness' sake."

She actually seemed prepared to do just that. He risked splitting his head in two by speaking to her.

"Do it, and I'll give you the whipping you desperately deserve."

Despite his valiant effort, Penelope was less than deterred.

She continued in her goal, and the drapes were rudely pushed aside, sunlight streaming in. Rastmoor groaned.

"Oh, for pity's sake, Anthony," she said, tsking and clicking her tongue loudly. "You've made yourself bog-headed today, haven't you? Stayed up drinking half the night, no doubt. Likely you dragged poor Mr. Nan . . . er, Clemmons, into your debauchery, too. Shame on you, leading the poor, injured man into your vices, and after you assured him you'd turned over a new leaf! Well, perhaps that explains why there was no answer when I tapped at his door."

"You tapped at his door?" Rastmoor roared. The room took a quick turn around him.

"Yes, but the poor man must be dead to the world. Poor, poor Mr. Clemmons. He might as well be dying up there for all you seem to care. And him about to become my fiancé, and all."

"Good God, he's not about to become your fiancé, Penelope."

"Oh? But you can't expect me to believe what Fitzgelder said about him being already married to Lady Dashford's cousin. He just doesn't seem the type to be married to that girl. Does he?"

Lord, he did not have the strength for this today. What on earth had gotten into Penelope? He never recalled her being so blasted annoying. What could Fitzgelder have possibly done to the girl to turn her into this . . . this raving shrew?

"I thought you wanted me to let you marry Fitzgelder."

Penelope simply shrugged. "I find I don't really like Mr. Fitzgelder anymore. I much prefer Mr. Clemmons. Don't you?"

Hell, yes he preferred Mr. Clemmons. "No. I prefer that you leave off any further talk of fiancés."

"Jealous?"

"What?"

"That I should find someone I wish to marry while you still grieve that actress."

"I'm most certainly not jealous."

Why, by everything holy, couldn't the girl keep her mouth

shut this morning? She seemed particularly unaware of his discomfort and continued. "Pity she had to die, though, wasn't it, Anthony?"

He saw absolutely no need to respond to that whatsoever.

But Penelope went on. "She did die, didn't she, Anthony? I mean, what a miracle it would be if she turned out to still be living somewhere."

The miracle was he didn't turn the little brat over his knee at that point. What a thing to say! What could she be thinking to bring up such a subject? By God, could she actually have an inkling of the truth?

Surely not, not given the way she'd been acting around Julia last night. Lord, but if Mr. Clemmons truly had been a mister, Rastmoor was fairly certain he'd have had to call the bugger out today. Thank heavens he wasn't, and Penelope was just a naive little girl who had no idea the game she was playing.

He rubbed his throbbing head. "You were hardly old enough to know anything about my affairs three years ago, Penelope."

She sniffed. Somehow she managed to do it loudly. "I was fifteen, and I've never been stupid, Anthony. I knew what people whispered about, that you had gone and gotten engaged to a lowly actress. I heard all about how horrible she was to run off with our cousin and then have the nerve to die a few months later."

"Then I should think you'd know enough to put a person like that far from your mind."

"Yes, as should you. Yet you didn't. So I assumed there must be more to the story, more to her."

"Don't assume things, Penelope. It's not wise."

"Assuming as in judgments or as in identities?"

"Either," he replied swiftly. "No more talk of things that are over and done."

"Are they?"

"I said no more, Penelope."

"But Anthony, you don't—"

Her words were interrupted as Lady Dashford came hurrying into the room. She seemed relieved to find them here. She had an odd look of concern on her face.

"Ah, here you are," she said. "Have either of you seen Mr. Clemmons this morning?"

Rastmoor didn't like the sound of that. "No, I haven't."

"I knocked at his door, and he didn't answer," Penelope said.

Lady Dashford merely frowned. "The servants say he is not in there. In fact, I was told it appears his bed has not been slept in. I thought perhaps . . ."

She glanced at Rastmoor then looked away quickly. He had a fair idea what she might have been thinking and was quick to properly inform her.

"The last I saw of Mr. Clemmons was last night, very shortly after our discussion in the study. He took his leave, and I assumed he was retiring for the night."

"Then where on earth could he be?" Penelope asked.

Rastmoor's jaw clenched nearly as tightly as the fists held tightly to his sides. "Fitzgelder."

But Lady Dashford shook her head. "I had the butler check. No one has been in or out of there all night. Mr. Fitzgelder was left quite uninterrupted. Alone."

"Perhaps Mr. Clemmons went for a morning ride?" Penelope suggested.

"But he doesn't know the area," Lady Dashford said. "Wherever would he go?"

Damn, but thanks to that map in the study Mr. Clemmons did have a passing knowledge of the area. Rastmoor suddenly had an idea just where their frustrating Mr. Clemmons might go—and why.

"Has Dashford received word yet from that troupe of actors?" Rastmoor asked.

"I don't know," the viscountess said with a shrug. "But why—"

Penelope broke into an excited little squeal. "Mr. Clemmons has run off with Signor Giuseppe and his Poor Players!"

JULIA SLEPT SURPRISINGLY WELL. OF COURSE, THAT could have been due to the brisk hour-long walk she took to find her way to the little cottage known as Loveland, but she also knew she must credit the surprisingly soft—if not a bit musty—bed she'd curled up in. Indeed, someone had once lived quite luxuriously here.

After leaving Rastmoor last night—a feat that had been far more difficult than it ought to have been—she left Hartwood. It had been easy to leave unseen, as most of the servants had been instructed to keep their eyes open for strangers trying to get into the house or for Fitzgelder trying to get out. As she was neither of these things, she simply strolled out into the garden and kept right on going. That map in the study had been a godsend.

In the darkness of late twilight she'd followed the road confidently until she came upon a fork. That, certainly, had given her a few moments of desperation—it must have been created after the map had been drawn. But panic never solved anything, so she caught her breath and tried to remember where Loveland was in relation to the river that ran the length of the estate.

She chose the correct fork and found Loveland not half a mile down that road. Her feet had not yet begun to ache when she came over the low rise of a gentle slope to see the cottage below. The whitewashed walls shone in the moonlight, and the sweet, damp smells of flowers filled the air around it. Really, with a bit of care, this would be a lovely place. No wonder Papa had thought to camp here. Lucky for them Dashford was kindly allowing them to stay.

Not that they could stay, of course. Not with Fitzgelder at Hartwood and his men prowling with no good intent. And most especially, not with Rastmoor so nearby. More than anything, she needed to leave him far, far behind.

Papa had opened the door immediately to her knocking. He'd seemed hardly surprised to find her and was far more concerned with offering her supper than he was in learning that Fitzgelder was at Hartwood. In fact, he assured her he knew all about it. Well, that was comforting. If he'd known Fitzgelder was there, he must have given an adequate excuse for turning down Dashford's generous offer to hire them for a performance.

"Ma petite chou," he'd said, shoving a bowl of stew and a chunk of bread at her. "It is all taken care of. Now eat, rest. You should be exhausted, coming all this way like that."

The only other female member of their troupe, the matronly Mrs. Maybelle Bixley—although Julia had never heard talk of any Mr. Bixley—fussed over her and nearly shed tears when she saw the state of Julia's hair. She pulled out a brush and set to coaxing out the tangles that had gathered under that blasted hat. Julia had to admit, it was heavenly to be back among her own people. She was free to let down her guard and be who she was. She could speak out loud, even.

But Papa hadn't let her say much. Instead, he enthusiastically filled her in on his exploits these past few days. He'd not led the group to Gloucester as they'd planned, but he'd been just half a day's travel from her all along. As she should have suspected, Papa had been watching out for her this whole time. Thankfully, he didn't mention anything about Rastmoor. She, of course, volunteered nothing.

It had been all too easy to feel safe and secure for the first time in days. She'd let Mrs. Bixley show her to a lovely bedroom—the cottage was surprisingly spacious—and then slipped into her very own night rail, courtesy of the entire collection of their personal belongings the troupe carted from London. Ah, how heavenly! She was sure she fell asleep the moment her head hit that pillow.

And now a new day had dawned, and the sun was shining. Julia stood in the doorway surveying the little, muddy yard in front of the cottage. Birds were singing, and she could almost be convinced that all was right with the world.

Until she caught a glimpse of Papa as he directed two of his young actors as they packed the troupe's belongings into their wagon. Good Lord, what was the man wearing? Her usually elegant father was dressed in blue and purple and orange so bold he appeared to be posing as some exotic bird. Oh dear, but wasn't this the costume he'd used in the past for the Great Giuseppe? Why would he be keeping up this particular masquerade? In half an hour's time they would be gone from this place. Wouldn't it be best if they did nothing to draw attention to themselves as they traveled along, assuming yet another group identity and hiding themselves in another little town?

"Ma petite!" he called when he saw her. "You had a good sleep, *non*?"

"Yes, Papa," she said, coming out to give him an affectionate peck on his cheek. "Thank you, but you shouldn't have let me sleep so long. I should be helping you."

He laughed and squeezed her into his huge, protective embrace. "You have not had enough sleep lately, I think. And besides, you should not be tromping out here, getting your lovely clothes ruined in all this mud. This dress has been lonely for you, *ma belle*. Let the men work while you stay pretty inside. We are nearly finished, anyway."

She had to admit she did enjoy being female again. Mrs. Bixley had pressed one of her favorite morning gowns and helped her into it. It felt wonderful on her body. She'd stolen a peek in a large mirror in the bedroom and then scolded herself for being vain. Then she'd had to scold herself for wishing Anthony could see her like this, garbed in fashionable muslin, freshly bathed with her newly short hair curling in a chestnut halo around her face.

But Rastmoor would never see her again—not if she could help it. She'd done what she could to protect him; now it was time to help Papa. And heavens, but he did need her help. The poor man must have been too long without an audience; he was practically burying her against his blue and purple and orange waistcoat while calling out orders to his actors in the most obnoxious, singsong Italian accent she'd ever heard. Lord, she supposed she ought to be thankful Rastmoor had made her Mr. Nancini mute.

"What on earth are you—" she began with a laugh, only to be cut off by Papa's whispered warning.

"It appears your absence has been noticed, *chouchoute*," he said.

She looked around his shoulder and squinted into the morning sun. Two men on horseback were just coming into view at the top of the hill. It took all of half a heartbeat for her to recognize them: Rastmoor and Dashford. What were they doing here? Oh, but Rastmoor would recognize Papa. Surely, even despite the flamboyant costume of the Great Giuseppe, Rastmoor would know the man who had once hesitantly given him permission to marry his daughter.

"Hurry, into the house, *ma chérie*," Papa instructed into her ear. "No fears. I'll take care of everything. You go inside and help Mrs. Bixley with your portmanteau."

Papa thought she could concentrate on packing when Rastmoor was so near? Just what would Papa say to him? He certainly had never really liked the idea of Julia marrying so far above herself, but he'd allowed the engagement because it made her happy. After things ended as they did, he'd been understandably bitter toward the man who'd broken his daughter's heart. No doubt he knew what must have been going on the past few days.

Oh, but this was dreadful! Papa would surely have more than a few unpleasant words for Rastmoor. They would argue, fight even. Dashford would learn who she was, things would all get out of hand, and no one would remember to run away and hide before Fitzgelder's men found them.

But Papa wasn't the only actor in the family, was he? Maybe if she hurried, she could salvage something from this. She kissed Papa lightly, then scurried into the house and set to finding Mrs. Bixley. And her portmanteau.

Chapter Seventeen

“I hope you remember to ask your bloody friend a few questions,” Dashford was saying as their horses clopped along the muddy roads. “Before you leap down and bludgeon him to death.”

“I have no intention of bludgeoning him,” Rastmoor said.

“Truly? That’s not what that storm cloud over your head seems to say. You’ve had murder in your eyes since the minute we left Hartwood.”

“It’s not Clemmons I’d consider murdering.”

“Giuseppe, then?”

Rastmoor rewarded his friend’s astuteness with a grunt.

Dashford shrugged. “That note would seem to convict them both.”

Indeed, it did, though not for the things Dashford assumed. He seemed to believe Julia’s note to Giuseppe indicated more than just an *affaire de coeur*. Dashford’s assumption was that Julia’s intercepted note to Giuseppe implied they both knew something about the missing Sophie. Well, of course Rastmoor knew the young woman Julia referred to in the note was herself, but he hadn’t figured out a way to convince Dashford without explaining the whole ruse. Julia and her lover were innocent of those charges. Still, Rastmoor didn't mind letting Dashford think what he would. He did rather like the idea of his friend making plenty of trouble for the unsuspecting Italian.

"I don't know exactly what this Clemmons fellow means to you," Dashford went on. "But I don't like him. I don't think he's precisely what he appears to be."

"He's not."

"Then what are you doing with him?" Dashford asked. "I mean, er, I don't really care what you do with him, but I do care that he's using your friendship against you."

"He's not."

"Oh? Then what in the devil is he doing?"

Blast it all, but Rastmoor didn't have an answer. Well, he did have an answer, but not one he could share with Dashford. He knew exactly what the devil Julia was doing. She was running off with Giuseppe. Despite what Dashford might assume, this had nothing to do with Sophie. Confronting Giuseppe would bring them no closer to finding Dashford's missing cousin. Rastmoor wasn't quite sure how to break this news to his determined friend.

"And it's theater folk again," his friend muttered. "I just hope this doesn't turn out like that fiasco three years ago—with that actress."

Rastmoor heard him plain enough. He understood, too. A warning bell rang out in his brain. If Dashford were to start piecing things together, things would not go well for Julia.

"If I thought for one minute *these* actors had anything to do with *those* actors, I'd have them booted from my lands and shipped back to the damn Continent. That little trollop forced her pretty hands down deep in your pockets then ripped out your heart. I promise you, Anthony, I'll not stand by to watch that again."

"This is nothing like that."

"Oh? You mean other than the fact that Clemmons is an actor rather than an actress?"

"You have no idea what's really going on here."

"I have eyes in my head, Anthony," Dashford declared. "I see how you look at him. Now, it's not my place to judge where you put your affections—or anything else—but in this case . . ."

"It's not like that!"

"Then what is it like? Is it like last time when you actually planned to marry that lying, traitorous little whor—"

Rastmoor found himself swinging a fist at his friend's face. Dashford ducked. His horse shied and sidestepped, while Rastmoor's mount balked at the way he'd tightened the reins. Rastmoor barely caught himself from falling off. The momentary distraction gave him enough time to realize he'd been about to leap from his saddle and yank Dashford to the ground for a thorough pummeling. He decided not to.

"What the hell was that for?" Dashford demanded.

"She's not a whore!"

"What? Oh, for God's sake, Rastmoor. That was three years ago. I distinctly recall you had more than a few colorful words to describe her yourself. Since when are you defending the worthless jade?"

"Since I learned a few things. And she's *not* a worthless jade."

"You mean she *wasn't* a worthless jade."

"Yes. Right. That's what I said."

"No, you didn't."

"Then I misspoke."

"Did you?"

"Of course."

But he was not nearly the actor Julia always was. His words sounded unconvincing even to himself. Surely Dashford would be able to deduce the truth, and then where would things stand? Despite the woman running away to this Giuseppe person, despite everything that note implied, despite those three long years between them, Rastmoor was not about to lose Julia again. He didn't particularly relish the thought of losing his oldest and dearest friend, either. How would Dashford react when he realized the truth?

He'd been an absolute fool to let his friend accompany

him on the ride to Loveland. What did he think he'd do once they got there and found Julia in the arms of her bloody actor friend? Hell, there'd be no keeping anything from Dashford at that point. The best thing to do right now was to come up with some brilliant excuse to send Dashford back to Hartwood.

Unfortunately, he was coming up empty on brilliant excuses. There was nothing to do but hold his breath and cringe as Loveland came into view just as they crested the last gentle hill. It took Rastmoor all of about two seconds to spot her. How could he miss her?

She was right there in the yard before the rustic cottage, snuggled up nice and tight with some bloody actor dressed like a bloody peacock. Two or three bloody others were scurrying about the two bloody wagons that sat waiting. It would appear the group was expecting to depart within mere moments. Despite Dashford's presence, Rastmoor was glad they'd made it when they did. A few minutes later, and they might have missed Julia altogether.

Damn, but could he have come that close? And double damn, but did she have to seem so comfortable there in that fellow's arms? Clearly any faint hope Rastmoor may have had that Giuseppe was nothing more than a passing fancy were completely in vain. Julia seemed more than happy to be with him.

Well, he'd just have to convince her she could be happier with *him*. He took a deep breath and made sure his shoulders were back. The cut of his coat was perfect, and he'd allowed Dashford's valet to adjust the pitiful cravat he'd attempted while the world was still spinning around him this morning. At the very least he could take comfort in knowing he looked a fair sight better than Julia's bloody peacock.

She hardly seemed impressed, though. She glanced up to see them, and joy was not exactly what Rastmoor could see in her face. Panic was more like it.

With a few hushed words to her lover, she gave him a disgusting buss on his cheek then ran inside the cottage. It was awful, and Rastmoor really wished he hadn't seen it. Hell, he wished Dashford hadn't seen it, either.

"What the . . . Who is that?" Dashford asked.

"Who?"

"That woman," Dashford said, nodding in the direction she had just gone. "By God, she looked like our man Clemmons . . . in a dress."

"It wasn't Clemmons."

"It looked like Clemmons."

"It *wasn't* Clemmons."

Dashford shook his head, clearly confused by the whole thing. "I suppose you're right. Clemmons would never look so damn delicious in a dress."

Rastmoor ground his teeth. He'd be damned if he was going to put up with Dashford drooling over an anonymous Julia; even if she did look so damn delicious in a dress.

"I'm sure a certain Lady Dashford would appreciate it if you confined your appetite to more domestic fare," Rastmoor reminded him.

Dashford merely laughed and got to the business at hand. "Hey, there!" he called out as they approached. "Which one of you fine men is the Great Giuseppe?"

The damn blackguard whose hands had been all over Julia replied. "*Si,* signore! I am-a zee Great Giuseppe, here to be at-a your service!"

By God, the man's accent was deplorable. If Rastmoor didn't already hate him, he'd certainly be halfway there already. He didn't bother to climb off his horse, content to stare intimidatingly down instead. Giuseppe, to his credit, didn't appear much intimidated. In fact, he moved to stand near Rastmoor and smiled boldly right up at him.

It was then that Rastmoor recognized him. *Albert St. Clement.* Oh, hell and double hell. This wasn't Julia's lover, it was her father!

Despite the fact that this man very likely would love to kill him, Rastmoor was suddenly overjoyed to see him. He was exceedingly and ridiculously overjoyed, as a matter of fact. He also was quite glad he'd not gotten down from his horse. There may still be need for a hasty retreat should Julia's father turn out to have any ready weapons. She'd had ample time to inform him what had been going on these past several days.

"*Buon giorno*, gentlemen!" St. Clement greeted, waving his arms in grand gestures. "You have-a heard of zee Great Giuseppe and have come-a to see for yourselves? Ah, perhaps you have wish-a to join with zee famous *compagni del teatro, si*? I know exactly the parts I would have you play! You, sir," he said with a flourish toward Dashford. "You are *il capitano*! Yes, I see it clearly—very brave. And you, signore," he said, turning to Rastmoor with an even brighter smile. "My Pantalone!"

Rastmoor glared. "Happily, sir, I am most definitely *not* your Pantalone."

"Regrettably, we are not here to join your troupe, Signor Giuseppe," Dashford said before St. Clement had the chance to heap on yet more insult. "I'm Dashford. You've agreed to come to my home for an impromptu performance today, I believe. We have some ladies who are most eager for pleasant diversion."

St. Clement cocked an eyebrow and leered at Rastmoor. "Ah? Two *vigorosi* as yourselves, and you can't-a give *molto diversione* for your ladies? For shame. But you ask Giuseppe to assist, and I accept zee very gracious invitation. See? My *compagni* are already preparing to go-a to your home, signore."

"Wonderful," Dashford said, seemingly oblivious to the embarrassingly crude caricature St. Clement was creating. In fact, Dashford got right to business, remembering what brought them out here in the first place.

"But you wouldn't by any chance have run into an old friend of yours here recently, would you?"

St. Clement made a dramatic frown. "Old friend? But who has need of zee old-a friends when he can make-a zee new friends like yourselves, eh?"

"You're too kind. But a young actor named Clemmons was recently a guest in my home," Dashford explained. "I believe he said he knows you. Have you seen him?"

St. Clement pretended to give the matter deep thought. "Ah, Clemmons . . . yes, I think I know him! He played in-a

Romeo and Juliet one year." Now St. Clement gave Rastmoor a meaningful glare. "I especially like-a zee part when Signor Romeo he died."

"You would," Rastmoor grumbled.

"But have you seen him recently?" Dashford asked. "He hasn't shown up here?"

"Here?" St. Clement repeated. "No one is here but my humble players, signore. As you see, we are busy getting zee wagons ready to go to your home. You are so very kind to let us stay in your most charming-a cottage last-a night."

"And you haven't seen Clemmons?"

"There is no one here zat is called Clemmons, signore. Just my simple band of players. So, finish your morning ride, and we'll see you for our performance after zee little while. Bye-bye, now. *Arrivederci!*"

Clearly St. Clement was trying to be rid of them. Rastmoor couldn't blame the man. In his position, he'd likely do the same. But he wasn't in that position; he was determined to find Julia, and no overly protective father was going to stand in his way.

Well, at least not figuratively. In actuality, St. Clement was standing in his way. He nudged his horse to move away, but St. Clement carefully compensated and kept himself very securely positioned right between Rastmoor and the cottage.

Indeed, if he was going to get to Julia, he'd have to pass through the very substantial St. Clement. It was obvious he had no intentions of letting Rastmoor so much as lay eyes on Julia again. The minute he and Dashford were out of sight, St. Clement would gather his troupe—and his daughter—and be off in another direction. Well, this was simply unacceptable.

Rastmoor loved Julia. Nothing was going to deter him from seeing her again, not angry fathers, long-standing friendships, or even bad acting. He was just calculating the distance between his horse and the front door of the cottage when everything changed. The cottage door opened, and there was Julia, tripping lightly out into the yard in full view of everyone. Rastmoor's mouth dropped open.

She was utterly beautiful.

Gone was the ill-fitting men's clothing. Gone was the rumpled hat she'd been wearing. Gone was every shred of the awkward Mr. Clemmons. Instead, before them all was the captivating form of a stunning young woman.

She wore a flowing gown of sprigged muslin, the color of new grass and as fresh as a Sunday morning. Her crisp bonnet was trimmed with lilac and ivy, while her cropped hair haloed her face with chestnut curls. A velvet ribbon went around her throat, drawing far too much attention to the graceful rise of her neck and delicate curve of her shoulders. Two precious mounds of ivory flesh bulged at the neckline of her bodice, just enough to torment him and not nearly enough to satisfy.

The gentle morning breeze tossed her skirts about her slight ankles as she made her way in velvet slippers quickly toward the group at the cart. An older woman followed behind her, but even in a garish burgundy gown and outrageously feathered turban, she was practically invisible beside Julia's perfection. The men in the yard seemed frozen in place as all eyes followed the presumably unintentional sway of Julia's hips. Her nut brown eyes were bright, and her smile was as innocent and guileless as a newborn babe.

By God, no wonder he was still her hopeless slave after all they'd been through.

"Here I am, Monsieur Giuseppe," she said with a lilting French accent. "*Mon Dieu*, have I made us late again? *Je regrette*, but this gown, it is too awful and . . ."

Her eyes locked on to Rastmoor as if she were only just now aware of his presence. He knew it was an act, but he simply couldn't help but ignore that fact when her face broke into a glorious smile. Lord, but his chest got tight when she looked at him that way.

Trousers, too.

"Why, *sacre bleu*! If it isn't zee Lord Rastmoor!" she exclaimed with a delicate squeal. "*Quelle surprise!*"

The turbaned companion was right at her side and spoke up before Rastmoor had a chance to so much as form a thought.

"Is this gentleman one of your admirers, Mademoiselle Mignonet?" the older woman asked.

Rastmoor frowned. *Mignonette?* So she was still not Julia but calling herself Mignonette now? He decided to keep his mouth shut until he had a better idea what the vixen was up to.

"Oui!" Julia said, her voice a luscious coo as she batted her lashes and smiled coyly. "Dear Rastmoor has admired my talents for quite some time."

No argument there. But what was she doing? It appeared St. Clement was in the dark regarding her new persona every bit as much as Rastmoor was. The older man cleared his throat and pinned Julia with a glare that implied warning. Papa did *not* approve. Blast it, but what was the girl up to?

"If mademoiselle might recall," St. Clement told her sharply, "we are expected for a performance today. You can let *il signore* go back to admiring you later."

"And look, he has a friend!" the burgundy lady remarked with a broad grin.

Julia glided toward the wagons being loaded in the yard. "Ah, but this is the only one I am looking at right now."

Then she leaned in to whisper to her companion, something that made the older woman giggle. One of the actors milling about helped Julia up into the waiting cart, but the older woman seemed to have forgotten something and trotted back into the cottage. Julia tucked and primped her skirts around her as she settled into a seat, all the while paying no mind to her fuming father. She did, however, keep her coy smile aimed right at Rastmoor.

She batted her eyes and beamed at him across the muddy yard. To his shame, he was helpless to respond in any of the ways he probably should have responded. Instead, he was clearly responding in ways he shouldn't.

The lilting voice went on. "Ah, *mon chéri*, you have come all ze way out to here for me? So *romantique*! But *quelle dommage*; I cannot leave Monsieur Giuseppe. *Non*, he has been too good to me."

"Has he, now?" Rastmoor muttered, letting his gaze roam over her delightful figure, only slightly regretting the lack of trousers that had previously flaunted her long legs. What the gown concealed in the lower areas, though, it easily made up for in the top. His eyes ate up every inch of her and only longed for more.

She paid him no mind and pressed her delicate white hand against her forehead, giving out a grand sigh. "Poor, poor Rastmoor. It is *très tragique, oui*, but you must learn to survive without me, *chouchou. Mais*, we will always have our memories, *non*?"

To be honest, Rastmoor wasn't entirely sure what she was talking about. All he knew was he did, indeed, have some rather vivid memories of Julia. *Very* vivid indeed. He would have loved to forget just about everything else, as a matter of fact, but slowly he recalled that he and Julia were not alone here, and that her very charming demeanor just now was merely an act.

Dashford was watching them with marked curiosity.

"So, this is another one of your actresses?" the man had the nerve to ask. Loudly.

Rastmoor winced, and Julia frowned, of course.

"What? Does he imply zere are others?" she asked with dramatic affectation. "But *mon chére* Rastmoor, you tell me I am zee only one!"

"How awkward," Dashford said. "What with Giuseppe mucking about, and all. And Clemmons, too, of course."

Julia frowned again. "But as monsieur has said, we have not seen Mr. Clemmons. Why on earth would you think he is here now?"

"Because he was trying to send a message here last night, and now he's gone missing," Dashford said. "We'd be ever so glad if you could produce him just now."

"But we can't!" Julia said quickly, minus a bit of the treacle-sweet accent.

"Clemmons is not here, sir," St. Clement said, cutting her off. "If he was trying to contact us, we've heard nothing."

Dashford studied him for a moment. "Haven't you?"

Julia nodded earnestly and batted her thick eyelashes. "*Non,* monsieur, we have heard nothing."

Suddenly, they all heard something. A gunshot. It rang

out loudly, an echoing crack from somewhere nearby. Julia shrieked.

"Well, *that* certainly sounded like something," Dashford said.

"IT CAME FROM INSIDE THE COTTAGE," RASTMOOR said.

Thank God Julia was right out here before him, or else he would have been tempted to panic right then. As it was, Dashford seemed a bit concerned by the unexpected gunfire. Then again, so did everyone else. Indeed, that must mean whoever was in there shooting was not exactly authorized to do so.

That must mean it had something to do with Fitzgelder.

"Damn it," Rastmoor muttered as he and Dashford instinctively leapt from their mounts and took off toward the cottage.

"Clemmons?" Dashford asked, sending him a worried glance.

Rastmoor wasn't certain if his friend was suggesting Clemmons was the shooter or the shootee, but either way he shook his head. "No."

"Fitzgelder." Dashford's words were a statement rather than a question. Rastmoor agreed.

He did not, however, agree with what he noticed behind him. Julia was there, trotting along beside her father as the whole group from the yard rushed toward the cottage. By God, what was the woman thinking? Someone in there was unexpectedly shooting! She ought to be running the other way, the suicidal ninny.

He purposely stopped in his tracks. She crashed into him from behind. It was not altogether an unpleasant experience.

Rastmoor took full advantage of her momentary loss of balance. He rounded on her, taking hold of her soft, slender shoulders, quite determined not to let go any time soon. He willed her into meeting his eyes.

"Where do you think you're going?" he asked.

She blinked in surprise. Did she honestly think he'd just

stand by and let her run into a house with random gunfire? She obviously didn't know him very well.

"Stay out here, where it's safe," he ordered. He could see plainly she had no intention of obeying.

Especially when the next noise they heard was loud, feminine screeching coming from the same general direction as the gunshot.

"Mrs. Bixley!" she exclaimed and nearly shook herself free from Rastmoor's grip.

Now, he had no clue who this Mrs. Bixley was, but if she was important to Julia and if she was in mortal danger, he knew, of course, Julia would not let a little thing like his demands keep her from rushing in there. Julia would be joining them indoors.

"Damnation," he said and released his hold on her shoulders. "Very well, come with me. But stay behind me."

Fortunately, there hadn't appeared to be any repeat of the gunfire, and as they drew closer to the house, it was obvious the screeching was not the weakening death cry of some helpless victim. It was, he quickly realized, the angry scolding of an angry woman. She certainly did not sound as if her life was in any immediate danger. Now, whoever she was yelling at, however . . .

The good thing about having taken that pause to make his vain attempt to keep Julia from rushing into the cottage was that now they were well and safely behind the others. Dashford led the way in through the front door, St. Clement followed, then came two actors before Rastmoor and Julia at last made it into the building. The screeching had stopped, and the ancient cottage resounded with footsteps clomping up the staircase. Rastmoor fell into step, careful to keep himself directly in front of Julia should their mysterious shooter suddenly appear from above.

He didn't really expect that he'd particularly enjoy being shot, but he knew he'd enjoy the alternative much less. Having already lost Julia once through betrayal, once through death, and once to the imaginary Giuseppe this morning, he was in no hurry to lose her to a crazed gunman right now. Besides, in that god-awful peacock coat, St. Clement made a much more obvious target.

He trailed the group of concerned men into what he recognized as the master bedroom of the home. As expected, there was a fuming woman in there, foot tapping and fists dug into her hips. She was none other than the burgundy nightmare from earlier. Her anger, it appeared, was directed toward a middle-aged man who stood across from her. He was the one holding the gun.

"What the devil?" St. Clement shouted in a voice that was surprisingly—and blessedly—devoid of Italian accent.

"He's tearing up the bloody house!" the woman shrieked.

Her clothes made St. Clement's seem pale in comparison, and a wilted ostrich feather bobbed in her turban. She was not altogether an unattractive woman of a certain age, though by her wardrobe it appeared she'd worked hard to conceal that. Rastmoor wondered what part she was supposed to be playing. He watched St. Clement carefully for anything he might learn from the man's expression, but it turned out to be a waste of time. The only hint of emotion on St. Clement's face was a slight quirk to his left eyebrow. Rastmoor decided he'd have to categorize that as a display of mild curiosity.

Well, at least that indicated St. Clement felt the danger here was minimal. Rastmoor could stand relieved that his chances of taking a lead ball while throwing himself in front of Julia were slim. He appreciated those odds. Still, it did all leave him a bit confused. What on earth was going on?

The ostrich feather flounced violently as the turbaned woman graciously enlightened them all. "This damn fool sneaks in here while the rest of us was out in the front. He thinks no one sees him, but I do. I see him and follow him up here, whoever the hell he is. He comes in here and goes to ripping out those floorboards! I swear, I told him not to."

"Of course you did, Mrs. Bixley," St. Clement said in a remarkably soothing voice.

She was not soothed. "I told him there'd be hell to pay if he didn't stop, but I guess he thought it was just fine that we'd be the ones getting in trouble for his mischief, the useless jackanapes. He wouldn't pay me no mind. He just went on yanking up those boards, and then he pulls out that bloody pistol and starts shooting at something he finds under there!"

An odd story, yet indeed, someone had quite truly ripped out several floorboards just near the foot of the bed. A shame, really. The cottage may be in need of certain repairs, but overall it still held quite a bit of charm. Dashford could not be pleased to find it so rudely vandalized. What must this mutton-headed gunman be thinking to make such a mess, right in broad daylight?

Rastmoor watched him. Like St. Clement, the puzzling housebreaker showed very little emotion. If anything, he seemed nothing more than peeved by the woman's ranting. Odd, considering that if she was to be believed, then he would soon find himself in a good deal of trouble. At any rate, it appeared he had just the one gun. Plus, he was thoroughly outnumbered. If he did get peeved enough by the accusations that he suddenly developed the urge to reload and put the ostrich feather out of its obvious misery, he'd be taken down long before a second shot could ring out.

"What in God's name do you think you're doing here?" Dashford asked, taking a step closer to the gunman and examining the hole in his floor.

The gunman glanced from Dashford to St. Clement and raised his eyebrows as if in question. St. Clement sighed.

"This is his lordship, Dashford," he said with a casual nod in Dashford's direction.

The gunman seemed to understand and nodded in reply. Still, he said nothing.

The turbaned woman made up for his silence. "I swear, it wasn't none of our troupe that did that there, my lord, sir. We're respectable people, we are. I don't know who this ruffian is or what he's trying to accomplish, but he's got nothing to do with us, and that's a fact."

No, it wasn't. Rastmoor had been witnessing a very telling display of silent communication between St. Clement and the other man. He had no clue what any of it meant, of course, but the nods, eye movements, and subtle gestures the two were making could not possibly be misinterpreted. They most certainly *did* have something to do with each other.

Dashford crossed his arms over his chest and glared at the gunman. "It's the treasure, isn't it?"

Aha! A trace of recognition stole across the man's face. So Dashford had struck a nerve, had he? Well, the fool ripping up the floor would be in for some disappointment. Rastmoor knew something about treasure.

Apparently Julia did not. "Treasure?" she asked.

If Dashford noticed the fact that she, too, was suddenly minus one ridiculous accent, he gave no indication. Instead, he chuckled. "The Loveland treasure, Miss, er, Mignonette. Surely you've heard of it?"

She shook her head. Great. Dashford just loved telling the story of his grandfather's mistress who'd been installed here at Loveland years ago and the rumors that had circulated for decades about a treasure hidden nearby. No doubt they'd all be forced to listen to it. Again.

"There've been stories around the countryside for years that some magnificent treasure was hidden here by smugglers," Dashford said, thankfully giving them the shortened version of the tale. "But I'm sorry to tell you we've once and for all put that rumor to rest. What treasure there was has already been discovered."

Now, that brought actual surprise to the gunman's features, while both of St. Clement's eyebrows twitched. Julia seemed no more shocked or confused than she already had been. Rastmoor decided that was a good sign. He'd remember to point it out to Dashford if his friend took it upon himself to prosecute the looters.

"You mean to say this fool is up here trying to steal treasure that's already long gone?" the older woman asked with a self-righteous sneer, her feather dancing overhead.

"Yes, unfortunately. That poor floorboard has suffered in vain," Dashford replied.

"The treasure's been found?" St. Clement asked. "How? By whom? And where is it now?"

Now Julia appeared somewhat more surprised. She completely forgot herself and turned to gape at her father. "Papa? You knew about this treasure?"

This time it was Dashford's turn to appear surprised. He refocused his gaze from the men onto Julia. "*Papa?* You mean Signor Giuseppe is your father?"

No one replied, so Dashford turned to St. Clement. "You're not really Giuseppe, are you?"

No one replied to that, either, so the man with the gun spoke up. "Who the hell is Giuseppe?"

St. Clement groaned and rolled his eyes. Whatever game the men—and Julia—had been playing was clearly not well-organized. It was falling apart right before their eyes. Rastmoor wondered just exactly what he'd learn as he watched it unravel. Then again, perhaps he ought to think of what Dashford would learn as things unraveled. All it would take was one person, one actor or one feather-headed matron, to call Julia by her real name, and Dashford would figure it all out.

He'd probably try to rescue Rastmoor from his own stupidity by having St. Clement's whole bloody troupe—Julia included—incarcerated for housebreaking and vandalism. Rastmoor didn't relish trying to untangle that mess. It seemed that the best thing to do, under the circumstances, was to take sides with the woman in the turban.

"I think it's obvious our housebreaker here doesn't even know these good people," Rastmoor announced. "Perhaps now that he knows the treasure is gone, he'll apologize for all the trouble and make the appropriate repairs to the floor. Then no harm done, right?"

"But it's not gone," the man said simply. "It's right here."

He pointed down into the hole he'd made in the floor. Hell. This was certainly going to slow down the process of extricating Julia from the muddle. He had a fair notion the only thing to be breaking loose any time soon was, well, *all hell.*

Chapter Eighteen

What in heaven's name was treasure doing buried under Dashford's abandoned floorboards? More importantly, how on earth did Papa know about it?

Oh yes, Julia had no doubt Papa knew about that treasure. Whether that was a part of his motivation to come here or whether he really had made his way to Loveland in an effort to be near her, she wasn't entirely certain. She'd like to believe it was the latter, but something about the glances he'd been shooting back and forth between that strange man with the pistol gave her doubt.

She recognized the man. She didn't know his name, but she'd seen him. Not quite two weeks ago, in fact. She'd seen him with Papa outside the home where they'd stayed in Oxford before their disastrous visit to London. She'd asked about the man—they'd seemed so deep in conversation and so hushed in their tones—but Papa explained he was merely an actor looking for work. She'd thought nothing more of it, although now she realized it had been precisely after that meeting that Papa had announced they'd be stopping in London before going on to an engagement in Gloucester.

Now, she'd never claimed to be a scholar of geography, but she knew enough to recognize that London was not anywhere near the route they would normally take from Oxford to Gloucester. It was, in fact, quite the opposite direction. Clearly their trip had not been a simple little detour.

What had this man said to Papa to make him divert their whole troupe as he had? Given how tight their finances had been lately, she couldn't deny the mention of treasure might have done the trick. Had Papa been plotting something with this reckless vandal all along? But why go to London—where they'd accidentally encountered Fitzgelder and been forced to embark on this recent debacle—instead of coming directly here?

She couldn't make sense of it. If only she had the opportunity to ask him. It was plain to see, however, that Lord Dashford was not about to allow for private conversation. His lordship eyed them all with heavy suspicion. That hole in his floor did not make him happy, nor was he glad to see a stranger reach into said hole and pull out a fairly large metal box: a metal box that gave every impression of being built to hold—and protect—a treasure.

She looked up at Rastmoor and found his eyes. He leaned toward her.

"You didn't know about this, did you?" he whispered.

She shook her head. Would he believe her? She wasn't sure. He turned back to the scene before them and watched as the metal box was brought into full view.

"Hand that here," Dashford directed.

The man glared from Dashford to Papa. Oddly enough, Papa nodded. The man seemed displeased by that but nodded in return. Grumbling, he relinquished the box. Dashford seemed to be doing his own grumbling, but he took the box and placed it on the washstand beside him for study.

"What's in it?" he asked.

"Honestly, I don't know," the man replied.

Julia wondered if Papa could say the same. His face was unreadable, which usually meant he was hiding something. But what?

"How does it open?" Dashford questioned after a moment or two of looking at the box from various angles and frowning.

Julia leaned closer to try to see, but Rastmoor was blocking her view. The more she tried to see around him, the more he seemed to stand in front of her. Drat the man! Did he think she would attempt to steal the treasure right out from under the noses of Dashford and all these gold-hungry men? Ridiculous.

She was not even convinced there really *was* a treasure. The man with the pistol, for instance, didn't seem the least concerned about Dashford's inquisition or the eager eyes leering at him. He simply shrugged. "You need keys," he announced. "Two of them—specially made." Before anyone could ask, he continued. "I don't have them."

"Who does?" Rastmoor demanded. He looked directly at Papa.

The room was silent. So was Papa. Julia could feel the tension starting to mount. If there really *was* treasure in that box, and someone here really *did* have the keys to open it, then something was clearly just about to happen. And it would probably not be good for Dashford. Even with Rastmoor to back him up, the man was hopelessly outnumbered.

Oh, what on earth had Papa gotten involved in?

"I don't know who has them," the man replied smoothly. "That's why I tried to shoot it open. Didn't work."

"Idiot," Papa grumbled. "You could have damaged it."

"Where are the keys?" Dashford repeated.

"I don't know!" the man snapped. "They may have changed hands over the years."

"But you have a reasonable idea that you can find them, don't you?" Dashford asked.

The man merely gave an unconvincing shrug, so Dashford continued. "Unless perhaps you plan to take a hammer to it and risk destroying whatever is inside. Hmm, perhaps we should do that right now?"

"No!" both the gunman and Papa chimed together.

Well, that answered one question. Papa obviously knew

what was inside, or at least he seemed to have a good idea what might be there. Botheration, why had he not told her he'd learned of a treasure hidden in an abandoned cottage? Heavens, if she'd known, perhaps she could have done more to keep Rastmoor and Dashford from finding them here.

"I think you should do it, Dash," Rastmoor said. "Surely we can find something heavy around here to bash it. It's your house, so whatever's in that box is yours, too."

Dashford contemplated this. "Actually, it's my wife's. This house—and everything in it—rightfully belongs to her. I should probably take this back to Hartwood so we can bash it open in her presence."

"Yes, excellent idea," Rastmoor agreed.

Julia did not agree. The dark look the gunman was sending to Papa hinted that he, also, did not agree. Rightful owner or not, it was obvious he had no intention of letting Dashford take the treasure and leave. But just what lengths would he go to in order to get the box away from Dashford? And would Papa help him? Lord, she hoped not! The law did not look favorably upon commoners who acted with violence against the peerage.

Dashford let the tension in the room build for just another heartbeat, then he tucked the box under his arm and straightened his coat. "Well, Rastmoor, shall we be off, then?"

"No!" the man shouted.

Things happened quickly. Before Julia even had time to blink, the man had leapt past Dashford and was grabbing poor Mrs. Bixley. Something flashed at her throat. Good heavens! The man had a knife!

"Stop, or she starts bleeding," the man warned as Rastmoor and Dashford together turned on him.

Thankfully, they stopped. Mrs. Bixley was wide-eyed and shocked into silence. That in itself was alarming. Julia had never known the woman to be silent. Ever.

"No!" Papa suddenly bellowed.

Julia jolted. So did the others. She glanced around the room, taking in the range of emotion swirling around. There was desperation in the eyes of the man with the knife, fear on Mrs. Bixley's face, and an eager anticipation on the two actors who had accompanied them. Dashford seemed tense and ready to move, while Rastmoor was deadly calm. She noticed that he'd managed to slide himself between her and the others—again—and she wondered if perhaps she'd been too hasty to interpret that as mistrust on his part.

Could it be, rather, that he was protecting her? That was kind of sweet, actually. What a pity this was hardly the time for her to revel in such a show of affection.

"Enough violence," Papa announced, glaring ice at the man with the knife. "What the hell do you think you're doing? Release her this instant!"

"But he's going to take the box!" the man protested.

"Let him bloody have it!" Mrs. Bixley wheezed, obviously somewhat recovered from her initial shock.

"It's not worth this," Papa went on.

"It is! You don't know, but I need it. I need all of it," the man declared.

"The only thing you're getting is a visit to the hangman if you cause that woman any injury whatsoever," Dashford said.

"That, and I'll give you a swift kick in the gooseberries," Mrs. Bixley assured her captor.

Papa sighed. "She'll do it; trust me. Just let her go and give it up."

"What, so he can bash it open? You think I'm going to let that happen? You know good and well it will be useless if he destroys it."

Papa sighed again. "I know. I won't let that happen. Lord Dashford, if you will refrain from bashing the box, I will tell you who has the keys."

"No!" the man protested.

His hands fell limp to his sides, and the knife clattered to the floor. Mrs. Bixley stood motionless for half a second, then quickly made good her word and nailed her attacker with a swift kick to the, er, gooseberries. He crumpled to the floor.

"That'll teach you, worthless mongrel!" she said over her shoulder as she scurried to stand beside Papa.

Dashford kicked the knife to Rastmoor who scooped it

up, lest anyone else get ideas. Julia let herself relax, but only slightly. The danger seemed momentarily averted, but there was still an awful lot she did not understand.

"All right, then," Dashford said. "I won't bash the box. But I need some answers! To start with, tell me who has the keys."

The man on the floor moaned. Julia didn't think it was entirely due to his injury. The greedy thing, he really did not want Papa to give up so easily.

"One belongs to an actress, my lord," Papa said, his silly, affected accent long gone. In fact, the only vestige left of Signor Giuseppe was, well, his vestment. Other than the insufferable clothing, Papa was very much his old self. No one seemed the least interested in this recent transformation, however.

"Which actress?" Rastmoor asked.

"Julia St. Clement," Papa replied with just the hint of an ironic smile.

"Hellfire," Dashford swore. "She's been dead three years! Her bloody husband likely took everything she left and sold it."

Julia was no less surprised than the others, though obviously for other reasons. What was Papa talking about? She didn't own any mysterious key. He must be fabricating this simply to buy some time. Good grief, was he planning to cross Dashford? She'd love to tell him that was likely not a very good idea.

She glanced at Rastmoor. No surprise, he was eyeing her with a questioning quirk in his brow. She spared him a slight, confused shrug. He turned back to Papa.

"Who's got the other key, damn it?" Rastmoor asked.

Papa winced. "Well, I'm afraid that gets a little bit tricky. I'm not sure who has it right this moment."

"Guess," Dashford ordered.

This time Papa deferred to the man with the gun. "Well?" he said, expectant.

The man frowned and dragged himself up off the floor. "I told you, I don't know. But if I had to guess, I'd have to say, er, what time is it?" The man made a great show of pulling up his watch to check. "Well, by now it's probably made its way to our dear friend, Mr. Fitzgelder."

Now it was Papa's turn to groan. Rastmoor joined him.

But Dashford simply nodded. "Well, then. I'd say we ought to go have a talk with dear Mr. Fitzgelder."

"Or something like that," Rastmoor grumbled.

"But if he knows where—" the gunman started, only to be cut off by a sharp word from Papa.

"We go with Dashford," he said, leaving no room for discussion. "You'll get what you need after we deal with Fitzgelder."

What on earth did Papa have going here? Julia found Rastmoor glaring at her. She tried to convey her own bewilderment, but it was impossible to know if he got the message. Likely he wondered if she was a part of whatever this was. She couldn't very well blame him for being suspicious. Drat it, but she was suspicious, too. Of her own father, for heaven's sake! Was he actually in league with such a slug like Fitzgelder?

"Come along, then," Dashford said.

He had the metal box tucked safely in his arm, and strode purposefully past them all out the door. Rastmoor gripped Julia's elbow and made as if to follow.

"You're coming, too, mademoiselle," he said.

Dashford whirled on them. "Indeed, you're *all* coming. I have the feeling I'll think of questions that even Mr. Fitzgelder won't be able to answer."

Julia shuddered, but there was no way out of it. Papa shrugged in her direction but seemed perfectly content to trail along after Dashford. So the man would be asking questions, would he? Indeed, this was bound to be just a little bit too enlightening. For all of them.

"YOU REALIZE, OF COURSE," RASTMOOR TOLD HIS friend as they rode the way back to Hartwood with the actors following behind in their wagons, "you're not forcing them to do anything they don't actually wish to do. If Giuseppe and his partner there had not decided to give you the box and accompany you back, there was nothing you could have done to make them."

"Yes, I do realize that," Dashford replied. "Lucky for me there's something valuable enough inside this box that Giuseppe—or whatever his name happens to be—is willing to risk it in favor of cooperation."

"You don't believe he's really Giuseppe?"

Dashford angled his head and raised an eyebrow. "You do?"

Of course it was pointless to lie. "No. I don't."

"I didn't think so." They were silent, save for the sound of their horses' plodding hoofbeats and the creaking of the ancient wagons. "So who is he?"

"What?"

"You've obviously had dealings with the man before. Last night when I mentioned he was nearby, I noticed your friend Clemmons wasn't the only one who had a reaction. And I noticed, too, that once you saw Giuseppe for yourself, you suddenly weren't nearly so concerned for your missing friend. I can only take that to mean you know more about what's going on here than you've seen fit to discuss with me. Am I right?"

"Dash, are you suggesting I was somehow involved in vandalizing Loveland?"

"No, I'm suggesting you know more than you've let on. So spill. What is your involvement with this Giuseppe person and his ever so charming little mistress?"

"She's not his mistress!"

"Oh? She truly is his daughter, then? Well, perhaps I begin to see your involvement. But what of Clemmons?"

"I'm sure he's fine. Likely he'll turn up somewhere."

"I don't know. I think perhaps I'll contact the magistrate and warn him that these actors are up to no good—that they might have done something nefarious to poor Mr. Clemmons."

"Really, it's not necessary."

"I'll exclude the women, of course. You may have your little actress; you do seem to love them so."

"They are not criminals!"

"They certainly were acting like it, tearing up my property and holding hostages at knifepoint!"

"I don't know who that man is. He acted alone."

"He acted under Giuseppe's control, if I'm not mistaken. I cannot in good conscience let these sorts of men run the countryside, can I? No. The minute we get to Hartwood, I'll have my footmen take them into custody, I'll notify the magistrate, and we will see about getting to the bottom of this bloody treasure box."

Oh, but Julia was not going to like this. She'd likely throw a fit and end up getting herself locked away, as well.

"Let me talk to them," Rastmoor suggested. "Perhaps I can get them to explain, to tell us the truth of what they were doing at Loveland. It could very well turn out to be innocent."

"He held a knife at a woman's throat, Anthony," Dashford reminded him. "That can hardly be considered innocent, no matter the explanation."

He had a point there. Still, for Julia's sake, he wouldn't give up. "At least let me try."

Dashford sighed but nodded. Rastmoor pulled up his mount to allow the trailing wagons to catch him. Julia was in the first, wedged between her father and the turbaned lady on a bench that rocked back and forth with the sway of the old conveyance. It was, by far, too precarious, and Rastmoor had half a mind right now to swoop her off of there and plant her safely in his saddle with him. He doubted St. Clement would let him.

The older man glared at him as they approached. Rastmoor had heard the quiet whispers between the three of them, but they were deadly silent now. He had no doubt that whatever they'd been discussing had not been for his ears. It was probably just as well. Rastmoor already knew enough curses; he had no need of picking up more.

"He's planning to have you arrested," Rastmoor said when St. Clement was near enough to hear clearly.

Julia and her female companion exclaimed in surprise, but St. Clement merely shrugged. "Of course he is. Wouldn't be much of a gentleman if he lets vandalism and violent threat go unpunished, would he?"

"Why don't you just tell me what's going on," Rastmoor said. "Then perhaps I can figure out some way to help you."

"We don't need your help," St. Clement assured him.

"I believe you do. Tell me what's in that box."

The older woman clicked her tongue. "Don't tell him anything, Albert. He just wants it for himself."

"I don't give a fig for your bloody treasure," Rastmoor declared. "But I might be able to keep you out of prison."

"As if we should trust the likes of you," the woman said.

"Mrs. Bixley, please," Julia said finally. "We can trust him. Rastmoor is . . . he's my friend."

"Is that true?" St. Clement said, leaning forward to meet Rastmoor eye to eye. "Are you her friend?"

Rastmoor hardly thought *friend* was adequate to cover just what it was he felt toward Julia. "I assure you, St. Clement, I will do whatever it takes to protect Julia *and* her family."

St. Clement didn't break off his unnerving stare. He was studying, contemplating Rastmoor's face. Thankfully, the man kept his thoughts to himself.

"You might find yourself regretting that commitment, monsieur," the man said.

"True, but you might be surprised by the level of my commitment, sir," Rastmoor responded. Hell, he was surprised himself by the solid resolve in his gut. St. Clement may not trust him—may not even like him—but no way in hell was Rastmoor about to let Julia down by seeing the man sent up on charges, deserved though they might be.

"Very well," St. Clement said, sighing as he turned to study his daughter. "I see there is no reasoning. I suppose you might as well know what's in the box. It isn't what you . . ."

But his words trailed off as the sudden rumble and pounding of hooves distracted him. Heading fast toward them was a carriage. It was elegant and gleaming, the gilded scrollwork flashing in the sunlight and the brightly painted wheel spokes a blur of fashionable yellow. Dashford didn't even need to see the driver to recognize the striking phaeton.

Lindley. By God, what was he doing here? And what was that cloud of dust following behind him? No, not dust. It was two riders in Dashford's familiar livery, that's what it was. Was he imagining it, or where they pursuing the phaeton? Rastmoor winced. Indeed it appeared that way. Given the speed all three were going, it could be fairly well assumed this was not good news galloping toward them.

"By Jove," Dashford exclaimed, pulling his horse up to a halt. "Is that Lindley?"

"Is that your men, chasing him?" Rastmoor asked in reply.

"Oh no!" Julia said with a precious little gasp.

"Who the hell is Lindley?" St. Clement asked.

"And how the hell is he going to stop that blasted gig in time to keep from running us over?" Mrs. Bixley cried.

Rastmoor had to admit, all of these were excellent questions.

FORTUNATELY FOR THEM ALL, LORD LINDLEY WAS AN excellent driver. Somehow—and Julia wasn't at all sure how—he managed to pull up his horses in time to finish his approach at something like a leisurely pace. Indeed, the frustrated creatures blew and stamped, but Lindley seemed not the least rattled. He greeted Dashford almost cheerfully.

"I say, Dash," Lindley said. "What on earth has gotten into your men back there?"

They weren't "back there" long, though. In moments two of Dashford's sturdy grooms came pounding up on their mounts, clearly having ridden hell-for-leather and even more clearly with intent of overtaking Lindley.

"Watch it, sir, he might be armed!" one of them called to his master.

Julia glanced up at Rastmoor, who was poised atop his horse, just on the other side of Papa. He eyed the situation suspiciously. Julia had to admit she was glad he was this close. With Lindley in front of their little caravan and that strange man they'd found at Loveland sitting in the wagon behind them, it was good to have the security of a capable man so close by. Not that she wouldn't have trusted Papa and the other actors to look out for her, but right now she wasn't entirely sure where exactly Papa stood. Was he somehow involved in things that connected him to the likes of Lindley? She shuddered at the thought.

"What's this about, Lindley?" Dashford questioned.

"I stopped at Hartwood to see you and was told you were out here," Lindley replied.

One of the grooms added to that. "When he left, her ladyship thought it might be a good idea if we came along, too."

"Did she now?" Dashford said.

"I say, is something going on that—" Lindley stopped short when his eyes fell on the man in the rear wagon. "You!"

The man seemed no less thrilled at the sight of the newcomer. "Lindley, you dog. What in the bloody hell have you done with my daughter?" he shouted, scrambling to get out of the wagon. Three of Papa's actors worked to restrain him.

"I was hoping to find her here with you, D'Archaud," Lindley replied calmly. "Am I to take it she's missing?"

"I'll murder you!" the man, apparently someone named D'Archaud, announced loudly. "What have you done to her?"

"I see you've been busy making friends wherever you go, Lindley," Rastmoor said.

"And just what, exactly, did you do to this man's daughter?" Dashford asked.

"I tried to keep her out of the mess this man is making of his life! Watch him, Dash, he's not to be trusted," Lindley replied.

"Oh?" Dashford responded. "Some would say you aren't, either."

"He's not," Papa said suddenly. Julia whipped her face around to look at him. "He's after the treasure."

"Hellfire," Rastmoor breathed under his breath. "Not another one."

"I'm afraid you're just going to have to wait your turn with it, Lindley," Dashford said. "Your friend D'Archaud back there got his hands on it first, but I claim right of ownership for my wife." He patted the metal box that he held securely in his lap. "And just what claim do you have on this?"

"That's the treasure?" Lindley asked.

"Don't get any ideas," Rastmoor warned.

Lindley frowned. "That's the treasure? Odd. I rather thought it would be bigger. I suppose I shouldn't be surprised. Those French . . . they always exaggerate."

Dashford picked up on this. "French, you say? The treasure is French?"

"Indeed. I know little about it, but I do know it's French," Lindley said.

Julia frowned. Well, that did nothing to exonerate Papa. True, just because he and this so-called treasure shared the same country of origin hardly proved his involvement in anything sinister. Still, she couldn't like the fact that he hadn't seen fit to mention it to her. That had to mean something.

Rastmoor glanced at Julia then slid his gaze to Papa. He must be piecing it together, too. Did he believe she'd known of this? She hoped not, but honestly, there was no reason for him to doubt her involvement. Especially when Papa said she'd possessed a key and that the other was with Fitzgelder. Truly, he must be losing faith in her by the minute.

"Well, no matter," Dashford went on. "Our friend here"—he gestured toward Papa—"has graciously informed us of where we might find at least one of the keys needed to open the box. Since the box was hidden in my wife's property, and since the holder of one of these keys is currently a guest at Hartwood, we are headed back there to see about opening it. Perhaps it did indeed come from France, but it's in England now."

"You already have one of the keys?" Lindley asked.

"Not quite," Rastmoor interjected. "It's en route to Fitzgelder, we believe."

"Are you certain of that?" Lindley asked.

"Not at all," Dashford replied.

"Well then, who has the other? Two are required, I believe?" Lindley questioned.

No one asked where he had come by this information, although Julia thought it might be important to know that.

"Sadly, that one belonged to an actress," Dashford said. "One Julia St. Clement."

Lindley looked from Dashford to Rastmoor, his left eyebrow arching prominently. "Then this would mean it is already in Fitzgelder's possession, wouldn't it?"

"Yes," Dashford said.

"No," Rastmoor said.

Everyone looked at him, but he offered no explanation.

"At any rate," Dashford went on, "Fitzgelder is in my possession. Lindley, what do you say to returning with us to Hartwood? My grooms, of course, will see that you encounter no difficulties on the way."

Everyone recognized that for what it was—Dashford's warning to Lindley. The man, like everyone else, would be watched carefully. The grooms would watch Lindley, Papa and his actors would watch D'Archaud, D'Archaud would watch Dashford, Dashford would watch Papa, and Rastmoor—it seemed—would watch her. Not that she really minded that, but she just wished she could know he didn't condemn her as he watched. She certainly hoped, for everyone's sake, that when they arrived at Hartwood at least one of those dratted keys would turn up.

Chapter Nineteen

Rastmoor breathed a bit easier when they finally made it back to Hartwood. Dashford's footmen were only too glad to help monitor the new guests, and the new Lady Dashford was only too glad to see her husband whole. For some reason she was convinced something grave had happened to Clemmons, and when Lindley showed up, then set off to follow Dash to Loveland, she feared the same horrible fate awaited her husband. It was going to be quite a chore to convince her Clemmons was well, and no one else was in any immediate danger.

Especially since he couldn't entirely be sure of that last part. Just who was this D'Archaud, and what was the connection between him, Lindley, and St. Clement? Where did Julia fit into it all? And how, in God's name, did Fitzgelder fit into the picture?

He certainly was looking forward to an explanation. He scanned the group as Dashford ushered them all into the large formal drawing room just off the great entrance hall. Rastmoor doggedly positioned himself beside Julia when she took a seat next to her father on a silk-covered divan. The other four members of his troupe made themselves comfortable wherever they could, Mrs. Bixley taking care to stay clear of D'Archaud. Lindley stood against the wall near the doorway. Was he planning a hasty exit, or making sure no one else did?

Of course Lady Dashford insisted on joining them, which of course forced Dashford to secure two extra footmen. Just in case. It was a motley gathering, and Rastmoor could hardly wait to see how it played out. Oh, he was about to hear plenty of explanation; he was sure of that. He just wondered how much of it would be credible.

"I've sent for Fitzgelder," Dashford announced.

Rastmoor groaned. Indeed, of course they must invite Fitzgelder. He held vital information and certainly the man's presence would add to the festive atmosphere. Clearly things were just about to get interesting.

The actors, for the most part, glanced around the room with worried, confused expressions. Rastmoor was ready to believe that of the troupe, only St. Clement and D'Archaud really knew anything about what was going on. But then he reminded himself that they were, after all, actors. This could truly be an elaborate scene they'd rehearsed beforehand.

Except that he was inclined to believe Julia's ignorance. Perhaps it was gullibility on his part, but he simply couldn't dismiss the shock and dismay on her face every time her father volunteered some unexpected information. He also could not overlook the hurt.

Damn that man! Had he lied to his own daughter? Had he set her up to be used, to be dragged into this mess so he could take advantage of her relationship with Rastmoor and now the Dashfords for some tasteless plot to steal wealth? If Rastmoor thought for one minute Julia would allow it, he'd give the man a thorough thrashing. And enjoy it.

But it was clear she would not. She adored her father; it was plain on her face. Even as she sat here, surrounded by scheming strangers, her concern for her father's well-being was evident. Rastmoor's anger faded. Blast it, but he'd vowed to protect St. Clement, and he'd live up to that—for Julia's sake. He doubted very much he'd particularly enjoy it, though.

"Now, where did you say you found this box?" Lady Dashford said, leaning forward in her chair to gaze at—but not touch—the metal box as it sat on the narrow table that Dashford had dragged to the center of the room.

"It was under the floorboards in the master bedroom," Dashford replied.

The viscountess nodded, then glanced over to D'Archaud. "And you were the one they found tearing up my grandmother's floor?"

D'Archaud seemed surprised by this. Indeed, Rastmoor was quite unprepared for the blatant shock that took over the man's face.

"Er, your grandmother, my lady?"

She gave him a cold frown. "Yes. Do you have any problem with that?"

"Certainly not!" D'Archaud replied and sent St. Clement a questioning glance.

"My wife's heritage is none of your damn business!" Dashford barked at the man, taking one menacing step forward.

"I'm afraid you are wrong, monsieur," St. Clement said.

Rastmoor couldn't help but roll his eyes. What was wrong with these men? Were they mentally deficient? Anyone could see they were in no position to argue with Dashford—especially about such a sensitive subject as his wife!

"You see, the Lady Dashford's heritage is very much our business. After all, her—"

And of course they were interrupted by the butler entering to announce the arrival of Fitzgelder. As if the man were some far-off dignitary come for tea. Dash the man, he strode in with the air of one who owned the place. From the looks on the faces of the other men in the room, however, it was clear he did not.

When Fitzgelder laid eyes on the newcomers, his expression soured. Rastmoor was rather pleased to see it.

"What the hell are you doing here?" he said, aimed at D'Archaud.

"Where the hell is my daughter?" D'Archaud shot back.

Really, the man ought to take better care of his daughter.

Leaving her with the likes of either Lindley or Fitzgelder was certainly not the mark of brilliant parenting.

"I told you where she was," Fitzgelder said. "If you didn't find her there, ask Lindley. He had her."

He let his snarky smile give additional meaning to that last phrase. D'Archaud very nearly had steam coming out his ears.

"I'll murder you along with him!" the furious father hissed.

"Gentlemen," Dashford interrupted. "There will be plenty of time for arguing and murder later. Right now, we have this other matter at hand."

He pointed to the box. "Open it."

"Is that it? You've got it?" Fitzgelder said, his eyes wide as he took in the box on the table. Rastmoor could see his hands clenching with the itch to grab it.

St. Clement ignored him with a sigh of frustration. "We can't open it. We need the keys."

"You said you believed Fitzgelder to be in possession of at least one of the keys by now," Rastmoor reminded him.

Fitzgelder scowled. "I was supposed to be in possession of *both* of the damn things by now. As it is, I'm sorry to say I have neither."

"You expect us to believe that?" Dashford asked. "These men claim your wife held one of those keys. Can it be that somehow you knew about this treasure business, yet when your wife passed away you didn't manage to keep track of such an important object?"

Fitzgelder growled a bit.

"Oh, yes. Mr. Giuseppe here—or whatever the hell his name is—told us your dearly departed wife had one of the keys," Dashford went on, taunting the man.

Rastmoor would have been happy to join in, if only things were the way Dashford assumed them to be. He, unfortunately, was not privy to all the facts. Clearly, Fitzgelder was. At least, most of them. The look in his eye was pure evil.

"Hell, that little bitch I got tricked into marrying had something I thought was the key, but it sure as shit wasn't the right one." Fitzgelder's lip curled back at the memory, and he gave a feral snarl as he turned to St. Clement. "Giuseppe, is it? Lying bastard! Go ahead, why don't you tell your friend Dashford here just where that other key *really* is. I'd like to hear that, myself."

"I don't think his lordship is quite ready to consider himself my friend," St. Clement said.

"That's not the point!" Fitzgelder yelled, pounding his fist against the nearest object, which just happened to be a spindly legged tea table that very nearly crumbled under the abuse. "You know where it is because you gave it to . . ."

His voice trailed off when his wild eyes settled on Julia. Rastmoor could sense her body tensing, cringing under his gaze. He readied himself for what was to come.

"Her!" Fitzgelder fairly shrieked. "That's *her*, isn't it?"

He jabbed a wicked finger into the air, pointing at Julia. If it had been a dagger, he'd have impaled her with it. As it was not, all he could do was slide his hateful gaze up to meet Rastmoor. "God damn it, but you were in on this all along, weren't you, Cousin?"

The idea seemed to give Fitzgelder so much agony that Rastmoor was perfectly content to let the man go on believing it. Indeed, nothing would please him more than to rob Fitzgelder of the perverted glee he'd found in ripping out Rastmoor's heart. Well, nothing except, perhaps, ripping out Fitzgelder's heart. That was assuming, of course, the creature had one.

"You never deserved a woman like Julia St. Clement," Rastmoor said after a long, tense pause. "And you never had her."

"He never deserved Kitty, either," Julia said under her breath.

Rastmoor began to understand some of the guilt Julia must have carried all these years, knowing that her friend had sacrificed herself with a monster like Fitzgelder and Julia had been the benefactor. He wished somehow he could simply make it go away, though he knew he could not. He had been a part of the horror; he had believed evil of her and left her to survive as best she could. His guilt in all this was twice what Julia's was.

"Hold up," Dashford said, although it was not really necessary. The sudden revelation seemed to have sent everyone into stunned silence. "Do you mean to say, *this* is Julia St. Clement?"

It was obvious to whom he referred. Rastmoor could only be glad his mother and sister weren't here. As it was, Dashford's reaction was difficult enough.

"You brought her *here*, Rastmoor?"

"Dashford, there are some things you don't fully understand. I—"

"You brought your lying, scheming whore *here*, into *my* home?"

"By God, Dash, you will not speak of her that way!"

Dashford threw his hands up and paced in tight circles. "The St. Clement bitch, right here, alive and well! Damn it, Rastmoor, are you touched in the head? After all the torment she put you through? Hell, I think you *must* be insane. One minute you're cavorting around with that Nancini pup, and now you've gone and—"

His wife put her hand on his arm as he made a pass near her chair. "Dearest, I believe we may have been wrong about Nancini."

He huffed. "Clemmons, then. Whatever it was."

Her ladyship pursed her lips and gave a sideways nod toward Julia. "Miss St. Clement, I believe."

Dashford was momentarily at a loss, but eventually his wife's hinted implication sank in. "What? Good God, are you telling me . . . oh, hell. Rastmoor, is this true?"

"I couldn't very well tell you who she was, could I? Besides, we had this mongrel chasing after us," Rastmoor explained, gesturing—impolitely, of course—at Fitzgelder.

"Wait a moment," Fitzgelder piped up. "Are you saying that Clemmons lout was *her*?"

"A fine little actress I raised there!" the senior St. Clement said with fatherly pride. A bit misplaced, given the situation, but glowing, nonetheless.

"Clemmons? Do you mean that worthless little fool who went around telling folks he was married to my daughter?" D'Archaud asked.

"Your *daughter*?" Lady Dashford said. "Do you mean Sophie Darshaw is your *daughter*?"

"Indeed she is!" D'Archaud announced. "And that makes me your uncle, doesn't it?"

"This is your uncle?" Dashford asked, clearly unimpressed.

"But I thought you were dead!" Lady Dashford exclaimed. "And so did Sophie!"

"So you can imagine her shock when I caught up with her at that posting house in Geydon. I followed from London so I could save her from an unfortunate elopement. Funny, you'd think she would have mentioned to me her new husband was actually a female!"

"So you're the one who took Sophie from the posting house in Geydon that night when someone was shooting at us?" Julia asked. "But I was sure it was . . . er . . ."

"You thought it was me, I know," Lindley finished for her.

"Well, it would have been you, bastard, if I hadn't gotten her first," D'Archaud said. "You didn't waste any time following us to Warwick and beating me half to death. What did you do with her? Where is she, Lindley?"

"You mean you *did* kidnap Sophie?" Rastmoor asked, frowning at Lindley.

"I *rescued* her!" Lindley defended himself. "That ass"—here he pointed at D'Archaud—"was dragging her into this, endangering her. He's been in Fitzgelder's pocket for years!"

"And you haven't?" Rastmoor asked with obvious skepticism.

"Of course not," Lindley replied. "Entirely too crowded in there for my taste."

D'Archaud launched into a string of French profanity.

"So where is she?" Rastmoor asked, pinning Lindley with an expectant stare.

He fidgeted slightly. "I don't know. She, er, got away from me."

Dashford threw his hands up. Again. D'Archaud's French became even more colorful. Only Fitzgelder laughed.

"I say, you didn't by any chance think to get that key off her while you had her, old man?" he asked.

"Wait a minute," Julia suddenly spoke up. "You believe Sophie had a key?"

"Of course she did," Fitzgelder growled back. "She took that damn locket from me when we scuffled, the sly little bitch."

"Do you mean to say the key is in the locket?" Dashford asked, although Rastmoor would have done it if he hadn't.

How on earth could his father's locket be in any way involved with all this?

"Not quite," Fitzgelder said simply. "The locket *is* the key."

"Oh, for God's sake!" Dashford grumbled.

Rastmoor would have said something a bit more colorful, but he decided to let this suffice. Instead he turned to Lindley. "You knew about this?"

Lindley smiled. "Of course I did. And, yes, I also had the good sense to think of getting the locket from her before she, er, escaped. Again."

He reached into his coat pocket and extracted a cloth. Unfolding it, he gently pulled out a gold locket and held it, dangling into space, for all to see. A small golden locket on a delicate chain.

"Aha! That's the very one!" Fitzgelder cried. "Go ahead, Lindley. Open it. I think everyone will be more than interested in what you find. Rastmoor, especially."

Rastmoor realized this could very well be the first honest phrase ever uttered by his abhorrent cousin.

"NO!" JULIA EXCLAIMED.

There must be some mistake. This locket couldn't be the key to some strange, Dashford family treasure. This was the locket that held something dreadful, something that Rastmoor felt would ruin his family. Something so horrid he feared his own sister would sooner marry Fitzgelder than let the contents become known. This had to be some trick, some scheme of Fitzgelder's to destroy poor Rastmoor.

And Lindley must know this. Surely, if he'd had the locket

since he was last with Sophie in Warwick he'd had ample time to investigate its contents. He must know why Fitzgelder wanted it so very badly.

And he was going to open it. She had to do something to stop him!

"Wait! I believe that locket belongs to the Rastmoor family," she said, hoping Dashford would care enough about his friend to listen. "I think Rastmoor should be allowed to examine it first."

She could feel Rastmoor's eyes on her, but the ones that mattered most right now were Dashford's. She kept her focus only on him and thought she recognized a slight hint of understanding cross his features. With any luck, Rastmoor had mentioned Fitzgelder's threats, and Dashford would realize the danger of opening that locket in front of everyone like this. Surely he'd protect his friend.

But instead, Dashford simply turned to Lindley. "What's in the locket?"

Lindley shrugged. "I haven't had time to look."

"If that's true," Rastmoor said, "then I'd very much appreciate it if the locket is returned to me. Unopened."

Lindley seemed surprised by this, so Rastmoor continued. "Now, if you please."

"Well, it is yours, I suppose," Lindley said with a shrug. Carefully, he handed the locket over to Rastmoor.

"No, it isn't!" D'Archaud cried. "It's mine! I gave it to his father for safekeeping!"

"What?" Rastmoor asked.

"Your father," D'Archaud continued, "was a good man. He helped me out when I needed it. He said he'd keep the locket safe when there were men who would have killed me for it."

"You knew my father?" Rastmoor couldn't help but question.

Julia was not at all pleased to hear that. D'Archaud wasn't exactly the fine, upstanding sort who would aid Rastmoor in defending his family from whatever slanderous scheme Fitzgelder might have in mind. Likely he was a part of the scandal, in fact.

"Your father was my friend," D'Archaud said simply.

"Well, he never said anything to me about this locket," Rastmoor said. "All I know is that when he died, it was among his things. Left to me with instructions never to lose track of it and to continue sending monthly payments to a certain party I assumed was associated with it. And that party was most assuredly not you."

D'Archaud shook his head. "No, it was for Sophie. Your father sent money to help support my Sophie after her mother died."

"I'm not as gullible as you think," Rastmoor assured him. His dark expression said he'd had very nearly enough of this whole business.

"I can prove it's mine!" D'Archaud declared. "I can tell you how it opens the box."

That seemed to pique Rastmoor's interest. "Oh?"

"I will have to admit," Dashford said, "I am a bit curious about what's in there."

"Then let me show you," D'Archaud coaxed. "I know the secret. And . . . and I won't even need to open it."

Now, that was a bit difficult to swallow. The locket could act as a key without even opening? How? Julia didn't trust the man. He'd likely get his hands on the locket, rip it open, and wave whatever contents there were in front of everyone, destroying Rastmoor. At this point she didn't know who—or what—could be trusted.

"Er, don't you need two keys to open that box?" she asked suddenly. "What good will one be?"

"Yes," Rastmoor agreed. "If you don't mind, I think I'll just hang on to this until we can dredge up that other key."

Dashford frowned. "If I'm not mistaken, Miss St. Clement is supposed to be in possession of the second key. That is what our fine actor here said, isn't it?"

"No, that's not precisely what I said," Papa uttered, but Julia cut him off.

"Honestly, Papa. It's a bit late for games. Why did you tell them I have the other key?"

"I didn't, *ma chérie*!" he said with a fabricated look of hurt.

"I told them you *owned* it. I never said you actually *possessed* it."

"Oh, bother," she grumbled. "What's the difference?"

"The difference, *ma belle*, is that you may actually own the key, but *I* have it in my possession."

"*You* have the other key?"

"But of course!" He smiled cheerfully. "Always have. I held it for you, and unlike my compatriot, I never cultivated friendships with such lowlife scum that I had to be concerned for its security. He may have given his elsewhere for safekeeping, but I have kept yours, *ma belle*. It is right here."

None of this made sense. She could barely believe it when Papa reached into his coat pocket—quite a chore, given the many flaps and flounces in his foppish attire—and pulled out his own little cloth. Unfolding it, he uncovered a locket. From what she could see of it, it seemed very much like the one Rastmoor held clutched in his fist.

"By God, he has it!" Fitzgelder said with something like reverence.

"So we can open the box?" Lady Dashford asked.

"Well, there's one way to find out," her husband replied. "With Rastmoor's permission, of course."

Rastmoor thought for a moment then glanced to meet Julia's eyes. She could have sworn the expression she saw there was one of question, as if he was asking her advice on whether or not to agree. But of course he really couldn't expect her to know what to tell him, could he? He must know she was clueless about all of this.

She attempted a feeble smile and shrugged. Not very good advice, she had to admit, but she hoped he recognized at least she was being honest with him. At last.

"All right, then," he said. "Let's open it."

RASTMOOR COULDN'T HELP IT. HE HAD TO WAIT FOR some sign from Julia before making up his mind. What a want-wit he'd become, that was certain. But truly, he knew she'd not steer him wrong.

Unfortunately, she didn't seem to be able to steer him at all. She was obviously as much in the dark about all this as he was. He rather liked that, actually. They were on the same side.

With a well-practiced flourish, St. Clement stepped forward and held his locket up. He seemed almost to be making ready for some sleight of hand or display of sorcery. All eyes in the room were riveted on him. Rastmoor had to smile. The man certainly could play to his audience.

Carefully, he turned the locket over. He seemed to be toying with the ring at the top where the locket was held on to the chain. Indeed, he turned the ring very slowly. He leaned very close, as if listening. Perhaps he was listening to the object as he worked it, or perhaps he was merely giving his onlookers a dramatic exhibition. Either way, at one point he suddenly stopped, and the back of the locket sprang up, fanning open in two halves like the wings on a beetle.

Gingerly and perhaps timidly, St. Clement twisted these wings. Rastmoor would have loved to get a closer look at the works inside this device. Certainly, this was like no locket he'd ever seen before. Would the locket he still held in his hand do something similar? He rather hoped it would. From what he could see of the first one, the front part of the locket—the part where any incriminating paper or other evidence could be hidden—was still undisturbed. St. Clement seemed to have been telling the truth when he claimed he could open the box without opening his locket.

How very unfortunate for Fitzgelder. Odd that the man was still so eager to follow this through. Rastmoor would have expected him to show much more disappointment at having his dearest plans totally destroyed while being forced to watch someone else discover a treasure.

But at this point, Fitzgelder was easy to ignore. St. Clement was twisting the pieces of that locket into the most unusual shape. At last the pieces seemed to snap into place, and St. Clement smiled, holding it up for all to witness.

"Voilà!" he said. "The first half of the key."

It was like no key Rastmoor had ever seen. The front portion of the locket looked as one would expect a simple heart-shaped locket to look. The back of it, however, was sprung out and flipped so that the points of the two halves jutted down and away from the body of the locket. It almost seemed the harmless object had just grown fangs.

St. Clement held it up toward the light streaming through the window. "See? There is a hole through it."

Rastmoor leaned forward to see. Indeed, there was. It was hardly more than a pinhole, but it went all the way through the locket. Not that it meant anything to Rastmoor, of course, but the design was ingenious.

"Now we will see how the other locket fits into it," St. Clement said.

Both St. Clement and D'Archaud reached their hands out to take the second locket from Rastmoor. He did not need another opinion on this, however. There was no question but that he felt more inclined to give it to St. Clement than his shiftless friend.

The man took it and held it up as he had the first locket. His fingers went immediately to the ring at the top, but after a moment or two, he paused. He held the locket closer for examination. He peered at it front and back.

"This isn't it," he said at last.

"What?" D'Archaud exclaimed, nearly yanking it out of St. Clement's hand. "*Mon dieu!* This is not my locket!"

Rastmoor was stunned. Not his locket? That was not good.

"Where is the real locket?" D'Archaud asked, glaring first at Rastmoor then turning his anger on Fitzgelder. "Where is it?"

Fitzgelder simply grinned. "What a shame, D'Archaud. You lost your fancy locket."

"Someone deliberately replaced it," St. Clement said. "This locket appears very similar, but it is not the right one. Someone has deceived us."

Fitzgelder laughed as if this were all great sport. "For once, I am innocent of the crime!"

Oh, hell. The locket had taken such a roundabout way to

get here—being smuggled by Penelope, given to Fitzgelder, stolen by Sophie, retrieved by Lindley—there was no way to know when the real locket had been replaced by this alternate. Clearly someone in that chain of handlers knew the secret and decided not to part with such a valuable object. But who was it? And why?

The most likely suspect was Fitzgelder. He'd made it very clear he had something in mind for what he believed was in that locket. Obviously he would have had ample reason to keep it close to him. But why chase after Sophie if he knew she had the wrong locket?

Lindley, on the other hand, had indeed chased after Sophie. He, in fact, was the one who took the locket from her, wasn't he? He would have had plenty of opportunity to open it and find the evidence Fitzgelder swore was inside. Lindley was just intelligent enough to figure out how to profit from that evidence. Hell, he was intelligent enough to discover any other unusual features of the locket, too. He would have realized it was part of something much bigger than simple blackmail.

Unless of course D'Archaud had lied from the start. He claimed he'd given the locket to Rastmoor's father for safekeeping, hadn't he? Well, Rastmoor still found that a bit shaky. Surely his father would have told him if he truly held a locket with damning family secrets or keys to untold treasure. Wouldn't he? Of course he would have. That left D'Archaud's story sounding very thin. He could have easily kept the right locket in the hopes that once the wrong locket turned up, someone else could be blamed while he went behind everyone's back and got the treasure for himself.

Damn it, there was just too much to consider, and frankly, there was still entirely too much about this whole thing that just didn't make sense.

"So," Rastmoor said with a heavy sigh. "Who has the real locket?"

As one voice, the group chorused, "Not me!"

Chapter Twenty

Julia pretended she could ignore the rapping at her door. After that fiasco in the drawing room, being allowed to come up here to peace and solitude was heavenly. She half expected Lady Dashford to throw them all out, but the viscountess had not. She'd been overly kind and had servants look to the needs of all of Papa's troupe. When her ladyship invited Julia to return to the room she'd been using during her brief, deceptive stay at Hartwood, she could have wept. Lord, but she needed some time to collect her thoughts.

Papa had gone with his troupe to the kitchens, where there was a luncheon being prepared for them. Julia was glad not to have to face him with all the questions running wild through her mind. She needed some time alone, time to process all she'd just seen and heard.

Surely the others were as confused as she. Presumably Fitzgelder had been placed back under guard in his room, where he could stew about his lost opportunities. Rastmoor had probably gone to confer with Lindley and Dashford while his mother and sister, as far as Julia knew, had not yet been notified of any of this. As far as she was concerned, that particular revelation could wait all year.

As for Lady Dashford, she was busily seeing to everyone as if they were guests she had invited into her home. Probably she had never envisioned her first few days of marriage to be like this. However, she appeared to handle it all with inherent grace. She even seemed quite eager to accept D'Archaud into her family, despite the man's questionable ethics. Julia could only guess how Lady Dashford must feel to suddenly be handed such a kinsman.

No worse, she supposed, than to suddenly discover her father was a treasure hunter who kept friends with such scabs like D'Archaud. Heavens, but that had certainly caught her unawares. She'd never known her father to be anything but honorable. True, he may not have been born a gentleman, but he had certainly always behaved as one. And he'd expected nothing less from her. Now to find out he was not what he'd seemed, Julia just wasn't certain of anything.

Well, she was certain whoever was knocking at her door was determined not to leave her in peace. Halfheartedly smoothing her hair and fluffing her skirts, she left the bed where she'd fallen lifeless just a few minutes ago. With a smile that was merely superficial, she opened the door.

It was Lady Dashford.

"I just wanted to make sure you have everything you need, Miss St. Clement," she said and gave every indication of being sincere.

"Yes, thank you. The luncheon plate your servants brought up was quite filling."

The viscountess smiled, but it was a nervous smile. "Good. I want you to be comfortable here. Truly, I do."

Since she didn't give any indication that this was the end of the conversation, Julia felt the polite thing to do would be to invite her in. Her ladyship graciously accepted. Drat. What on earth could she need to discuss? Julia was almost afraid to find out.

Lady Dashford glanced around the room then made herself

comfortable in one of the chairs at the window. Julia joined her there, but could not really say she was comfortable. Certainly she owed their hostess quite a bit of explanation.

But before she could start, Lady Dashford spoke. "I, er, I know my husband may have said some unkind things. Some horrible things, really. But please do not hold that against him. He's a good man, and he cares deeply for his friend. It was just such a shock, that's all. In time he will soften."

Now Julia really did not feel comfortable. How on earth did one begin to make amends after such fraud? She should be begging her ladyship's forgiveness, not the other way around.

"Please, my lady, he had every right to be upset. I came to your home under false pretenses. I knew very well I would not be welcome if my identity were known. You've been more than kind, but I'm sure my father is eager for us to be on our way and out from underfoot as soon as possible."

"I'm afraid Dashford has requested that your father remain here until we have some resolution on this. Really, it is a fascinating situation, isn't it? Imagine, we find you alive, my cousin's father also is alive, and now we learn that the Loveland treasure is not merely a myth or a joke, but it is real, as well! How remarkable."

"Yes, I suppose it must be," Julia replied. "But aren't you worried there might be some danger in this for you? After all, someone has gone to great trouble to keep that other locket, and poor Sophie is still missing."

Lady Dashford's face clouded. "Yes, poor Sophie. But Lindley assures us the minute she went missing, he sent a man to find her. Since she obviously didn't come here, then she must have gone the other way, and he seems quite sure his man will find her before anything dreadful happens. I believe Lindley is quite honestly concerned for her."

"I believe Lindley is quite honestly concerned only with himself," Julia muttered.

Lady Dashford, obviously, had known only comfort and compassion in her life and, therefore, must see only that in others. Such a pity to pop the lady's bubble now, but the notion of treasure did that. It brought out the worst in people, and apparently even Papa was not immune.

"We will find Sophie," Lady Dashford assured her. "I take it you are her friend?"

Julia shook her head. "I barely know her. We met very recently when my father's troupe was hired to perform at what turned out to be Mr. Fitzgelder's home in London."

Of course Julia had no intention of explaining the whole sordid story to her very proper hostess, but Lady Dashford seemed so interested. In the end, Julia gave her most of the tale, at least as far as it pertained to Sophie, all the way up to the point when Sophie was kidnapped at the posting house. By her father, apparently, which truly had been unexpected.

"So, do you believe it was her father who tried to shoot one of you at the posting house?" Lady Dashford asked.

"From what I've seen of him so far, that would seem to be the case. He appears to be a very violent man." Too late, she remembered D'Archaud's connection to Lady Dashford. "Oh. Sorry, my lady."

But her hostess merely chuckled. "Believe me, even if he is a vandal and a cutthroat, I'd still choose him over my other living relatives any day. I'm just glad you and Sophie were able to get away from London without that dreadful Mr. Fitzgelder finding you. Posing as a man was brilliant, really. You were most convincing."

"Really?" Julia couldn't help but ask. "There were times I wasn't entirely sure you didn't suspect."

"Well, I must say I was a bit confused when I noticed his boots on the floor in your chamber," her ladyship answered with a blushing grin. "After all, it was difficult to reconcile my image of Lord Rastmoor with, well, *that*."

By God, Julia felt her own cheeks reddening, also. "Yes, that episode was somewhat, er, discomfiting."

"But now it all makes sense. It's rather humorous in fact, don't you think?"

Well, Julia didn't know if she'd go so far as to call it that, but she was happy enough that her hostess did. It helped ease the mortification she would otherwise be feeling. Heavens, what must this lady think of her? Perhaps she ought to explain that entertaining gentlemen while a guest in someone's home was not something she often engaged in.

"Really, I'm very sorry that—" Julia began, only to be interrupted by more knocking at her door.

Lady Dashford's shrug confirmed that she had not expected anyone. Julia left her seat—which was just starting to feel comfortable—to see who was there. She cracked the door open only to have it shoved wide as some massive form swept through and gathered her into his arms.

Rastmoor. He held her tight and breathed into her hair. "Sorry I left you so long. I hope—"

Lady Dashford demurely cleared her throat. Rastmoor quickly pried himself off Julia and took a step backward. He wore the expression of a guilty child. Julia couldn't help but smile.

"You know," Lady Dashford said, "I just recalled that I promised to meet with the housekeeper this afternoon. If you don't mind, I'll just go take care of that now."

Rastmoor sputtered something about not wanting to interrupt or make the lady leave on his account, but she brushed him off with a coy smile and the wave of her hand.

"Miss St. Clement and I can continue our pleasant conversation at another time," she said, passing them on her way to the door.

Julia thanked her for coming and gladly accepted the polite little hug the viscountess offered, though for the life of her she couldn't guess what it was for. Perhaps her ladyship was just an affectionate sort. It was truly a shame she wouldn't be at Hartwood long enough to actually establish a friendship with this kindhearted woman. Rastmoor gallantly held the door for her, but she paused to smile at him just as she headed into the hallway.

"You might try not to leave your boots sitting out in plain view this time," she advised. "Just in case someone should drop by."

With a knowing wink, she left them and let Rastmoor close the door behind her. Julia was only slightly surprised when he locked it.

"So what were you two ladies discussing?" he asked.

Julia sighed as if the subject matter bored her. "Oh, she wanted to know if you are as much the raging tiger in the bedroom as you've always bragged about being."

He choked. "What? She didn't really say that. Did she?"

Julia laughed and slid back into his arms where she'd been a moment ago. "No, I'm funning you. Lady Dashford is very proper and gracious, of course. She was merely making certain I was comfortable here and all my needs were being met."

"Are they?" Rastmoor asked, pulling her closer to him.

"Well, for the most part. The food is excellent, and the accommodations are quite inviting."

"And what of your other, er, needs?"

"Up until last night they were fine," she said, hoping his manly pride wouldn't be offended at the mention of it.

"Oh? And is that why you left?"

She could feel his arms go loose around her. Indeed, he was offended. She supposed at the very least he deserved an explanation.

"I left because I was worried for my father," she said. "Giuseppe is a name he's used before when we needed to avoid Fitzgelder. When I heard Dashford announcing he was here, at Loveland, I was afraid Fitzgelder's men might find him there. I tried to send that note to warn him, but, as you know, that didn't work out so well."

"No, not so well at all."

"So I had to go to him. Besides, I was afraid if I stayed here, I'd end up married to your sister!"

He smiled, but clearly he was not ready to laugh at the matter. "Yes, that was a bit awkward. Still, you should never have run off without telling me."

"Would you have let me go if I had told you?"

"Hell no!"

"That's why I didn't tell you. Really, I thought it was for the best. You said it yourself: We distract each other. You need to focus on your family, on putting a stop to Fitzgelder's schemes. That much hasn't changed—we still don't know where that locket is or how dangerous it is. And your sister . . . she's so young and impulsive! She needs you, Anthony."

"And I need *you*, Julia."

She did love the way his fingers pressed into the small of her back as he said that, dragging her closer and wrapping her tight. It was easy to believe he really did need her, that his life was as meaningless without her as hers would be without him. But she knew, of course, it wasn't true. Fitzgelder may have lied about many things three years ago, but he'd been right on one point: viscounts did not marry actresses.

Rastmoor might very well *want* Julia, but he did not *need* her. Not the way she needed him, and that was never to be. The longer she tormented herself by pretending she could enjoy Rastmoor today then somehow face the future without him, the more miserable that future would be.

"No, there isn't time," she said as his head dipped to bring his lips close to hers.

"Shh," he said, brushing her lips with a featherlight kiss then going on to kiss her chin and her neck. "We have all the time in the world."

"No," she repeated. "There are too many other things . . ." But Lord, it was difficult to form words when he was doing this to her.

"Later," he said. "We will deal with all those other things later."

"But by then it will all be so much more complicated, more difficult," she said, or rather, she tried to say. It was hard to talk with Rastmoor's tongue introducing itself this way.

But really, she knew it didn't matter. Rastmoor wasn't paying attention to what she was trying to say, and neither was she. They were only interested in what they were trying to do, which was eagerly remove each other's clothing. Once again, they were both far too distracted to worry about such silly things as tomorrow or forever.

"HOW MUCH LONGER BEFORE YOU'RE MISSED?" JULIA asked.

"Years, I'm sure," he said and snuggled her more tightly against him.

"But won't Dashford be looking for you? He must be eager to get that other locket or find some other way into that box."

"No, he's taking this time to gather men to go track down his missing cousin. We still haven't heard from Lindley's man, so Dashford has sent out some of his own."

"Sending out a few men won't take all afternoon."

"No, but you forget the most important thing he's got to do."

"What's that?"

"His poor wife is quite distraught. I'm sure he'll want to spend hours and hours comforting her. And I assure you, I will not be needed for that."

"Well, you've done an excellent job of comforting me," she said and added a satisfied sigh just so he'd know how truthful she was.

He'd managed to loosen some of the fastenings at her back so her gown was drooping off one shoulder, and her skin prickled where he'd lavished hot kisses and hungry caresses. Indeed, though she had no doubt what the future would inevitably bring for them, she would allow herself to be content right now, wrapped up in Anthony's arms.

"But what about, er, your mother?" she couldn't help but ask. "She's going to hear about this, that you brought me here. You need to talk to her."

He sighed and pulled himself away from her. "Woman, you do know how to kill the mood."

"She's your mother, and she cares about you. I can't imagine she'll be happy to find out I've been here, lying to her, all along."

"She knows what a monster Fitzgelder is. She'll understand."

"Will she?" Julia asked. "I wouldn't, not if I were in her position. No, I'd be furious and, well, hateful toward the both of us. You need to go to her."

"Are you trying to get rid of me?"

"No! Of course not, but she needs you."

"And what about you, Julia? Do you need me?"

She smiled as best she could, realizing her answer would send him away. "Not for another hour or two, I suppose."

* * *

HE HONESTLY WISHED SHE'D TAKEN HIS QUESTION A bit more seriously, but of course she hadn't. Things between them had been serious once; it would take some time to build up to that level of trust again. He could wait, at least for that hour or two, he supposed.

"Very well, I'll do as you command," he said, leaning in for a quick kiss then detaching himself from her again. "I'll go present myself to my mother and convince her you are not the devil incarnate. Then while I'm at it, I'll break the sad news to Penelope. Her dreams of marrying an opera singer will be crushed."

She did laugh at that. He'd hoped she would. "Don't be too very surprised if she's not as crushed as you might expect. I think Penelope is a bit smarter than you give her credit."

"Oh, indeed," he said, adjusting his trousers and smoothing out his coat. "After all, she gave the locket to Fitzgelder and tried to get herself engaged to a woman. Yes, she's a bright one."

"I don't know . . ." Julia said, helping him straighten his cravat with a practiced hand.

In return, he moved behind her and retightened her gown. "I'll make sure to give Penelope the distressing news in a kind, gentle fashion. In the meanwhile, I want you to assure me you'll stay here."

"Don't worry. Lady Dashford informed me her husband is insisting Papa stay until things are cleared up. It appears I have no choice but to stay here."

"Wonderful! But what I meant was I want you to stay here, in your room."

"In my room? But I should go down to find Papa."

"No. Now that Fitzgelder knows who you are, you're in danger. I'm convinced he's not given up his efforts to take his petty revenge, and I don't know that we can trust this D'Archaud fellow, either. Plus, Dashford has given Lindley free run of the place. To tell the truth, he's who I find most likely to be the one to have switched the lockets."

"What? But what would Lindley have to gain by that?"

"I don't know. But if Fitzgelder switched them, why would he have been so motivated to find Sophie to get it back? I would simply feel much safer for you if I knew you were not aimlessly roaming about. Will you promise?"

"I will stay safe."

"But will you stay *here*?"

"I will stay here unless I'm needed elsewhere. No unnecessary wandering. Is that satisfactory?"

"No, but I assume it's the best I will get out of you."

She smiled and shook her head. "No, Anthony, you've already gotten the best out of me."

No, she wasn't entirely correct about that. He loved every precious thing he'd ever gotten from Julia St. Clement, but there was more. One thing eluded him, and he was determined to get that, too. He needed her forgiveness.

If she could give him that, trust him once again with her whole heart, *that* would be the best.

"I'll check on you soon," he said, pulling the door open.

"I know," she replied.

He managed to get one more quick kiss before leaving her. He closed the door behind him and felt as if he walked from the sunshine into shadows. She let him go far too easily, and he didn't beg to stay.

When would he finally have the courage to beg?

AND THEN HE WAS GONE WITHOUT FURTHER DISCUSSION. But what had she expected? That he would profess undying love and promise to go against his family and all of society to marry her? No, of course she did not expect that. She didn't want it.

How happy would she be as the outcast wife of a peer? He lived in a world she couldn't hope to comprehend; he had duty and responsibility that would only ever draw him further and further away from her. Her father would certainly not be a welcomed guest of the well-connected Lord Rastmoor. His blue-blooded connections would undoubtedly shun her and perhaps shun him as well because of her. And what if there were children? They would be denied the happiness of honor and respect, too.

No, she did not want that. She wanted Rastmoor—she needed him—but not at that cost. Not at the cost of his own happiness.

She had to let him go. Indeed, the sooner the better. She knew him well enough to know that he was not merely using her to pass the time. When all this was over, and his family's security and that silly treasure were assured again, he would probably see about making their arrangement more stable. He would offer to set her up, to fund her father's theater, to have a decent and respectable affair with her. The mistress of a gentleman could have a fine life, indeed.

But she would have to watch him marry another. She would see his legitimate children grow up in the happy embrace of society and comfort. She would have to be content to share him with them all.

No, that was something she simply could not do. She needed to make perfectly sure she spent the rest of her life far away from Lord Rastmoor and his damned blue-blooded existence. Like so many unpleasant things in life, the longer she waited to make that happen, the harder it would be to do it.

So what about now? Could she just leave? Surely she was not a prisoner here. At least, she didn't think she was. She went to the door.

It opened. Of course it did—she had not locked it after Rastmoor left. No, she was not a prisoner. The hallway was empty. Yesterday there had been footmen placed as guards near Fitzgelder's room. Today there were none. Well, perhaps Fitzgelder was not in his room. Maybe he was off wandering somewhere, looking for trouble. Or maybe Dashford no longer considered Fitzgelder a great enough threat to merit a guard. Either way, there was no one to tell her not to leave her room.

But then footsteps climbing the nearby staircase caught her ear, and she shut her door quickly as if she'd been caught escaping from Newgate. How ridiculous. She cracked it open again, slowly and carefully, just in case. She saw Lindley as he reached the top of the staircase.

He glanced up and down the hallway but didn't seem to notice that her door was not fully shut. She held her breath and watched. Indeed, Rastmoor had been wise to suspect him. Everything about Lindley said he was up to no good.

Silent as a cat, he moved directly toward the room Fitzgelder had been occupying. Odd: how could Lindley have known that? Clearly, though, he knew what he was doing.

He approached the door and noiselessly knelt before it. With deft determination, he drew something small and metallic from his sleeve. A knife? No, it was too narrow. A key? Perhaps.

Whatever it was, he used it to quietly work the lock on Fitzgelder's door. She heard the whisper of a click, and then Lindley stood to his full height and casually returned the metal object to his sleeve. He reached for the knob, and it turned easily. The door swung open with an ominous creak.

"What the hell . . . ?" she heard Fitzgelder yell.

"Shut up. It's me," Lindley said, stepping inside. "And I believe I have something you might be interested in."

"Well now," Fitzgelder's oily voice replied. "It's about damn time."

Then the door was shut tight, and she heard nothing more.

But good heavens, she'd heard enough! Lindley had the locket, and he was giving it to Fitzgelder. Rastmoor was still in danger!

She had to do something. Obviously she couldn't very well burst in on the two schemers and demand they hand her the locket. No, but she couldn't very well just sit here and let them get away with it, despite the fact that she'd promised Rastmoor she'd do just that.

But she hadn't promised that. She'd promised to be careful and not wander around aimlessly. Indeed, she had no intention of being aimless. But she needed a plan!

Papa would know what to do. Of course, she'd go to him. He was probably worried for her, anyway.

Just as quiet and stealthy as Lindley had been, she crept

from her room and scurried downstairs. The footmen at the front door nodded as she passed. Indeed, she truly was not a prisoner here. Dashford, hate her though he must, had not instructed them to keep her confined.

Good. She turned and smiled at the footmen.

"Do either of you have any idea where the performers are?" she asked sweetly. "I heard they were enjoying luncheon in the kitchens."

The footmen very kindly directed her to the kitchens. She thanked them and went on her way. Rastmoor would be pleased—she was not wandering aimlessly at all.

HIS MOTHER WAS IN HER ROOM. THE MINUTE RASTmoor entered and caught a glimpse of her there, ramrod straight in her chair as she plucked away at her embroidery, he knew that she knew.

Damn it, but news traveled fast. Then again, he hadn't exactly hurried here. He should have, though.

"Is this my son?" she asked. Her brittle voice cracked through the air.

"Hello, Mother," he said.

"Yes, I suppose it's you." She managed to take her eyes from her work long enough to study him. "Although I hardly know you these days."

"Yes, Mother, it's me. I take it you're a bit angry with me."

The embroidery was tossed violently to the ground. "No, I'm furious. You brought that woman here! That whore, that actress, that filthy deceiver—you brought her here and had the nerve to introduce her to us."

"Mother, you're overreacting. Julia isn't—"

"Don't speak her name! I can't even think of all the damage this will do to poor Penelope."

"Good grief. How could this possibly damage Penelope?"

"She was positively friendly with her, a fallen woman like that."

"I doubt that a few hours' acquaintance will ruin our Penelope. Besides," he said, stooping to retrieve the embroidery, "she'll no doubt be getting to know her much better in the future."

"You are not threatening to bring her around again, are you?"

"Absolutely not! I'm *promising* it. I fully intend to marry her, Mother, as I should have done three years ago."

For once his mother was at a loss. She simply stared at him, limp. "You intend to *what*?"

"I'm going to marry her."

"Why? Has she gotten herself enceinte to snare you? Well, that's no reason to marry her!"

"I'm going to marry her because I love her, Mother. I should think that is reason enough."

"Well, it isn't. Not for a woman like that."

"Once you get to know her, you'll understand."

"I most certainly will not!" She refused to take the embroidery that he tried handing back to her.

In fact, she slapped it from his hand as if anything he'd touched had suddenly become foul and disgusting. She rose to stand facing him. Lord, but he remembered why he'd thought as a child she must be ten feet tall. The woman could be terrifying when her dander was up.

"And I will not remain under the same roof with her," she said with iron resolve. She marched to the bellpull and tugged it several times. "I'm going to take Penelope and leave this place. It can't be soon enough."

A maid appeared almost immediately, which gave him to wonder if she hadn't been listening from outside the door. Indeed, she probably had been. Surely the servants were aware of the unusual activities around here today. They must be enjoying the intrigue.

"Really now, Mother," he said, knowing his attempt would be useless, but he ought to at least try. "There's no need to be rushing off. You don't even know that it's safe to go traveling while—"

"I'll take my chances out on the open highway rather than stay here with the unseemly vermin you bring around," she sniffed.

She turned her back boldly on Rastmoor and then spoke in a much more affable tone to the curtsying maid. "Please go to Miss Rastmoor's room and ask her to join me here."

But the maid seemed almost afraid to answer. "Er, well, my lady . . . er, Miss Rastmoor is not in her room."

"Oh? Where is she?"

"I believe she went down to the kitchens. With those actors. She, er, was rehearsing a scene with them."

Rastmoor thought his mother's head was going to explode. Somehow, though, she kept herself calm and simply turned to give him a look that said more than her words could. "This is your influence," she hissed at him.

He refused to let her know he could still feel such guilt at her censure after all these years. "I thought I hadn't been around enough lately to have an influence," he said with casual disinterest.

"I will deal with this," she announced, then turned back to the servant. "Take me to the kitchens."

Oh, Lord. This was not going to be pretty. Well, it looked like he was making a trip to the Hartwood kitchens.

Chapter Twenty-one

Oh, drat. Now she *was* roaming aimlessly. Did Dashford intentionally hide his kitchens? Julia grumbled under her breath as she realized she was passing the same laundry room she had already passed twice before. This lowest level of the grand Hartwood estate was a labyrinth.

And oddly enough, there seemed to be no servants around to ask for directions. Well, here was a corridor she had not taken yet. At least, she didn't think she had.

She turned and followed it some ways. Wait, did she hear laughter up ahead? Yes, indeed, that was laughter. Lots of it! And the smell of food and the waft of heated air. By Jove, she believed she had found the kitchens.

She followed the sounds and the scents and soon came to a set of narrow steps. She followed them up and found herself in a wide corridor with another set of steps at the far end. Ah, but she recognized it from earlier. The footmen had directed her here, but she must have come down and taken a wrong turn, going off into an entirely different section of the house. If she had come down that far stairway and come here, to this end of the corridor, she would have found the kitchens just off to her left.

Well, she'd likely only wasted ten minutes. Obviously the laughter was proof Papa and his troupe were still there, doing what they did best. It would do her good to be reminded of the life she'd loved for so long. Especially since that was the life she would be leading forever.

She crossed the corridor and went through the wide opening toward the sounds of laughter and happiness. Papa certainly knew how to please his audience. He was good at that; always in control of the things around him. He would surely know what to do about that dratted locket.

But she didn't quite make it into the larger kitchen area. Suddenly a form leapt out from a doorway, and hands grabbed at her, covering her mouth and pulling her into a shadowy alcove. She was entirely caught unawares, and it was a full heartbeat or two before she could think to struggle. By then it was too late.

She felt the cold edge of a knife against her throat.

"Well, well," that hated voice she now recognized immediately purred in her ear. "You feel pretty damn good for someone who's been dead for three years."

She couldn't see him, but there was no doubt her sudden captor was Fitzgelder. While she was wandering lost, he must have left his room and come down to wait for her. Drat. She glanced around and realized they were in a little storage room. There was another door at the other end that presumably went out to the kitchen areas, but there was little hope of getting there. Fitzgelder held her like a vise.

She wasn't quite panicked yet, though. Her eyes caught on some familiar items. Scattered about the small room were trunks, Papa's trunks. They were opened to expose the props their troupe used in their performances. They must be using this room between acts! Papa couldn't be that far.

Still, she couldn't be exactly comfortable with the situation. Some of their acts ran rather long, especially when Papa let Mrs. Bixley do all the Lady Macbeth speeches. It could be a while before Julia was found. The fact that Fitzgelder's solid form was strong enough to hold her against her best efforts didn't do much to help calm her, either. Her shoulder was wedged in the vise of his arm, and his hand was clenched over her mouth. His other arm pinned her fist helplessly to her side and flashed a deadly knife quickly before her eyes, letting it rest again at her neck.

Well, a swift kick aimed carefully ought to do the trick. She tried that. It only resulted in his grip increasing, smothering her, grazing her with that blade. Apparently Fitzgelder had enough experience with unwilling women to be prepared for something like that. Damn him!

"So this is the real Julia St. Clement," he said, and she could feel his horrible eyes raking over her body. "I wondered what my deluded cousin saw in that first one, but now I understand. You truly are exquisite. I should have known that other was not the right one. But I suppose the fault was not entirely mine. You went to great effort to make a fool of me, didn't you? You and that slut I was tricked into marrying."

His fingers were digging, bruising her, and her lungs were crushed under his angry force. Still, she forced herself to stay calm. Fainting and hysteria never helped anyone. Somehow Fitzgelder would make a mistake, and she'd have her opportunity to escape. All it would take was just one moment, one cry, and the others would hear and come running. She just needed to wait.

"I suppose you're wondering what I have planned for you," he said.

As if she could answer. The idiot. She muttered curses she had no hope of him understanding. It was safe to assume he got the gist of it, though.

He laughed at her. "Talkative, aren't you? Well, I'll make a bargain. I'll release your mouth so you can speak, but if you make any peep louder than a whisper, I'll slit your throat. Fair?"

Hell, no! But given the circumstance, she'd agree to it. She nodded as best she could, considering there was a lethal knife at her throat.

For the first time ever, Fitzgelder was true to his word. He relaxed his fingers just enough for her to gasp out a reply.

"You'd best pray my father doesn't learn of this," she said.

He actually spat on her. "Your father? Hell. I care nothing for a broken-down, insignificant actor. No, my focus is entirely on my magnificent cousin, the wonderful Viscount Rastmoor. That title should have come to me! My father was the older son, you know."

"I've heard," she said. It was probably unwise, but she didn't stop there. "You, however, are nothing more than a bastard."

She winced as the knife blade pressed painfully into her skin. Yes, it had been unwise to say that. But she'd enjoyed it.

"You really are in no position to insult, Miss St. Clement. Given the circumstances, I would expect you to be much more agreeable. After all, I have your life literally in my hands."

Ouch! The tip of the blade pierced her. She could feel the first drops of blood trailing down her neck. Indeed, now would be a very good time to scream!

"One extra sound from you, and you will be dead before your precious father finds you here," he said as if he'd read her mind. "And I will be gone. Lindley was kind enough to unlock my door for me."

She had plenty more to say to him, but this time she thought it through before babbling something that would only result in further injury to her person. "How did you manage to get a man like Lindley to side with you in all this?"

He laughed at her apparent stupidity. "Money, my dear! Everyone knows Lindley's father squandered the family fortune. The man may have inherited an earldom, but he got a king's ransom in debt with it, too. He's had to lie, cheat, and steal to keep a roof over his head—and Lindley prefers an expensive roof. All I had to do was mention that I knew the secrets of a hidden French fortune, and he's been my bosom friend ever since. Everyone has their price, you know."

He seemed to honestly believe that. And perhaps he was right. She would have never guessed her father could be won over by simple treasure, but it seemed that he had been. But perhaps she could use this to her advantage.

"It must be a very large treasure," she whispered.

"Enormous," he whispered back.

"How did you find out about it?"

"Ah, suddenly you're not so eager to be free of me, are you? Yes, everyone can be bought for a price."

"My father and that other man seem to think they have rights to this treasure." It was a dangerous thing to say, and she held her breath, but he seemed to be enjoying the conversation.

"Perhaps they do. Obviously they were a part of bringing it into the country to fund some of their countrymen who were here, working for their little emperor and spying on the Crown."

"What? You mean this treasure was used to support French spies, right here on English soil?"

"Dastardly, isn't it? Do you really expect me to believe you had no idea your father was a spy? That he was betraying the country that had housed him and supported him for so long? My, but that is tragic, my dear."

No, it couldn't be true! Papa was a spy? She would not believe it.

Fitzgelder's shoulders shook against her. He was laughing. Damn him, but he was laughing at her again.

"Poor little actress. I'm tempted to believe you truly did not know. Well, perhaps he never intended to share it with you."

That she knew would never be true. But Fitzgelder didn't. He must have never known a parent who would sacrifice and give up his own hopes and dreams for the sake of his child. On some level she supposed Fitzgelder should be pitied, but it was a little difficult to do that right now while he held a knife to her throat and breathed his sticky breath all over her.

But now that she understood his weakness, she would find a way to use it against him. She'd done it before, hadn't she? And this time she'd not hide behind someone else. She'd defeat the man on her own.

"He was so disappointed in me when I failed to marry Rastmoor," she said, feigning a tremble in her lip. "He wanted me to make a match there; he helped convince Rastmoor I was more than just a common actress. When you came to tell Papa that Rastmoor had learned the truth and wanted no part of me, he was furious."

Fitzgelder rumbled with prideful mirth. "Yes, I remember that. I told him I had my cousin's vowels, that he'd wagered you at the table and purposely lost you to me. Oh, but the old man was livid. Threatened to kill me if I tried to claim that purse, as I recall."

She was silent. The conversation was taking a dangerous turn—she was certain Fitzgelder would not like to be reminded of what happened next, when Kitty approached him and claimed to be Julia.

"That's why he sent that actress, wasn't it?" Fitzgelder said. "He thought if he appeased me with her, then perhaps he could still snag Rastmoor for you. Silly man. He should have realized Rastmoor is a gentleman. He could never really take a wife like you, a common slut from the gutter, no matter how charming and delicious."

"Yes, we found that out. Papa was furious about that, too," she lied.

"Your father must not know human nature, Miss St. Clement," he said, his voice lulling her as his grip relaxed.

Yes, this was what she wanted. She let herself lean into him; listen as if the sun and moon hung on his very words. Years of experience on the stage came in rather handy right now as she let go of her disgust and willed her body to react to his nearness. She even gave out a tiny sigh as he let one finger trace the edge of her jawline.

"Rastmoor is a man of stature, a peer of the realm," he went on. "When he can take a wife with beauty, breeding, and a healthy dowry, why would he settle for one with merely beauty? Your father overestimated your charms, my dear."

"I did the best I could," she whimpered. "In the end, he wouldn't have me."

She felt him exhale, the moist air prickling the back of her neck. He was bending into her, caressing her. He spoke, and his voice took on the tone of a lover. "Rastmoor is a fool. I am not. I will have the woman of beauty *and* I'll have the treasure."

"Can you get it? Do you have the missing locket?"

"Yes," he said, kissing her neck where the blade of the

knife had cut her. "Our friend Lindley was kind enough to tell me where I might find it."

"Then all you need is the other locket, and you can get the treasure!"

She didn't bother to mention the fact that the box was probably locked away somewhere under Dashford's care, and it would likely take more than a scheming Lindley to get his hands on it.

"And that other locket rests with your father, doesn't it?"

"I know where he keeps it," she said. "I can get it."

"Can you? Can I trust you, Miss St. Clement?"

"As you say, Mr. Fitzgelder," she said, letting her voice drop low and her lips angle up toward his, "we all have our price."

His kiss was vile. His touch made her skin crawl. She turned in his arms to help him, though, as he sought to possess her mouth. She managed to keep from vomiting by focusing on the knife. Slowly, she felt the harsh metal leave her skin and trail harmlessly down her back to withdraw entirely just before she heard the sound of metal clattering on the cold stone floor.

Ever so gingerly, she edged her foot out behind her until finally she felt the hilt of the knife under her slipper. Carefully, she slid the knife in closer, letting Fitzgelder ravage her mouth with his awkward kiss and enduring his hands as they ranged over her body. Eventually the entire knife was safely under her foot, concealed by her gown and waiting for just the right opportunity.

She'd killed once. She could do it again.

"IT'S DOWN THIS WAY," RASTMOOR SAID, GUIDING HIS mother down the narrow staircase toward the kitchens located in the lowest level of Hartwood.

"I don't even want to know why you are so familiar with this area of Dashford's home," his mother said with an imperious harrumph.

"When we'd come visiting years ago, you and Father

would be abovestairs discussing very adult things with Dash's parents," he explained for her. "Dash and I would come down here and do very adult things with the scullery maids."

She didn't even bother to slap him as he'd half expected. "I'm going to assume you're teasing me."

He just shrugged. "Assume whatever you like."

Well, at least she was speaking to him. He supposed that was something to be grateful for. He'd have to come up with more outlandish lies, however, if he hoped to produce a chuckle. Clearly she was even more upset about Julia than he'd expected. He wondered how Julia was going to take it.

"It's just through here," he said, indicating the wide opening that led from this section of the house to an older one.

Raucous laughter was filling the corridor. His mother rolled her eyes and shook her head.

"It sounds as if your sister is developing similar tastes in entertainment as you. Honestly, Anthony, I don't know what to do with either of you. I'm almost afraid what we'll find in there."

Hmm, maybe she had a point. Perhaps it would be best if he went ahead of her.

"Mother, it *is* a kitchen," he said in his gentlest voice ever. "It might be rather warm in there and may not smell quite right. Perhaps I ought to go in and bring Penelope out here to you. Look, there's a little room over here where you can wait."

He pushed the door open to a storage room and smiled at his mother, hoping she'd take his advice. But she didn't. Instead, she gaped into the room as if Napoleon himself were in there. Rastmoor's head jerked around as he heard something metallic clatter against the floor.

His mind couldn't even fathom what his eyes were seeing. Julia? Kissing Fitzgelder? It couldn't possibly be. Could it?

He must have stared forever. She seemed to be inching ever closer to the man, allowing him to paw all over her like some drunken letch, and she was doing absolutely nothing to stop it. He blinked a couple times just to be sure the vision was real.

"See? Just what I told you. She's a whore!" his mother announced.

Rastmoor barely heard her. All he could think of was getting Fitzgelder away from Julia. So he did. He dove for the man, grabbed him by the neck, and threw him against the wall. A bag containing flour toppled over and sent up a white, dusty cloud. Julia shrieked, then coughed.

Fitzgelder probably would have been coughing, too, except that Rastmoor had him by the throat and was in the process of strangling him.

"You are going to wish you hadn't done that, Fitzgelder," Rastmoor growled.

In the background he could hear his mother bellowing. Strange, but she was not crying out in concern for her battling son or even for the trauma of having witnessed such a frightful scene as the octopus Fitzgelder pillaging poor Julia. She was hollering at the top of her lungs for Penelope.

"Miss Penelope Rastmoor, you get yourself here to me at once," she roared. "This instant, young lady! Cavorting with theater persons? Not in this lifetime!"

The distant laughter stopped, and presently Rastmoor was aware of the rumble of approaching footsteps. Good. They could deal with his mother. He already had his hands full with the still somewhat living Fitzgelder.

"Anthony, stop," Julia said.

He had to pause for a moment in his murderous endeavor to glance over at her to make sure he'd heard right. "Stop?"

"Don't kill him until he tells you where the other locket is," she instructed.

Ah, sensible girl. So that's why she was allowing his advances. Julia always did have a good head about her. He glared at Fitzgelder. "Where's the other locket?"

His cousin shook himself back to consciousness and actually had the nerve to smile. "I don't know. I just told her I knew so she'd let me climb on top of her. It worked, now, didn't it?"

"No, bastard, it didn't work. Instead, you got me climbing on top of you. Now, where's the other locket?"

"I tell you, I don't know!"

The door at the other side of the little room opened up, and suddenly Julia's father and D'Archaud burst in. One look around at the floured floor and Rastmoor's aggressive position, and it was clear they had an idea what had been going on. St. Clement ran to his daughter, while D'Archaud observed things from the doorway. It appeared there was something in his hand . . .

"Watch yourself!" Rastmoor heard his mother cry out. Bloody hell, did she give up on Penelope and decide to come in here now to critique his actions?

"Mother, I think I can handle things—" he began, only to be silenced by his mother's insistent pointing.

But she was staring past him, waving a finger toward D'Archaud. "He's got a gun!"

Sure enough, Rastmoor peered over his shoulder to find his mother was correct. D'Archaud had a gun. Wonderful.

For a moment, the Frenchman looked confused, but after a quick glance and a nod from St. Clement, he stood up taller and held the gun toward Rastmoor.

"Yes," he said. "I do have a gun. And I'm not afraid to use it."

"I say, see here now, D'Archaud . . ." Rastmoor said, torn between turning around to negotiate for his life and staying right were he was to rob Fitzgelder of his.

"Just say the word, Rastmoor, and I'll blow off his *stupide* head for you," D'Archaud went on. "He's nothing but a worthless bag of worms."

Julia wiped her mouth on her sleeve. "So that's what it was," she muttered.

Her father was horribly concerned. He was fussing over her, and she turned her head just enough that Rastmoor noticed the blood. Damn it, this bastard had hurt her!

Julia must have noticed their stares and felt the boiling rage in the air. "It's all right," she said. "I'm fine. I, er, distracted him, and he dropped the knife. I've got it here." She stepped sideways and pulled up her skirts. Sure enough, there was a cold, deadly little knife right there on the floor.

That must have been what Rastmoor heard dropping. By God, he knew there had to be some reasonable, rational excuse for Julia to be kissing the man like that. She was simply preparing to jab him with a knife. That made perfect sense.

"I truly was going to use it," she said, glaring at Fitzgelder.

Rastmoor threw the man back against the wall and stepped away, brushing flour from his coat. No sense further mussing himself if D'Archaud and his pistol had Fitzgelder firmly under control.

Unfortunately, he didn't.

Fitzgelder took advantage of his momentary freedom to leap up to his feet and lunge across the small room toward D'Archaud. He knocked the man backward, sending him staggering out the door and the pistol flying out of his hands. Fitzgelder caught it with unexpected grace.

He smiled and turned to the group. "All right, now who's got the upper hand? Everyone over there, in that corner. Now! Or Miss St. Clement gets a hole in her chest to go along with that little scratch on her neck."

They complied. Even Rastmoor's mother was forced to gather with them, helpless in the corner while a very angry, very twitchy Fitzgelder took pleasure in every moment of his authority.

"Well, since you're all here, and I've got such a lovely target standing right in front of me, perhaps one of you can give me what I need."

"I'll give you what you need . . ." St. Clement mumbled before dropping into some very impolite French that even Rastmoor wasn't sure he'd heard before.

"I'll tell you what I need. I need the location of that other locket. Tell me, and I'll let Miss St. Clement live. Don't tell me, and she dies."

"How can we tell you what we don't know?" D'Archaud argued.

"It's a trick," Julia said. "He already knows where it is. Lindley told him."

Fitzgelder shook his head and laughed. "No, he didn't. I

lied to you, Miss St. Clement. Honestly, did you really think Lindley would ever do anything to help me?"

"But I saw him! He broke the lock on your door . . . he said he had something you'd be interested in," Julia said, her eyebrows crinkling adorably.

"Yes, the bastard, he did have something for me, but nothing I wanted. He came to show me a letter he had from the Home Office implicating me in some rather unsavory activities over the past few years. He thought I'd just gladly fill him in on the missing details, maybe give him the names of my associates. Ha! He got nothing from me. Nothing but a bump in the head."

"What have you done to Lindley?" Rastmoor asked.

"I left him locked in my room. Don't worry, I don't think he's dead. Yet."

"But I thought you said you were paying him to work for you?" Julia asked.

"Yes, well, apparently the generous people in our office of the interior were paying him more to work for them."

"You mean Lindley has been investigating you?" Rastmoor said it, but even the very question sounded incredible.

"It would appear so, the Judas Iscariot. I thought he was my friend!"

"No, he's nobody's friend," D'Archaud announced. "He's a damn spy hunter, and he doesn't much care who gets punished for what crimes."

"Papa! Does that mean Lindley has been investigating you, too?" Julia asked.

"Well, if he has, I'm sure he's been disappointed, *ma belle*. I'm afraid I've never been so adventurous as to engage in any of those goings-on. No, life in the theater has been adventure enough."

Julia glanced back at Fitzgelder. "You said that Papa . . ."

"Lies again, Miss St. Clement!" the bastard said, mocking her. "Really, for such an accomplished little trollop, you're hopelessly naive. But all this distracts me from my purpose. Tell me where I might find that locket! One of you switched it. Was it you, D'Archaud? You, Rastmoor? Or even our sweet Julia? Tell me, or she dies!"

They all just looked at each other. Rastmoor wondered if that was because no one had an answer, or if someone was simply risking Julia's life for his own personal gain. He watched them all closely, especially Fitzgelder. Unfortunately, the man was becoming more and more unhinged by the minute. With that gun trained constantly on Julia, there was no telling what might happen.

He had to do something about that.

"Did you think to ask Lindley about it before you bashed in his head?" Rastmoor asked, inching away from Julia and hoping Fitzgelder—and the gun—would follow. "Did it ever dawn on you that he would have had the most opportunity as well as the most reason to switch that?"

"Of course I asked him," Fitzgelder said. "He claimed he didn't know—he thought I had it."

"Oh, and he couldn't possibly have been lying, could he? I say we go up and ask him, if he's not dead already. All of us, right now. We could force the truth out of him."

"Look, I'm the one deciding what we do," Fitzgelder said, his voice rising.

Rastmoor continued his slow creeping away from Julia, separating himself from the group. "Are you? I don't hear much deciding, Cousin. All I hear is complaining about how everyone else isn't doing things the way you like it. If you're really the one in charge here, why not be decisive. Go to the one who has your answers."

"No, stop it! I know what you're trying to do," Fitzgelder was waving the gun wildly now. "You always think you can tell me what to do; always the head of the household. Just because your damn father was married to your mother, you think that makes you better than me. Well, it doesn't. I know things about your father! I know what he did—things Lindley would love to know about, too—things I've got proof of all neatly tucked away in that locket."

"What are you talking about?"

"Ha! Why do you think your father had that locket to begin with? It belonged to D'Archaud, didn't it? Well, he gave it to your father—gave it to him as insurance that your father wouldn't do anything to upset the applecart, as they say. It was a reminder that D'Archaud knew things that your father wouldn't want made public, and vice versa. I guess neither of them counted on your poor papa sticking in his spoon quite so early, did they?"

"I think you'd do well to shut up right now, Cousin," Rastmoor warned.

His cousin, of course, paid him no mind. "But he did die, leaving D'Archaud in a bit of a bind. How was he going to get his precious little locket back now? Rastmoor's widow wasn't likely to let something like that get out into the world. Poor, poor D'Archaud. All he could do was get drunk and wallow in his own self-pity. He left his wife and brat and went off with the only people who seemed to care about him: actors. That's how I came to know of it. Dearest mother was rather a friend of his . . . for a time. Now, isn't that ironic?"

Fitzgelder laughed, although Rastmoor didn't find any of this very funny. "Can you imagine?" the bastard rambled on. "I learned the secret to your ruin, my dear, legitimate cousin, from my own unsainted mother. An actress! Yes, by God, my mother was a filthy little actress. Good enough for my father to bed and breed, but not to make her a decent offer. I'm a bastard, Rastmoor, because my frigging mother was a bloody actress, but this ruddy bastard over here told her about the locket! Ah, but that's poetic justice, isn't it?"

"Really, that's kind of pathetic," Rastmoor admitted.

"Don't patronize me! And don't think I'll let you live to marry this damn, filthy actress of yours."

Suddenly Fitzgelder was coolly in control again. He leveled the gun squarely at Rastmoor. His eyes said he'd fire it, too. Well, Rastmoor had to confess this visit to Hartwood was proving even more adventurous than the last.

"Come, Miss St. Clement," Fitzgelder called to her, his eyes and his pistol never leaving Rastmoor as he backed toward the doorway. "I think you and I should be on our way."

"She's not going anywhere with you!" Rastmoor declared.

"Oh, but she is. Unless, of course, she wants to see you dead. Aw, hell. Maybe I'll just kill you anyway." His arm straightened, and the gun rose just a bit, just enough so that the barrel was pointed directly at Rastmoor's heart.

"No!" Julia cried and leapt in front of Rastmoor.

It was at this very moment that Penelope finally decided to respond to her mother's earlier bellowing. She came tripping through the doorway and plowed right into Fitzgelder.

The gun in Fitzgelder's hand exploded, the loud crack echoing in the tiny storeroom. Females shrieked, and Rastmoor threw himself into Julia, desperately hoping that bullet could rip through his own body and not touch hers. Engulfing her, he fell to the cold floor.

Rastmoor was conscious of activity around him. Feet scuffled, and he heard St. Clement's angry cry, followed by a thud with moaning in the general vicinity of where the bastard had been standing. Penelope was screeching for someone to tell her what had just happened, and his mother was somewhere nearby, shushing her.

But none of that mattered. All Rastmoor could think of was Julia. Dear God, but she'd been right there, right smack between that damned pistol and his heart. He moved himself away from her and was almost afraid of what he'd find when he gazed down into her lovely face.

Her eyes were closed. No, hell no! She couldn't be . . . no, he would not let her be. He propped himself up and eagerly scanned her, looking for any evidence of a scarlet-soaked wound that he might quickly bind it and save her. He found nothing.

"Julia . . . Oh God, Julia! Are you all right?" he murmured as he ran his hands over her, frantic in his search for the injury that might be, even now, draining her life from her.

Suddenly she dragged in a deep gasping breath, and her eyes flew open. Thank heavens. She was still with him.

He knelt over her and cupped her face in his hands. "Darling, where are you hurt?"

Her brows knit together, and she bit her lip, seemingly confused. The poor thing, she was in shock. But he would save her.

"Tell me, where does it hurt, Julia?"

She thought about it for a moment then winced as he shifted slightly to get a better look at her.

"Oohh, my hand!" she groaned weakly.

That was unexpected. "Your hand? You got shot in the hand?"

She shook her head, cringing in pain. "No! You're kneeling on it."

He jumped back and quickly she pulled up her hand, cradling her fingers.

"Good Lord," he muttered, taking those fingers and kissing them gently. "I'm so sorry."

"It's fine. But what of you? Are you hurt, Anthony?"

He mentally checked himself. "I'm fine. God, if you're alive, I'm fine."

She smiled at him. Indeed, she looked healthy enough. He pulled her to him and nearly crushed her in his embrace. Never again did he ever want to lose this woman.

How odd, then, that he should hear St. Clement laughing. Did he not realize he could have just watched his daughter die? Rastmoor did not see how this was any time for laughter.

"Of course you're fine, my boy," the man said.

Rastmoor looked over to see him standing with Fitzgelder sprawled at his feet. D'Archaud was crouched beside him, holding the knife to Fitzgelder's throat. A happy sight to be sure, but still not quite an excuse to laugh.

"It wasn't loaded," St. Clement went on. "The gun; it was a prop for a spectacle to entertain the servants. To be sure, it's loud, but there was no ball inside. Fitzgelder could have never harmed anyone with it. The fool."

St. Clement kicked the man just for good measure. Fitzgelder started to curse him, but D'Archaud silenced him with a warning flick of the knife.

"Thank God," Rastmoor heard his mother breathe in amazement from the corner where she hovered over a still inquisitive Penelope. "It wasn't loaded!"

"No, but this one is," a new voice said from the doorway.

Well, damn it to hell. *Lindley.* And he had a gun, which most likely really was loaded.

He also had a goose-egg-sized lump on the side of his head and a surly demeanor. This did not bode well.

Chapter Twenty-two

Julia sat up, glad for Rastmoor's nearness. Her eyes found Papa's across the crowded storeroom, but she couldn't quite read his feelings. That meant he wasn't exactly sure what Lindley was up to. Drat. She was getting rather fatigued of all the worrisome excitement.

"I suppose you can kill him if you want to," Lindley said to D'Archaud in a tone far more commanding than his usual. "But I'd really much rather turn him over to some people I know who have excellent ways to extract information. I'm sure Mr. Fitzgelder still holds a few secrets my friends would be very interested in hearing."

Oh, dear. She knew what that meant. Fitzgelder would be tortured into revealing all he knew about Papa . . . and the previous Lord Rastmoor.

"No!" she said, scrambling up to her feet. "Please, let him go. Make him leave the country or whatever you wish, but please don't turn him over to your, er, friends!"

Lindley raised an eyebrow at her. "Well, Miss St. Clement. I can appreciate your compassionate soul, but this is taking mercy just a bit too far, don't you think? This man just tried to kill you."

Rastmoor, for some reason, agreed. "Julia, I think in this case, we should let Lindley do his duty and take Fitzgelder to the proper authorities," he said in his kindest tone.

She practically snarled at him. Didn't he realize what this might do to him, to his family's honor? She flashed her eyes emphatically, hoping he would understand. She decided to use the voice she'd use on a small—and very thickheaded—child. "But Anthony, dearest, think about it. They might be cruel toward your poor cousin. They will want him to tell them the things—*all the things*—he knows about this business with the spies."

Ah, now he got it. "Yes, I see what you're saying," Rastmoor agreed and turned to Lindley. "Indeed, Lindley, this man is my cousin. You don't think for my sake you could make an exception this time? The war's over, after all. I doubt Fitzgelder can be much of a threat to the Crown at this point."

But Lindley's grim expression didn't change. "Oh, he's still a threat, unfortunately. But don't think you need to worry, Miss St. Clement. My friends know all about your family. Rest assured, they are not our targets."

"But what about Rastmoor's . . ." she caught herself, but not in time.

"Rastmoor's *what*, Miss St. Clement?"

Rastmoor sighed, and she realized he was going to tell. Drat, but she'd left him little choice, had she? She tried to stop him.

"I meant Rastmoor's poor cousin, of course," she said quickly. "He's had a difficult life already, and we wouldn't want—"

"No, Julia," Rastmoor interrupted her, laying his hand on her arm. "No more lies. We've had too many already."

She was going to speak again, try to make him see reason, but he boldly went on.

"Fitzgelder claims he has proof that my father was involved in funding the French efforts against our king," Rastmoor said.

He looked so secure, so sure of himself as he spoke those damning words. She hated to hear him say it, but Julia had to admit it was most attractive. Imagine, a man of wealth and position who was willing to risk his social standing just for the sake of honesty and truth. My, but how appealing. In fact, she found she rather wished they were alone together here in this storeroom just now. Although of course the irony was that if they were alone here, the very trigger for her sudden craving would not exist.

Then again, as long as Rastmoor was present, she was fairly certain that would be trigger enough.

Lindley, however, didn't seem nearly as smitten with Rastmoor for his confession. He frowned at Rastmoor then turned back to Fitzgelder. "What the hell are you talking about? Damn it, Fitzgelder, is there no end to your lies?"

"It's no lie," Fitzgelder said, his words muffled and slightly slurred by the way his face was pressed into the floor as D'Archaud sat on him, knife still in hand. "The proof is there—it's in the locket."

"Which locket?"

"The one that got switched, you lobcock," Fitzgelder said. D'Archaud eased up on him just enough to make speech easier. "And you know where it is, don't you?"

"As if you even deserve an answer to that."

"You do know! Ah, I see. You already found the locket and are determined to protect dear old Rastmoor. That's how it works for you damn gentlemen, isn't it? Justice only when it suits you."

"You'd better hope justice isn't what I give you, Fitzgelder! By God, you need to be praying we *do* find that missing locket," Lindley said.

"Is this *really* all about that silly locket?" Penelope suddenly chirped from her corner. "The one Fitzy asked me to give him?"

"Yes, Penelope," Rastmoor replied. "That's the one. You caused quite a lot of trouble, you know. That locket was fairly important, and now someone switched it."

Julia almost felt sorry for the girl; she seemed so calm amid this disaster. Once she finally figured out exactly what it was she'd done, she was going to feel terribly low. Rastmoor was not likely to go easy on her about it, either.

"Yes, I know," she said, obviously still clueless.

"No, you don't, Penelope. There was something in that locket."

"Yes, I know," she repeated.

"And someone switched it, so we don't know where it is!" Rastmoor explained, becoming exasperated.

"Yes, I know."

"No, you don't, Penelope!" he nearly shouted at her. "You don't seem to know what you've done!"

"Yes, Anthony, I do," she replied, sounding a bit snippy. "I know exactly what I've done. I switched the locket; therefore, I know where it is."

"You *what*?" several disbelieving voices chimed together. Julia's was not one of them. She was struck speechless.

"I switched the lockets," Penelope explained carefully and slowly. "You don't really think I was fool enough to be taken in by Fitzgelder's ridiculous sweet talk, do you? I assumed that if he wanted that locket so badly, there must be something to it. So, I took the locket out of Mamma's things—sorry, Mamma—and investigated."

"And you found something inside it?" Lindley asked.

Penelope nodded. "I did. There is a note inside it. And more! If you turn the ring on the top just right, the back opens into the most unusual shape. Well, I knew better than to let Fitzgelder get his smutty hands on something like that. I simply gave him another. He'd never seen it, so he wouldn't know."

Rastmoor was shaking his head in disbelief. "Amazing. And you still have this locket?"

"Of course not," Penelope said, to the great sighing and consternation of others. "It's packed safely upstairs with Mamma's things. I put the locket right back in her jewel case after I looked at it, and she brought that case with her."

"It's here? At Hartwood?" Rastmoor asked.

"Dashford can open the box!" Julia exclaimed.

"After I take a look at what's inside that bloody locket," Rastmoor amended.

Julia glanced at Papa. He was, understandably, smiling. "Well, D'Archaud," he said to his friend with the knife. "It seems our lockets will be reunited at last."

"Wait, did you just say, D'Archaud?" Penelope asked. "Is that man's name D'Archaud?"

"Yes . . ." St. Clement replied, hesitant.

"Well, that's the name on the note inside the locket. It says—" she said.

Julia cringed, and Rastmoor tried to interrupt her, but she rattled on anyway.

"—for Sophie D'Archaud with deepest love," she recited. "And it's signed, simply, Papa. I never knew what that meant."

D'Archaud smiled through misty eyes. "I left that there for Sophie, in case something happened to me. I was in a bad way back then, fallen in with a bad crowd and down on my luck. I'm ashamed to admit it, but I met your father, Rastmoor, when I tried to rob him on the street."

"You vomited on his boots, if the stories I've heard are true," St. Clement said with a wry chuckle.

"Then fell in it," D'Archaud replied, wincing. "Still, your father chose to help me. He got me sober and helped me escape the men I'd been forced to work for. To be safe, I left the locket with him. He promised he'd look after Sophie for me . . . in case of the worst."

"Oh, that's so very sweet," Penelope said.

"Wait." Lady Rastmoor disrupted their warm moment. She glanced from her daughter to her son and then on to D'Archaud. "You mean, *you* are the father of Sophie D'Archaud?"

"I am, and quite proud of the woman she grew into, I might add, despite the fact that she never seems to stay in one place very long."

But this seemed to confuse Rastmoor's mother. Slowly her hand rose to her lips, and her confusion turned into something resembling a smile. "Then he was not . . . he did not . . . Oh, but this is wonderful!"

"Mother?" Rastmoor asked. "Do you know this Sophie D'Archaud?"

"No," she replied, nearly breaking into giggles. "I never even heard of her until I found that note in that locket after your father died. I was going through some of your father's things and . . . Oh, but this is too wonderful!"

"Mother!" Penelope said, scandalized. "You did not think that note was from our father, did you? But then that would mean he had, er, that Sophie D'Archaud was . . . but Mamma, that wasn't even Papa's handwriting."

"Well, what was I to believe? I found that note right there in his things, hidden in this strange locket I'd never seen. Your father was gone; I couldn't very well ask him, could I? Then, when your stupid cousin there started bragging that he had information to damage our family, I just assumed it had something to do with that note."

"Well, I suppose you were partially right about that," Penelope allowed.

"Happily, I was mostly wrong," Lady Rastmoor replied.

"Damn it, get off me!" Fitzgelder complained from his place on the floor. "You're breaking my back."

"Why don't you let him up, D'Archaud," Lindley said. "I think it's time we find our host and catch him up on what's transpired. If you'd be so kind as to allow us the use of your locket, Lady Rastmoor, I think we'd all be interested in seeing some treasure today."

"Treasure?" Lady Rastmoor questioned.

"Ooo, that sounds exciting!" Penelope was practically bouncing.

"It's quite an amazing story," Lindley said. "You and Miss Rastmoor will be fascinated. D'Archaud, bring Fitzgelder along. This dreadful dampness down here is ruining my lines."

And with that, the group began to file out of the little basement storeroom. Julia turned to follow her father, but Rastmoor grabbed her arm to hold her behind. She looked up to meet his eyes, smoldering with the same desire she felt inside for him.

"Come along, you two," Papa said from the doorway.

"Sir, I'd like to request that I have a few moments alone with your daughter," Rastmoor said. "There's something I wish to discuss with her."

Papa knew good and well Rastmoor's intentions had little to do with discussion. Still, he smiled and gave Rastmoor a nod. "Very well, but two minutes and no more. She's a lady, you know, son."

"Indeed she is," Rastmoor replied.

Oh, the male posturing was nauseating. "I'll be fine, Papa," she insisted. "Go on with the others. We'll be along."

Papa grunted. "Two minutes."

At last he left them and followed the group. They were alone once again. So why on earth was she suddenly anxious? Honestly, these last few days had played havoc with her nerves.

"You're trembling," he said, moving closer to her. "Are you certain you're not injured?" He touched the place at her neck where Fitzgelder's knife nicked her.

"I'm fine," she assured him, placing her hand over his. "I'm just happy it's all over. Fitzgelder is apprehended, and that terrible family secret turned out to be nothing at all."

"A happy ending for everyone, it would appear."

"And for your mother, as well. How dreadful she must have felt all this time, thinking that your father, er . . ."

Rastmoor shook his head. "But she shouldn't have worried. The man was devoted to her; he worshipped her. He was faithful to her until the day he died."

She couldn't help but smile. The sentiment was beautiful.

But then Rastmoor continued. "Just the way I'm going to be with my wife."

She felt her smile vanish. Those words cut her worse than Fitzgelder ever could. So this was how it ended, with a polite discussion of the way things had to be. She knew he was doing the right thing, but a sudden panic took over her as she faced the reality of a future without him.

She wanted to pretend she hadn't heard him. She wanted him to sweep her into his arms and ignore the truth of reality. She wanted him to devour her with that blinding passion she'd never share with anyone else. She wanted him to tell her somehow she would survive.

But he did none of that. To her great surprise, he dropped down to one knee and gazed up at her the way she had seen hungry hounds gaze at their masters.

"Julia St. Clement, now that my family honor is not about to be obliterated and my good name raked through the mud, I simply must beg you to do me the great kindness of agreeing to be my wife."

Her breath caught in her throat, and her vision inexplicably began to blur. Her nose itched and tingled. Good heavens, had the man just asked her to marry him?

"Anthony, I . . ."

"Say yes, Julia!"

"But I can't. Truly, you know I can't."

His face fell. "Why not?"

"Well, because I'm an actress. You have your duty to society, to your title, to generations of properly genteel Rastmoors!"

His countenance improved, and he breathed out a sigh of relief. "Oh, thank God, Julia. For a minute there I thought it was because you haven't fallen back in love with me again."

My, but the man certainly was full of surprises today. He asked her to marry him? Oh, he was a fool! It would be wrong, so scandalous and condemned. He'd only just regained the security of his good standing; she couldn't destroy that now by agreeing to marry him, could she?

Hell, how could she *not* marry this man? Her resistance was nil, and he was still gazing up at her with love and devotion and desire and a hundred other wonderful emotions she could simply not exist without. Basically, she was incapable of denying him any longer. If he was fool enough to ask for her, then he deserved whatever fate he got. She melted into him, falling down into his arms and tumbling him into the overturned bag of flour.

"Drat it all, Rastmoor. I fall back in love with you every time I breathe."

* * *

"AH, HERE THEY ARE!" JULIA HEARD LORD DASHFORD saying loudly as she and Rastmoor tried to inconspicuously rejoin the group.

It had been a ridiculous attempt. Clearly they'd been missed. Dashford and his lovely wife had been located, and the whole group from the storeroom—minus Fitzgelder—were waiting patiently in the large, formal drawing room. Rastmoor took his hand off her backside as they stepped in through the door.

"Sorry to keep you all waiting," Rastmoor said cheerfully. "I had to, er, help Miss St. Clement with something."

She nervously patted her hair to make sure her cropped curls were all in place. An obvious sprinkling of flour came sifting out. Drat. She thought she'd shaken all that off downstairs.

Penelope giggled. Julia refused to look at Lady Rastmoor to see what horror might be etched on her classical features. She focused instead on the floor, only to be appalled as more flour came filtering down like snow when she took a deep breath. Penelope giggled again.

"What is everyone staring at?" Rastmoor demanded. "You think you have an idea what transpired while we were elsewhere? Very well, I'll tell you. I was downstairs asking Miss St. Clement if she would do me the great honor of becoming my wife."

"You damn well better have been asking that, my boy," Papa said, but she recognized the little glimmer in his eye. He approved.

"And she has consented," Rastmoor finished.

Julia stared at the whitening carpet and waited for the explosion of weeping and gnashing of teeth that would surely come from Lady Rastmoor. But it didn't come. All she heard was the happy chorus of well wishes from everyone else. Penelope especially. Finally, Julia made herself look at the woman who, for better or worse, would soon be her mother-in-law.

"So, this is the woman who will take my place at Gaberdell Abbey, is it?"

Julia's nerve failed her, and she looked back down at the carpet. She felt woozy, to go from feeling such utter joy to be suddenly cast down to such wretchedness. She'd promised herself to Rastmoor not ten—well, perhaps fifteen—minutes ago, and already their trials had begun. Would he soon come to regret his choice of bride?

"I think she'll make a marvelous sister-in-law, Mamma," Penelope said with far too much perky anticipation. Heavens, but just what did she think she and Julia were going to be doing as sisters-in-law?

"Don't expect to be allowed much to do with her, Penelope," the viscountess said regally.

Julia pinched her eyes closed and felt Rastmoor come up close behind her. She willed the tears not to form in her eyes. She loved Anthony, and he loved her; somehow they'd get through this together.

"At least," his mother went on. "Not for some months. I have a feeling your brother is going to be rather jealous of his new wife's time."

"I most certainly am," he said. "And protective of her if anyone should attempt to make her life unpleasant."

Julia glanced up when she heard the woman begin to chuckle. She must have started at the sight, because another fall of flour drifted past her view.

"I'm sure you will be, Anthony," Lady Rastmoor said. "But don't get your hackles up on my account. You've made up your mind, and there's nothing I can do to change it. Besides, I just witnessed this woman try to throw herself in front of a bullet for you. As a mother, I couldn't hope for a better mate for my son. As long as you are happy, I will be happy."

"Thank you, Mother," he said. She could hear the honest gratefulness in his voice.

"So it's official, is it?" Dashford asked. "You're determined to marry her, come what may?"

"I am, though I'd hate to lose a good friend over it," Rastmoor said.

Dashford paused, then shook his head. "You won't. I'm the first one to acknowledge matters of this nature rarely follow common sense. Please forgive my earlier behavior, Miss St. Clement. My wife assures me it was inexcusable, but I beg your pardon, anyway."

She could hardly believe it, but Dashford was actually waiting for a word from her. She swallowed hard before words would come. "Yes, thank you, my lord. Any offense is forgiven."

"Very well, then," Lindley said, moving toward the center table where, once again, the metal treasure box was resting.

Only this time, to Julia's amazement, the box was open!

"Shall we get back to the business at hand?" Lindley suggested.

"You opened it!" Rastmoor declared.

"We got tired of waiting," Penelope said. "It seemed you would be a while."

Lindley cleared his throat and, thankfully, changed the subject. "The D'Archaud lockets fit together perfectly and made the exact key that unlocked the box."

"You mean the D'Archaud locket and the St. Clement locket," Rastmoor corrected.

"No, he had it right," Papa said. "The treasure belongs to the D'Archaud family as do the lockets that open the box."

"But I thought half of it belonged to you, Papa?" Julia said, confused. "You had one of the keys."

"Yes, but I never claimed to own the key. The key, *ma petite*, belongs to you."

"Honestly, Papa, how can I possibly own a key I've never even seen before?"

"I've kept it safe, *chérie*. It was your legacy from your dearest *maman*."

"From my mother?"

Now D'Archaud spoke up. "We did not tell you for your own safety, my dear."

She couldn't much like being called "dear" by the likes of D'Archaud. What on earth could the man possibly know about her safety?

"It was a difficult time back then," D'Archaud went on. "In the revolution. My father lost his life. Oh yes, he was a good man, but he had a great many things the people did not. And others wanted it. My brother and sister and I feared for our lives, as well."

"It was a very dark, dark day," Papa said. She knew it was true. All her life she had never been able to get him to talk about his life in France, those years before he crossed the Channel and began a new life.

"But your father was smart," D'Archaud said. "He made a way for us to escape. Only my brother would not go. He insisted that one day he would regain all that the revolution had cost us. He refused to help our escape or give us our share of what was left of the family fortune."

"So we took it anyway," Papa said, making the long story short. "D'Archaud and his beautiful sister took their share of the treasure, and we sailed for England. His brother was furious."

"*Mon dieu*, he sent men after us to retrieve the treasure. But, again, St. Clement saved us. He convinced us not to go to friends in London, where my brother would surely find us. Instead, he took us with him, to the life he knew—the theater. And we were safe there. My brother never thought to look for us among such common people as actors! I told you your papa is smart. And that's why my sister married him."

Julia thought by now she must be getting used to the constant string of surprises. She was not.

"My mother was your sister?"

"*Oui*, such a lady, your mother was." D'Archaud sighed as he gazed past her, unseeing and lost in a memory.

"She was the daughter of a great man, *ma belle*. A gentleman of high rank. As I've always told you, you are a lady."

She was becoming numb to the amazement. "But how come I never knew this? Why have you never told me any of this?"

"We couldn't," Papa said. "It wasn't safe."

"My brother was obsessed!" D'Archaud continued. "He hunted us for the treasure, threatened our lives and those of our children! Year after year, living like paupers and constantly on the move, it was terrible. I'm afraid it was too much for me. I got desperate and made some mistakes."

"I couldn't trust him any longer," Papa said. "We parted ways but agreed to hide the treasure so that one day, when it was safe, our daughters would get what belonged to them. Trouble was, neither of us was sure the other wouldn't go back for the treasure later on. So we found a solution."

"We would each take a key," D'Archaud explained. "It would take both of us to open the box."

"And now you've done that!" Julia remarked. "So, what is this treasure?"

She stepped forward to look inside the box. To her surprise, which really should have been no surprise at all, given the way her day had been going, it was empty.

"It's empty!" she exclaimed.

"No," Papa said. "It has the code."

She glared at him. What on earth did that mean?

"If you look, there are symbols etched on the box, one on each of the interior surfaces and, apparently, some on the outside. The box itself is the code."

D'Archaud nodded enthusiastically. "That's why we simply couldn't let Lord Dashford bash it to pieces."

"So where is the treasure?" Rastmoor questioned, clearly getting a bit weary of the endless journey they were on.

"Buried somewhere." Both Papa and D'Archaud replied at the same time.

"And the code will tell us where?"

"Yes," they echoed again.

"But wait a moment," Julia said, confused again. "If you came up with the code, wouldn't you therefore know where you buried the treasure?"

Papa laughed. "Of course! That is, if we had come up with the code. But we didn't, *ma belle*. We let others do that for us."

"Who? Who on earth could you possibly trust with something like that?" Rastmoor asked.

"Lord Dashford, of course," D'Archaud said.

Now Dashford jumped into the conversation. "What? I never came up with any code or buried any treasure!"

"No, not this Dashford," Papa said, laughing again. "It was your grandfather."

"His mistress—who lived at Loveland—was my wife's mother," D'Archaud said.

Julia had to think a moment to let that all sink in. "So, your mother-in-law was old Dashford's mistress, and because of this you let that man hide your treasure for you?"

"Quite so! Capital old man, he was. He buried the treasure, she hid the box, but they made out the code together."

"So just how do we decipher this code?" Rastmoor asked.

Papa scratched his head. "Well, that's become the sticky part."

"We can't find the book," D'Archaud said.

"The book?" Rastmoor asked.

Papa looked decidedly uncomfortable. "It's a slim volume, very plain binding, about so big . . . unremarkable to look at, I'm afraid. It was supposed to have been left in Loveland, but Dashford managed to find it and bring it here several years ago, apparently."

"The cover was unremarkable, but I had the good fortune of opening it," Dashford said with a wide grin.

Oddly enough, Lady Dashford was grinning as well. And blushing.

"Well, what sort of book is it? Did you check the library here?" Rastmoor asked.

"Of course we did," Dashford replied. "We had ample time, waiting for you to finish helping Miss St. Clement in the basement."

"And it's not there?" Julia asked quickly, changing the subject.

"No," Papa said. "Unfortunately it's the sort of book that, if discovered, might be rather . . . engrossing."

"We're afraid someone might have taken it," D'Archaud finished.

But Julia thought she had an inkling why everyone was being so cryptic about this book and why Lady Dashford was still blushing.

Botheration. She had to tell them, didn't she? "Er, I think I may have been the one to take it."

Papa gaped at her. "You?"

"Is it the sort of book you'd wish me to read, Papa?"

"Absolutely not! You're a lady, Julia St. Clement."

"Well, then this sounds like that book. I took it up to my room."

Rastmoor gave her a questioning look, but she just shrugged. It would be a shame to let him know she'd borrowed a few, er, techniques from that book. She'd rather he simply go on crediting her with superior creativity.

Lindley gathered up the box, and the whole group of them trooped up the stairs to Julia's bedroom. Sure enough, the book was right where she had left it. Hidden plainly behind the loose panel under the drapery in the far corner beside the bureau. At least there was little risk that anyone else had found it and taken it to their room.

Dashford did the honors and took the book. He thumbed through a few pages, and Lady Rastmoor gasped and threw her hand over Penelope's eyes. Lady Dashford was blushing again. Julia almost thought perhaps Rastmoor was, too.

"It appears the symbols on the box match symbols handwritten in the book," Dashford said. "Perhaps if we match them with the letters or numbers they are drawn nearest to, we will decipher the code."

"Or at least we'll get a fair useful education, eh?" Rastmoor chuckled, reading over Dashford's shoulder.

Lindley asked for a paper and charcoal, so Julia found some that Mr. Nancini had used during his mute phase. Quickly the men ran through the symbols on the box, finding the corresponding one in the book and making note of any numbers or words it seemed to indicate. Some of the symbols seemed a bit more difficult to match up, but Julia decided those were the ones that fell on pages with the most intriguing illustrations.

Before long—although it must have seemed ages to Lady Rastmoor, who was stuck with a fidgety and inquisitive Penelope across the room—one certain pattern emerged. The symbols on the outside of the box each corresponded to numbers, from one to six. The symbols inside the box—and there were two on each of the surfaces—corresponded to letters.

"I see it!" Rastmoor exclaimed. "The numbers tell us what order to place the letters. Each panel of this box has an interior side and an exterior. The numbers on the exterior panel tell us what order to place the letters on the inside panel."

He seemed to be correct. Lindley carefully wrote out letters in the order that Rastmoor called them off to him. Julia peered closely, having to strain to see between her father and D'Archaud. As the tenth letter was written down, she couldn't help but frown.

This was it? This was the great secret code that would lead them to the D'Archaud treasure? She couldn't see how.

"Strawberries?" she said, reading what Lindley had written. "All this trouble, and that's the only clue we have? The code spells *strawberries*?"

But to Dashford, Rastmoor, Papa, and D'Archaud this seemed to make perfect sense. "Strawberries!" they said together.

"The old man must have put it in his strawberry patch," D'Archaud said.

"He did love his strawberries," Papa said with a nod.

They laughed again and slapped one another on their backs. Penelope finally broke away from her mother and demanded to be allowed to go along to the strawberry patch. The men bundled up their code-deciphering tools—Lindley ending up with the armload of box and charcoal and symbol-scrawled papers—and traded suggestions for treasure hunting in a strawberry patch. Julia was surprised to hear that the strawberry patch was actually under cover of a greenhouse, but Dashford assured them all this would have kept the treasure safe from any prowlers or other dangers.

Papa seemed to have no doubt they would find it just as the long-deceased Lord Dashford had left it for them. It still seemed too incredible for Julia, but her father and D'Archaud couldn't have been happier.

"Ah, *ma chérie*," Papa said as they began to file out of the room. "There is a string of pearls in there that will look ravishing against your porcelain skin."

Rastmoor was at her shoulder, and he leaned down to whisper in her ear, "I'd love to see you in pearls."

"Heavens, I have nothing to wear with pearls," she said.

Rastmoor smiled. "All the better, then."

A thrill of anticipation coursed down her spine. She could go her whole lifetime and never tire of his voice. And she would, too.

"Hurry now, Julia," Papa called as he followed the excited group. "Don't you want to find your treasure with us?"

Julia just smiled at him. "I already have, Papa. All the treasure I need."

Epilogue

It was late, and Rastmoor was tired. More than that, he was not looking forward to another long and lonely night. Three days now he'd been kept from her—surrounded by Julia's ever watchful papa and her whole nosy theatrical family, not to mention his own nosy family. It seemed the lot of them were determined to keep the couple painfully chaste until the wedding, nearly one whole month away.

Damn their well-meaning meddling! Rastmoor found it downright torture to spend his days in Julia's presence but be forced to spend his nights bereft. True, he understood the need for respectability, but Lord, it was tough. Every minute that passed, he seemed to love Julia more. Their whole lifetime together would never be enough.

His mother and St. Clement were adamant, though. Tomorrow they would leave for London, where Julia and her father would begin living the life that should have been theirs years ago. The D'Archaud treasure was safe at last. It had turned out to be as rich and remarkable as one might hope; jewels, coin, even a tiny portrait of Julia's maternal grandfather. Julia and her relatives would never want for anything and could finally count themselves free of any further threats from the continental arm of the D'Archaud family. Julia had no further need to hide from anyone. Their engagement would be announced by the end of the week, as would her connection to an old and honored aristocratic French family. Julia truly was a lady.

But, by God, he wouldn't treat her like one if he had his way about it tonight. He had a rather lengthy list of things he might love to do to Julia, but none of them seemed suitable for ladies. Why the hell had he agreed to this drawn-out engagement? He would lose his mind in a fortnight.

He stepped into his room and pulled the chamber door shut behind him. How was he to pass these next weeks without her touch, without her breathing beside him in the dark? He wondered if anyone had ever died from frustration or if he'd likely be the first.

The evening was somewhat chilly, but a gentle fire had been lit in the grate. Candles flickered their warm glow around the room. If he wasn't so blasted alone here, he would have to say the place was downright inviting. And then he realized he wasn't alone.

Julia was there in his bed, her hair tousled on his pillow and the covers pulled up around her. She wasn't asleep, though. Her warm, nut brown eyes flashed a desire that equaled his own, and she smiled.

He smiled in return. "Well, Miss St. Clement, it seems you've ended up in the wrong bed tonight."

"No, my lord, this is quite precisely the right bed."

Instinct told him to kick off his boots and dive into that bed with her, but sheer force of will held him back. She was, after all, a lady. He supposed he owed her at least a moment or two of conversation before he ripped off her covers and devoured her with passion.

"However did you manage to escape your father's eagle eye?" he asked.

"You were gracious enough to keep him distracted downstairs, my lord," she replied, her voice teasing him almost as much as the curves of her lovely form beneath those bed linens. "Whatever did you find to discuss for so long?"

"Plans for your arrival in London, of course. Oh, and there's good news, my love," he said, moving slowly toward her. "Word has come from your uncle. Sophie is found, and all is well. She's been staying with some friends she met along the road once she left Lindley's company. It seems she traveled back to London with them and has been quite worried for you this whole time, in fact. You'll be seeing her in London when you make your grand debut."

"Wonderful! And, er, what of her child? Lady Dashford assures me she received a letter from Sophie months ago mentioning a blessed arrival. What on earth happened to Sophie's child?"

Rastmoor shook his head with a grin. "It was not her child."

"Not her child? But how could Lady Dashford have been so mistaken?"

Rastmoor shrugged. "Apparently our hostess had not gotten all the correspondence that had been directed to her. Sophie assured her father she sent two letters to her cousin those months ago. The first explained that a dear friend of Sophie's was expecting, and the second simply mentioned that the child had arrived and all was well. The first one must have been lost and Lady Dashford, understandably, drew the wrong conclusion. The child Sophie referred to was not hers, but a friend's. See? All truly does end well."

Julia sighed and relaxed back into the bed, her huge eyes still flashing at him. "Indeed, but it would be even more well if you would stop making chitchat and please remove your clothing, my lord."

"Oh?"

"Yes. I took special pains to make my apparel pleasing to you tonight, and I shall expect you to do the same for me."

"Indeed! And just what delightful confection have you robed yourself in for me, Miss St. Clement?"

She didn't answer but merely gave a coy smile. Hell, he'd

been too long without her to play at this game. He strode to the bed and yanked at the covers. They sailed off of her, and she giggled up at him. His eyes took in the scene, and it was several moments before he could speak.

"Ah, how thoughtful. You wore your new pearls."

KEEP READING FOR A PREVIEW OF

THE NEXT HISTORICAL ROMANCE

BY SUSAN GEE HEINO

Temptress in Training

COMING SOON FROM BERKLEY SENSATION!

Chapter 1

What? There would be no usual Thursday orgy? Indeed, this was a relief.

Sophie Darshaw could not be too grateful for a break from her household duties. Tidying up after Mr. Fitzgelder's constant debauchery was quite exhausting. She honestly didn't believe she had it in her to spend another night restitching some randy reveler's trousers or hunting down new lacing for some doxy's willfully dismantled corset. After all, Sophie had her own troubles to tend. She'd learned several long hours ago that a grave error had been made in the design of her latest undergarment invention.

Velvet pantalets, as it turned out, were a decidedly unwise construction. They chafed particularly.

This was a problem, and not merely for the obvious reasons. Madame Eudora, her former employer, had commissioned this project and seemed convinced such an object would suit nicely. Sophie would be obliged to send a carefully worded note tomorrow stressing the, er, unfortunate drawbacks.

Would the Madame still pay the agreed price for the pantalets if she were to fashion them from some lesser, more comfortable fabric? It hardly seemed likely. Or ethical. Sophie couldn't in good conscience allow it. She would simply have to take a loss on this project and encourage Madame Eudora to settle for something a bit more conventional, like those lovely little silk pillows she'd created to fit snugly into Madame's bodice to force the woman's forty-year-old assets back into proper position. Now *that* had been a useful invention and certainly there would be nothing like this god-awful rash today's endeavor had got her.

It was this problem precisely that she sought to correct when she spied the linen cupboard. Conveniently, someone had left the door ajar. Sophie would just tiptoe in and make use of the blessedly private and unoccupied space.

At least, she'd assumed it was unoccupied.

Sophie was suddenly face-to-face with her horrible employer, the always-eager Mr. Fitzgelder. That fretful chafing was quickly forgotten. Good heavens, what was the man doing in here? Her first impulse was to glance around for whichever of her unfortunate fellow servants the man must have dragged into the small room for unimaginable purposes, but it appeared this time he was uncharacteristically alone.

In his thin, pasty hand he held what appeared to be a locket hung from a long golden chain. He was working the locket, studying it so intensely she almost believed that little bit of jewelry might hold his attention long enough for her to slide out of the room unnoticed. And unmolested, with luck.

Apparently, though, it could not. He saw her and smiled. The locket was instantly forgotten, folded into his sweaty palm as he moved toward her.

"Well, if it isn't the proper little miss from Madame Eudora's," he said.

His thick, drawling voice irritated her like sand in a shoe, and she knew he chose his words intentionally. Mr. Fitzgelder was not about to let her forget where he had found her and, supposedly, rescued her. He didn't have rescue on his mind now—that much was certain.

"Beg pardon, sir," she said, staring at his feet and backing away. "I'll just . . ."

"You'll just stay here with me, little dove," he said, grabbing her wrist and tugging her back into the room.

He kicked the narrow door shut. Now it was dark. Just a thin line of light escaped into the room on three sides around the door. Sophie choked on her panic but forced herself to stay calm. She would find a way to get out of this. She had to.

The room was small. She knew shelves lined each wall, piled high with towels. Bedsheets and all other manner of upstairs linens surrounded them—it would be the perfect place for the unpleasantness her master clearly had planned. Even a fool like Fitzgelder would not overlook such a golden opportunity. Lord, but she should have been more careful. She knew what sort of man her employer was.

Well, she was not ready to give up without a fight. Not that she could count on help from anyone outside that cupboard door, of course. No matter what ruckus she might make in here, Fitzgelder's servants knew the force of their master's wrath—they wouldn't dare interrupt. Especially not for the likes of her. Indeed, although she was ostensibly in training as a maid, everyone knew the real reason Fitzgelder had brought her from Madame Eudora's brothel to his home. And it did not include polishing his silver, unless of course one was not really talking about actual silver.

But Sophie was not interested in polishing anything—real *or* hypothetical—for this man. She hadn't spent the last month repeatedly escaping his groping hands and roving eye only to succumb in a linen cupboard of all places. She'd survived four years as a seamstress—and only that—for Madame Eudora. She was not about to quietly give up what was left of her virtue to a putty-faced, perpetually drunk bastard like Fitzgelder.

And she was certainly not about to let the man find out she'd been wearing velvet pantalets!

"Get off me, sir! I do not wish for this."

"What fine airs you take on." He laughed, his thick fingers digging into her shoulders. She knew it would leave bruising.

"Leave me alone or I'll scream!"

He simply shrugged—she could feel the slight movement in the dark. "Go ahead and scream. I like screamers."

Well, then screaming was out of the question. She'd conserve her energy for other purposes. Like scratching his eyes out.

But in the dark she had a hard time finding them. Her nails

had barely scraped his pock-marked face when he caught her hands in his and clenched them tight. She winced in pain and realized things were not going well for her. She shoved against him but it had little effect. Heavens! Whatever was she to do?

Desperation took over and she slammed her forehead against his chin. Something warm dripped onto her face. Was that blood? Good. With luck she'd caused him to bite his own tongue off. If there were any justice in the world, he'd choke to death on it now.

But he merely sprayed her with warm moisture as he laughed—actually laughed!—at her fury. With one hand fisted in her hair so she could no longer move freely, he loomed nearer, breathing heavily and filling the room with the smell of whiskey and tobacco. She was hopelessly pinned.

"I'm going to enjoy this," he hissed.

No, she was fairly certain he would not. With every ounce of fury she felt, she brought her knee up between them. God was merciful and she caught him dead-on right where she had hoped to aim. He let out an injured yelp.

"Damn it, you're going to regret that!"

Now he was grabbing at her again, but she'd been able to move slightly to one side, and in the dark he'd not known exactly where to find her. She knew the room was far too tight to escape him for long, but there was no way in hell she'd make this easy for him. Too soon, though, he had her pinned in the corner. Now her arms were wedged behind her and she admitted he was not likely to allow her a second chance at attack.

Curse those velvet pantalets that brought her in here! And to think she'd hoped the money she earned from their design might be enough to finally free her from this man and his employment. How mistaken she'd been. She should have known a girl in her circumstance would never earn enough honest wage to set herself up as a proper dressmaker. It was just a foolish dream that—

She blinked in surprise when the door suddenly came open and light flooded into the cupboard. Fitzgelder released her immediately, adjusting his sagging breeches and disheveled coat. Sophie was torn between hiding from the shame of being discovered like this and rushing out to embrace her savior.

As her eyes adjusted to the relatively bright light from the hallway, she did neither. Instead her words of thanksgiving died in her throat as she recognized the intruder. Good Lord, could it really be *him*? Here, wandering the halls and linen cupboards of Mr. Fitzgelder's home as if it were his own?

How awful that he should see her this way! What must he think? He stood there in the doorway, his tall, elegant form perfectly silhouetted, taking in the full panorama of what he could not possibly mistake as anything other than what it was.

Richard Durmond, Earl of Lindley. The finest man she'd ever laid eyes upon and one of the few who'd treated her with something like respect when she'd been introduced to him at Madame Eudora's. Thank heavens he happened to find her here!

Yet he gave no appearance of shock or surprise or even the least bit of distress at her plight. That struck her more than anything. Why on earth was he not distressed?

Honestly, he seemed barely miffed. His voice, when he finally spoke, was disappointingly calm and dripping with ennui.

"I say, Fitz, why didn't you bother to tell me the festivities had begun already? You know how I deplore coming in late on the entertainment."

LORD LINDLEY CURSED HIMSELF AS HE PROWLED THE deserted halls of Fitzgelder's garish town house. Marble statuaries peered at him from the crowded alcoves built to showcase them. Reproductions, of course, but still they represented a great deal of investment. Even upstairs the walls were lined with expensive silks and gilded tapestry. All in all the effect was quite overwhelming, but even the casual observer would have to wonder where a shiftless bastard like Fitzgelder came up with the blunt to furnish his home in such lavish fashion.

Lindley was convinced he knew the answer. Oh, for a while Fitzgelder tried to pretend his wealth was inherited from his father, but Lindley knew this not to be the case. He'd spent the last year conjuring a friendship with Fitzgelder's legitimate cousin and learned some intimate details of the family's situation. Fitzgelder was a bastard whose father had seen little use for him. He'd died without heir and left his wealth and his title to his brother. Upon the brother's death, the Rastmoor wealth passed even further from Fitzgelder's grip to his younger cousin. This current Lord Rastmoor was not inclined to share.

Yet somehow Fitzgelder did quite well for himself. By all appearances, his bills were paid and he could afford the lascivious life he led. In all his prying, Lindley had found little explanation for this. Clearly, then, that was its own explanation. Fitzgelder was his man.

Frustrating as it was, he couldn't yet move on it, though. Captain Warren would want details, names, places, and proof. Lindley had none of these, nothing more than suspicions and a deep, churning sense in his gut that told him Fitzgelder was rotten. Just how rotten, he was determined to find out.

He supposed another night spent in carousing and in false friendship with the man would likely not kill him. Then again, it would probably give him a strong headache in the morning and another load of guilt to carry around. But he was getting used to that now. No matter of guilt for a few lies here and a liaison or two there would ever come close to comparing to the loss that still festered in his soul. If Fitzgelder was his man, by God he'd do what it took to catch him.

Then he'd see him hanged.

First, though, he'd have to find him. Where had the bloody bastard gone? They'd only just returned from that dreadful reading of erotic poetry one of Fitzgelder's tasteless friends had arranged. What a waste that had been.

At least, he hoped it had been a waste. Had the man met with his contact in the dark secrecy of the event? Damn, he hoped not. He'd hung on Fitzgelder like a horse bur for the last two weeks but still he was no closer to confirming his intuition about the man. It would be a shame if he had to put up with all this only to miss out on catching Fitzgelder in the act.

So where was the man now? They had returned to Fitzgelder's home to find a parcel waiting for him, delivered by messenger. Lindley had seen the delight written on Fitzgelder's face, yet he'd not gotten any clue who had sent the parcel. Fitzgelder deposited a frustrated Lindley in the drawing room and instructed him to wait, saying he was off to refresh himself but would return momentarily and they might resume their evening plans.

Well, Lindley wasn't about to let Fitzgelder go off to deal

with that secretive parcel alone. By God, if this was the evidence he'd long been looking for, Lindley was going to find it. He had quietly followed the man upstairs but promptly lost him.

So where the devil was he? And what was in that bloody parcel?

A commotion from farther down the hallway snagged his attention. It seemed to be coming from behind a narrow door, probably a closet or cupboard. Lindley heard the low drum of Fitzgelder's voice, and the panicked high pitches of a female. Well, it would appear he might yet catch Fitzgelder in the act, although sadly this was far from the act he was hoping for. Apparently the parcel had turned out to be less enthralling than Fitzgelder expected.

Really, Lindley knew he ought to leave the man to his efforts. He'd worked hard to insinuate himself into Fitzgelder's confidence. A good friend would never interrupt a gentleman—or rather, in Fitzgelder's case, a ruddy lecher—from availing himself of an opportunity for a little tussle with a willing maid. An interruption just now might actually sever what measure of trust that had been established between the men. Was Lindley prepared to sacrifice that?

Yet the female's protest and the sounds of struggle were obvious. She was clearly—and not surprisingly—unwilling. Lindley decided he was not game for heaping that guilt upon his shoulders along with all the other. He'd no doubt kick himself for it later, but right now he must certainly intervene.

And he was glad that he did.

Light from the many sconces in the hallway poured into what turned out to be a linen cupboard. Fitzgelder, startled, struggled to right his clothing. Lindley politely averted his gaze. What his gaze landed on made him temporarily forget his disgust, his guilt, and his mission to implicate Fitzgelder.

Sophie Darshaw. Hell and damnation, it was she who had been struggling with Fitzgelder. By the looks of it she'd been giving the man quite a fight, too. Her clothing was in dreadful disarray, her fair hair was mussed and tangled in clumps, and were those droplets of blood spattered on her pretty, ashen face? By God, he'd kill the man.

No, he couldn't. He'd come too far and had too much at

stake. Sophie Darshaw was just a minor player in this, and Lindley reminded himself he wasn't even entirely sure yet what part she played. He'd interrupted and that was enough. He would not give in to ridiculous sentiment when there might still be a chance to salvage things.

He wiped all trace of loathing from his face and carved out a disgruntled pout.

"I say, Fitz, why didn't you bother to tell me the festivities had begun already? You know how I deplore coming in late on the entertainment."

"Bloody hell, Lindley," Fitzgelder growled. "What in damnation are you about, tearing in while a fellow's readying to plug himself a little laced mutton?"

Lindley simply shrugged and allowed a lengthy—and welcome—look over Miss Darshaw's disheveled person. It appeared he'd come just in time. The girl was shaking and as pale as the crypt, but he was pleased to see a healthy spark of defiance left in her crystal blue eyes. She'd done well for herself, all things considered. Fitzgelder sported a bloody lip while she was merely untidy.

"Well then," Lindley said, unbuttoning his coat and placing his hand as if to begin unfastening his trousers. "If the mutton's willing, I might fancy a go at her myself."

"The mutton most certainly is *not* willing!" Miss Darshaw announced firmly.

She shoved Fitzgelder and pushed her way out of the tiny room. Lindley stood aside to let her. He could well do without a bloodied lip tonight and Miss Darshaw seemed every bit capable of giving him one. Hell, if he hadn't interrupted when he did, poor Fitzgelder might have ended up singing soprano. The way Miss Darshaw glared murder at them both, he wasn't entirely convinced she had needed his intervention after all. The girl showed ferocity enough to do serious damage.

But Fitzgelder was a fool and paid no notice. He brushed past Lindley and made as if to follow the hellcat. Lindley latched on to his arm.

"Oh, let her go," he advised, careful to seem unconcerned. "She's not but a little slip of a thing, Fitz. Hardly woman enough for men like us. Come, what more creative pleasures do you have scheduled tonight? It is Thursday, after all."

Miss Darshaw shot him a hateful glance before scurrying up the hall and disappearing around a corner. Fitzgelder watched after her, steaming. Indeed, he was too proud to admit his frustration but Lindley knew this matter was not settled. As long as Miss Darshaw chose to remain in this household—whatever her reasons might be—she was going to be her master's choice prey. Clearly this was not something she wished, but at the same time she did not disdain it enough to leave. That, of course, must mean something.

If only he could discern what.

"I swear, that minx needs a good thrashing to put her in her place," Fitzgelder was muttering.

"Thrash her later, old man. I'm nearly bored to death after that abominable poetry party tonight. Why ever did you drag me to such a gathering of stiff-rumped nobs? In faith, I could have enjoyed myself more with my Methodist grandmother. You know I come to you, Fitzy old man, to save me from such dreariness."

He glanced back into the cupboard behind them and noticed the wrappings from Fitzgelder's parcel lying discarded on the floor. Damn! Whatever had been in it, the man had already taken possession of it. But perhaps there was some clue in that abandoned wrapper. He'd have to get a look at it.

In hopes of distracting his friend, he stepped aside to allow Fitzgelder to leave the cupboard and join him in the hallway. The man did. Lindley casually shut the cupboard door behind them.

"So where shall we be going next?"

Fitzgelder finally took his focus off the direction Miss Darshaw had gone and brought out a handkerchief to dab his lip. "Well, I'm afraid tonight's entertainment might seem a bit tame for your lordship's high standards," he said.

"Nothing aimed to better my mind, I hope."

At last Fitzgelder lost a bit of his anger and made a sound that was likely akin to laughter. "No, nothing like that. I've had my man engage a theatrical troupe to present for us. They should be already preparing down in the blue salon and our other guests should be arriving presently. I suppose we can expect the odd Shakespeare scene, a tableau or two, and the usual buffoonery. Personally, though, I'm quite looking forward to it. Why don't you go do some damage to my brandy while I find my man to put me in a fresh cravat, eh?"

"By all means," Lindley said. "But see that the man ties it with both hands this time, Fitzy. All evening long it's looked wretched, like someone strapped a wet cat around your neck, or what."

Fitzgelder laughed at him. By faith, the stupid man actually seemed to enjoy the ridicule Lindley found all too easy to heap on him.

"I'll tell the man you said so," Fitzgelder assured. "He'll be mortified, of course, so perhaps you'll encourage the sluggard to do better. There's no better judge of the complicated knot than the Earl of Lindley, after all."

"Precisely," Lindley agreed.

Fitzgelder left him then, still chuckling—presumably—over the amusing image of a wet cat around his neck. Honestly, the man thought himself quite the fashion plate when really he was a complete simpleton. Lindley watched him go. So just what was the muttonmonger up to? Was he really off to attend his neckcloth or to conduct secret business without Lindley's watchful eye? Or perhaps the bastard was planning to hunt down Miss Darshaw and finish what he'd started.

Lindley would see that it was not the latter. But first things first. The minute Fitzgelder was out of sight, he ducked into the cupboard and retrieved the wrappings. He didn't dare examine them here, but shoved them quickly into his pocket and left the cupboard. Should Fitzgelder come back to look for them, with luck he might assume a dutiful servant had removed them and not suspect Lindley.

Calm and casual, Lindley took himself down to the ground floor. Miss Darshaw was nowhere in sight, so he headed to the room where Fitzgelder indicated the actors would be. He couldn't help but wonder how the hell a theatrical troupe fit into things. Mangled Shakespeare or pirated French farce was a bit tame for Fitzgelder—hardly the usual fair offered at his frequent routs. Could this simply be a cover for something more furtive? Would he be meeting with someone in regard to that parcel? Or were tonight's theatrics to be of a tawdry nature simply to feed Fitzgelder's insatiable appetites? It was hard to say with the fellow. Lindley could only hope he hadn't ruined any hope of uncovering the truth of that parcel by thwarting Fitzgelder's efforts with Miss Darshaw.

Whatever was to come, though, Lindley could not regret rescuing the girl. Surely she was not party to the worst of her master's sins. She must have some simpler, less sinister reasons for being in the man's employ. Perhaps she might not even know the full extent of his treachery. The sooner he learned Fitzgelder's secrets, the better.

And perhaps along the way, he'd learn Miss Darshaw's secrets as well.

SOPHIE DID HER VERY BEST TO PRETEND THE LAST FEW minutes in that insufferable linen closet had not happened. She was blissfully anonymous here in her master's busy blue room, surrounded by bustling actors and the hectic preparations for tonight's entertainment. She could make herself useful here, blending safely into the hustle and forgetting what had very nearly occurred—and who had fortunately interrupted it.

Heavens, but what was Lord Lindley doing here? Not that she cared a fig for where the man was or wasn't; it simply surprised her, that was all. Just because he'd seemed a decent sort certainly did not mean he was. He'd been in company with Madame frequently, after all. What sort of upstanding fellow would do that? And now here he was with Mr. Fitzgelder. Clearly she'd been grossly mistaken regarding his character.

How ridiculous that she should waste one ounce of brain matter contemplating one of the dissolute blackguards from her former life. Indeed, she'd left her previous situation to prove she could be better than all that, to become better than that. She may not have been able to find work for anyone more respectable than Mr. Fitzgelder, but she fully intended to use this as a step in the right direction. She would have that dress shop one day. It merely appeared it would take a bit longer than she'd first envisioned.

Clearly she needed to find a different position. She could be a ladies maid, for instance. That was a fine, respectable occupation, and the pay would no doubt be higher and put her that much closer to her dream. All she needed was a bit of experience and a reference. Perhaps she could start on that very thing today. It appeared the acting troupe Mr. Fitzgelder had hired did include a lady or two.

She approached the middle-aged woman who was clearly one of the actors and offered to be of assistance. The woman eyed her curiously, then jabbed her thumb in the direction of a young woman who was just now entering the room.

"There you go, miss, that's the lady you need to be presenting yourself to," she said with a smile. "That's our, er, Miss Sands. She'll know what to do with you."

Sophie curtsied, thanked the woman, and hurried over to this Miss Sands. She was young and pretty and gave every appearance of being horribly respectable. At least, as respectable as an actress could be. Sophie knew a thing or two of actresses. Hopefully she could use that to her advantage and make a favorable impression on this one.

"I was told you might be needing some help dressing for the performance, Miss Sands," Sophie offered with a cheerful smile.

She watched the young woman bustle about, selecting her wardrobe and giving instructions to other troupe members as they hauled in the various paraphernalia needed for Fitzgelder's entertainment. Thankfully, there was not a single thing of it that suggested "orgy." Good. If she could impress Miss Sands with properly attentive service, perhaps this might be just the opportunity she needed to secure a decent enough reference to move on.

Nervously, Sophie smoothed her apron and patted her hair in place. Everyone knew a proper ladies maid needed to be properly turned out.

"Thank you," Miss Sands said, her focus clearly torn between the lovely blue silk gown she held in one hand and the more elaborate golden one in the other. "I suppose if our host tonight favors the more classical pieces I ought to go with the embroidered neckline, but I do so prefer the blue. Tell me, is your master a great lover of Shakespeare or will he be more inclined to request . . ."

And now the lady finally turned to look at her. Oh, bother. By the look on Miss Sands's face it would seem Sophie's hasty attempts to put herself to rights after that dreadful episode upstairs had failed dismally.

"Good God!" the actress exclaimed. "You poor dear! What in heaven's name has happened to you?"

Sophie stared at the floor. "I'm sorry, miss, I didn't realize I, that is, I should go tend to my appearance." She curtsied and tried to leave, but Miss Sands would have none of it.

"Gracious! Are these bruises at your wrists? And there's blood on your apron! Who did this to you, girl?"

Sophie knew it would be the height of impropriety to lie to her mistress, but since Miss Sands was really only a guest in the house, she supposed it was a forgivable offense this time. Besides, Mr. Fitzgelder would likely not take kindly to having his dirty secrets aired for these entertainers.

"No one, miss," Sophie replied. "I fell."

It seemed Miss Sands had brains as well as beauty. "My arse, you fell. Come, my girl, I recognize the print of a man's hand when I see it. Who did this to you?"

"It's nothing at all, miss. I managed to get away."

"Not before he welted your eye!"

"What?" Sophie's hand shot up to her face. Indeed, her eyelid felt puffy and tender. Bother, but when she slammed Fitzgelder with her forehead she must have also succeeded in bruising herself.

"Come," the actress ordered, pulling Sophie over toward a row of chairs against the wall.

"Truly, I'm quite fine," Sophie began, politely trying to fend off the other woman's examination.

"This is very fresh, isn't it? Heavens, we'll have to put something on it immediately."

"No, really I don't need—"

Miss Sands cut her off by turning her to face a lovely round mirror that hung on the master's wall. Sophie had no other option but to stare at her own face and catch her breath at the ugly red welt that showed quite plainly at her swollen eyelid. It throbbed. Merciful Lord, how would she ever hide this from the other servants? They would not need to question who had done such a thing—or why.

And they would not be pleased about it, either. If Mr. Fitzgelder was in a foul mood after this—and of course he would be—he'd naturally take it out on the staff. As far as they would care, this injury would be undeniable evidence of her insolence while they would be the ones paying the price. Unsurprisingly, they'd take it out on her.

"Oh," was all she could say as she stared back at her reflection.

"Don't worry, I'll help you," Miss Sands said. "What is your name?"

Her first instinct was not to trust this stranger, not to give any information that could somehow be used to further damager her place in this household. But as she cautiously met the actress's gaze she wondered if perhaps she could indeed trust Miss Sands with something as innocuous as her name. After all, what more did she have to lose?

"I'm Sophie Darshaw, miss," she said.

The actress smiled. "Well, Sophie, you look like an honest girl. I can't imagine there's anything you could have done to deserve such treatment that would leave you like this."

"*He* would clearly disagree." Sophie wasn't quite able to keep the bitterness out of her voice.

"And who is *he*?" the actress asked gently. "Your husband?"

Sophie was only too happy to set her straight. "No, thankfully he's nothing more than my employer."

"But surely that doesn't give him the right to do this!"

"At least this is all he did," Sophie assured her. "I know how to handle his likes, Miss Sands."

"And just look how he handled you," the actress replied. "You don't need to suffer this, Sophie. No position is worth it. You simply must leave his service."

"Leave? To go live on the streets?" Sophie shook her head, one unruly lock of her disobedient honey-colored hair bouncing loose of the prim cap where she'd tried so hard to tuck it. "No, I know all too well what leaving would bring, miss. Trust me, I'm better off here."

"Surely there is somewhere you can go?"

"With no references?" Sophie shook her head. "No, miss. And I assure you, Mr. Fitzgelder is not likely to authorize a reference."

Oddly enough, this statement seemed to have quite the effect on Miss Sands. Her eyes grew suddenly huge and her face paled as if she feared a dragon might suddenly leap out and eat them. Sophie wondered if the woman wasn't going a bit overboard with her outpouring of sympathy.

"Did you . . . Did you say Mr. Fitzgelder?"

Sophie nodded. "Yes, miss. He is my master."

The actress appeared as if she were going to be ill.

"I'm sorry," Sophie stammered quickly. "Did I, er, did I say something wrong?"

"Your master is called Fitzgelder? But surely not Mr. Cedrick Fitzgelder, is it?"

Sophie nodded. "Yes, miss. The very same. Do you know him?"

Miss Sands didn't answer. By her nervous hand wringing and the way her brown eyes darted around frantically, she didn't need to. Yes, Miss Sands obviously knew Sophie's master. Apparently her dealings with him had been as pleasant as Sophie's.

Without warning the actress grasped Sophie by the hand and was pulling her toward the other side of the room, toward the doorway that led out of the salon at the rear of the house. Deciding it might be best to find out what this was about, Sophie went along. They made it to the doorway just as an older gentleman carrying a crate came through it. Miss Sands nearly plowed into him.

Good naturedly, he urged the young actress to be careful. What caught Sophie's attention, though, was that he did it in French. Such a simple thing, yet her soul reacted. The dull pain of loss throbbed to life, catching her off guard by its force, even after all this time being dormant. How silly that words from a stranger could evoke so much of the past!

She carefully pushed old, best-forgotten feelings back into that dark corner of her heart. Her life today had no room for such memories. Things were as they were and she'd do well to keep her mind on today's troubles, not useless memories of things dead and buried.

Miss Sands was breathlessly informing the man—also in French—what she had learned from Sophie. He appeared similarly affected when Fitzgelder's name was mentioned. He scanned the room, then hurried them into a corner where they could duck behind a screened wall that had been erected for concealing musicians during an entertainment. He lowered his voice and rattled a string of questions. Was Miss Sands certain it was him? Had he seen her? What else did she know?

Without bothering to answer him, Miss Sands responded with a barrage of her own questions for the man. What could he have been thinking when he scheduled this performance? Did he not realize this was London and they should have been more careful? What did he suggest they do now?

From what Sophie could gather from their hurried, harried conversation, the gentleman insisted he *had* been careful. He was quite certain Mr. Fitzgelder's name had not come up when arrangements were made for this event. In fact, it appeared he thought he'd been hired by a man named Smith.

Then he noticed *her*. Miss Sands gave him her first name and explained—tactfully—the reason for Sophie's lamentable bruising. The man's distress was even more pronounced. He swore.

"And you've believed her story?" he asked gruffly, still in his elegant French.

Well, that was far from the sympathy she'd hoped for!

"Of course I believe her," Miss Sands replied. "Just look at her."

"You trusted her, just because of a little bruising?"

The man was eyeing Sophie with a dark suspicion. She didn't much care for the intensity of this scrutiny. What exactly did he think she had done?

"I haven't told her anything," Miss Sands went on, also in a very cultured French. Sophie got the idea they had no clue she could understand them.

"Good. Fitzgelder could be using her to get information," the man said.

What? But that was ridiculous. Whatever could they be talking about? She knew nothing about any information. She wasted no time setting things straight. In French.

"Mr. Fitzgelder certainly was not interested in me for information, monsieur."

They seemed surprised.

"You are French?" the gentleman asked.

"My father was French," Sophie responded. "But Mrs. Harwell scolds me if I do not speak English."

"So you understood our conversation," Miss Sands said.

Sophie shook her head. "Not in the least."

"Don't lie to us," the man said, leaning over her so that she was forced to take a step back. "Did Mr. Fitzgelder send you to find out about us?"

"Find out about you? Heavens, if that was all Mr. Fitzgelder asked of me I would not be wearing this," Sophie replied, touching her swollen eyelid. "Besides, you're in his home. He must know about you already, I would think."

"What did he tell you of us?" the man demanded.

"But he did not mention you at all! I came to you hoping to avoid him."

The gentleman did not seem entirely convinced. "You had no other reason to ingratiate yourself with my daughter?"

So this was his daughter, was it? No wonder he was concerned. Any father with a pretty young daughter who suddenly found himself in Mr. Fitzgelder's home had good reason to be concerned.

Sophie swallowed and forced herself to meet his flashing eyes as she replied. "Well, I had thought perhaps if I took extra care, Miss Sands might give me a reference so I could find a position elsewhere."

"See, Papa?" the actress announced. "Surely you can't believe she would ever help Fitzgelder. Look at her! We ought to go while we can and take her with us."

The man frowned, this thick brows nearly touching above his prominent nose. "But if we leave, that will only alert Fitzgelder that something is not right. No, we must think this through first."

"It's too dangerous. We must go now!"

"If we go he'll only follow. No, I must think of something else."

They argued a bit and Sophie felt as if she really ought not be privy to their conversation. Clearly these people had some great, dark reason to fear her master and it did appear as if Mr. Fitzgelder must have lured them here intentionally. She felt sorry for them, of course, but at the same time she couldn't help but realize things would go especially bad for her if she were discovered in their company.

She tried to excuse herself.

"But you cannot go back to work for that monster!" Miss Sands suddenly protested, grabbing at her hand to keep her hidden with them there.

Suddenly Sophie was inclined to agree. She'd barely poked her head out from around the screened wall and quickly ducked back in. *He* was here.

Miss Sands's father noticed and leaned forward to peer through the openings in the screen. Miss Sands did the same, her breath catching in a way that Sophie could truly not find surprising. Women often did that upon sight of the tall, impeccably dressed gentleman and his arguably perfect features.

"Is that him?" she asked with a mix of awe and astonishment. "Is that Fitzgelder?"

Sophie had to stifle a laugh. As if there could be any comparison!

"No, it's someone else," her father replied. "I don't know him."

"Lindley," Sophie informed them. "His name is Lindley."

"The earl?"

Sophie nodded.

"We are in trouble, then," the actor said.

Sophie joined Miss Sands in sending him a curious glance. He ran his hand through his thick, dark hair and sighed. Could these people have something against Lindley, too? Sophie watched intently as a careful determination stole over the older man's face.

"Papa, who is this Lindley? What does he have to do with us?"

"Nothing, *ma chou-chou*. He is merely a friend of Fitzgelder's. But this tells me what I must do."

"It does?"

"Indeed. I must leave."

"No, Papa. *We* must leave. Together."

He shook his head. "No, people must merely *think* we've left together. Remember, *ma belle,* he's never seen you. You must stay here where you will be safe."

"Safe? *Here?* You cannot be serious, Papa!" Miss Sands protested.

Sophie voiced her agreement. "Beg pardon, monsieur, but Mr. Fitzgelder will surely take notice of Miss Sands, even if he does not know her. I cannot think she'll be safe here!"

The actor simply smiled at them. "She will if she gives the performance of her lifetime."